On *The Walls of Jericho*

"Fiercely intelligent."

—*Publishers Weekly*

"The trail is as tortuous as a John le Carré tale. . . . Land's writing is slick and the action is swift."

—*The Denver Post*

"Better than anything by Tom Clancy."

—*Hartford Courant*

"Land has managed, in *Jericho,* to get the feel of the land, of the hot and dusty alleyways of the current capital of the Palestinian entity, and to create believable Israelis and Arabs. . . . There are enough unexpected twists in the plot, which I will not give away here, to keep you turning pages until its finale."

—*The Jewish Voice*

"Some unexpected plot twists make *The Walls of Jericho* quite a read."

—*The Detroit Free Press*

"The fuse is burning, and the Middle East is ready to explode in this gripping roller-coaster ride of crime and intrigue. *The Walls of Jericho* has the impact of a punch to the solar plexus."

—*Stephen Coonts*

"Jon Land has clearly landed amidst the top writers of political thrillers."

—*The Midwest Book Review*

"Land's diabolically clever thriller is packed with emotion and suspense, offering larger-than-life heroes and a nightmarish glimpse of life in today's conflict-ridden Middle East. A highly entertaining thriller."

—*Booklist*

OTHER BOOKS BY JON LAND

The Alpha Deception
The Council of Ten
*Day of the Delphi
*Dead Simple
*Dolphin Key
The Doomsday Spiral
The Eighth Trumpet
*The Fires of Midnight
The Gamma Option
*Hope Mountain
*Kingdom of the Seven
Labyrinth
The Lucifer Directive
The Ninth Dominion
The Omega Command
The Omicron Legion
The Valhalla Testament
The Vengeance of the Tau
Vortex
*A Walk in the Darkness
*The Walls of Jericho

*Published by Forge Books

JON LAND

THE PILLARS OF SOLOMON

A TOM DOHERTY ASSOCIATES BOOK
NEW YORK

For Natalia,
an editor from before page 1

This is a work of fiction. All the characters and events portrayed in this book are either products of the author's imagination or are used fictitiously.

THE PILLARS OF SOLOMON

Copyright © 1999 by Jon Land

A Forge Book
Published by Tom Doherty Associates, LLC
175 Fifth Avenue
New York, NY 10010

www.tor.com

Forge® is a registered trademark of Tom Doherty Associates, LLC.

ISBN 0-812-56672-6
Library of Congress Catalog Card Number: 98-46710

First edition: March 1999
First mass market edition: April 2000

Printed in the United States of America

0 9 8 7 6 5 4 3 2 1

ACKNOWLEDGMENTS

THIS IS THE one page of the book where I get to talk directly to you, and it's time I took advantage of that. *The Pillars of Solomon* is my twentieth book and, I think, my best. Part of the credit for that lies with me, but just as much lies with the professionals around me who have contributed in various and countless ways. One thing I have learned after twenty books is that the more you write, the more you need to work and to listen, and I am fortunate to have some truly gifted individuals helping me do both.

Toni Mendez and Ann Maurer have been there through every single title, challenging me to get better every step of the way.

The Tor/Forge team, under Tom Doherty, enlarged old doors and opened new ones for me thanks to the loyal dedication of Linda Quinton, Yolanda Rodriguez, and Jennifer Marcus. (About my editor, Natalia Aponte, see the dedication page.)

For this book special thanks goes to the always brilliant Emery Pineo, Nancy and Moshe Aroche, Rita and

Wiley Archer, Irv and Josh Schechter, David Onik, and David Schechter.

And my most important thanks goes to you—the reader, without whom I am nothing. Whether you have been with me before or are picking me up for the first time, make yourself comfortable, sit back and enjoy the tale. Am I right about *Pillars* being my best book yet? You be the judge.

So the LORD said to Solomon: "Since this is what you want, and you have not kept my covenant and my statutes which I have enjoined on you, I will deprive you of the kingdom and give it to your servant. . . ."

1 KINGS 11:11

PROLOGUE
THE FOUR FRIENDS

TELL ME A *story, Papa.*"

The old man lifted his granddaughter onto his lap, his aged body strained even by so small an effort. "Which story would you like to hear, Tali?"

"You know, the one about the four friends. That night they first met."

"Again?"

"It's my favorite, Papa. Please," Tali pleaded, and widened her eyes.

The old man could never refuse her anything when she looked at him like that. She was ten years old; he would have thought the much-told tale from his past would bore her now. But Tali never tired of hearing it, just as he never tired of telling it.

"Very well," the old man said, letting his mind drift backward. "This is how the story starts. . . ."

THE MEDITERRANEAN SEA, 1947

The freighter thrashed against the choppy seas, battling each swell as it drew closer to land. The storm had ended hours before, but its residue of wind and waves made the final stretch of the long journey the most difficult of all.

Two days after slipping out of port under cover of darkness, she was now approaching the British blockade lying in wait at the three-mile limit off the coast of Palestine. Blockade runners had not encountered much success getting past the British, but tonight God must have been in a generous mood; the patrolling boats would be hard-pressed to find the freighter in the thick fog that had settled over the sea before she off-loaded her cargo of 206 Jewish men, women, and children.

There had been 209 at the outset, but the journey had taken the lives of 3, 2 elderly and 1 infant. The seas were too rough to risk opening the hatches to ventilate the cargo hold that had become their home. As a result, the stench of sweat, mixed with urine and vomit from seasickness, hung in the stale air like a thick paste. But most of the passengers had experienced much worse than this. First in the concentration camps of the Nazis, who knew exactly what they wanted to do with them, and then in the refugee camps of European nations, who had no idea what to do with them at all.

According to the registration filed at her port of call, the freighter was named the *Silver Princess,* after her original color before rust had taken over during long years at sea. Before setting out on this voyage, though, she had been rechristened with a name more befitting the nature of her journey:

The *Gideon.*

Her passengers had been "liberated" from a French camp by the Jewish underground determined to populate Palestine with the future of a Jewish state. All the refugees knew where they were headed, just as they knew that the odds of making it were long. Few spoke of that, and most, after the first few exciting hours, did not speak at all.

But some did.

In the darkness of the hold, three young men had found each other early in the journey and remained together through its duration.

"They'll be sending us to the lifeboats soon," said Hyram Levy, his voice cracked with fatigue and thirst. He was the smallest of the three, a slight, bespectacled young man who had not weathered the trip well at all, but never complained.

"How can you know that?" demanded Max Pearlman, squeezing a filthy rubber ball to make his forearm flex, keeping his muscles strong. Pearlman had exercised moderately throughout the entire voyage, increasing his efforts as it wore on. His lean, sinewy muscles looked like coiled bands of steel beneath his thin flesh. His veins protruded obscenely.

"I just do, that's all."

"Wait," said Jacob Rossovitch in a deep voice that resonated through his barrel chest. He was a monster of a man, every bit as strong as he looked and, incredibly, none the worse for wear, it seemed, after their time at sea. His hair remained knotted in thick strands the texture of steel wool and his features retained their granitelike immutability, as ridged and angled as a statue's. "I think he's right. I think we're slowing down."

"Take to the lifeboats in this sea?" moaned Pearlman. "Hell, the waves will get us before the British have a chance to."

"Where will they leave us off?" asked Levy.

"Caesarea," Pearlman answered.

"What's that?"

"Not very much anymore. An ancient port built by Herod. Just rubble and ruins now."

"Rubble and ruins," Levy repeated, shaking his head.

"Places to hide," said Pearlman.

"Quiet!" ordered Rossovitch, as the clanking sound of a hatch being opened echoed through the hold.

The vague shape of the captain's oil-streaked face appeared behind a wavering flashlight almost directly above them. "It's time."

Pearlman, Levy, and Rossovitch were among the first to climb the ladder to the deck, settling into one of the eight lifeboats that had been readied in the dark. The ship's crew lowered it gently, and it kissed the surface with a soft plop. The water smelled rancid and dank, and the bite of the cool fog felt like needles prickling their flesh.

"The Palmach spotters we were told to look for will never see us," said Pearlman, referring to the Jewish group dedicated to bringing settlers safely to Palestine. He pulled his oar powerfully through the thick, motionless sea, a torrid pace set for the boats following in their wake.

"But neither will the British," followed Rossovitch.

"We'll never reach shore."

"Rubble and ruins coming up any second now," said Levy breathlessly, and both Pearlman and Rossovitch turned as a beam of light swept back and forth from what must have been the shoreline. Little more than a flicker that looked to be only a few hundred yards away through the fog.

"The spotters!" yelled Pearlman.

"I told you." Levy smiled, and inhaled deeply to catch his breath.

The three friends reached the beachhead minutes later. Tempted to join the first wave of refugees rushing away, they decided instead to help their fellow pilgrims in the next boat disembark. By then, though, another two boats, packed with elderly, had come in, and the one after that carried mostly children. Before they knew it, Rossovitch, Levy, and Pearlman had fought the crashing waves to off-load all their fellow refugees, turning them over to the Palmach escorts to be hustled across the beach toward safety.

"Trouble," said Levy when the last boat was almost to shore.

Suddenly the lights of a British patrol jeep swept down the beach and surged toward the dozens of refugees fleeing across the sand. If they ran, the three friends would have a chance too. But that would mean abandoning eight others now struggling to pull their boat through the last of the shallows.

"Go!" Rossovitch yelled, and he dragged the final boat ashore by himself.

The eight passengers scampered out of it and rushed in all directions. Machine-gun fire sounded and one man went down, then another. The three friends swung together and saw the headlights of a second patrol jeep burning closer toward them through the night, riding the shoreline.

"Bastards!" wailed Pearlman, arms held like iron bars by his sides. "Damn British bastards!"

He rushed the jeep with nothing but his scraped raw hands as weapons. Bullets kicked up the sand around him as Rossovitch and Levy hurried to give chase, screaming for Pearlman to get down.

Rossovitch got there first and tackled him to the sand. Levy dove next to them and watched the jeep bear down close. It twisted to the side and skidded to a halt to give the shooter a clear shot as he stood upon the rear floorboards.

All at once a single gunshot split the night from somewhere behind the three friends. The British gunman who had them dead in his sights crumpled in the backseat. A second shot followed, and the driver slumped over the wheel. A third soldier in the passenger seat just managed to draw his side arm before a final shot snapped his head backward.

Heavy footsteps pounded the sand, and the three friends turned to see a lone figure streaking toward them with an old carbine rifle in his hands. He stopped almost nonchalantly and extended a hand down to Pearlman first.

"I'm David Wollchensky. Welcome to Palestine."

MORE, PAPA," TALI *whined sleepily. "Don't stop."*

"It's late," the old man said, and lowered her gingerly out of his lap. It was a well-practiced ritual between them, a shared moment the old man cherished above everything else. Someday his granddaughter would no longer hunger to hear the story of his life. Someday he would lower her from his lap and she would never return.

"I'm not tired. Please."

This time even his granddaughter's pleading eyes were not enough to dissuade him. His legs felt as if someone had wrapped tight steel cord around them, and he knew if he tried to stand right now they might give out beneath him. "Tomorrow."

"Does David save his friends?"

"We'll see."

"What happens when they get off the beach?"

"Tomorrow," the old man repeated.

Tali looked at him quizzically. "What about the part of the story you always leave out?"

The old man felt a chill pass through him. "What part?"

"The secret you've never told me. I know there's a secret the four friends kept to themselves. I can tell."

"It comes much later in the story," the old man said, unable to lie.

"I'm old enough to hear it now. You know I am, Papa."

"Someday."

"Tomorrow?"

"Maybe."

"Promise?"

"We'll see," the old man said, stroking his granddaughter's hair. "We'll see."

DAY ONE

CHAPTER 1

MY DAUGHTER," HANNA Fatuk pleaded, clutching the framed color snapshot tightly in her hands. "You will find her. You must find her! *Min fadlak!* Please!"

Ben Kamal set the sweet mint tea she had served him down on the table and leaned forward. "How long has she been missing, Umm Fatuk?"

"Three days. I called the police the first day, but no one came. Same thing yesterday. This morning I called again." Hanna Fatuk extended the picture frame toward Ben's outstretched hand. Her fingers were still trembling after he took it. She laced them together in what could have been a position of prayer. "And now you are here. *Haududallah!*"

The look of utter reverence she gave him embarrassed Ben because it was pure luck that had led him to the Fatuk home in the center of Jericho this morning. He happened to be walking past the desks where calls to the ancient city's Palestinian police headquarters came in when Hanna Fatuk phoned; he could hear the anguish in her shrill voice through a receiver six feet away. He had the call transferred to his office before he even knew what it was about. This in spite of the fact that he hadn't worked on a case himself in over six months.

Ben sipped some more of his tea, his teeth filtering the cooling liquid through the mint leaves that floated on top, and studied the missing girl's picture again. It was a casual pose, catching Leila Fatuk leaning over the kitchen table he had seen as he entered the home, dark hair tumbling leisurely over her shoulders. Her smile looked very natural, her teeth perfect and very white. He thought of the pictures of his own daughter he still kept, cherished since there would be no more, and did some fast calculations in his head. If his daughter had lived, she would have been about the same age as this missing girl.

The Fatuks lived on the outskirts of Jericho in a two-story stone house that showed the rectangular abutments of several additions made as the family grew. Based on the home's age and the number of additions, Ben could tell it had been in the family for several generations. He had passed through a gate at the edge of the property into a garden full of roses and geraniums. Ivylike vines wrapped themselves about the front of the house, adding to the fresh and succulent aroma that had greeted him.

Inside, that scent was replaced by a strong, fresh smell Ben recognized as *malfulf*, a cabbage dish stuffed with rice. He remembered the same smell as a child, both in Detroit and Nablus.

His eyes looked up at Hanna Fatuk and her husband, Amir. They were holding hands now. Another man, big and brawny, wearing a wrinkled white shirt untucked, hanging over his trousers, hovered by the window. Arms crossed. Sneering. The impatient look of a man already late for work. Ben hadn't been introduced to him yet, but guessed he was a relative. The number of plates stacked neatly in the kitchen sink indicated he had joined the Fatuks for breakfast. The lack of other place settings told Ben the older generation that had once shared this house had passed on, just as he assumed that the two young men pictured with Amir and Hanna Fatuk on the wall must have moved off on their own.

"Umm and Abu Fatuk," Ben began, "there are questions I must ask you. Some of them might be uncomfortable and I want to apologize in advance."

"There is no need, *sidi*," Amir Fatuk said humbly.

"Inspector will do. Please."

"Inspector," Amir repeated.

Ben nodded, flipped open his notebook.

"Why don't you wear a uniform?"

Ben turned toward the big man still standing by the window. "Excuse me?"

"You are a policeman, but you don't wear a uniform."

"I'm a detective."

"I know what you are. I know *who* you are."

"And who are you?"

The man gestured toward Hanna Fatuk. "Her brother. The missing girl's uncle."

"What's your name?"

"What does it matter?"

"You said you knew who I was. I'd just like to know who you are."

"Nazir Jalabad. I came to watch the great Bayan Kamal, the famous hero. I came to watch you do nothing like the rest of them." The man made a slight spitting motion. "Three days, it takes *three days* before they send you over so you can ask your useless questions. Like always."

Ben felt something scratch at his spine. "This has happened before?"

"Not with my Leila," Hanna Fatuk answered. "Please

excuse my brother's temper, but he is her godfather."

"How old is your daughter?"

"Thirteen. My youngest. Her brothers are gone. One lives in Jordan."

"Then this picture . . ."

"Taken over a year ago. But it is still a close likeness."

"She left the house at what time Monday?"

"Nine o'clock at night. She was going to the store on an errand." Hanna Fatuk's hands shook a little. "I . . . sent her."

"What store?"

"The grocer up the street. Number ninety-one."

"Six blocks away," Ben noted. "That means she disappeared within five minutes of leaving here. But you said the grocer never saw her."

"No. No one saw her after she left the house."

"Always the same," Nazir Jalabad snickered. "The damn Israelis never leave witnesses."

"Why do you think the Israelis are responsible?" Ben asked him.

"Everyone knows their soldiers steal our girls. Take them back to their bases, have their way with them, and then drop them off whenever they are finished. Usually not this young, though. They must be getting desperate."

Hanna Fatuk shuddered at her brother's comment.

"There are no longer Israeli patrols active in Jericho," Ben said, but he didn't sound very convincing. The truth was, withdrawing from Jericho and other cities in the West Bank had done little to curb the power of the Israeli army and at times seemed to only increase it. Patrols continued to ride in whenever they liked, although they didn't stay very long. The homes of suspected terrorists were still bulldozed, entire villages punished for the crimes of the few terrorists who seemed as determined to destroy their own people as the Israelis.

The big man snickered. "They are still here. Everyone knows. For a while the girls filed reports. They stopped bothering when none of your police would listen."

"You know someone else this happened to?"

"I've heard about it."

Ben returned his attention to the Fatuks. "Has your daughter ever been gone for a time before?"

"No."

"And she had no reason to run away that you're aware of?"

"No!" Hanna Fatuk said. "Of course not!"

"I'll need to take this with me," Ben said, realizing he was still holding on to the picture. "Do you have any others?"

"Recently, just of Leila with a school group."

"Hanna," her husband interrupted.

"They were part of an exchange program with an Israeli school in Jerusalem."

"He doesn't have to hear about that," Amir Fatuk said, sounding embarrassed. "I told you it was a bad idea."

"Not to Inspector Kamal," sneered the hulking Nazir Jalabad. "He is a great believer in the benefits of peace."

"I'm going to need a list of your daughter's friends," Ben said to the Fatuks, ignoring him. "People she spent time with outside of this house. Teachers, too. Anyone she might have had contact with."

"That night?"

"Anytime," Ben told Hanna Fatuk. "Also anyone who might have a reason to harm either of you."

"You think . . ."

"I don't think anything. Not yet. We simply must cover all the possibilities."

And the possibilities, Ben had to acknowledge to himself, were not pleasant. Once a child had been missing this long, the odds of her returning on her own diminished significantly. He wondered what would have happened if he had taken Hanna Fatuk's call on Tuesday instead of today.

"We have no enemies," Amir Fatuk said staunchly.

"What is your job?" Ben asked Amir.

"I am a mechanic. Cars."

"I'll need a list of all your customers as well."

"Why?"

"Because I assume your daughter has been to your shop, where someone may have seen her."

Back in Detroit, Ben would have gathered the assembled lists and run all the names through a computer. And, if he was lucky, the names of several possible suspects would emerge. But in Jericho no such database existed. The closest thing to it remained the files the Israelis turned over, which often had no listings for crimes actually committed, and hundreds of listings for crimes that either never happened or were exaggerated to provide cause for arrest and incarceration. And that was assuming he could gain access to them, which these days was hardly a foregone conclusion, since he was no longer considered an investigator.

Amir Fatuk shrugged. "She's been to my shop a few times."

"And I want you both to think of vehicles you may have seen that didn't belong in the neighborhood."

"The day she disappeared?" Hanna Fatuk asked him.

"As far back as you can remember."

"Anything else?" Hanna Fatuk asked him.

Ben turned toward Nazir Jalabad. "You said before that other girls have disappeared."

"Ask anybody."

"I'm asking you."

"I already told you."

"Not names, you didn't."

"I don't know names."

"But you can find out, can't you?"

"Why should I do your job for you?"

"Because your goddaughter is missing."

"Wait," said Hanna Fatuk suddenly, "I just remembered something else. . . ."

CHAPTER 2

"PAKAD BARNEA?"

Danielle Barnea entered the crime scene alone, moving into the gift shop past the uniformed police and other detectives, who were obviously surprised to see her. "Spare me the welcome and just tell me what we've got here."

Two of the uniformed officers looked at each other.

"Seventy-five-year-old male with his head bashed in behind the counter," one of them said.

Danielle continued stepping through the cluttered confines of the shop. Furniture was strewn about and broken. Tables and display cases had been toppled everywhere, their shattered contents scattered all over the floor. She knew enough about antiques to recognize the real thing among the few pieces left whole. The shop had only a small sign outside, and Danielle noted the absence of any price cards or tags attached to the pieces on the floor.

Located near the start of the covered lane that formed Jerusalem's bustling Mahane Yehuda marketplace, the shop was squeezed in between open spice and fruit stands. The result was a lusciously sweet smell of cinnamon, cumin, and ripe figs that reminded Danielle of her mother's kitchen long ago. She was almost sad when the smell faded away once she closed the door to the shop behind her.

Careful of where she stepped, Danielle headed toward the photographer snapping off pictures behind a counter upon which rested an old-fashioned cash register. A detective hovering near him brushed against it accidentally and bells jangled. The detective turned when he heard Danielle approaching.

"Good morning, Pakad. They told me you were coming."

The young man looked familiar. He wore his curly hair long, and his deep-set brown eyes blinked often.

"Do I know you?" Danielle asked him.

"We met once before in East Jerusalem. You were investigating the work of that serial killer they called the Wolf. I was a lieutenant in charge of a sector where one of the murders was committed." He extended his hand. "Yori Resnick."

Danielle gave back his firm grasp. "I remember."

"I was surprised when I heard you had been assigned to this case," Resnick said innocently enough, but the implication of his words was clear: Two years ago Danielle Barnea was a member of Shin Bet and a national hero. What was she doing assigned to a routine murder investigation in Jerusalem's Mahane Yehuda marketplace?

My job, Danielle wanted to tell him.

She had returned to work at the National Police ten days before after a meeting with Commissioner, or Rav Nitzav, Hershel Giott. Giott was a small, stoop-shouldered man whose grandfatherly demeanor belied the stern, uncompromising fashion in which he executed the duties of his office. He had welcomed Danielle with a firm grasp of both hands and light kiss on her cheek, inspecting her as a seldom-seen relative might. In fact, they hadn't seen each other since her father's funeral six months earlier.

"You're looking well," he said, face quickly sombering. "All things considered."

"I got your note. Thank you."

"When I heard . . ." He flapped a hand before him. "Accch, in the past. We must move on, all of us. Come, sit down."

Giott led her to a pair of leather chairs fixed before his desk and waited for Danielle to take one before seating himself in the other.

"This isn't a social call, Rav Nitzav."

"I didn't expect it was."

"I want to come back to work for you."

He scratched his bald dome. Danielle realized this was the first time she had seen him without his ever-present yarmulke. "Your leave of absence is in effect from Shin Bet, not the National Police."

"My relationship with Commander Baruch was strained from the beginning, as you well know. I think he will welcome my reassignment."

Giott scorned her with his small eyes. "Commander Baruch will not want to lose you any more than I did when you were transferred the first time."

"Much has changed since then," Danielle said, and looked down.

Giott reached out and took her hand. "I'm sorry things did not work out. And I'm not speaking of Shin Bet."

"I know."

"What was his name?"

"Eli Bourne."

"Israel Defense Forces?"

"A captain." Danielle smiled slightly. "We met at a firing range, of all places."

"And who was the better shot?"

"He, apparently." Danielle had hoped for levity with the remark. It didn't happen.

"He never proposed?"

"I don't think it was what either of us was looking for."

"Even after you became pregnant?"

Danielle shrugged. "Maybe he would have. Who knows? But not now."

"I'm told it was a boy."

"Yes."

"I'm also told you had an unusual visitor after the miscarriage."

Danielle stiffened a bit. She had told no one about the strange-looking man who had appeared at her bedside that morning, she was certain she hadn't.

"He wouldn't tell me who he was. Wouldn't answer any of my questions."

"What did he say?" Giott asked her.

"He asked if there was anything he could do."

"And you told him . . ."

"I told him there was nothing. He said he'd be back, but I checked myself out before he had the chance."

"Perhaps he was from the hospital."

"Maybe," Danielle said, remembering how the dark of the man's eyes seemed to have swallowed the whites. He had a gaunt, almost skeletal face and gold, weathered skin that looked as though it had shrunk back on the bone. "I don't see how he could have known so much otherwise. Not just about the miscarriage, but about what it might mean for future pregnancies."

"The doctors aren't sure yet themselves, are they?"

"No," Danielle replied, aware now that Giott must have already conferred with them. "I thought the man was a therapist, some kind of counselor."

Giott nodded. "And?"

Danielle shrugged. "I don't need therapy." She straightened a little. "You sent him, didn't you?"

"What makes you think that?"

"Who else would be so concerned for me? But it's not counseling I need, it's work. A different kind of therapy."

"You're still young, Danielle."

"That's why I'm here."

Much to her relief, Danielle had been reinstated at her old rank, before serving in Shin Bet, of *pakad,* or chief inspector. And now, ten days later, she had been assigned her first case since her return.

"Who was the victim?" Danielle asked Yori Resnick, still having made no move to inspect the body herself.

"They called him the Engineer for his ability to arrange procurement of any item a customer desired," Yori Resnick told her. "I remember him from my days in the army. He did business with Jews, Arabs, Christians. Everyone. *Anyone.* Culture stopped at the front door."

"Too bad the killer didn't do the same."

Resnick frowned regretfully. "He was killed early in the morning. Between two and four A.M. would be a fair estimate."

"Has the medical examiner arrived yet?"

"En route."

"Who found the body?"

"An army patrol noticed the spilled merchandise from the street. The door was locked, but they forced their way in."

"Locked? Is there another way out of this shop?"

"A back door. Also locked, Pakad."

"Did you check his body for keys?"

"I thought it better not to until the medical examiner arrived."

"Let's have a look, shall we?"

Danielle slid around the counter. The Engineer lay on his back with his head and legs turned to the side. She couldn't see his face, but the large pool of blood beneath and around it more than revealed the level of damage done. The smashed contents of a curio cabinet covered the floor around him in a mosaic of ruined china and crystal. The crystal picked up some of the shop's stray light and bounced it back at her as Danielle crouched over the Engineer's small, slight body. She felt the shape of a large set of keys through the fabric of the first pocket she checked and didn't bother to extract them. Stood back up and faced Yori Resnick.

"Well, Detective, our victim still has his keys on his person, and yet both doors were found locked. Interesting, don't you think?"

Resnick gave her a slow nod, muttering an acknowledgment.

Danielle did a slow pan of the shop. A breeze blew through the broken windows and started a number of exquisite wind chimes tinkling gently together.

"All this damage," she started. "Happened when he struggled against his attacker, you think?"

Resnick shook his head. "His body shows no other sign of wound or bruising."

"You checked his hands?"

"No lesions or lacerations. Nothing under the fingernails my preliminary examination could detect either."

"Meaning . . ."

"Unlikely there was a struggle at all."

"The Engineer knew his killer?"

"The locked doors indicate the killer must have had a key of his own. That indicates an employee, or close friend," Resnick surmised. "I think the Engineer must have come especially to meet him here. That would explain his presence in the shop so late."

"Where did the victim live?"

"A house just across Navron Street."

"That close? So he didn't have far to go," Danielle said, thinking out loud. "This meeting could have come up suddenly."

"Is that important?" Resnick asked her.

"Everything is important at this point."

Resnick thought briefly. "The Engineer did business with a number of Palestinians, Pakad."

"In what capacity?"

"Mostly procurement of items from the West Bank traditionally unavailable in Jerusalem these past few years."

"Items that were smuggled in?"

"Yes."

"And nothing was done?"

"No."

"Why?"

"The Engineer was a man to be left alone, Pakad. I have known this since my days in the army on patrol in East Jerusalem."

"Apparently nobody told his killer."

Danielle looked back at the Engineer's body lying amid the shattered pieces of his life's work. She came around the far side of the counter and crouched low again, this time to fasten her hands under the corpse's legs. The doctors had cautioned her against lifting anything heavy for several weeks, warning about future complications. But it had been more than a month now since she had left the hospital.

Danielle eased the Engineer's legs upward. Beneath him the floor was barren, clean. The cracked pieces of crystal and china formed a perfect shadow around the outline of his corpse.

She eased the legs down again. "I think, Yori, we can safely assume that all this destruction occurred after the attack."

"To make it look random, a simple robbery and nothing more?"

Danielle hit two keys on the cash register. Bells jangled and the cash drawer slid out, revealing a modest amount of Israeli shekels. She lifted the tray and found an unkempt assortment of American currency as well.

"A robbery that leaves the cash behind . . . No, Yori,

I believe whoever killed the Engineer was looking for something. Now we need to find out what."

"How, Pakad?"

"Asking a few questions."

"Asking whom?"

Danielle flicked her eyes toward the Engineer's corpse. "Him, for starters. You'd be surprised what the dead can tell us when asked. They're often the most eager to talk." She looked back at Resnick. "What was the Engineer's real name, by the way?"

"Levy," the young detective replied. "Hyram Levy."

CHAPTER 3

A WHITE VAN!" Hanna Fatuk had realized. *"When I watched Leila go, there was a white van parked down the street!"*

Now, as a long hot day of canvassing the missing girl's neighborhood stretched on, Ben replayed the rest of the conversation in his mind.

"It was old and rusted. I didn't give it a second look."

"Did you see anyone inside?"

"I saw it only from behind. If there was someone in the cab . . ." Hanna Fatuk finished with a shrug.

"Anything else, Umm Fatuk?"

"I only glanced at it. The van was halfway down the block. I was watching my daughter." Tears welled up in the woman's eyes again. "She looked back at me. She waved. I saw her smile. Then I went back inside."

Hanna Fatuk had broken down at that point and Ben had left her in the collective embrace of her brother and husband. He took the picture of Leila Fatuk at the kitchen table with him, figuring the van at least gave him a place to start, something to question residents about in addition to the missing girl.

He realized from the start that he would have to manage the entire effort on his own. Recent unrest in the larger cities of Nablus and Ramallah had led to the reassignment of Palestinian police officers out of more "quiet" zones like the district of Jericho. As a result, the detective squad remained skeletal. And the uniformed officers spent much of their time hovering protectively around the tour groups, composed mostly of professional and would-be archaeologists who came to Jericho to join a dig. Or stopped on their way to the larger digs ongoing in Petra just over the Jordanian border.

Beyond that, several ranking officials of the Palestinian Council, along with a number of Yasir Arafat's cabinet ministers, had chosen to buy or build lavish villas in Jericho as opposed to the Gaza waterfront. This had been good for the economy when construction was at its peak, but now, with many of the homes occupied, increased security precautions were required, which meant more patrols and manpower had to be expended when they could plainly be better used elsewhere. The police force administered by the Palestinian Authority had become thirty-five thousand strong, twice the number originally planned. Virtually all of these, though, were assigned to security and patrol units of the various, often competing branches, with only a few having been assigned to investigative duties.

So the job of canvassing the neighborhood in search of any information pertaining to Leila Fatuk's disappearance was left to him alone. Ben started by going door-to-door, finding no one who had noticed either Leila Fatuk or the white van. It could have been making a delivery, but no one on the street remembered receiving one in the time frame that Hanna Fatuk insisted she had seen it.

It was no wonder. After he left the Fatuk home that

morning, Ben stood at their door and imagined the van in the position where Hanna Fatuk recalled it. In the dark, set against buildings of only a slightly darker shade, the van would be virtually invisible.

As for the neighbors, after dark many of the old stone homes would have the shutters closed over their windows. On a street like this people kept to themselves. For many of them the day began early and ended early. Still, it seemed strange that nobody had seen the girl. Ben counted eighteen homes between the Fatuk residence and the grocer, where he spoke with two groups of men playing backgammon at tables shaded by the facade. The men told him they had not been playing Monday night but others almost certainly had. Ben would come back tonight to speak to them and complete his canvass around the same time of night Leila Fatuk had disappeared.

Even then, as it always was with an investigation, people would be reluctant to speak to him. Authority for so long had rested in Israeli hands that it remained difficult for Palestinians to trust anyone who announced himself with a knock on the door. Perhaps, too, the rumors of Israeli involvement in other such abductions would have potential witnesses fearful of the repercussions if they told what they had seen.

But that hadn't stopped the missing girl's uncle, Nazir Jalabad, from mentioning the disappearance of other girls to Ben that morning. Besides the white van, that unsubstantiated assertion was the only clue he had. So late that afternoon Ben returned to the Fatuk home and knocked gently on the door. Hanna Fatuk answered, looking slightly hopeful as the stronger scent of the *malfulf* pushed past her.

"Have you found out anything?"

"Not yet, Umm Fatuk," Ben said respectfully. "May I come in?"

"Of course," she said, stepping back so he could enter.

"I would like to speak to your brother Nazir," Ben said after she had closed the door behind him.

Hanna Fatuk looked down, embarrassed. "I apologize for his behavior this morning."

"I would like to speak to him about his claims that other Palestinian girls have disappeared."

The woman looked back up. "He's at work now."

"Where does he live?"

"Just down the street."

"*This* street?"

Hanna Fatuk pointed a finger out a nearby window. "Two blocks down."

"Where the white van was parked?"

"I don't know. Close, I guess. But he doesn't remember it." She backpedaled a little. "Is that . . . important?"

"No," Ben lied. "Probably not."

Chapter 4

BEN WAS STANDING in the shadows outside Nazir Jalabad's house, in the dusty confines of an untended garden, when Jalabad returned from dinner at his sister's home at nine-thirty that evening. Ben waited until Nazir was almost to his door before stepping out from beneath the cover of an olive tree.

"How was dinner at your sister's, Nazir?"

The big man swung awkwardly, startled. "You . . ."

"We should talk."

"I have nothing to say."

"I'm not surprised. Otherwise, you might have mentioned to me this morning that you were Hamas."

Nazir Jalabad's eyes sharpened. He straightened up and glared down at Ben. "Who told you that?"

"You just did."

Jalabad tried to relax. "I don't know what you're talking about."

"Perhaps your sister Umm Fatuk will know."

Jalabad took a menacing step forward. "This has nothing to do with her."

Ben could smell *biera kbiera*, a strong Arabic beer, on his breath. "It does if you're the reason her daughter disappeared, if she was abducted by an enemy of yours who was after revenge. Someone who was watching your house. Someone in a white van."

"The Israelis," Jalabad snarled.

"Back to that again, are we?"

"They've been watching me."

"What about the uncles of the other Palestinian girls who disappeared? Were the Israelis watching them for the same reason they were watching you?"

"I wouldn't know."

"Would you know how to come up with that list for me of the other victims?"

Jalabad gritted his teeth. "I told you, that's not my job."

Ben took a step closer to the big man, surprising Nazir Jalabad by drawing within range of his huge hands. "It is now."

AFTER HE HAD finished his business with Jalabad, Ben drove to the Palestinian Authority headquarters on the outskirts of Jericho. The building was a chiseled white stone structure that at four stories was the tallest in the area. A security guard patrolling the lobby let him in after he flashed his identification against the glass.

Ben thanked the man and proceeded down a first-floor hall toward the sound of classical music emanating softly from one of the offices. He stopped in the doorway and found Colonel Nabril al-Asi, head of the Palestinian Protective Security Service, sitting in his leather desk chair, eyes closed and hands resting comfortably atop the armrests.

"One of my favorites," al-Asi said when the selection ended thirty seconds later.

"Who was it?"

"Bach." Al-Asi turned his chair around to face Ben. As always he was wearing an elegantly tailored suit. "You are well, Inspector?"

"As well as can be expected."

"Your phone bills indicate otherwise."

"Have you been spying on me, Colonel?"

Al-Asi looked genuinely hurt. "Looking out for you, Inspector. I couldn't help but notice the number of calls you made to the United States over the past two months."

"This troubles you?"

"More calls than you had made in the previous two years combined. That troubles me, yes."

"It's nothing."

"Unless you're thinking about going back there." Al-Asi leaned forward and straightened his tie. "I have few friends, Inspector. I can't afford to lose one," the colonel said, and held Ben's stare.

"I haven't felt like I've done much good here lately, much of anything, that's all."

"That's enough, apparently."

"I haven't made any arrangements, Colonel."

"I know. But you left the United States for a reason, Inspector. Do you really think anything there will be different for you?"

"Maybe I'm ready to go back," Ben said, not sounding very convincing. "Maybe I've done all I can here."

"Patience, Inspector. These are difficult times. The rules keep changing. But men like you and me, men who can change with them, will emerge better off eventually."

A strange way of putting it, Ben thought, since al-Asi was one of the people who wrote the rules. Under a less dignified leader, the Palestinian Protective Security Service would have been little more than a thuggish secret police. But al-Asi had molded his department in his own image, successfully leaving his true intentions and loyalties moot to the point where nobody really knew the true agenda he was pursuing. Al-Asi thrived precisely because no one fully understood him. He was known, more than anything else, for his elegant appearance and wardrobe of European designer suits. Few knew whether to call him a friend or an enemy, or whose ends he was actually serving.

"You're working late tonight," Ben said.

"Waiting for a conference call with the Israelis. Apparently they caught a pair of alleged suicide bombers about to enter the country. Their car had Israeli plates. It's a miracle they thought to stop it."

"Amazing that with nine other Palestinian security agencies, the Israelis thought to contact you."

"Yes, isn't it?"

Ben had come to realize that al-Asi's world was lived between the lines, the understated that was never quite said and could never be safely assumed.

"They will call as soon as they confirm the men's identities in search of information about their families and friends," the colonel continued. "Whom they associate with. Who else should be watched."

"That's what I wanted to ask you about."

"Go ahead."

"A Hamas soldier lives on Tafaret Road. I need to know if the Israelis are keeping an eye on him."

"What's his name?"

"Nazir Jalabad."

Al-Asi nodded. "The Israelis are keeping an eye on him. How did you know?"

"A white van was parked in clear view of his house Monday night."

Al-Asi shook his head. "A waste of gasoline. Jalabad is no longer active in the movement. I told the Israelis that but they wouldn't listen. Why are you interested in him?"

"It's the van I'm interested in: a girl disappeared on the street the same night the van was seen."

"You suspect the Israelis were responsible?"

"I doubt it. Under their typical surveillance tactics, though, there would have been a camera operating. That camera may have recorded what happened to her."

"We, on the other hand, don't use cameras. Makes altering reality too difficult later. Better to film only when you know exactly what is going to happen."

"I need to see that tape."

"Officially it doesn't exist."

"What about unofficially?"

"Same thing, which means you'll have to pay your own way on this one. Know anyone who can get you a pass?"

"Maybe," Ben said.

CHAPTER 5

"PAKAD?"

Danielle looked up from her desk and found Yori Resnick standing in the doorway. She realized she had been nodding out and tried to chase the fatigue from her voice.

"Yori, I didn't know you were there."

"I knocked. You didn't hear me."

"Long day." She noticed he was holding a manila folder in his hand. "What have you got there?"

"Hyram Levy's phone records, dating back six months," Resnick said, advancing into Danielle's office.

She rose to take them from him, placed the folder on her desk.

"Can I get you something else, Pakad?"

"No. Thank you."

"Have you eaten?"

"Get on home, Yori. We have an early day tomorrow."

"You're sure?"

Danielle nodded.

"Good night, then."

She waited until he was gone before walking from her office to the coffee station down the hall. There was enough left in the pot to fill one cup and enough pastry from that morning sitting out to fill her stomach. The pastry was stale and the coffee bitter, but she felt herself coming back to life. She had forgotten what the pace of a high-profile investigation was like.

Of course, she hadn't realized how high profile Hyram Levy's murder was until halfway through the morning, when the block around his Jerusalem shop became a portrait in chaos. The entire city seemed in mourning, Danielle reflected. These were people used to violence and terrorism but, strangely, not to civilian murder, especially the murder of a man as popular in the community as the Engineer. All day long her investigation had been slowed or stalled by an endless parade of dignitaries coming to visit the scene.

It started with the mayor just an hour after she arrived. He brought his entire entourage, and Danielle had all she could do to make sure the crime scene was not compromised. He was followed by a ranking member of the Palestinian Authority who came surrounded by the press and made a statement praising Hyram Levy as a man whose door was always open to all peoples. The Israeli media were represented all day as well, and no fewer than two cabinet ministers, as well as the assistants of three more, made appearances too.

It was from these and others that Danielle learned of Hyram Levy's background. She could not say exactly how much was truth and how much could be passed off instead to the legend of the Engineer. Several pertinent facts were plain enough, though:

Levy had come to Israel in the days after World War II and become one of the early defenders of freedom: a soldier, and a terrorist by some accounts, who fought the British to secure a state and then the Arabs to keep it. Unlike the other legends whose names were often mentioned in the same breath with his—men like Ben-Gurion, Begin, and Dayan—Levy had never formally entered politics. After retiring from the army as a general in the wake of the Yom Kippur War of '73, he had opened the shop in Jerusalem where he was murdered over twenty-six years later.

Danielle would fill in the rest of his life as the investigation wore on. For today she was content to follow through on the basic procedures and principles. Obtaining a report from the medical examiner, for instance, and reconstructing Levy's final days. This meant carefully scrutinizing Levy's appointment book and phone records. Receipts for all purchases made in the past weeks. A list of all special orders he might have been trying to fill, thus providing a corresponding list of those individuals who had reason to be in the shop in the most recent past.

Complicating her task here was that Hyram Levy's filing system consisted of sheets of paper stuck in the tabs of his desk blotter, pinned to a corkboard in his office set in the back of the shop, and bulging out of every drawer. It would take some time to sort them out, considerably less to obtain phone records and go through his address book, or Rolodex, if he had one.

Toward that end, Danielle had dispatched Yori Resnick to the Engineer's house across from the Mahane Yehuda marketplace on Navron Street in the company of a forensics team. They had returned with another box full of material. She decided to leave the task of sorting through the mountain of notes and memos to Yori, while she scrutinized Levy's phone records, store receipts, and Rolodex if one was ever found. In this case it seemed abundantly clear that the victim had known his killer, and that meant somewhere amid these reams of information would likely be the murderer's name.

Danielle returned to her office, a half cup of coffee in her hand, and began to go over the phone records.

She had spent the first part of the evening checking through his most recent store receipts and orders, setting up a database for the information on her computer so she could search for a pattern later. A person repeatedly billed who owed Levy money, a dissatisfied customer who felt he'd been bilked on a purchase, even someone on the unscrupulous side of the antiquities trade—one just never knew. The Engineer might have been one of the most popular men in Jerusalem, but it only took one person to want him dead.

The preliminary medical examiner's report arrived when Danielle was well into the pile. There were no surprises. Hyram Levy had died of a single blow to the head that had caved in his skull and crushed his brain. The preliminary examination, rather extensive in itself, had found no signs of any other wound or injury on his body indicative of either repeated beating or a struggle. Levy had been standing behind the counter when his killer lashed out. All indications pointed to the fact that the Engineer had been struck from behind—more evidence he was well acquainted with his killer.

The most intriguing missing piece now, besides the murder weapon, was motive. Danielle still believed the killer had met with Levy to obtain something from him. When Levy failed to produce it, the killer had struck and then ransacked the shop postmortem in search of what he had come for. Based on the shop's condition, the odds were he hadn't found it, which meant there was a piece of evidence still out there, somewhere, that would very likely incriminate the Engineer's killer.

Instead of collating the receipts and orders, Danielle decided a scrutiny of Levy's home and business phone records made for much easier work at this hour of the night. She took a deep breath and opened the manila folder, careful to keep her cooling cup of coffee a safe distance away.

Although Israel is small geographically, calls between major cities like Tel Aviv and Jerusalem fall under the toll variety and are listed on the bills. As a service to the police, the phone company also provides the name of the person called, or at least to whom the number is registered, on the printout. Danielle's intention, after initially perusing the phone records, was to compare them to the database she had been in the process of assembling. Names that appeared most often would give her an initial list of potential suspects who, if not guilty themselves, might have information ultimately crucial to solving the case.

Most police work is more drudgery in the office than chasing down suspects on the street, and Danielle embraced it now as an alternative to going home to her empty apartment. Once the last of the coffee wore off, she could curl up on the small couch against the wall to her right. It was made out of some leatherlike material that matched her desk chair and most of the other furniture on this floor of offices at headquarters.

She had been the youngest woman ever to achieve the rank of chief inspector at National Police, and she looked forward to rediscovering the same drive and determination that had accompanied her original tenure. But it hadn't returned yet. Those who knew her, or of her brief stretch with Shin Bet, regarded her differently. Those who didn't know asked, were told, and were too awestruck to approach her at all. To all of them, the events of two years ago that had branded her a hero might as well have been yesterday. To Danielle, though, it felt like, and in many ways was, another lifetime. At first she passed her discomfort off to sensing it in. others, then realized her own was much deeper. She couldn't simply go back and pick up where she had left off. Too much. had changed, not here but inside her. ·

Bearing the legacy of a hero was more curse than blessing because it set expectations in the minds of others that could not possibly be met. She was just a person, and a much different one at that. She had returned to the National Police hoping to melt into the framework and disappear into the routine. That, clearly, was not going to happen. The events of two years before had left their mark, and she could not simply pick up her life again as if they had never taken place. She could see that in her own eyes, just as she could see it in the eyes of her fellow detectives, who expected more of her than she might be capable of providing.

Danielle went to the bathroom down the hall to freshen up and was relieved to find it empty. She splashed water on her face and tousled her hair. Even in the bathroom's dim light, most would say she hadn't changed outwardly at all in two years. Her auburn hair still fell evenly past her shoulders and her skin maintained its bronze, healthy tone. Danielle studied her eyes and wondered if that's where the difference was. Their sultry radiance had always been her strongest feature, but their gaze seemed empty to her now, somehow lengthened.

She returned to her office and continued scanning the phone records of Hyram Levy. A recurring number on the second-to-last phone bill in the folder snapped her alert again. Several calls had been made from Levy's shop in Jerusalem to a Tel Aviv exchange that was not identified. She flipped fast to that same month's bill from Levy's home on Navron Street, and, sure enough, the same number had been called numerous times from there as well, also not identified.

That could only mean a protected, secure line the phone company's computers could not access. The number was very likely a dummy exchange, just a routing source that had transferred Levy's calls elsewhere. Only the highest government and military officials were afforded such treatment. The calls were various lengths in duration, long enough to indicate an interested party on the other end of the line.

Danielle checked the dates on both phone bills. The calls had begun just over two months ago and had increased in frequency in the weeks since. The last call had been placed yesterday afternoon, just hours before the Engineer's murder.

Danielle forgot about the rest of her coffee. Commissioner Giott had left the building hours ago, and this was a piece of information she must share with him. Only his authority could help reveal the identity of the person Hyram Levy had been so intent on conversing with for the past eight weeks.

Danielle looked at her own phone, flirting with the notion of dialing the number Levy had contacted so many times in the past few months. It was not the soundest or most prudent of strategies, but in the end it came down to not being able to resist.

She picked up the receiver and pressed out the number. It rang twice, then stopped. Nothing.

Dead air.

The line had been disconnected.

Danielle hung up the phone just as a shadow crossed her open door. She gasped, snapped to her feet so fast that her desk chair was sent sliding backward against the wall.

"I'm sorry I startled you, Pakad," said Yori Resnick.

Danielle gripped the edge of the desk with both hands. "I thought you had gone home."

"I promised myself, just another half hour."

"It's been more than that. You shouldn't lie to yourself, Yori."

Resnick didn't return Danielle's forced smile. "I found something, Pakad, something I thought you should see immediately."

"What is it?"

Resnick approached her desk stiffly, holding a crinkled piece of notepaper in his hand. "This was found in the top drawer of Levy's desk in the study of his house. I'm . . . not sure what to make of it."

He said no more, just handed the notepaper across the desk. Danielle took it and read Levy's scratchy writing:

Her name was scrawled across the top of the page, followed by the numbers 5-1-3.

The room she had been in at Hadassah Hospital in Jerusalem last month.

DAY TWO

CHAPTER 6

BEN HAD COME to his office early the next morning after a fitful night's rest. He had fallen asleep staring at the phone in his apartment, had dreamed mostly of picking it up and making the call he had avoided while awake. He had promised himself he would make that call this morning. Better not to disturb her at home anyway, so as not to confuse the professional with the personal.

Nabril al-Asi had made it clear Ben was on his own when it came to obtaining a surveillance tape that, if it existed, had been made around the time Leila Fatuk had disappeared. For al-Asi to exert his influence would be to admit he knew the Israelis were in Jericho, and that was something the shrewd head of the Palestinian Protective Security Service could not afford to do. Pursuing such an inquiry through conventional channels, though, would lead Ben nowhere. That left the unconventional, and the only person in Israel he could call upon for help.

Seated in his office now, Ben picked up where he

had left off at home: staring at the phone. Coming up short every time of picking it up and dialing the number.

He hadn't spoken with Danielle in months, no correspondence at all other than the sympathy card Ben had sent after al-Asi told him what had happened to her in the hospital. She had not written back, and that had been almost six weeks ago.

Staring at the phone again, practicing the words, what to say when she answered. The right thing, it had to be the right thing. Yet Ben knew whatever he said, it would be wrong.

The phone rang as he stared at it, jolting him. He snatched the receiver to his ear.

"Hello," he said, clearing his throat.

"Can you meet me in an hour?"

"Who is this?"

"Don't say my name. Just answer the question."

Ben recognized the voice. It was Nazir Jalabad, godfather of Leila Fatuk.

"Where?" he asked.

"Baladiya Square. The butcher's shop in the market. I'll be in the back."

"Yes. One hour."

Click.

Did Nazir suspect Ben had brought him to al-Asi's attention? Had al-Asi acted last night after their conversation? No, that wasn't the colonel's style at all. Nazir's request for a meeting must have been spurred by something else.

Ben went back to staring at the phone, willing himself to pick it up. If only he had visited Danielle in the hospital. He had tried, he would tell her that, but it had been a tension-filled time right after the Israeli special election. By the time Colonel al-Asi secured him the VIP pass he needed to enter Jerusalem, Danielle had already left the hospital.

Not that Ben was sure he would have used it anyway.

In truth he was angry, bitter, jealous. The emotions scraped him raw and took turns exacting misery. It should have been *his* child she was pregnant with, and when she lost it Ben was racked by guilt over seeing what he had childishly wished for come true. He would never get over her, could not move on as she insisted he must. And now, eighteen months after their parting, far more than a phone stood between them.

Ben promised himself he would call her as soon as he returned from his meeting with Nazir Jalabad. In the meantime, he had just enough time to keep his weekly coffee session with newspaper editor Zaid Jabral before heading off to Baladiya Square.

Ben walked from his office to an outdoor coffee shop set on a nearby corner shaded by olive trees, eliminating the need for canopies over the tables laid out on the sidewalk. He got there a few minutes early and ordered two coffees and a plate of *kenafeh,* a sweet cheese pastry, before Jabral arrived precisely on time.

Jabral was the senior editor of the Palestinian daily newspaper *Al-Quds.* He had been a teacher until he was beaten by student leaders for not agreeing to dismiss his students early so they could take part in a protest. It did not seem to matter to the leaders that his class was in the midst of their *Tawjini,* final high school exams. But it mattered to Jabral. His reporting had long presented an objective, if somewhat cynical, view of the peace process. His latest series of articles had chronicled how individual lives in Palestine had changed through the various stages of peace and how these individuals felt about Ari Bar-Rosen. The incoming Israeli prime minister had won a special election eight weeks earlier on a platform that promised to pursue peace again in bold, sweeping strokes on a landscape marred by scars and mistrust.

Ben's own personal history with Jabral was scarred as well. He had returned to his native Palestine from Detroit four years earlier to establish a detective bureau within the fledgling Palestinian police force. One of the first investigations he supervised directly was the murder of a cabdriver who was a suspected Israeli collaborator. The trail led to three members of the Palestinian police force who had tortured and executed the man, later found to be innocent. All three were sentenced to life in prison by a militarylike tribunal.

Jabral's scathing articles on the case had branded Ben a *kahyin*, a traitor to his people and collaborator in his own right. He had been ostracized and nearly exiled until his capture of a serial killer known as *al-Diib*, the Wolf, redeemed his worth. Thanks in large part to another series of articles by Jabral, Ben was not only returned to good standing among his people, he was lauded as a hero in the same tradition as his late father. He became a celebrity who came to represent the great hope of peace, or at least peaceful coexistence for the benefit of both the Israeli and Palestinian peoples.

By connection, though, when peace failed miserably due to the installation of a more militant right-wing administration under the Likud Party in Israel and a scourge of terrorist attacks, Ben became just another figure the Palestinian people could turn their wrath upon. He had become so identified with peace that functioning amid its breakdown had become nearly impossible. As a result he had been spending all of his time teaching at Jericho's police academy and handling an ever growing load of administrative duties at the office.

Going nowhere fast and finding himself increasingly frustrated over a different form of ostracism he had fallen victim to: instead of being hated, he was ignored. Lumped together with the politicos who preached and promised peace, then continued to increase their own standing when it didn't come. These men had white license plates with red numerals that permitted free passage throughout the West Bank and even Jerusalem. Ben had no such plates, but those who considered him party to the same lie never seemed to notice.

Of late, he had shared his frustrations with Zaid Jabral, who had brushed off his consideration of a return to America as overreaction. *What do I have to keep me here?* Ben would challenge. *A lot more than you will find when you get back to the U.S.*, Jabral would snap in his typically caustic tone. But Ben wasn't so sure the journalist was right anymore.

Despite the cane clacking on the side of his bad hip, Jabral had a spring to his step today.

"I have to take a rain check," he said when he got to the table Ben had taken.

"Was it something I said?"

"Haven't booked your plane tickets yet, have you?"

"I was waiting for you to talk me out of it again."

Jabral gazed down at the plate of pastry that had come ahead of the coffee. "You'll find the *kenafeh* back in Detroit sadly lacking."

"Is that the best you can do?"

"I have an interview scheduled."

"You always have an interview scheduled. Who is it today?"

"Fayed Kabir."

"Ah, the Authority's eminent finance minister."

"We're not going to be discussing finances, Ben," Jabral said, not bothering to hide his excitement. "I'm onto something big."

"Bigger than the last story you did on me?"

"Perhaps." Jabral leaned on his cane and checked his watch nervously. "I'd tell you if I could, but you wouldn't believe it. *Nobody* would believe it."

Ben lifted a piece of the pastry but stopped short of biting into it. "Sounds like the story of the year."

"Try century, Ben. If I'm right, our world is going to wake up a much different place the morning this story runs. That's why I need proof."

"It's a good thing you don't need a loan, based on

Kabir's handling of the Palestinian Authority's budget."

Jabral fidgeted, eager to leave. "Same time next week, then?"

"Wait," Ben said, "one more thing."

The journalist put all his weight on his cane and leaned toward Ben. "If you leave Palestine, who would I have coffee with?"

"There was an article you did a while back about an old woman from Jerusalem who claimed her baby had been stolen fifty years ago."

Jabral's back stiffened, as if a jolt of electricity had coursed straight up his spine. "What about it?"

"I think there may be some vague connection between her story and a case I'm working on."

"I thought you weren't permitted to work on cases. You keep trying to convince me that's why you want to leave our tranquil home here."

"You think I'm lying?"

"A lie of ommission. Leaving out the part about the Israeli detective, Ms. Barnea."

Ben bristled, returned the pastry to the plate and wiped the sticky glaze from his hand with a napkin. "That was over a long time ago."

"So was your active casework."

"I'm pursuing this investigation unofficially," Ben said, glad Jabral had changed the subject. "I was wondering if you could put me in touch with the old woman you wrote about. I'd like to ask her some questions."

"Of course. Anything that helps keep you in the country a little longer," Jabral said, his sarcasm typical but his eyes uncharacteristically evasive. "I'll call you tomorrow, the day after at the latest." He started to turn around to leave, then changed his mind. "You'll keep this between us?"

"Of course," Ben said, "whatever you say."

He watched Jabral move off, cane tapping tentatively ahead of him as if he had suddenly lost his way.

BEN ENTERED THE butcher shop Nazir Jalabad had directed him to and headed straight through to the rear of the store, where workers cut, cubed, and chopped away at meat and chicken in their bloodied white aprons. In addition to serving local patrons, this shop daily shipped meats and poultry to others in nearby towns where hard times had cut demand well below the need to buy in bulk.

"Over here," a voice said, and Ben turned toward a collection of steel containers into which the excess fat, gristle, and bone had been dumped.

Standing among those containers in the cold refrigerated air, Nazir Jalabad was wearing a white apron too, only his was unbloodied.

"Outside," he said when Ben got to him.

They moved through a wide rear door onto a raised porch that trucks backed up against to load the refuse.

"Why didn't you tell me last night you weren't part of Hamas anymore?" Ben asked.

"Because you wouldn't have believed me."

"You're sure you did nothing to upset them?"

"They had nothing to do with what happened to my niece," Jalabad insisted. He fished a hand under his apron and came out with an envelope, which he extended toward Ben. "Inside you will find the names of three other girls who disappeared, like my goddaughter."

Ben took it, surprised.

"I asked around to get those names. There were some who were not pleased with my inquiries."

"Your former friends from Hamas?"

Jalabad flashed his sneer. "They threatened me. I do not like being threatened." He moved a step closer to

Ben and lowered his voice. "I understand there is going to be a suicide bombing today. In Tel Aviv. Atarim Square at one o'clock." Jalabad checked his watch dramatically. "You can still make it, Inspector."

CHAPTER 7

A LONG NIGHT, Pakad?" Hershel Giott asked as Danielle Barnea settled into the chair before his desk.

"Not really, sir," Danielle lied.

She waited for Giott to take his seat and then leaned forward to set down before him the pages she had been holding. "These are some of Hyram Levy's phone bills. As you can see, he made repeated calls recently to someone the phone company computers were unable to identify." She watched Giott's brow furrow as he began to count, and continued, "Thirty-one in total over the past two months."

Giott picked up the pile of phone bills and began to study them. His eyes off her, Danielle let herself yawn. She had slept little the night before, plagued by the note that had been found in Hyram Levy's desk with her name and hospital room number on it. She never remembered meeting the man, but it was possible he had attended her father's funeral. Although Levy was ten years older than her father, the fact that he had been a much decorated general in the IDF meant their paths had likely crossed on more than one occasion. The two men had, after all, fought many of the same wars together.

So when Danielle went back to her apartment well after midnight, she had checked the guest signature book that had been at her father's funeral as well as the shivah mourning sessions that followed.

Hyram Levy's name was nowhere to be found. Nor had he written her a condolence card, or sent flowers, or made a donation in her father's name to a charity.

But there had been so many handshakes, so many polite gestures of grief. Levy's could have been among them, but Danielle couldn't be sure one way or the other. And even if it had, how would that explain his notation of her hospital room number that Yori Resnick had discovered?

In studying the names in the memorial book, Danielle came across Ari Bar-Rosen's and recalled how impressed she'd been that he had made time from his busy schedule to pay a condolence call. He had drawn her aside and explained simply that he had served under her father and had come to admire him greatly. He was handsome and strong, and Danielle could tell that his grief was honest. Just a few months later he had been elected prime minister, and she had recently received an invitation to attend his installation ceremony, to be held on Masada in a week's time.

"You think these conversations may have something to do with Levy's death?" Giott asking, snapping Danielle alert again.

"At the very least, the ultimate *reason* for his murder might have been discussed. Clearly something was bothering him, something he may have mentioned to the person at the other end of that phone number."

Giott was holding the pages almost protectively when he finally met Danielle's gaze again. "And you are asking me to find out who this person is."

"Yes, Rav Nitzav."

"So you can contact and question him."

"Yes."

"No."

"No?"

"It is not the way such things are done, Pakad," Giott said in the voice of a parent scolding a petulant child. "In your absence you have obviously forgotten the way they *are* done."

"I thought—"

"You thought to come to me first and that is good, so I can tell you how." His voice grew even more stern. "Has anyone else examined these records?"

"No."

"Are there any other copies?"

Danielle shook her head.

"Very well. You will leave this material in my possession. I will make some calls. After determining whom this phone number belongs to, I will speak to this person myself and decide, myself, whether they have information pertinent to this investigation. Then and only then will I decide whether or not to put you in touch with them. Clear?"

"Clear, sir."

"And if I decide not, you will forget about the presence of this number on the murder victim's bills. Yes?"

"Also clear, sir."

"Very well, Danielle. Now leave me."

DANIELLE WAS SUMMONED back to the commissioner's office less than an hour later. His expression was etched in stone. He was wearing his yarmulke now. He barely met her eyes as he spoke.

"This is a very delicate matter, Pakad."

"I understand," Danielle sighed.

"No, you don't, I'm afraid. The man Hyram Levy called all those times is a deputy cabinet minister for the outgoing government. He has served for six different governments in all, both Labor and Likud, over a twenty-five-year period."

That would make him about Levy's age, Danielle calculated for herself.

"His name is Max Pearlman," Giott continued, "and you are meeting him for lunch this afternoon. Twelve-thirty at Atarim Square in Tel Aviv."

CHAPTER 8

BEN DROVE MADLY through the streets of Jericho to the Palestinian Authority building. He rushed through the door and hurried to the offices of the Palestinian Protective Security Service.

Nabril al-Asi was not in his office. No, nobody knew where he was. No, he couldn't be reached. Yes, he had a cell phone, but no one in the building seemed to know the number.

Ben charged up to the fourth floor and Ghazi Sumaya's office, but, as usual, the mayor of Jericho was elsewhere too. His receptionist promised to try and reach him and have Sumaya call Ben at police headquarters.

Ben raced back down the stairs, reaching the lobby again out of breath. Who else would listen to him, what else could he do to ensure the information Nazir Jalabad had given him about an imminent terrorist attack reached the proper parties in Israel before it was too late?

Ben saw the phone resting atop the security desk and burst toward it.

"Hey!" the on-duty police guard yelled when Ben snatched the receiver to his ear.

Ben flashed his identification as he pressed out a number in Israel. Phone service between the West Bank and Israel, even Jerusalem, was only two years old, but he thanked God for it. He had to call Danielle now; he had no other choice.

Nothing happened. The call hadn't gone through.

He tried again.

Still nothing. Dead air. All too familiar.

"What's wrong with this thing?" he screamed at the nearby cop.

"Where are you calling?"

"Israel, goddamn it, Israel!"

"They shut off all long-distance service this morning," the uniformed cop told him. "To punish us."

And themselves this time, Ben thought, standing utterly still.

He checked his watch. It was almost eleven-thirty, giving him no time to try any more channels.

Then Ben remembered the pass into Israel that Colonel al-Asi had finally secured for him so he could visit Danielle in Hadassah Hospital. He hadn't used it because she had checked out on the very day he intended to visit. The pass was still tucked in his glove compartment.

And he would use it now.

CHAPTER 9

DANIELLE ARRIVED AT Atarim Square just before twelve-thirty. Located on the corner of Tel Aviv's fashionable Hayarkon Street and Ben-Gurion Boulevard, the square was built on an elevated platform and lined with shops and cafés on both sides of a boulevard that had been closed to traffic.

The establishments were all doing a brisk business, and under other circumstances Danielle could have enjoyed strolling down the center amid tables, benches, and canopies set atop the street-sized promenade's checkerboard pattern of white and beige stone. It seemed to her that more big-name franchises like the Gap, Benetton, and Au Bon Pain had opened since she'd been here last, but she hadn't been paying nearly as much attention to her surroundings then.

She had come to Atarim Square with Ben in the final days of what had become a relationship impossible to maintain. The square had not been the site of their final breakup, but Danielle remembered watching other couples walking hand in hand and thinking that it was never going to work out no matter what they did. There were limits to how much culture could be overcome, even in their own minds. Passion had fooled them, and when the intensity slowly wore off, reality had set in. They'd fought it for a while, but in the end they couldn't overcome reality's harshness, and they had separated a year and a half ago.

She approached a deli called Moshe's, where she'd been told Max Pearlman had lunch whenever he was in Tel Aviv. Since he would be out of the government in less than a week, that might soon be every day. Of course, it was still possible the new prime minister, Ari Bar-Rosen, would add Pearlman to his government in some capacity; he had served in six of the last seven, after all.

Danielle could see Pearlman sitting at a canopied table set on the edge of the square itself, close enough to reach out and touch the strollers and cyclists. Even the most recent photos she had seen of him must have been old, picturing a man with more hair that had barely begun to whiten. He was seated, but a young man with watchful eyes stood not far away surveying the scene from behind dark sunglasses. His bodyguard, she guessed.

The bodyguard watched Danielle approach, sliding over to make it obvious she had to go through him to reach Pearlman.

"It's all right, Lev. This must be my luncheon guest," she heard Pearlman say.

The bodyguard stood aside and Danielle walked straight to Pearlman, who rose to greet her.

"How did you recognize me?" she asked him.

"Attractive young women don't approach me very often these days." He took her hand warmly in both of his, then opened a palm to the table. "Please, join me."

Danielle chose a chair that gave her a view of the promenade. Old habits. "How much did Rav Nitzav Giott tell you about what I wanted to talk about?"

"Some. Enough. Because of your medical examiner, we can't hold Hyram's funeral for at least another three days."

"I'm sorry."

"Don't be. I understand." Pearlman sipped what Danielle thought was iced tea. He must have been almost the same age as Levy, early seventies. His eyes were a piercing shade of gray and looked as though they belonged to a much younger man. "You know the truly sad thing? There won't be a single family member at the funeral. Hyram never married, claimed he never had time. I think he was very lonely these last few years. It's not a very good way to die."

"Being murdered never is."

Pearlman's free hand balled into a still formidable fist. "The man lived through every war this country ever fought to be killed in his own shop. God's justice, *acccchhhhhhh!*"

"According to Mr. Levy's phone bills, the two of you hadn't spoken much at all in the past year up until two months ago, when he began calling you on a regular and increasing basis."

Pearlman shrugged. "Like I said, he had gotten very lonely." He leaned forward. "And I'll tell you something about my friend Hyram. He got feelings sometimes. Ever since I've known him, he got feelings like premonitions about things. I can't remember many times that he was wrong. In fact, I couldn't recall even one for you now."

"You think he knew he was going to die?"

"He never said that, not in so many words, but I think he was expecting it. I think he kept calling me for reassurance. I think he was scared."

"Some of the calls were very long."

"*A lot* of reassurance." Pearlman smiled sadly. His teeth were crooked and stained by tobacco. "And we had a lot to talk about, much to rehash. Many adventures."

"You knew him a long time."

Pearlman straightened, looking proud. "Since the very beginning."

"As children?"

"No," he said, "a different beginning . . ."

And as Pearlman began to tell his tale, Danielle's eyes strayed to the promenade, where for a fleeting second she thought she caught sight, impossibly, of Ben Kamal weaving his way through the crowd.

CHAPTER 10

YOU'RE DOING IT all wrong!" said David Wollchensky when Max Pearlman missed the target yet again.

The rifle felt ridiculously heavy in his hands and looked ridiculously light when Wollchensky snatched it from him. He was dressed as a beggar, the disguise he often chose when he wandered the streets in Arab-controlled areas, trying to pick up tidbits of intelligence.

"Here, let me show you."

Barely a week had passed since Wollchensky had saved Pearlman, Jacob Rossovitch, and Hyram Levy from the British patrol on the beachhead at Caesarea. But already they were being trained as soldiers in the service of Israel. None of them had known what to expect when they embarked on this journey. Like everyone else, they came in search of fulfilling a destiny. They came home.

David Wollchensky turned out to be a soldier of the Haganah, an underground resistance movement determined to take Palestine back, at least enough of it to forge a nation, no matter what means that required. The stakes were too great to even consider costs; that much Pearlman understood very well. Like Rossovitch and Levy, he had lost his whole family and history to war. As a survivor, the value of his own life paled in comparison to living in a place where it could never happen again. Becoming a part of the movement toward a new state was what provided purpose when everything else was gone. The dream of Israel gave him a reason not just to exist, but to live.

As dramatic and tragic as Pearlman's own story was, though, it was nothing compared to David Wollchensky's. He had been imprisoned in a Polish ghetto, where he watched his mother die of disease and his father of a Nazi bullet to the head. The Nazi commander would celebrate the Jewish Sabbath every Friday night by gathering the town in the square and reading the names of ten young men of bar mitzvah age. The boys would draw marbles from a box, half of them black and half white. The ones who drew black were hung on the spot, in full view of the entire town.

But that wasn't even the worst of it. The worst was the boys lucky enough to draw white marbles were forced to escort their doomed friends up the gallows and fasten the noose around their throats as they stood on a stool. Then when the commander shot his pistol in the air they were to jerk the stools out from beneath their friends' feet. To refuse, or delay, meant they would be shot on the spot along with their families.

Seven times David Wollchensky had reached into the box held by the grinning Nazi, and seven times, incredibly, he drew a white marble. Incredible, but not fortunate. Not when seven times his "luck" meant David had to lead another friend to his death upon the gallows. The Nazis would not allow the use of hoods, but he learned to avoid the eyes of his friends when he tightened the noose around their throats. Yanking the stool out was the hardest. Standing there as they kicked and thrashed. It took a few of them a very long time to die, and a part of David Wollchensky died up there with his friends every time.

By his sixth and seventh turns, it became a game for the Nazis to see if his luck would hold out. They cheered and applauded when he opened his hand to reveal a white marble yet again. The last two times he escorted friends to their death, a line of laughing Nazis slapped his back fondly on the way.

But he never wished for a black marble, not even once. He maintained his will to live by fantasizing what he would do to these Nazis once the war was over. His soul was already dead while his body lived on, and he would make good use of that body as soon as the opportunity presented itself down the road. By the seventh Sabbath, he felt nothing as he half carried a boy his own age to his death. Heard not his sobs, nor smelled his fear. Did not turn away from his twitching feet or hands clawing at the noose around his throat beneath his bulging eyes.

It was all fuel for David Wollchensky's resolve, and after the seventh week that resolve took shape.

The depravity in the ghetto had reached a point where bodies were literally piling up in the gutters and needed to be hauled away on a daily basis. This unenviable task fell upon a team of Jews who grasped for anything that might keep them alive a little longer. They were provided with no gloves or sanitary equipment. Many who took on this duty, their immune systems already worn hopelessly down, caught any number of diseases from the corpses. Their reward thus became a slow death rather than a quick one.

On the morning after the seventh Sabbath, David was waiting outside in the street when the old open truck lumbered through the street, stopping every time it came to the husk of what had been a human being only a day or so earlier. After the truck passed his hiding place, David rushed to catch up and hurled himself to its bed amid the corpses. He hid among them, camouflaged by death, until the truck came to a huge flaming pit, again manned by more Jews, where the bodies were to be dumped. The Jews here wore makeshift masks to keep from passing out due to the stench. If they did pass out, the Nazi soldiers overseeing the operation would either shoot them or simply dump their unconscious bodies into the fire with the corpses.

David slid out and hid beneath the truck before the process of unloading the corpses began. He waited until most of the bodies had been tossed into the pit, so that the smoke would be at it thickest, before crawling out. He wormed on his stomach all the way into the woods and cried when he was well hidden amid the trees, because he was leaving the only home he had ever known. Only then did the enormity of the task he was taking on occur to him. But if God had not meant him to survive, He could have made sure David picked a black marble instead of a white one on any of seven different occasions. That belief gave David the faith needed to strengthen his resolve. It also kept him from ever looking back.

David would often tell Max Pearlman that the next few years formed a blurry patch in his memory. He remembered things in blotches, out of order chronologically to the point that he really could not say in which month, and sometimes even in which year, an event had happened.

A sense of order did not return to his thinking until he reached Palestine. He arrived with an early group of refugees before the British blockades, those that the *Gideon* had successfully avoided, were set up. He became a member of a secret army of Jews called the Palmach, dedicated to smuggling other refugees into the country and organizing them once they got there. By the time the *Gideon* dumped its lifeboats into the Mediterranean outside Caesarea, he had joined the

Haganah, a group of Jewish resistance fighters who had extended their mandate to conducting operations against the British occupiers.

Max Pearlman realized early in their friendship that David Wollchenksy, having determined his dream of revenge against the Nazis of the ghetto would likely never be realized, had turned all his wrath upon the British in their stead. And when the British finally relinquished their mandate following Israel's declaration of independence in May of 1948, David turned that same thirst for vengeance upon the Arabs who were so determined to deny the Jewish people the homeland that God, and the United Nations, had deeded them.

In the early days of their friendship, David's determination drove Pearlman, Levy, and Rossovitch to master the skills needed to join him in the Haganah. The British occupation of Palestine, and their increasingly brutal repression of the resistance fighters, was too much for him to bear. He could not live through another ghetto, and with Jewish refugee camps springing up first in Palestine and then in Greece, his fuse burned down to its end. It was as though Wollchensky had lost his soul in the ghetto, and the attainment of a homeland was the only way he could see to get it back. Nothing would get in his way. He would rather die than face another internment aimed at breaking the spirit as well as the body.

For two weeks, the three friends who had come to Israel aboard the *Gideon* did nothing but drill and study the methods and tactics of the Haganah. They provided backup and cover on a number of operations and raids that included blowing up a British oil refinery before David told them they were ready to move to the front line. In fact, the four of them had been approved for a mission.

It was a relatively simple operation and should have required no violence at all. Many of the British officers were sympathetic to the Jews and did their best to covertly aid their cause whenever possible. David had made contact with one of these men, a major at a large weapons depot, who offered to "lose" six crates of rifles, ammunition, and grenades to David's possession. The Haganah agreed to the plan and to provide backup in the hills surrounding the warehouse on the outskirts of Haifa.

The four friends drove to the warehouse in a covered supply truck stolen by another Haganah team months before, Max up front with David, Hyram Levy and Jacob Rossovitch in the back. David had flashed a forged letter of transfer for the weapons, which was just a formality since the major in charge was expecting them. Still, they wore pilfered British uniforms just in case, and David was under strict orders to abort the mission should anything be amiss.

"Trouble," David said as he slid to a halt in front of the depot.

"What?" Pearlman asked.

David fixed his gaze on a British major striding purposefully in their direction. "That officer approaching us isn't the man I've been dealing with."

"Abort. You know our instructions if anything goes wrong, abort."

"Too late," David said, and he threw the big truck into reverse, backing it up toward the garage's huge bay doors.

The British officer in charge had to leap out of the way to avoid being struck. "Hey!" he shouted, trotting after them. "Hold it, you bloody idiot! I said, *hold it!*"

David obliged only when the rear of the truck was in easy range of the bay. He started to open his door as the officer approached angrily, and Max Pearlman saw him cover his drawn pistol with the forged transfer order.

"Here you are, sir," David said to the major in a perfect British accent, firing twice before the man's hands had even closed on the paper.

Two more soldiers heard the shots and came running. David felled them with one shot each.

"Drag the other two bodies under the truck!" David ordered Pearlman.

Max, aghast, stayed frozen in the passenger seat.

"Did you hear what I said? *Do it!*" And David leaped out to pull the major from view himself.

Max recovered enough to jump down and join David on the ground. "This mission was never approved, was it?" he said accusingly as Rossovitch and Levy dropped out of the truck's rear. "This whole thing was your plan."

"Shut up and do what I tell you!"

"You never spoke to any sympathetic British officer."

"I said—"

"There's no backup, is there? We're on our own."

"That's right," David rasped angrily. He grabbed Pearlman by his British uniform top and slammed him against the truck. "And you'd be dead now if it wasn't for me. They would have buried you in the sand at Caesarea. So now you're going to help me, and if you don't like it, when we're done you can go to hell."

The hulking Rossovitch and diminutive Levy stood next to them with rifles in hand, transfixed.

"The two of you get the other bodies out of sight," David ordered them. "Then take up their posts. Keep your faces down." He swung back toward Pearlman. "Max, you and I will load the truck."

There were far more than six crates inside the warehouse, but most of them were too heavy to manage in the brief time they had left. After hoisting eight into the rear of the truck left them sweating and gasping, Max began to plead with Wollchensky that they had enough. David reluctantly agreed and lowered the bay door behind them. Rossovitch and Levy took their places back in the truck's now cluttered rear, but before they set off David popped open one of the crates and drew out a trio of machine guns. He passed them out, along with magazines from another crate, and told his friends to be ready, this in spite of the fact that none of them had ever fired such a weapon or could even locate the safety until he pointed it out.

The alarm did not sound until they were within sight of the gate. David didn't slow down, didn't hesitate. He jammed one hand out the window and opened fire with his pistol while the other stayed glued to the wheel. Max leaned out his window and drew down on the guard with the machine gun, the kick from its initial spray driving his head up against the truck's door-jamb.

Return fire shattered the windshield an instant before they crashed through the gate. Now Rossovitch's and Levy's bullets replaced theirs, blazing out the truck's rear as it tore away from the British camp. They were long gone before the British could summon vehicles to take up the chase, and safely nestled inside a Haganah stronghold before an effective dragnet could be mounted.

David Wollchensky was reproached for his maverick operation, but congratulated for its results. Weapons were the most precious of all commodities for the fledgling Jewish underground, especially since those leaders with the most foresight could see a much more violent struggle coming in the days ahead.

After their unauthorized mission, the three young men who had come to Israel aboard the *Gideon* talked about parting ways from their reckless friend. This was their chance. But they didn't take it. Wollchensky's passion was contagious. Later Pearlman would see that passion as being rooted in the desire to atone for the seven deaths he believed himself responsible for. Like David, Max figured, they all had something if not to atone for, then at least to recover from. Wollchensky made them feel like they held the future in their own hands, after being so helpless against the past. So the four friends, together, would fight for the establishment of a Jewish state.

Whatever it took.

Wherever it led them.

CHAPTER 11

THAT WAS ONLY the beginning, of course," Pearlman said to Danielle. In spite of the tale's brave and heroic text, he showed no joy in telling it. On the contrary, the process had seemed almost painful to him.

"I thought you were going to tell me about your friendship with Hyram Levy, Mr. Pearlman," Danielle told him, as politely as she could.

"That voyage on the *Gideon* brought us together, but it was David Wollchensky who *kept* us together. Everything we became, our very identities in Israel, we owe to him. There was no going back after that raid on the British weapons depot, no turning away."

"And does this have anything to do with what Hyram Levy has been calling you about these past few months?"

"It has *everything* to do with it, Pakad." Pearlman shifted his chair closer to Danielle's. "You haven't gotten the autopsy results back yet, obviously."

"Not the complete report, no," she acknowledged,

and her eyes wandered again to a man she could have sworn was Ben Kamal moving anxiously along the promenade as if he were looking for a lost child.

"I'll save you the trouble of waiting," Pearlman said grimly. "Hyram was dying of cancer. He never went to the doctor, but he knew all the same." His voice drifted. "He always knew those kinds of things."

"You stayed in touch with him all these years?"

"As I said, the story I just told you is only the beginning. The three of us survived all of the wars. If we'd had the time, we could have watched history forming around us."

"You mean four."

"Excuse me?"

"You said three, but with Wollchensky there were four of you."

Pearlman's shoulders drooped. His head sank toward his chest. "One of us did not make it all the way. But that's another part of the story."

"Is there a part which might help me learn who may have killed Hyram Levy?"

"Hyram outlived all of his enemies, Pakad, and most of his friends."

"It only takes one, sir."

Pearlman shrugged.

"I need to ask you something else," Danielle said. This was probably a bad idea, but she couldn't get the fact that Levy had jotted down her name and hospital room number out of her head. "Did Hyram Levy ever mention anything about me? It might have been about six weeks ago."

"*You?*"

"Yes or no?"

"Not to me. Why would he?"

She ignored his question, regretted raising the issue in the first place. "Did you ever discuss anything that gave any indication that Levy thought he was in danger?"

Pearlman leaned even closer to her. "Tell me what else you've learned, and maybe I will remember something."

Danielle decided not to hold back. "He knew his attacker. He was struck from close behind. There was no struggle."

"And the shop?"

"Ransacked. The killer was looking for something."

"Did he find it?"

"We don't know yet, sir."

"A diary, a journal, even a tape, perhaps?"

"What makes you ask?"

Pearlman smiled slightly. "How old are you, Pakad?"

"Thirty-two."

"In forty years you will understand. The past two months, since Hyram knew he was dying, have been about the past. That's what all our phone conversations were about. He was trying to come to terms with his life. You have children, of course."

"No." Danielle tried not to sound as uneasy as she felt.

"Oh." Her answer had clearly surprised Pearlman. "Someday, yes?"

She smiled politely.

"Well, Hyram had run out of somedays. He had begun to question the choices he had made in his life, what he was leaving behind. Like I said, in forty years you will know. I think he may have been writing it all down, sorting things out. Making his peace with the world."

"I understand. But why would someone kill him for such a journal?"

"I didn't mean to suggest they did, Pakad. Only that there might be things written in such a journal that plenty of people would have reason never to want to see get out. Enemies *and* friends."

"Any of them Palestinian, Mr. Pearlman? I ask because in his business he associated with a great number of Palestinians."

"An interesting suspicion coming from someone with your reputation."

"Reputation?"

Pearlman's eyes scorned her. He smiled almost playfully. "Come now, Chief Inspector Barnea, do you think I would not have read your file before this meeting? I am aware of your being paired with a Palestinian counterpart on a rather crucial investigation two years ago."

"And how did Hyram Levy feel about Palestinians, Mr. Pearlman?"

"You already know the answer to that. You told me so yourself."

"I know Hyram Levy worked with Palestinians. I know he did business with Palestinians. But I don't know how he felt about them."

Max Pearlman slid his chair away from her now. For a moment Danielle didn't think he was going to speak again, and let her eyes wander the cluttered promenade in search of the man who looked so much like Ben Kamal.

"Then let me tell you," Pearlman said suddenly. "After we established our state, during the war with the Arabs, the Haganah left the underground and became full-fledged soldiers. Some of the towns we were forced to take were filled with Arabs that Jews had always gotten along with, who bore us no ill will. We took their homes from them, Pakad. Sometimes we burned their homes after they fled. Hyram Levy cried over it, actually *cried*. He told me we had made refugees out of *them* now. We had turned them into ourselves. The hate we saw in their eyes for us, Hyram said, was the same that had once been in our eyes for the British. Ironic that we had so fast forgotten what it felt like, isn't it? I don't think his heart was ever in the war again after that day.

Even after we won I don't remember ever seeing him celebrate."

Danielle was about to ask another question, when she again spotted the man who looked like Ben Kamal. She watched him dart through the crowd and launch himself toward an Israeli soldier who had stopped for a cigarette.

CHAPTER 12

BEN HAD CONSIDERED all his options, reduced them finally to this desperate one.

He had spent nearly a half hour since arriving at Atarim Square walking up and down the crowded artery centered between two rows of shops and cafés, searching for the Hamas bomber. He concentrated on furtive movements, any anomaly that would give the bomber away. And when that failed he began to focus on people's eyes in search of a look of fanatical resolve swimming in them, mixing with terror as the final moment grew near.

Ben checked his watch. It was 12:56. According to Nazir Jalabad he had only four minutes left to find the bomber.

He was running out of time, goddamn it!

Ben felt himself growing desperate, realizing that if he failed he would very likely end up among the bomber's casualties: a promenade full of lunching Israelis and one Palestinian—he wondered what the press would make of that. There seemed to be no choice other than to evacuate the square, risk the panic that would ensue. The bomber could still detonate his explosives, if he was here, but at the loss of significantly fewer lives.

Ben started toward an Israeli soldier, intending to enlist his aid.

Wait! The soldier was wearing *a backpack*, the only one in the square to have anything but a Galil machine gun slung from his shoulder. And this soldier had no rifle, only a side arm.

My God, maybe that's him!

Ben looked at his watch just as the time ticked to 12:58. He had no gun, having left his pistol back in Jericho since his pass into Israel did not include permission to bring it. He knew instantly what he had to do, never even considered the consequences once the other soldiers saw him attacking one of their apparent fellows.

He started toward the soldier wearing the backpack, suddenly racked by doubt. What if the real bomber was someone else, some*where* else? Could he even be sure Nazir Jalabad had been telling the truth?

Ben quickened his pace through the crowd, approaching on an angle that would keep him on the soldier's blind side until he struck. Just before he made his move, he spotted the wire strung around from the backpack, saw the pen-sized detonator clutched in the Hamas terrorist's fist.

All doubt vanished.

Ben lunged.

Impact jolted his insides. He felt his ribs give a little, but maintained the sense of mind to go for the hand holding the detonator while he took the man down. He failed to wrench it completely free but managed to close his fingers over enough of the detonator to keep the suicide bomber from triggering the explosives.

They hit the polished stone of the promenade together with Ben on top, working a knee hard into the man's groin to further weaken his grasp. Around him people lurched away in all directions. A few screamed. For Ben, the moment was suspended in time. He struggled with the thrashing soldier, yelling,

"He's got . . .

. . . **A** BOMB! . . . *"*

Danielle lurched up from the table. Her chair crashed backward at the same time Max Pearlman's bodyguard hurled his body atop the old man and spilled the table over for cover.

It *was* Ben Kamal! It really was!

But what the hell was he doing? Why was he yelling about a bomb as he struggled with an Israeli soldier he had just attacked?

Soldiers and plainclothes officers converged on Ben from all angles in the promenade, rifles or pistols raised and ready. They screamed at bystanders to clear the way and shoved the ones who didn't listen brutally aside. Danielle whipped out her National Police badge and held it before her as she stormed forward.

"Police! Police! Hold your positions! Nobody fire!"

The authority in her voice made the soldiers obey for the moment. She didn't know how long it would last, but she had to make it last long enough to sort all this out.

Halfway to Ben her eyes strayed to a young blind man standing utterly still beside his guide dog. Her stare lingered long enough for the man to look away.

Blind men don't look away. . . .

The soldier beneath Ben lay still on the promenade. Ben rolled off him, one of his hands thrusting a portable detonator toward anyone who could see.

"Check his pack! Check his pack! He's got a bomb!"

Danielle drew her gun and sprinted toward the blind man, the second bomber in keeping with Hamas procedure, who was standing stock-still in the midst of the horde of patrons evacuating Atarim Square. But the explosives, where were his explosives?

She noticed the saddlelike bags strapped to his dog's shoulders and shuddered. He must have been waiting for maximum effect, the most people possible gathered around him before he blew himself up. Using the fleeing throngs for cover, she watched the bomber's hand let go of the dog's guide lead and move toward his pocket.

Danielle raised her pistol. A shot aimed at the bomber would have to be perfect—unlikely from this angle, with so many people in the way. So she steadied her gun lower, angled it so the bullet would come up just short of the dog.

This had to work!

Danielle fired through the slightest of gaps in the crowd, and the bullet ricocheted off the pavement a foot from the dog's hindquarters. Startled, the animal sprinted away.

Yes! she thought. *Yes!*

The blind man tore off his sunglasses and tried to move but was caught off guard by the surge of the crowd, jostled one way and then another, as the dog reached a winding staircase leading to the street.

Danielle bolted toward the second bomber on foot, taking the most direct route over tables set in a neat row at the edge of the promenade, leaping from one to another. Plates and glasses crashed to the ground beneath her rush, until she finally gained a clear shot and fired.

The bomber reeled backward, looking as though he'd been kicked hard in the gut. His legs wobbled. His hands clutched for his chest.

Danielle noticed one of them closing around something dark.

The explosion was deafening, the force of it enough to spill her from the last tabletop she had mounted. She heard the familiar screech of brakes from the pavement, followed by the crunching thud of cars slamming into each other. But the screams of agony and terror she knew all too well from similar incidents did not come, just a few voices wailing in fear and the rising scent of burning metal that formed the blast's aftermath.

Danielle climbed back to her feet and saw a tangle of twisted, smoking steel in the middle of the street. People were being helped from the burned husks of cars, some bleeding, but all, it appeared, alive.

She swung back toward Ben, who was being handcuffed and manhandled even as he fought to explain who he was.

"I'm in charge here! I'm in charge!" Danielle announced, rushing toward the tight grouping of soldiers who had engulfed him. She kept flashing her badge. "National Police! National Police! This man is one of ours!"

"But, Detective, this man is—"

"Shut up and take those cuffs off him! Do you hear me? Take those cuffs off him and *back off!*"

Danielle's tone left no room for argument. The soldiers around Ben did as they were told. The rest dragged the surviving terrorist off into custody. His backpack had been stripped off. It lay on the pavement, where it was enclosed by a trio of soldiers who kept their backs to it to keep everyone else clear of its contents.

Ben rose slowly and cautiously onto his knees beneath Danielle's protective stance. She scanned the square again, searching for the canopied table at which she had been seated just a few minutes before.

Max Pearlman was gone.

CHAPTER 13

"So WHAT BRINGS you to Israel?"

Seated in the back of the unmarked Israeli National Police car, Ben smiled at Danielle's question. It hurt to turn toward her. He could feel his back and shoulders starting to stiffen up from the pummeling he'd received from the soldiers back in the square above. Technically, he was under arrest. The whole situation needed to be sorted out. He would be questioned as to the source of his information, but Danielle had already assured him that she would not leave his side during the brief interrogation. Besides, Ben's face was not unknown inside Israel. Once the authorities realized who he was, he trusted, things would go smoothly. It was the first time he had actually welcomed the celebrity status that had made him more a pariah in the West Bank than anything else.

"It seems," Ben said to Danielle, "that fate is about to make us heroes again."

"I can see the headlines now," she said, nodding. " 'Palestinian and Israeli cops thwart suicide bombing

in square. Dozens saved.'" Danielle's gaze sharpened.
"How did you know an attack was coming?"

"A source in Jericho."

"And you decided to handle it yourself?"

"I had no choice, believe me," Ben told her, and
proceeded to explain.

Danielle was smiling when he finished. "It's a good
thing I left the hospital early. If you had used that pass
when you planned to . . ."

"I'm still sorry I didn't."

"How did you find out?"

"About today?"

"About me. Was it your friend Major al-Asi from the
Preventive Security Service?"

"He's a colonel now. He was kind enough to keep
me informed."

Danielle tried to smile again, but failed.

"I'm sorry it didn't work out for the two of you," Ben
said, trying to sound like he meant it.

"Are you more sorry it didn't work out for us?"

"You know I am. If you had any idea how much I
missed you . . ."

Their eyes met, and for that moment everything was
as it had been two years ago, when the latest phase of
the peace process they had preserved had been
greeted by both sides with optimism and celebration.
For the Palestinians, the road to an autonomous state
seemed clearly paved. For the Israelis, the end of terror
seemed a very real possibility. But the illusions didn't
hold.

Hamas terrorists enacted a desperate, all-out campaign of suicide bombings and random attacks that
sent the peace process reeling. The great hope of
peace became the great lie, with accusations and re-
criminations launched by both sides. And Danielle and
Ben found themselves trapped within that lie, held
hostage by it while they tried to foster a relationship
handicapped by geography and strained by politics.

With the West Bank and Gaza sealed for all but officials of the Palestinian Authority and its elected representatives, Ben could no longer enter any part of Israel without one of Colonel al-Asi's special passes. For a time he was not even supposed to leave Jericho, and he had been detained by roving Israeli patrols the two times he had tried to leave the district. The few occasions he and Danielle were able to see each other were uneasy at best. From the start they had expected the need to weather that storm, but they had misjudged its intensity. As the tension between their peoples escalated, they lost favor with their respective coworkers and faced being ostracized for carrying on a relationship that was *haram,* forbidden by both sides.

Danielle suggested they let things cool for a while, and although Ben didn't disagree with her, he knew the process, once started, would be difficult to reverse. Especially when the tensions between their peoples continued to escalate to the point of nearly nullifying the original Oslo agreement and threatening a return of the *intifada.*

Ben recalled following the most recent Israeli special elections for purely selfish reasons, rooting for Ari Bar-Rosen and his promises of renewed peace efforts out of hope it could renew his relationship with Danielle. But then he learned she was pregnant and counted the months backward a hundred times before conceding that the baby could not be his. After losing his family back in Detroit, he never thought he'd have any desire to have children again. Finding out that Danielle was pregnant with someone else's child, though, pitched him into a deep depression from which he had not yet fully emerged. He felt he had lost an opportunity he hadn't realized he wanted until someone else had seized it. Would she have come to live in America with him if he had asked her? He would never know. Too stubborn. Not only because he hadn't asked, but also because a part of him still clung to Palestine, even though what he was looking for, he realized, wasn't here.

Danielle was what he was looking for. A second chance at life, not a career or just a home. Now he had squandered that chance, and more than anything that was why he was on the verge of returning to America. He had come "home" because he had nothing left in America, then found he had even less here. He would always be an outsider, a foreigner in spite of the fact he'd been born on the West Bank. In his four years back, Danielle—an Israeli—had been the only person who had accepted him. And without her there seemed no reason to stay.

Ben wanted to reach out and take her in his arms right there in the car, started to tremble just thinking about it.

"There's something I need," he said to distract himself. "A tape."

"A tape?"

"A surveillance tape of a former Hamas operative. Made in Jericho five nights ago."

"Mossad?"

"Or Shin Bet. A white van was parked in clear view of the ex-operative's home. It stayed only long enough to record him on tape."

"Is this operative important to you?"

"Not at all. I think your people may have caught something else on that tape inadvertently: the abduction of a young girl that occurred around the same time."

"But you're not sure."

"That's why I need the tape."

"Difficult to obtain."

"After today, Pakad, I'd say your country owes me the favor."

* * *

A PLAINCLOTHES OFFICER finally climbed behind the wheel and drove them to National Police headquarters in Jerusalem. Ben's car had been impounded and would be returned to him upon his release.

Danielle promised to do everything she could to obtain the tape, if it existed, making no promises since cooperative police efforts had been few and far between as of late.

"Actually," Danielle said when they were alone again in a debriefing room at National Police headquarters, "there's something you can do for me as well. A shopkeeper was murdered in Jerusalem's Mahane Yehuda marketplace two nights ago: an Israeli named Hyram Levy, better known as the Engineer. Levy was acquainted with a number of Palestinians."

"And, naturally, they are suspects."

"Just among the usual ones we'd like to round up. Smugglers, specifically, the kind Levy was known to consort with."

"If he was known to do business with them, what do you need my help for?"

"Because Levy employed an unusual filing system—a bunch of scribbling on memo pages, mostly. We have first names and nicknames, but no last names."

"So you need a list of known smugglers in the West Bank and Gaza to find potential matches."

"Exactly. We're doing the same with Israeli smugglers and criminals connected to Levy. Whoever killed Levy locked the door behind him after he left. That means someone capable of making a key, or working a lock without one."

"Or given a key by your victim."

"We're looking into that as well."

Ben considered the prospects. "This list in exchange for that surveillance tape?"

Danielle shrugged. "Why not?"

"It's good to be working with you again, Pakad," Ben smiled.

CHAPTER 14

HERSHEL GIOTT'S BROW crinkled as he listened to Danielle's request. He waited until she was finished before responding.

"You understand that our intelligence services are no longer permitted to conduct operations in Jericho and the other cities ceded to Palestinian control."

"Yes, Rav Nitzav."

"So you are asking me to produce something which by all accounts cannot exist."

"That's right, sir. Only because in return it could yield us something of substantial aid to our investigation into the murder of Hyram Levy."

"This list of smugglers from your Palestinian police contact . . ."

"Who assures me he wishes to view the tape only to see if it captured the abduction of a young girl. Should the tape not include that, he will have no use for it."

Giott sighed deeply. "I see."

The sadness that lengthened his expression and deepened the baggy circles beneath his small eyes was something Danielle had never seen before. "You knew Levy, didn't you, sir?"

"In Israel those of us in certain positions know most others in comparable ones. Ours is a small country, Pakad."

"Did my father know Levy?"

"I'm sure he did. Why?"

"Because I think Levy knew *me*. My name was found on a note tucked in his desk." She let that sink in before continuing. "Along with my room number when I was in the hospital."

Giott remained utterly expressionless. "I don't think this is something you should be concerned about."

"It's only that—"

"Listen to me, Pakad," Giott said, more sternly than he had meant to. When he spoke again, his voice was lower, laced with a false calm. "Let it go. For your own good."

His eyes had gotten that fatherly look of concern Danielle remembered so well from her first tour of duty with the National Police. This man *could have been* her father as he stared across his desk at her. A small man, an old man. It was a paradox of Israel that so many people of age held positions of great power. Here experience was valued above all else, and people like Giott formed an impenetrable bottleneck for the younger generations to advance. As if they weren't ready to be trusted yet. As if only those who had lived through all of Israel's wars had the ability to lead her properly.

"Let it go," Giott repeated.

Danielle looked into his tired eyes and knew she would be better off if she did that, just as she knew that she couldn't.

Giott's phone rang. He picked it up, listened briefly, and then looked again toward Danielle.

"That was for you, Pakad," he said, replacing the receiver on the cradle. "You're wanted in the Mahane Yehuda marketplace as soon as possible. Apparently, they have found a witness."

CHAPTER 15

BEN RETURNED TO the West Bank via the main road that ran between Hebron and Jerusalem so he could stop outside Bethlehem at the Deheisha refugee camp, from which one of the three girls on Nazir Jalabad's list had disappeared.

Deheisha was one of more than a dozen camps still active in the West Bank. Surrounded by a crumbling twenty-foot fence, it remained the most populous. Ben had had few occasions to visit Deheisha since his return. The camp's militant reputation made it a prudent place for him to avoid, given his established association with a peace process the residents felt had betrayed them.

Nonetheless, today Ben parked his car in a packed-dirt lot and walked past the first of the seemingly endless rows of ramshackle homes squeezed close to one another en route to the office belonging to the United Nations camp administrator. He told the administrator he was looking for the Shabaz family and was surprised when the man produced a card with their address within seconds.

"Can you tell me anything about them?" Ben asked hopefully.

The administrator consulted the card as a ceiling fan spun lazily above them. "A mother and six children, according to this. The house belongs to the grandmother who still lives with them. The children's father has been in an Israeli prison for the past five years."

"How long have they been here?"

"It doesn't say. But the daughter and her children were born here; I can tell you that much. Would you like me to have someone show you to their house?"

"I'll find it."

The previous night's rain had dragged up from the earth a musty stench that clung to the air like an invisible shroud. Ben tried to shut his nose to it as his feet sloshed through the soggy ground en route to the address the camp administrator had provided. The cement houses of Deheisha were squeezed closely together, often separated by no more than a small yard fenced in with corrugated aluminum. Virtually all the yards contained gardens, some no more than a few potted plants placed atop the fence, but a garden all the same. Many of the houses showed the effects of growing families in the form of neatly erected concrete extensions, their color unmatched from that of the main structure and their bulk shrinking the space between adjacent homes even further.

The Shabaz home was a simple rectangular structure, one story built upon a cement-block base with a rather large yard since it lacked the additions enjoyed by many of its neighbors. Ben could hear chickens squawking, and a few goats meandered near the rear of the property, munching verdant weeds that seemed to grow out of the fence. He spotted a woman clipping clothes to a rope line that extended between her house and the next. Her feet slogged through a thick layer of mud as she fastened the clothes tight. When the earth grew sodden like this, the rancid smells of sewage permeated the air, seeming to hang over everything and casting a pall over the whole of the camp.

"Umm Shabaz?" Ben called.

She turned, regarded him fearfully. "Who are you?"

He showed her his badge. "Inspector Bayan Kamal of the Palestinian police."

She looked him over again. "Where is your uniform?"

"I'm a detective."

"I haven't done anything."

"I've come about your daughter."

The woman dragged her basket of clothes free of the mud and stood facing Ben, the basket lying between them. "Which one? What have they done?"

"Nothing, I'm sure." He consulted the card Nazir Jalabad had given him. "It's Assira I've come about."

Mrs. Shabaz started to kick her basket back toward the line. "Then you've come for nothing. She's not here."

"I know. That's why *I'm* here."

"You're late. She's been gone for almost six months now. *Eib.*"

"How old is she?"

"Thirteen," the woman said matter-of-factly. "My oldest."

"Did you report her disappearance to the police?"

Umm Shabaz simply chuckled and went back to hanging her clothes. A pair of boys—twins, Ben thought—rushed out through a patched screen door chasing a dog. The door stayed open and an older woman, their grandmother, he guessed, emerged lugging a tray of dough toward an outdoor oven called a *taboun.* Soon the fragrant smell of bread baking would fill the air, battling the odors of refuse in one of the paradoxes of Deheisha and all the camps.

Ben followed Umm Shabaz into the mud. "Your daughter isn't the only young girl who's disappeared recently."

She still didn't look at him, continuing to sound like anything but the grieving mother. "She didn't disappear, Mr. Policeman. She left, she ran away. She's gone because she wants to be gone."

"Do you know where she can be found?"

"No."

"Why did she leave?"

Umm Shabaz smirked. "Just look around you. Who wants to stay? My children sleep in a single room. Our toilet doesn't work. Wherever she is, she probably has more space, can go to the bathroom when she wants, I hope."

"Have you seen her again since she left?"

"No."

"If I could find her . . ."

"Don't bother," the missing girl's mother said, and turned her back on him. The line was sagging now, the clothes in the center flirting with the mud's reach. Ben could see the next few items she hung trembling in her hands.

"Have others left the camp, too, like your daughter?"

"I wouldn't know."

"People talk."

"I don't listen. I keep to myself, so when the police come I don't have to lie."

She still wouldn't look at Ben. She dropped a tattered shirt into the mud, fished it out, and hung it on the line even though it was soiled now.

"I can help you."

"You want to help? Look around you. Where would you like to start? My daughter wanted to leave. She left. She hasn't come back and maybe she never will. *Fi Idein Allah*. It's in God's hands. I have nothing else to say."

With that, Umm Shabaz picked up her basket and retreated back through the mud into her house, leaving the door open behind her.

CHAPTER 16

THE WITNESS'S NAME, Danielle learned, was Abdul Samshi, and he operated a food stand in the Mahane Yehuda marketplace, just around the corner from Hyram Levy's shop. Wrapped around the intersection of Chaim Street and Apple Alley, the stand lay on the street parallel to the covered lane. It was situated next to an open-air market featuring all varieties of meats hanging in display from a small over-head rack and smelling strongly of the salts and spices with which they had been smoked. Samshi, an Israeli Arab, was in fact part owner of the stand, rewarded by its elderly Jewish proprietor for fifteen years of loyal service.

To reach the stand, Danielle had to dodge the tables of card players clustered on the sidewalk. Older men watching the world go by between hands completed amid the fragrant smells of the marketplace.

"What is it that you saw?" she asked Samshi as some of the card players looked on, attracted by the slight commotion.

"Not what I saw, Pakad," Samshi said impatiently, repeating what he had told Yori Resnick, "what I *didn't* see."

"Very well."

Samshi checked on some grilling meat that smelled strongly of salt, then returned to the counter. He was a dark man with a furrowed brow and a pitted but gentle face. His mustache was thick, well groomed, and mottled with strands of white. "Every day the Engineer comes here to my stand for his lunch. Every day I can remember. If he's in town he comes here. Nowhere else. Picks up his food, always the same thing: *magluba,* a chicken, rice, and eggplant dish I make special for him in a pita sandwich. Picks it up and takes it back to eat in his shop. Stops and talks to people on his way."

"Except on the day he was murdered," Danielle said, recalling Yori Resnick's preliminary report.

Samshi nodded. "That afternoon another man came up and asked for *magluba.*"

"For the Engineer?"

"He didn't say." Samshi shrugged. "But who else would know to order it?"

"You had never seen this man before."

"No."

"Was he Israeli or Arab?"

"It was hard to tell. The sun was in my eyes and he kept his face tilted down."

"Would you recognize this man," Danielle said, "if you saw him again?"

"I don't know." Samshi shrugged again. "I think so."

"Then I would like you to give a description of what you did see to someone else from the National Police."

Samshi looked troubled. "When I get off work. I'm alone here right now. Just an hour or so. Is that okay, Pakad?"

Danielle nodded. "I'll have a car bring you to his house."

"He is not a policeman?"

"He's an artist. Based on what you tell him, he will create a likeness of the man you saw."

"Anything if it helps you find the killer of the Engineer," Samshi said sadly. "He was a great man, a true *mukhtar.*"

"I don't know what that—"

"An elder, Pakad," Yori Resnick translated. "One held in the highest esteem by his village."

"This was the Engineer's village," Samshi said passionately. "The street, the marketplace, all of Jerusalem. He was loved by everyone."

"Almost," Danielle corrected.

CHAPTER 17

"COME IN," THE woman named Arra Rensi greeted Ben an hour later in Ramallah. "It's about time."

Then she practically grabbed Ben to drag him inside.

"Umm Rensi—"

"My neighbor's dogs. Something must be done about them, I tell you."

Ben's foot smacked into a box, rattling a collection of framed pictures piled inside. He looked down briefly.

"We have only lived here a month," Arra Rensi said apologetically. "Please excuse the mess."

But the two-story home did not look messy at all. The double-door entrance opened into a traditional salon, the walls of which were lined with low cushions used during the day for sitting and at night for sleeping. To the right was a Western-style living room furnished with a long couch, a love seat, and four matching chairs upholstered in a brick red fabric.

"I have not come here about your neighbor's dogs."

Arra Rensi, who appeared to be in her early forties, suddenly looked suspicious. "Oh?"

"I have come about your daughter, Zahira. The one who has been missing for five months now."

The woman hesitated just slightly. "But I have no daughter by that name."

"There must be some mistake," Ben said unsurely. "Yours, I think."

"You have no daughter?"

"I have *two*, and two sons as well. But they're all here. None is missing." She seemed eager to close the door. "If you don't mind . . ."

Ben consulted Nazir Jalabad's note again. "And neither of your daughters is named Zahira?"

"No."

"Are they home?"

"Playing."

Ben gazed beyond her. "Can I see them?"

"No."

"You would like me to come back with more police, then?"

The woman glared at Ben fearfully. "What have I done? Why do you pester me?"

"Why are you scared?"

"I'm not scared! I want you to leave!"

Ben retreated slightly. "If you have done nothing, you have nothing to be frightened of. I'm only conducting an investigation."

"Into *nothing!*" Arra Rensi said, and pushed forward against him.

Ben reached the door. "Into missing children."

"You must have the wrong address."

"I would like to see your children. I promise I will not be long."

"*Kus Okhthum,*" Arra Rensi said just loud enough for Ben to hear, and pushed him outside.

The double door slammed in his face and Ben

started to head back down the walk. He was almost to
his car when something struck him: the family portrait
he'd glimpsed inside the box his foot had struck had
pictured *five* children, not four. *Three* girls, even
though Arra Rensi was quite adamant about the fact
that she had only two daughters. One could have died
recently, he supposed.

Or Arra Rensi could be lying.

HIS INTEREST PIQUED, Ben decided to call
on the final name on Nazir Jalabad's list. The Khaladi
family lived in a neighborhood on the outskirts of Nablus. Night was falling by the time he arrived, yet Ben
still could hear the sound of bulldozers blocks before
he neared their address, only to find that the Khaladi
home was the one being bulldozed to the ground. A
woman wearing a traditional *hatta* stood in a neigh-
boring yard wailing hysterically and screaming at the
Israeli workmen.

More punitive actions being dispensed by the Israeli
government in the outgoing administration's final
days, Ben thought, feeling anger gnaw at him. He felt
so helpless standing there, imagined how the Khaladis
must have felt. Obviously they had built their home
without obtaining the proper permits. Strange how in
the West Bank the most dreaded weapon was not tanks,
but bulldozers.

The rest of the neighborhood joined Umm Khaladi
in yelling at the crew, which paid no attention to them
whatsoever, safe in their buffer behind a ring of Israeli
soldiers. Ben moved closer to a woman who had just
brushed some tears from her eyes.

"A terrible thing," he said.

The woman looked at him sadly. "The land is theirs.
They have a right to do with it what they wish."

"Are you a neighbor?"

"A lawyer," the woman replied.

"From around here?"

"From Israel. I represent Palestinians in Israeli courts." Her gaze turned a bit angry. "This is a case I lost. First their daughter and now this . . ."

Ben feigned surprise. "The girl who disappeared was Umm Khaladi's daughter?"

The woman nodded. "She and her husband searched for her every day for weeks. Where they could not drive, they walked. Left notes in everyone's mailbox." The woman peered at Ben. "I haven't seen you here before."

Ben showed her his badge and identification.

"Can you arrest some of my fellow Israelis?" she asked him, and turned her attention back to the demolition crew.

"I would like to arrest whoever kidnapped the Khaladi girl."

"They called the police. I think someone came by, took lots of information. The Khaladis never heard from him again."

"I'm different. How old was the girl?"

"Eight. She'd be nine now."

The age his own daughter had been when she was killed, Ben thought.

"How long ago did this happen?"

"Five months, maybe six. I'm not exactly sure."

Before Ben and the Israeli lawyer, Umm Khaladi collapsed to the grass, still shrieking as neighbors tried to comfort her.

"How did it happen?" he asked softly.

"She left school and never came home."

"The girl disappeared in the middle of the day?"

"So far as we know."

"Inquiries must have been made," Ben said, surprised by the news. "Someone at the school *must* have seen something."

"I don't believe the school was ever contacted."

"I can't believe the police wouldn't at least have followed that up."

"It's a bit more complicated than that I'm afraid, Inspector. You see, the school the Khaladi girl attended was in Israel. She was part of an exchange program."

CHAPTER 18

WHAT HAVE YOU learned about Levy's employees?" Danielle asked Yori Resnick in her office that night. Abdul Samshi, the closest thing she had to a witness, had been with the Israeli sketch artist for some time now, and she awaited word that the resulting portrait was ready.

"It's difficult to say."

"Let's start with a number."

"That's what's difficult to say. Levy employed everyone part-time on irregular hours. Mostly he called the night before to tell people when he needed them."

"But you have accumulated a list," said Danielle.

"As few as five, as many as ten. Most don't even know any of the others, except by name. Levy seldom had more than one working at the same time. I'm still checking their alibis for the night of the murder."

"Do any of them meet the description Samshi gave us?"

"Not that I've met so far, and they're all Jews. The Engineer may have done plenty of business with Palestinians, but he didn't employ any."

"I'll want the employees to be the first ones to see the sketch of the man who brought Levy his lunch the day he died. See if they can tell us anything. Now, what did you learn from the medical examiner?"

"Max Pearlman was right about Levy having cancer: pancreatic, according to the report. Late stage and totally untreated. Not even a trace of painkillers in Levy's system."

"So he wasn't being treated at all."

"Not in any Israeli hospital, anyway. From what I can gather, he had no doctor whatsoever. I don't think the man ever even had a checkup."

"What about fingerprints?"

"So far we have lifted twenty different sets from the shop. Since a cleaning woman insists she thoroughly dusted the shop the morning of the murder, we can safely assume the fingerprints came from people who came and went that day."

"Not a very good day for business," said Danielle.

"Many visitors would have only handled merchandise, much of which was regrettably destroyed by the killer."

"Any luck locating potential witnesses?"

"I have had two plainclothes officers with me on the street each of the last two nights. We have stopped everyone who walked or drove past the main entrance to the marketplace closest to Levy's store. Most deny they were out the night of the murder. But a few who admitted they were claimed to have seen a beggar in the vicinity."

"A strange time for a beggar to be out," Danielle noted.

Resnick consulted his notes. "Actually, they said he *looked* like a beggar. Two of the witnesses made a point of saying he also looked old." He flipped his pad closed. "Any luck locating Max Pearlman?"

"None. I haven't been able to reach him since he disappeared from Atarim Square yesterday. No one seems to know where he is. I think he's gone into hiding. I think it's possible Pearlman fears the same people who murdered Levy are after him."

"You think the attack at the square was—"

The phone rang before Yori Resnick could continue. Danielle snatched it up.

"Thank you," she said, and replaced it as she looked up at Resnick. "Our sketch of the suspect Abdul Samshi described is ready."

DANIELLE DROVE OUT personally to pick the drawing up, as much to protect the artist's identity as for expediency. Moshe Goldblatt opened the door before she could ring the bell and looked up from the wheelchair he had occupied since taking a bullet in the spine during the Yom Kippur War of '73. Goldblatt had turned his attention from guns to brushes and, later, a computer keyboard. To Danielle, his wild shock of hair and bright omniscient eyes made him seem more fit for an easel than a keyboard.

"I did the best I could," he said. "Your witness didn't get a very good look. This was one of the few times I was glad for the software they keep sending me."

He wheeled himself toward the bank of computer equipment set up in the far corner of the room, and Danielle followed.

"Fascinating work, really," Goldblatt explained. "I create a base outline from what the witness clearly remembers and the computer extrapolates the material and fills in the rest of the features, drawing from a million-strong database. Apparently facial features often fit a pattern, like everything else. It isn't exact, but it gives me something to show the witness and work from. Spurs the memory, if nothing else, and that helps a lot."

Goldblatt stopped at the ink-jet printer and fished out from the tray a copy of the computer-enhanced color likeness of the man Samshi had seen at his food stand. He handed it to Danielle, who took a long look at the man's narrow, wedge-shaped face. His receding hairline and hollow, empty eyes that even in the picture were difficult to get a fix on. The shadow of a beard that must have been there always.

My God, Danielle thought, the picture trembling a little in her hand, *this can't be!*

"You know this man, Pakad?"

"I've seen him before," Danielle said vaguely. "Once."

In the hospital, Danielle almost continued, *after I had lost my baby.*

This was the man who had appeared at her door, promising he could help her.

DAY THREE

CHAPTER 19

"**Y**OU SHOULD HAVE conferred with me before leaving Jericho, Inspector," Captain Fawzi Wallid told Ben the next morning, sounding more disappointed than angry.

"I'm sorry. I didn't feel there was time."

"Perhaps I could have expedited matters from this end. You know, made a few calls."

"I wasn't thinking."

"You thought of contacting your friend Colonel al-Asi."

In the absence of a functioning chief of police, daily administrative duties at police headquarters in Jericho had fallen on Captain Wallid's shoulders. Wallid was a young man—about thirty, Ben guessed, which made him almost ten years Ben's junior. He had been a Fatah fighter since boyhood and had spent a number of his formative years in Israeli prisons or under administrative detention. He had been among those prisoners released as part of the original Oslo Accords and had worked his way quickly through the ranks of the

Palestinian police. He had not attended either of the two academies in the West Bank, but had gone through an abridged program in Cairo.

Wallid was of average size and build with a dime-sized scar on his right cheek. He was extremely ambitious and seemed, to Ben at least, to be always considering future advancement as he carried out the daily duties of his job. That meant taking few chances and thinking every step out, in order to achieve his goal of being named chief of police en route to bigger things on the Palestinian Council.

"It's a matter of trust, Inspector," Wallid continued. "I have great respect for your work and your experience. But I must know you are willing to work within the system, and by that I mean work with me."

"I am entirely willing to do so, *sidi*, and am at your service."

Wallid leaned a little back in his chair. "And when were you planning to advise me of this investigation you decided to involve yourself in?"

"When I had something specific to advise you about," Ben responded.

"You notice I did not criticize you, Inspector, even though I know you are under strict orders not to actively involve yourself in any investigation. I do not believe you have been treated fairly. But that doesn't mean I am prepared to circumvent a policy already in effect when I was named captain. At the same time, I trust your judgment and would always welcome any thoughts you might have on a matter brought to my attention." Wallid interlaced his fingers. "This matter of missing Palestinian girls, for instance. How many was it?"

Ben studied Wallid briefly before responding. "Four I'm aware of so far. I believe there could be many more."

"And who do you suggest is behind these disappearances?"

"My source blames the Israelis, but I have found nothing to indicate that yet."

"Reprisals, perhaps," Wallid suggested. "Have you checked the backgrounds of the families involved?"

"That would require a more official approach, *sidi.*"

Wallid smiled slightly and touched a finger to the scar on his cheek. "You were asked to relinquish your investigative duties because you became too recognizable. Punishment for making your mark. But a mark can be a good thing, if it can help you get what you want."

"Sometimes that means taking risks."

"A liability to be minimized wherever possible. Leaving an out can be as important as leaving a mark." Wallid stopped, as if waiting for something. "You understand what I'm saying."

"Yes, Captain, I think I do."

"When being used, you must know exactly where you stand, what you have to gain as well." The captain's expression turned straight and flat. "Of course, if you had come to me yesterday . . ."

Ben looked into the captain's eyes and understood the intent behind his glare. "The phones to Israel were out. You had no choice but to send me to Tel Aviv, to Atarim Square, after learning of the planned attack."

"Despite your status with the department?"

"My established relationship with the Israelis made me your only choice."

"I do not recall reading that in your report."

Ben recognized the folder lying on the top of Wallid's desk. He reached out and snared the report he had already filed, buried it in his lap.

Wallid's finger circled his scar this time, as if searching for it. "And what of this inquiry made to the Israelis?"

"Strictly unofficial."

"But if it were to yield something . . ."

"We would have no choice but to reveal our methods. Submit them for review."

"I quite agree," the captain said, finally poking his scar like a bull's-eye. "Yes, I do."

They rose together and Ben gave him a light salute before heading for the door, the folder containing his soon-to-be-revised report in hand.

"Keep me informed," said Captain Wallid.

AFTER A QUICK stop in his office, Ben decided to pay another visit to Nazir Jalabad. He was out the door of the Municipal Building when a policeman called his name. Ben stopped and turned. The young policeman reached him, out of breath.

"I'm glad I caught you, Inspector," he huffed.

"I think you need to work on your conditioning," Ben said.

The policeman didn't smile. "A call for you just came in. You are wanted on Tabar Road."

"Why?"

"There's been an explosion at number twenty-seven. The man who called said you'd know what that meant."

Ben felt himself going numb. Twenty-seven Tabar Road was the office of his journalist friend, Zaid Jabral.

CHAPTER 20

"THAT IS THE tape you requested, Pakad," said Commissioner Hershel Giott as he pointed toward a videotape lying near the corner of his desk.

Danielle barely had to come out of her chair to take it. "Thank you, sir."

"I am advised to tell you that all material not directly related to the investigation being conducted by your Palestinian counterpart has been deleted," he continued.

"I understand."

"I am also advised to tell you that the tape cannot be transported and can only be viewed in this building. Copying it is not possible and it must be returned to me by tomorrow morning at this time."

"Yes, sir."

"Very well," Giott said, and rose.

Danielle remained seated.

"Is there something else, Pakad?"

"Yes, sir, there is."

"You sound very formal this morning."

"The investigation into Hyram Levy's murder took a disturbing turn last night when we were able to produce a likeness of one of the last men to have seen him alive."

"And why is this disturbing?"

Danielle removed a copy of the computer-enhanced portrait Moshe Goldblatt had given her the night before. She handed it to the Rav Nitzav, who was still standing.

"Do you know this man, sir?"

Giott put on his glasses before studying the picture. "No, I don't think I do. Should I? Who is he?"

"We don't know yet. He brought Levy lunch on the day he was murdered."

Giott's eyebrows flickered at that. "What else, Pakad?"

"This is the man who came to see me in the hospital."

Giott showed no reaction. "I remember your mentioning that."

"He said there were things he could do to help me. All I needed to do was ask. He told me to think about his offer. Said he'd be back. I left the hospital before he had the chance to see me again."

"I recall your mentioning that as well."

"Levy had written down my name, my hospital room number. Levy was well acquainted with this man."

"Go on."

Danielle took a deep breath. "You were the one who had this man sent. You told me that the day you agreed to take me back."

"I do not recall telling you anything of the sort."

"Suggested it, then."

"Have I become part of your investigation, Pakad?"

"Only if you have information relevant to it, Rav Nitzav."

"I see." Giott looked at the picture again. "So you have connected this man to Levy."

"And Levy to you. By your own admission."

"I was confessing a friendship."

"You called Levy and Levy dispatched this man to my hospital room."

"And if this were true . . ."

"How was he going to help me?"

Giott thought for a moment. "What would you say if I told you the answer to that question has nothing to do with this case?"

"That I'd like to make that determination for myself."

Giott looked like a man trying to choose his steps in the darkness.

"Rav Nitzav?" Danielle prodded.

"That tape I gave you, Pakad," Giott said suddenly.

"Yes."

"You did not ask how I came by it."

"Because it doesn't matter how."

"You trust my judgment. You know where to draw the line between relevance and necessity. You are a professional and a professional understands the way things must sometimes be done." Giott's small, sharp eyes bored into hers. "I'm asking you to trust my judgment again now when I tell you that this man's appearance in your hospital room has nothing to do with this case."

"Personal, instead of professional, is that it?"

"Judgment, Pakad. Let's leave it at that."

"But you did send him to me, didn't you?"

Again, Giott did not bother to deny it.

"You sent him to help me. But why? What could he have done?"

"Something that no longer matters."

"Even though it's connected to Levy . . ."

Giott narrowed his gaze, scolding her. "I took you back, Danielle. I didn't have to, was advised against doing so in fact, yet I did."

"But you knew Levy."

"Yes," Giott said reflectively. "I knew him."

"Can you at least tell me how?"

The commissioner of the National Police finally took his chair again. "What did Max Pearlman tell you?"

Danielle summarized Pearlman's tale of the four friends and their early days in the Haganah as quickly as she could.

"Very well then," Giott said when she had finished, nodding in concession. "But be prepared, Pakad: you might not like what you're about to hear...."

C H A P T E R   2 1

KEEP YOUR HEADS *down! Wait until this wave of firing passes!"*

The order was repeated down the Haganah lines. The battle to retake Fort Halev had been raging for hours and Jewish casualties had been very high. This would prove to be one of the most costly battles to take place during the first of Israel's many wars. But the fort's strategic location, perched on a hillside overlooking a valley road accessing Jerusalem, made taking it a must, no matter the cost. Otherwise Jerusalem would surely be lost.

Through the long hot day that had come two months after Israel declared her independence, Haganah fighters fought for every inch of ground up the narrow slope, each inch precious. Mortar and light artillery fire rained down on them, killing indiscriminately.

By nightfall, though, the front lines of the Haganah fighters had reached the final ridge. If nothing else, they were close enough to actually hit something with their old rifles and at least consider using some of their precious few artillery shells.

Hyram Levy, Max Pearlman, Jacob Rossovitch, and David Wollchensky were among those who had waited beneath the last ridge, having followed a trail of blood and bodies to reach it.

"The fucking British," Wollchensky sneered. "They promised this fort to us before they left and then gave it to the Arabs. I wish they had stayed so we could have killed them, too."

"We're going to take that fort," Levy said suddenly, peering up over the ridge.

"Of course we are," Pearlman agreed routinely.

"No, I mean *we* are going to take the fort. The four of us."

The friends looked at each other.

"After the sun goes down," Levy continued.

"And just how are we going to do that?" the massive Rossovitch asked him. Unshaven, his skin dark with grime and his long hair matted, he looked like a huge ape.

"I don't know," Levy confessed.

"I do," said Wollchensky, standing straight up to tempt the Arab fire from the fort.

Rossovitch dragged him back down. "You're mad."

"No, I have an idea, a plan."

But the Haganah commander was not too keen on Wollchensky's plan when he heard it. He grimaced in pain the whole time, a bullet having shattered his arm and left it dangling bloody by his side.

"The back side of the hill? It'll never work. Too exposed, even at night."

"For an entire force, yes," Wollchensky acknowledged. He looked at his friends one at a time. "But not for four men."

"Four men with four rifles . . ."

"Or four men with two mortars."

The Haganah commander couldn't believe what he

had just heard. "Carry those overweight dinosaurs all the way around the hillside?"

"That's right."

"And risk the futile loss of half our artillery complement?"

"We won't lose it. You draw the Arabs' attention with a skirmish and we'll shell them from the rear, opening the way for a full frontal assault."

"No," said Pearlman, "a skirmish won't work. Send half our force back down the mountain."

"Make them think we're retreating!" Rossovitch realized.

"They'll let their guard down," picked up Wollchensky. "Pull out their hashish pipes to celebrate their victory, before we send in the real smoke."

Hyram Levy simply smiled, as if he had known this all along.

The commander wavered, beginning to weigh the possibilities. "You'll need to position a spotter to direct your fire. That means taking two of our five radios."

"We'll make it well worth it."

Rossovitch carried one of the ancient mortars himself, the other toted between Levy and Pearlman, while Wollchensky took point. The route around the hillside he chose offered the most cover over the hardest terrain in a long, sweeping half circle. The four friends set up the mortars as close to the fort as they dared draw, its rear watched over by only a token Arab presence.

"Stupid bastards," muttered Wollchensky.

"This is going to work," said Levy.

"Only if we can get these blasted things to fire," huffed Rossovitch, working the second steel monster into position. "World War I leftovers, God help us."

"How many shells do we have?" Pearlman asked.

"A dozen," Rossovitch answered, since it was he who had carried them as well. "But I can't believe the barrels will survive even half that many."

"They better."

It was agreed that Rossovitch and Pearlman would man the mortars and Levy would serve as spotter, leaving Wollchensky to coordinate their efforts with the remainder of the Haganah force. At precisely midnight he nodded to Rossovitch and Pearlman and signaled Levy that the false wave of retreat was under way.

Within seconds, the four friends could hear a spontaneous cheer rise up within the walls of the fort. As planned, Wollchensky waited several more minutes, until the enemy celebration was well under way, before contacting the Haganah commander again.

"Sixty seconds," was all he said.

The mortars were both packed and primed, the ancient mechanisms cumbersome to fire under the best circumstances, never mind perched unsteadily on a hillside.

"Now!"

The first two shells rocketed into the air without a hitch, deafening all the friends except for Levy in his spotter's role. With his binoculars, he followed one direct hit into the center of the fort and one strike into the rear wall.

"Samuel dead on target!" he radioed down. "Adjust Elijah fifteen degrees rising!"

Another pair of shells thumped out behind deafening roars. Four more followed in rapid succession, the angles carefully readjusted to Levy's specifications each time. Elijah's barrel cracked before it could be loaded again, leaving them only with Samuel to handle the chore of firing the remaining four shells.

By then, though, the main body of Haganah fighters had already stormed the fort's gate and used their other two ancient pieces of artillery to further confound the now desperate enemy. The Haganah commander had actually ordered Wollchensky to cease fire before their final shell could be loaded, because their forces had broken through.

* * *

*T*HE BATTLE WAS one of the many great victories in a war no one outside of Israel believed she could win. But it never truly ended, not with hundreds of thousands of displaced Arabs who had fled or been forced from their homes taking up residence in the West Bank. Their new homes were refugee camps that quickly became dens of famine, squalor, and disease. Their leaders resisted all Israeli overtures to make peace, relying instead on militant leaders from Jordan, Lebanon, and Syria to ready them for another war. Fedayeen fighters, meanwhile, stirred up the masses, especially the young, confronting Israel with the one opponent she would never be able to best:

Terrorism.

The fedayeen would cross over from Jordan and enter the refugee camps. There they found waves of angry, eager recruits who had nothing left to give but their lives. Martyrdom appealed to many, and most of the raids carried out over the Israeli border were hopeless forays conducted by untrained and ill-equipped youngsters who died for nothing.

A few were not.

By 1950 Jacob Rossovitch had settled on a kibbutz outside the village of Sefir on the road between Tel Aviv and Jerusalem. He had been the first of the four friends to take a wife, Revkah, who was now seven months pregnant. Pearlman, Levy, and Wollchensky had been the first he contacted with the news, and they all pledged to gather for the birth.

Rossovitch was asleep when the warning siren sounded that night. He jumped out of bed and grabbed his rifle, as he had done a hundred times, each only a bad dream or a drill. But this time it was real. This time the kibbutzniks on guard duty intercepted a contingent of well-armed fedayeen terrorists a dozen strong. The terrorists had crawled their way through the fields before being detected, accounting for the little advance warning the guards were able to provide.

In a strange way, the presence on the kibbutz of the legendary Rossovitch might have been responsible for them letting their guard down. Having a man of his prowess and reputation on the premises imbued all the residents with a false sense of security, a belief that his presence made them impervious to attack.

Under most circumstances they would have been right. This time, though, the Arab raiders were well armed, and half of the twelve had either military or fedayeen training. The terrorists had no strategic purpose other than to kill as many Jews as they could before they themselves were slain. Two of their party fell to the initial response from the guards, but ten slipped through the lines and made straight for the residential structures.

They tossed surplus World War II grenades through windows, causing chaos and havoc. It would have been much worse if the kibbutz's women and children had not followed their explicit orders to take cover the instant they heard the warning signal. Still, the grenades blew glass and wood shards in all directions, disabling and distracting a substantial number of men who, like Jacob Rossovitch, were outfitting themselves to defend the compound.

Rossovitch himself had two rifles in hand when he came upon the ten remaining terrorists advancing on the children's dormitories. He opened fire earlier than he should have to keep them from lobbing more grenades, and the fedayeen answered with an intense barrage of fire from rifles that flashed like fireflies in the night.

When both his rifles clicked empty, Rossovitch drew a pair of American .45-caliber pistols in their place. And when these were exhausted, he resorted to a knife.

Rossovitch killed seven terrorists on his own that night, and an eighth would die of his wounds the next morning in the same Israeli hospital where Rossovitch was taken. Doctors pulled six bullets from his massive steel-skinned frame, three of which should have been instantly fatal. Nonetheless, he hung on to life for four days before finally succumbing.

So when the three surviving members of the four friends finally gathered at the kibbutz, it was for a funeral instead of a birth. Max Pearlman, Hyram Levy, and David Wollchensky stood stoically through the proceedings, though each shared the same grim resolve. In two short months Jacob Rossovitch's child would be born, and they would now turn their devotion and loyalty from their dead friend to his wife and unborn baby. To honor his memory, they pledged neither his wife, Revkah, nor his child would ever want for anything. That child had been denied the one father God had meant for him.

But now he would have three.

The three friends said nothing of this commitment out loud, said virtually nothing throughout the course of the somber afternoon, until the fall of night left them alone on Jacob Rossovitch's last battleground.

"The raiding party came from a refugee camp just outside Jericho," Wollchensky began.

"How do you know this?" Pearlman asked him.

"The bodies of the men Rossovitch killed have been identified. The information wasn't hard to come by." He looked at both of them. "We have to do something."

"What about blowing up the Allenby Bridge the fedayeen use to cross over into the West Bank?" Levy suggested bitterly.

"You miss my point," Wollchenksy said. "We *know* where the terrorists came from. They must be made to pay."

"They're dead."

"Their families aren't. Their friends aren't. And these camps will remain breeding grounds for more raids unless they are made to understand the price for taking innocent civilian lives."

"What do you have in mind?" Pearlman asked.

Wollchensky told him.

"Even you could never get approval for that!"

"Who said I was going to ask for it?"

"The repercussions would be—"

"Fuck the repercussions!"

Pearlman and Levy looked at each other, then back at Wollchensky, who stood before them like a statue.

"I cannot do this thing without you," he said finally.

"Innocent lives will be lost," Levy noted, his voice cracking a little. "Women, children . . ."

"It is the only way to stop this from happening again and again. The youth who strike out at *our* women and children must know their families and homes will pay for their martyrdom."

"And if it wasn't Jacob we buried today?" Pearlman challenged. "If it was a stranger to us instead?"

"Then I hope that man's friends would be having the same conversation we are. Then the responsibility would lie with them."

One week later, the three surviving friends entered the West Bank at night disguised as refugees. They reached the camp in question without incident and entered without so much as a question; it was not a place into which people had much reason to sneak.

Pots, pans, and other paraphernalia hung from their backpacks, clacking together as they moved purposefully through the darkness. To those Palestinians who saw them, the three friends appeared to be headed for the tent or shanty of a relative. Displaced persons arrived regularly almost every day, after all.

Inside their three backpacks, though, were crude homemade bombs David Wollchensky had learned to make in the Haganah. Just chopped-up glass and nails

mixed in putty affixed to one or two st
The fuses were the only tricky part. Tin
was not something Wollchensky had ma
meant lighting the fuses manually. This
synchronizing the explosions difficult and e
haps, even more so.

But Wollchensky had come up with the idea of placing a lit, filterless cigarette against the fuse. Once it
burned down to the end, its flame would ignite the
fuse. David had tested it ten times before that night
and it had worked each time. Four minutes for the
cigarette to burn down, another one for the lit fuse to
work its way to the dynamite. That meant the explosions would commence five minutes after they began
setting their bombs and continue to crack off sporadically over the next four. This left only one minute for
the three friends to begin their escape. They intended
to use the utter chaos that would follow the initial
blasts to make good their flight.

The plan went off without a hitch, all going perfectly, until the first cries and shrieks of agony accompanied the sight of burning bodies crawling through
the dirt. This was different and much more terrible
than war, and none of the three friends had been quite
prepared for it. As they fled the camp, though, leaving
the screams behind, they thought of Jacob Rossovitch
dying for no reason other than he was a Jew and an
Israeli, killed by those whose hate dimmed their reason. Rossovitch's death had taught his friends to hate
in a whole new way as well, and to realize that fear of
a much worse reprisal was the only thing that could
keep terrorism in check at all.

"What have we done?" Pearlman wondered when
they stopped to catch their breaths, still close enough
to the camp to see it aglow in flames and hear the
lingering screams that echoed through the Jordan Rift
Valley.

"What we had to do, my friend," Wollchensky told
him stoically. "That and no more."

CHAPTER 22

TWENTY ARABS WERE killed that night," Commissioner Hershel Giott continued. "Another hundred were wounded, some critically. Some of the survivors were crippled for life."

"The Jen Geret massacre," Danielle said, nodding.

"I see you've heard of it, Pakad."

"A black mark on our history. I always thought lingering elements of the Irgun were behind it," Danielle said, referring to the most militant of all Jewish resistance groups from that era.

"Because that was what we wanted the country to think. It would not have looked good for three war heroes to be blamed."

"But you knew who it was."

Giott looked at her impassively. "I was the chief investigating officer for the military. Understand that we had no comparable civilian authority at the time."

"There was an investigation?"

"We had no choice. Ben-Gurion had been flooded with protests from the UN, the Red Cross, the Arab

League. He even got an earful from the Americans. He had to do *something*."

"And what did you do?"

"What I was asked to. The type of bombs used clearly pointed to elite Haganah commandos. Narrowing the list down even further proved to be a simple task, especially after I located the intelligence officer who admitted identifying the terrorists responsible for Rossovitch's death to Wollchensky."

"Wait, you're saying you knew it was these three men all along?"

"Yes."

"But you never arrested them. You didn't even detain them. It would have shown up in Levy's file if you had."

"I interrogated Levy myself. He was the only one of the three I spoke with directly. That is how I learned the story I just told you."

"He *confessed?*"

"Off the record. On the record, he and the others had an ironclad alibi. There were no witnesses and no evidence that linked them to the massacre that I could find."

"Did you look?"

"No."

"*No?*"

"I did my job, Pakad, exactly what was expected of me."

"Your job was to *investigate!*"

Danielle's stinging retort drew no emotion from Giott whatsoever. If anything, he seemed to grow even calmer. "Are you able to travel our country much, Danielle?"

"Not as much as I'd like to."

"It's the same for me. But when I travel south I always like to stop at Solomon's Pillars. You are familiar with them?"

"Huge red sandstone rocks that stand at the entrance to the Timna mines."

"They are far more than just rocks, Pakad. They are guardians of the past, having stood as they are today unchanged since the beginning of our recorded history." Suddenly Giott's eyes grew piercingly sharp, changing just like that. "Everything around them has been wiped out, laid waste and rebuilt two, three, a dozen times over. But Solomon's Pillars have endured, and I have great reverence for them, as I have for anything that has endured while all around it has crumbled."

"People are different."

"Are they really? You ask how I became acquainted with Hyram Levy. Now you know. You ask why I cannot tell you anything more about what Levy's associate was doing in your hospital room. Now you know that, too."

"But I don't know what that associate might be able to tell me about Levy's death."

"This man had nothing to do with that, Pakad."

"He may know someone who did."

"Something you will never be able to find out."

"Unless I find him."

"You won't."

"And I won't be able to find Max Pearlman again, will I? He's gone into hiding, but not from me. First Levy was murdered in Jerusalem, and then an attempted suicide bombing takes place in Tel Aviv where Pearlman ate lunch every day."

"What are you getting at?"

"What if this was not a terrorist operation at all, Rav Nitzav? What if the entire attack was set up to get Pearlman?"

"That's absurd!"

"But if I'm right, Wollchensky's life may be in danger. Perhaps something else these men once did is behind what's happening. Perhaps that will tell us who killed Levy and orchestrated the attack on Pearlman."

Danielle tightened her stare. "We must reach Wollchensky, Rav Nitzav."

"We must remember the lesson of the Pillars of Solomon, Pakad," Giott said, unmoved by her emotion, "before we do anything at all."

CHAPTER 23

THE FRONT OF Zaid Jabral's small street-level office had been blown out entirely. Glass and rubble were scattered a half block in each direction, and a pair of firemen were hosing down the blackened, charred remnants of the building, which continued to smoke.

It was obvious to Ben from viewing the scene that he hadn't been among the first called. In fact, judging by the activity, the presence of police and other municipal officials, and the amount of water pooling in the streets, the explosion had occurred several hours before.

He searched the crowd for Jabral, hoping he had not been caught in the blast. But the presence of a converted rug van a pair of brothers now used to haul bodies, along with Jericho's bulbous medical examiner, Dr. Bassim al-Shaer, indicated otherwise. Al-Shaer lingered outside the smoldering building, the sweat making his wrinkled khaki suit stick to him. Ben judged from the black dust staining it that he had already been inside.

"They really didn't need me for this one," al-Shaer said, seeing Ben's approach.

"A bomb?"

"Tossed in through the glass, the police think. What was left of the victim was found near his desk. He never had a chance."

"Any evidence or suspects?"

"You're the detective."

"It's not my case."

"Then find whose case it is and ask them. Leave me alone."

Ben gazed through the remnants of what had been the glassed front of Jabral's Jericho office. "I'll want a complete report on this."

"You just said it wasn't your case."

"He was my friend. I'm taking a personal interest."

"Then let me give you my report now: a bomb blew him up."

"I was hoping for something more specific."

"Like how flying glass nearly decapitated your friend? Or how most of his flesh was burned off by the fire before the authorities arrived to put it out."

"Then how can you be sure it's him?"

"He was blown out of his chair. Was anyone else in the habit of sitting in it?"

Ben was about to continue to press al-Shaer, when he saw Colonel Nabril al-Asi's Mercedes arrive. One of the colonel's men opened the rear door for him and he stepped out, dapper as always.

"I see you got my message, Inspector," he said, joining Ben in the street as al-Shaer took his leave.

"It was you who called me," Ben realized.

"I knew you were a friend of Jabral's."

"Just as I know you weren't. It's a good thing this isn't my case, Colonel. I might have to put you on my list of suspects, considering the criticism Jabral continually leveled at the Authority. That's one of your jobs, isn't it? Making sure critics of the Authority don't stay in business very long."

Al-Asi looked unmoved. "Jabral has appeared on *Nightline*. Under the circumstances, I would have chosen something more subtle. But the truth is he wrote as many articles favorable to the Authority as not, and the international press picked up more of the favorable ones." Al-Asi gazed at the blackened shell of a building. "You can be sure I would have handled things differently."

"In what way?"

"I would have asked you to speak with Jabral first. Now, Inspector, if you'll be kind enough to join me in my car . . ."

"The smoke and ash too tough on your suit, Colonel?"

Al-Asi brushed off what he could. "Thank God for dry cleaners. Actually, I have something for you."

When they were together in the backseat, the car's windows closed and its cabin cool thanks to a still-blowing air conditioner, the colonel handed Ben an envelope. "The names of known smugglers you requested are inside. Too many to furnish complete files on each, but I can make files available once you and your Israeli friend have narrowed down the list a bit."

"Thank you, Colonel," Ben said sheepishly, embarrassed.

"Don't mention it. You owe me a tie. In the meantime I would like to ask you if you know anyone, besides me, who had reason to want your journalist friend dead."

"Not by name."

"Any idea what he was working on?"

"Only that it was big; that's what he said. He was excited. I got the feeling he was about to break a story that would make headlines all over the world."

"Anything more specific?"

"No," Ben lied, holding back the fact that Jabral had

canceled their weekly coffee two days ago to interview the Palestinian Authority's finance minister, Fayed Kabir. If this was about corruption in the Authority, al-Asi could easily be here to protect suspects instead of investigating them. No sense making his job easier until Ben was sure.

"I have another question for you," al-Asi said, leaving things at that. "Have you told me everything about this case you're working on?"

"Yes."

"Missing girls and no more?"

"Isn't that enough?"

"Ordinarily I would say no. Ordinarily I would find myself curious as to why an investigator of your caliber would concern himself with something so mundane, when the West Bank does not lack for crime. So my first thought is that there must be more going on here."

"If there is, I haven't found it yet."

"I suppose I should be appreciative of anything that keeps you in the West Bank."

"Still checking my phone calls?"

"None to the United States in the past several days. Getting back to work suits you well."

"I'd like to find out who murdered my friend."

"That can be arranged."

"A stretch even for you, Colonel."

"Not if you were working for me, Inspector. Think about it."

Ben didn't say he would or wouldn't.

Al-Asi looked disappointed by his silence. "You should know that someone has been following you," he said, almost as an afterthought.

Ben reflexively turned to look out the big car's rear window.

"Whoever it is isn't with us now. But yesterday, when you returned from Israel, he was there."

"Which means someone from your office was following me as well."

"For your own protection."

"It seems I owe you thanks for many things, Colonel."

"If you want my help, you need only ask for it."

"I already have," Ben said, holding up the envelope al-Asi just handed him.

"You will give it to the Israelis."

"Yes."

"In exchange for that tape."

"Right again."

Al-Asi nodded, as if his point had been made for him. "It could be someone does not want you to view the contents of that tape."

Ben started to open the door. Al-Asi grasped him gently on the forearm.

"You will keep me informed, Inspector?"

"Don't I always?"

BEN FOUND NAZIR Jalabad in the front section of the butcher shop this time. He loitered about until the big man was free, then moved up to the counter.

"I'm being followed. I want to know if your friends in Hamas are responsible."

Jalabad's eyes shifted slightly. He looked tentative, even frightened. "I can't talk now."

"Just answer my question."

Jalabad reached into the display case and weighed out some bloodred tenderloin. "Keep your voice down. I've talked with more people. I think I may know what's going on here. I think I may know what happened to my goddaughter."

"I'm listening."

"I told you, not now." Jalabad wrapped the meat in brown paper and taped it tightly closed. Then he scrawled the price across the top. "That will be three dinars."

Ben gave him the bills. Jalabad took them and stood there, warning him off with his eyes. Ben backed wordlessly away from the counter with package in hand.

"Come again," the big man said before Ben reached the door.

And outside when he glanced at the package he saw Jalabad had written something on it besides the price in thick black letters:

Tonight. Here. Eleven o'clock. Rear entrance.

CHAPTER 24

DANIELLE SAW BEN Kamal standing outside her office when she returned from a meeting with Yori Resnick.

"You look as bad as I feel," she said, managing a slight smile.

"You remember my friend Jabral?"

"The journalist. Of course."

"He was killed this morning. His office was blown up."

"I'm sorry. You could have called. You didn't have to come."

"I needed to see you. We still have work to do."

"Why didn't you wait inside my office?" she asked him.

He shrugged. "I would have felt uncomfortable."

"Well, I felt uncomfortable seeing you standing in the hall," Danielle said, ushering him in. She closed the door behind her.

"How did your meeting with your superior go?"

Danielle shrugged. "I wish I knew."

Ben smiled slightly. "I see things around here haven't changed at all."

"And in Jericho?"

"I have some leads, but I'm not sure what they mean. The only thing of substance so far is the fact that a second girl who disappeared was enrolled in the same program Leila Fatuk was."

"The Israeli-Palestinian student exchange?"

Ben nodded. "Aside from that, everything's different. Leila Fatuk was still in a Palestinian school; the Khaladi girl was attending one in Israel. They share nothing in common, other than they're both missing."

"But if the list of enrolled students yields any more who have vanished . . ."

"I'm having trouble tracking down such a list. No one at the Palestinian Authority seems to know who's in charge of the program. Most don't even know it exists."

"Maybe I can help," Danielle offered. "You said this Khaladi girl was enrolled in an Israeli school as part of the program. I'm sure that school has a roster and that there must be a master list available somewhere. Let me see what I can do."

"Speaking of which," Ben started, reaching into his pocket for the list Nabril al-Asi had produced for him, "I have the names of Palestinians most known to smuggle goods into Israeli shops."

Danielle unfolded the single piece of paper. There were about thirty names and accompanying addresses.

"I cannot tell you which did business with Hyram Levy."

"Shouldn't be too hard to determine that," she said, still studying it. "Why are these men still at large? I thought doing business with Jews was against the law."

"Selling land to Jews is against the law. But these men are mostly brokers who sell merchandise on behalf of Palestinians who desperately need the money. It's become quite a thriving industry, one of the few that has prospered during the bad times."

Ben didn't bother hiding the displeasure in his voice over what punitive measures dispensed over the past two years had done to the Palestinian economy. Danielle, though, did not react to it, not wanting to begin a rehash of the old arguments that had helped drive them apart from each other. Looking at Ben now, the good memories had started to resurface again, and she wanted to leave it that way.

Danielle refolded the list and pulled the videocassette Hershel Giott had provided from her pocket. "Quid pro quo, Inspector," she said, and handed it to Ben.

His eyes bulged, scarcely believing she had managed the feat.

"It can't leave the building and it can't be copied," she continued, recalling Giott's conditions.

"I'll have to watch it here, then."

"That can be arranged," Danielle told him.

A PAIR OF quick phone calls allowed her to reserve one of the National Police's four video labs, located on a subbasement level. In order to access that secure level, Danielle had to get Ben a pass with a high security clearance programmed into a bar code. With that and her identification card, they were finally permitted access to the video lab.

"Now let's see what we've got here," Danielle said, and moved for a videocassette recorder built into a NASA-like control panel.

Ben marveled at the level of technology around him in the cubicle-sized room. Since he had returned to the West Bank from Detroit, he had forgotten how much modern police work had come to depend on high-tech equipment like this. It made him nostalgic as well as jealous, considering a simple computer was a rare commodity in Jericho, especially one allocated to the police.

Danielle popped the tape in and the VCR swallowed it. Instantly one of three twenty-seven-inch television screens before them came to life, then filled with a shot encompassing the front of Nazir Jalabad's narrow home. Several seconds passed before a figure walked down the sidewalk in front of his house.

"Stop the tape!"

Danielle froze the screen. "Is that her?"

"I don't know. Go back a little."

She rewound until the shape was centered on the screen. "Hold on while I enhance this. . . ."

Using a computer mouse, she maneuvered a red circle about so it enclosed the general area of the figure's head. Danielle pressed a button and the next effect was similar to a camera zooming in for a close-up.

Ben continued to watch as a face filled almost the entire screen. He removed the picture of Leila Fatuk from his pocket and compared the two. The picture was faded, grainy and washed-out, but there was no doubt of the identity.

"That's her."

"Let's go forward again."

And with that Danielle worked the console. The red circle disappeared and Leila Fatuk returned to being a dark shape walking toward the edge of the screen. Disappointed, Ben had begun to think she was going to walk out of the frame, when something made her stop and retreat slightly.

The front end of a car appeared in the scene. Two people lunged from inside it and swallowed the girl in their bulk, dragging Leila Fatuk out of the frame toward the rear of their car.

"Can we get better shots of those two men?" Ben asked.

Danielle rewound and played the scene again in slow motion. The closer of the men who had grabbed Leila

Fatuk had his back to the camera, but the face of the other was in plain view. Danielle planted the red circle over it and clicked on the mouse again. Seconds later that face, made ominous by the long dark shadows cast across it, filled the screen, enlarged enough to clearly reveal that one of the man's eyes was sealed shut by scar tissue. The socket was empty and recessed behind it.

"Not the prettiest face I've ever seen," Danielle commented. "Recognize him?"

Ben stood up, came right up to the screen as if he intended to introduce himself. "No," he said distantly. "I'm going to need a hard copy of this."

Danielle shrugged to herself. "Well, my superior never said I couldn't make a copy of an individual frame. . . ." And she double-clicked on the mouse. "It'll take a few minutes."

"Can you try for the license plate?"

Danielle waited until the PROCEED command replaced WORKING on the LED readout, then worked the mouse about on maximum magnification. "Sorry, the camera was pointed too high to catch any of the figures."

"What about the color?"

Danielle zoomed in on a single corner of the plate the camera had caught. "White with green numerals."

"Palestinian," said Ben.

The hard copy of the abductor's face churned out of a laser printer perched on a table against the side wall.

AFTER BEN LEFT, Danielle began the arduous task of using the list of suspected Palestinian smugglers he had acquired for her to compile a list of possible suspects. The National Police database, networked as it was with Shin Bet's, contained the files of every Palestinian ever incarcerated in an Israeli jail or detention center. Almost invariably, these files would include fingerprints.

Danielle intended to cross-reference the prints lifted from Hyram Levy's shop with those of all Palestinians on the Israeli database in the hope that any name revealed would match one from the list Ben Kamal had provided. She gave the massive undertaking of sorting through years of files to a computer technician, who promised to get to it as soon as he could. Then Danielle returned to her office to set about finding the third man she felt certain was in grave danger:

David Wollchensky.

According to the files she was able to access, Wollchensky's exploits following his retaliation for the murder of Jacob Rossovitch made him a hero in every sense of the word. He had led an elite group of commandos in a parachute drop behind Egyptian lines in the war of 1956. He had commanded a force of troops that helped take the Sinai in 1967. And he had overseen the defensive line that had repelled the initial Arab attacks from the Golan Heights in 1973.

Wollchensky's entire military career was marked by assignments no one else wanted. Inevitably, he volunteered for and received the most dangerous commands where the percentage of casualties was likely to be the highest. But final tally of those casualties seldom exceeded figures for troops on much more mundane lines, as if Wollchensky was able to will the same determination and heart he possessed, so evident in the tales told her by Pearlman and Giott, into his troops. True to form, defeat became no more an option for them than it was for him.

According to everything Danielle read, Wollchensky had progressed beyond hero to legend. A number of his campaigns and operations still came up in formal Israeli military training. Danielle studied each of his files, waiting for one to reveal his current position, residence, and phone number. The problem was that every scrap of information she was able to access on Wollchensky ended in 1976, as if his very existence had ended there. He hadn't died, or been wounded or reassigned, nor had he retired. He had simply disappeared.

Danielle was baffled, left with an Israeli war hero who hadn't been seen or heard from in almost twenty-five years. She switched to another menu and logged on to the files of the major Israeli newspapers, the *Jerusalem Post, Haaretz* and *Mareev*. If government files had stopped following David Wollchensky, it didn't mean the press had too.

Apparently, though, they had. Her search did not uncover a single mention of him in any of the papers from 1976 on. David Wollchensky, by all indications, had ceased to exist, and unless he happened to be listed in the phone book, Danielle had no idea now of how to go about finding him.

Suddenly she shivered.

Of course, what was I thinking?

Danielle realized she had something much better than a phone book:

Hyram Levy's bills for the past several months!

If he had called Pearlman on so many occasions, it stood to reason he also would have called Wollchensky. And she seemed to recall a number of calls made to overseas exchanges. They hadn't attracted much of her attention at first because she was much more interested in the most frequently called numbers, all inside Israel. Beyond that, the calls located outside the country were not identified by either person or address.

Excited, Danielle extracted the folder in which she had placed Levy's phone records from her top desk drawer and opened it.

The folder was empty.

CHAPTER 26

THEY WOULDN'T LET you keep the tape this was pulled from," Captain Wallid said regretfully, looking up from the uneven picture of Leila Fatuk's abductor.

"No, I'm afraid not," Ben told him.

"You realize we have no firm evidence without it."

Ben took back the picture of the one-eyed man from his superior officer. "We need to find the man in this picture, Captain."

Wallid ran his teeth over his lower lip. "That would require us to make the investigation official."

"I'm aware of that."

"With you in charge."

"A chance I'm willing to take."

"Assuming I am, as well." Wallid seemed to be weighing the prospects. "And just how exactly would you propose we proceed?" he asked noncommittally.

"Intensive distribution of his likeness through all the West Bank, for one thing. Alert the other Palestinian security agencies, for another."

"Can I see that picture again, Inspector?"

Ben handed it across the desk to Wallid.

"Difficult to get a firm identification based only on this."

"It's all we have right now."

"And it could cause significant complications. The request for such an alert would have to be signed by me. That means the responsibility will be mine, should anyone identify this man erroneously."

"He has a rather distinctive look."

"All the same, you are suggesting that I recommend dedicating a significant amount of manpower to a case most would rank considerably low on our list of priorities."

"You have children, Captain?" Ben asked Wallid.

"Yes. Three. *Haududallah*."

"You go home from here, secure in the knowledge they will be waiting for you, safe and sound. It is a terrible thing to come home and find that not to be the case. You can't know, because you have not experienced it. But I have, and I can tell you that never since that time have I slept straight through the night."

Captain Wallid simply sat there.

"How many mothers and fathers in the West Bank are facing that same fate already? How many more will follow them unless we act now?"

Wallid scribbled a note on a scratch pad. "I am going to allow this picture to be distributed through every Palestinian police headquarters both here and in Gaza. I do not want officers carrying it around, trying to match up faces. I do not want it posted all over our cities. Agreed?"

Ben nodded.

I'M SORRY IT'S not Armani, Colonel."

Colonel al-Asi held the tie Ben had purchased for

him in Jerusalem at arm's distance, scrutinizing it under the light.

"The clerk said it was a Zegna," Ben continued. "The next best thing."

Al-Asi looked genuinely pleased. "I quite agree." He stood up and moved to a seascape print covered in glass that made it an adequate mirror. Then he stripped off the tie he had donned that morning and began to knot the Zegna in its place. "The Israelis were pleased with the list of smugglers we came up with for them?"

"Very."

Al-Asi looped the larger side of the tie around the smaller. "You haven't mentioned the tape they were supposed to provide in return."

"It was enlightening."

"What you expected?"

"I didn't know what to expect."

Al-Asi tightened the knot and slid it upward. "That is one of your great strengths, Inspector. You are able to control your expectations."

"I've learned not to set them too high."

"All the more reason why you should consider coming to work for me."

"I'm afraid I'd find the work . . . tiring."

"At least there's plenty of it, easily enough to keep you from making airline reservations anytime soon." Al-Asi turned from the glass. "What do you think?"

"It goes well with that suit."

"You know, I believe you're right."

Ben handed him a copy of the picture of Leila Fatuk's abductor. "The Israelis were able to lift this off the tape."

"I don't know him," al-Asi responded curtly after inspecting it.

"There's something else. The bombing suspect they have in custody. The Israelis would like to know whether he is truly Hamas."

"What does the suspect say?"

"His story is typical."

"So is his file: Recruited from the Tukarim refugee camp several months ago. Two brothers, both dead. Minimal training. No brain. The perfect suicide bomber." The colonel gave Ben a sharper look. "Why would they doubt he was really Hamas?"

"The Israelis are of the opinion that the Tel Aviv attack was not random, that there was a specific target."

"Israelis plural or singular?"

"My contact," Ben conceded.

"Your female friend again."

"Yes."

Al-Asi went back to the seascape and began checking his new tie once more. "You have good taste, Inspector, in more than just fashion."

CHAPTER 27

BEN FOUND **F**AYED Kabir, the Palestinian Authority's minister of finance, on the site of the lavish villa he was building on the eastern edge of Jericho. He had purchased a pair of abandoned, rundown houses with a view of the palm trees, banana groves, and even the Jordan River only to demolish them in order to build his new home. Kabir's rationale, and the rationale of other Palestinian officials with similar projects under way, was the need to be close to the Authority headquarters.

The appointment of Kabir, a member of the political wing of Hamas, had been meant to placate the more militant elements of the movement. Whether it had or not was difficult to say. But it had obviously suited Kabir quite well.

Ben didn't particularly care about Kabir's politics. Nor did he care how Captain Wallid would respond should he find out that Ben was pursuing yet another unauthorized investigation. What mattered to him was the fact that Kabir had been one of the last, if not the last, person Zaid Jabral had interviewed. And if Kabir could shed any light on what had led to Jabral's murder, then the risk was well worth it.

Kabir was a tall, thin man with a perpetual stoop caused by a childhood bout with meningitis—not a beating endured in an Israeli prison, as was often reported. "It's nice to finally meet you, Inspector," he greeted.

Ben shook his hand and noted the thin film of sawdust coating the man's clothing. Kabir immediately turned his attention back to the heavy equipment flattening and clearing the last of his land. Wood was stacked up in huge piles covered by plastic that flapped in the breeze off the Jordan River. Bags of cement waited to be mixed and poured to form the villa's base.

"Can you believe this?" Kabir asked, shaking his head. "Months behind schedule, months! I hired an American construction company that retained an all-Palestinian work crew. Then the Israelis canceled the Americans' visas and told their company to send them home. Can you imagine?"

"Terrible luck."

"What it took to get them new visas." Kabir shook his head dramatically. "The Israelis must think they are the only ones who deserve good homes. Well, the most patient hunter always reaps the biggest catch." He finally gave Ben more than a passing glance. "Now what can I do for you?"

"You've heard about Zaid Jabral's murder?"

Kabir looked regretful for a brief moment, until his eyes turned to a front-loader that had prematurely dumped its load. Then he grimaced. "What a tragedy . . . Of course I have."

"The other day he told me he was coming to see you."

Kabir nodded, straightening slightly. "He wanted to do a profile of me. He said he thought I would make a good story for the international press."

"Because of your . . . wound?"

"No. Jabral was more interested in my youth, the theft by the Israelis of my family's land. You know in 1948 it was the great peacemaker Rabin who issued the order to expel all Palestinians from our villages. And people still wonder why we don't trust the Jews. . . ."

Kabir suddenly shook his head and angrily stormed toward the site foreman, yelling his name.

Ben hurried to keep up. "You told this to Jabral?"

"Among other things."

"Like what?"

Kabir stopped. "That I came from a village that enjoyed excellent relations with our Jewish neighbors, until we were banished from our land. My family was among the first of the Palestinian refugees, Inspector. We settled in a camp outside of Ramallah. Jabral wanted to know what life was like in that camp."

"That's all?"

"I was eighteen years old. I left my village with only the possessions I could carry. We had to fight for every scrap of food, every drop of water. There was no organization, no leadership. People came and went. People died, my brother and sister included. Once I sneaked over the border to the land the new Israel had claimed for itself—our land. A town was being built right before my eyes. They were laying irrigation pipes, electrical lines, already planting their crops in our fields. Until that moment I had stupidly clung to the belief that someday the Jews would be vanquished and we would be able to go home. I think realizing that would never be was harder than leaving in the first place." Kabir took a deep breath to steady himself. "But Jabral was more interested about what I had to say about life in the camp."

"Specifically?"

"What we had to do to survive. It wasn't pretty. Little accurate has ever been written of those days before."

"So what did you do to survive?"

Kabir started toward the foreman again. "Whatever it took, Inspector."

"That's what you told Jabral?"

"I had to return to Authority headquarters before our interview was completed. I promised to call him next week to make another appointment. A shame he won't be able to finish the story now." Kabir cupped his hands in front of his mouth. "Come over here!" he shouted at the foreman, then turned back to Ben while the man trudged over. "You know what I told Jabral before he left, Inspector? I told him I had never gotten over seeing the Israeli machines laying a new town over ours. But now I have my own machines. I feel I have gotten the last laugh on the Israelis, and this home, I will tell you, they will never take from me."

CONTINUING TO RETRACE Zaid Jabral's final days, Ben drove to Jericho's small library, where back issues of his newspaper, *Al-Quds*, were stacked neatly on steel shelves against a far wall on the first floor. He couldn't remember exactly what day Jabral had run the story on the old woman who claimed her baby had been stolen fifty years before. He started three weeks back and worked forward, covering six papers before he found the article in question.

It was shorter than he had recalled and contained very few hard facts, accompanied by a picture of a near toothless old woman named Ramira Taji who had the saddest, most plaintive face Ben had ever seen. Even in black and white, her skin looked like thin, wrinkled paper a pull away from tearing. Her eyes were blank and her hair bald in thin patches along the nearest edges of her scalp.

Her baby, she claimed, had been stolen from the squalor of a refugee camp. The story went on to relate how Ramira Taji had fought her way out of the camp her family had fled to after their village had been overrun by Jews in 1948. She had spent the next fifty years relentlessly, and futilely, searching for her lost child.

Ben couldn't help but be struck by the similarities between Ramira Taji's story and that of Palestinian Authority finance minister Fayed Kabir. In fact, their lives had almost mirrored each other's, even though Kabir was now building a villa on the Jordan River while Ramira Taji lived out her life in a Bethlehem rooming house. The last paragraph of Jabral's article on her promised a follow-up the next week.

Ben searched back issues of *Al-Quds,* wondering if he had somehow missed that follow-up. But he could find no trace of it, and, after scanning additional issues up through yesterday's, he determined it had never run. Even more strangely, not a single article penned by Jabral had appeared in the two weeks since his story on the old woman had been published.

Had something she told him set Jabral off on his story of a lifetime, a story somehow linked to Fayed Kabir?

Maybe there was a way the journalist could still tell him.

FROM THE LIBRARY, Ben drove to Jabral's modest apartment in the center of Jericho. He kept another apartment in East Jerusalem he preferred to this one, but current Israeli travel restrictions had made it inconvenient for him to use, and, as a result, he had been spending more time lately in Jericho. Ben had visited Jabral once in East Jerusalem. Sipping wine on the front veranda of Jabral's two-story residence, Ben had a postcard-perfect view of the walled Old City and the golden-domed Qubat al-Sakhra. Beyond, the hills of southern Jerusalem stretched to the horizon. He had asked Jabral how he could ever leave such a home. His friend's answer had been to take Ben around to the back, where the only view was that of a recently built Jewish housing complex.

Well aware of how slowly his fellow officers worked, Ben knew the detectives assigned to the case would not get to the apartment until tomorrow at the earliest, so he would be the first to see its contents. But he didn't have a key and had never been much for picking locks. Fortunately, the owner of the building lived downstairs and let him in after Ben showed the man his identification.

Jabral's Jericho apartment was a single reasonably sized room with a small bath. The room's lone window had been left open to keep it cool through the long, hot day; Jabral, of course, had had every intention of returning tonight when he had left this morning. Somehow that thought stirred by the open window deepened Ben's regret, and he returned his focus to the apartment. It was sparsely and simply furnished, clearly a secondary residence. The sofa must have pulled out into a bed, though judging from the flattened and unkempt cushions Ben guessed Jabral had been sleeping atop them instead.

There was a thirteen-inch television and an ancient VCR on top of which rested a rented video Jabral would never be returning. A small wooden desk set near a window contained numerous pieces of correspondence and notes that yielded nothing of any help to Ben.

Lying on the floor beneath the desk, however, having been blown off by the breeze, was a sheet of paper with Hebrew writing printed across the top. Ben retrieved it and saw that Jabral had been issued a warning summons by the Israeli army for presence in an unauthorized area. Only the fact that he was a journalist had probably saved Jabral from instant arrest. Ben smiled sadly at the thought of his friend trying to talk his way out of jail.

The summons had been issued four days earlier, just

two days before Jabral's meeting with Fayed Kabir. Ben studied the location of the offense listed on the simple form and memorized it, then moved on.

He checked the rest of the apartment carefully and found nothing that seemed to have any significance to the story that had gotten Jabral so excited. Ben ended up sitting in his late friend's easy chair, picturing him at work behind his desk, remembering him for his tenacity and honesty. That honesty had made Jabral more than his share of enemies, any number of them a candidate for tossing a bomb into his newspaper's Jericho bureau. Such an explosive was easy to make and even easier to come by.

Before leaving, Ben retrieved the video, intending to return it to the store for no real reason, other than he thought that was what Jabral would have wanted him to do. He opened it up, curious as to the journalist's taste in film, expecting the case to contain some classic movie.

Instead he found a plain, unmarked tape that could be purchased in any convenience store, not a rental at all. As did everything else in the apartment, the tape's plastic housing had a thin coat of white dust on it, evidence it had been in the apartment for some time.

Feeling his heart quicken a little, Ben slid the tape into Jabral's VCR. Then he turned the small television on and pushed PLAY.

CHAPTER 28

"YOU WANTED TO see me, Pakad?"

Danielle Barnea was waiting behind her desk when Yori Resnick knocked on her open door.

"Yes, Yori. Please come in. . . . And close the door."

"We finished lifting the fingerprints from Hyram Levy's shop late this morning. I'm sorry it took so long but the damage done made finding prints almost impossible. I'm sure we have many duplicates and it took much more time getting them printed on that—"

"There is no need to apologize. I asked you to be thorough. You were."

"I've already passed all the prints we gathered on to the tech people downstairs. We'll know soon whether any of the names on the list of smugglers you provided match up with them."

"There's something else, Yori." Danielle shifted slightly behind her desk. "Something unfortunate has happened. The phone records you delivered to me the other night have been mislaid. I called to obtain a duplicate set, but apparently there's been a computer malfunction, a head crash or something, and the records have been permanently lost." She leaned forward. "Now I assured the Rav Nitzav that there were no other copies in existence. But then I remembered the order I gave you."

"Order, Pakad?"

"I know, I know. It was such a long and busy night, I almost forgot myself: I made sure you made copies before you delivered the originals to me. You did make those copies, Yori, didn't you?"

Resnick was silent and still for a long moment before saying, "Yes, I did."

Danielle rose happily. "You are the model of efficiency. I don't know what I'd do without you." She met him in front of her desk and grasped his arm tenderly, steering the young detective back toward the door. "You hid them safely, of course, as I instructed."

"Of course, Pakad."

"And you can get them for me now."

"Instantly."

"Very well then."

She stopped at the door. Resnick proceeded tentatively into the hall alone, gazing silently back.

"Oh, and Yori . . ."

"Yes, Pakad?"

"One copy is sufficient. We don't need any more lying around."

RESNICK DELIVERED THE photocopies of Hyram Levy's phone records minutes later, stiffly and without comment. Danielle thanked him and locked the door behind her. She went through the records again, noting on her scratch pad any unidentified numbers outside of the country. Originally, when she was simply searching for Levy's killer, there seemed little need to note the foreign numbers. But now that she was searching for David Wollchensky, things were altogether different.

Danielle found that Levy had called only two overseas phone numbers: a Manhattan exchange three times and a Connecticut exchange once. Each of the calls had been brief in contrast to his conversations with Max Pearlman.

This time she decided not to be subtle, simply picked up her phone and dialed the long series of numbers to reach the United States. The phone began to ring.

"Wolfe Enterprises."

Danielle swallowed hard.

"Wolfe Enterprises," the polite female voice repeated.

She decided to take a chance. "Is Mr. Wolfe in, please?"

"Who should I say is calling?"

A pause. "Levy, from Israel."

"I'm afraid he's out of the office, Ms. Levy. Would you like to leave a message?"

"No. No, not now," Danielle said.

She hung up and then immediately dialed a second New York number.

"Directory assistance."

"The number for Wolfe Enterprises in Manhattan, please."

"One moment . . . Hold for the number. . . ."

A computerized voice repeated it twice and Danielle jotted it down, comparing it with the one she had just called. The number ended in 5000, meaning it must have been the main listing for Wolfe Enterprises. The number Hyram Levy had called three times, meanwhile, was probably Mr. Wolfe's direct line. And she guessed the Greenwich, Connecticut, number was his home.

Danielle slid over to her computer and keyed into the Internet. It took longer than usual, but when she

finally got on line, she ran a search under WOLFE EN-
TERPRISES. Seconds passed, the time kept by a small
round clockface in the right-hand corner.

Finally the screen jumped to life:

1,275 ENTRIES FOUND

Danielle did a double take: 1,275 entries would have
made this a major company indeed. She began scanning them, gaining a rapid education on Wolfe Enterprises in the process. It was a major conglomerate, with
holdings in a variety of industries, concentrated mostly
in the media but including oil and gas. A major motion
picture studio, a newspaper, book publishing, radio,
even a growing television network. A public company
for which the controlling interest continued to be held
by its founder, a man named David Wolfe.

The on-line search had cross-referenced a number
of entries on Wolfe himself, including profiles in *Time*,
Newsweek, and *People*. He was mentioned in the same
breath as Rupert Murdoch and Ted Turner among
high-flying media moguls. And, like Turner, Wolfe
prided himself on being a philanthropist, by all accounts one of the most generous and giving men in
the world. His charitable foundation had funneled
over a billion dollars in the past ten years into schools,
hospitals, scholarship programs, college endowments,
research, and virtually every other grant imaginable.

A hundred million dollars given away every year!

The figure was too large even for Danielle to imagine. Intrigued, she tried to find more information on
the foundation, yet came up empty when she searched
under WOLFE FOUNDATION. A closer scan of the entries
pertaining to it told her why, because it was called
something else entirely:

THE FOUR FRIENDS

I've found him! . . .

Other than changing his last name, Wolfe had done nothing to disguise the fact that he was really David Wollchensky. In fact, every profile of the man himself mentioned his heroic past in some depth, some even touching on stories almost identical to the ones told to her by Max Pearlman and, later, Hershel Giott.

It made such great press that Wolfe's entire life seemed the creation of a public relations machine. A brave hero who became a business phenomenon while never losing his compassion for others. Danielle skimmed dozens of versions of the many stories and legends that were already well known to her. For reasons that none of the articles could make clear, though, in 1976 Wollchensky had left Israel for the United States, where he surfaced again in 1980 as David Wolfe, by all accounts already an immensely successful businessman.

Then how had he become a millionaire?

It seemed impossible that Wolfe, who came to Palestine penniless as a teenage boy in the early 1940s, would have taken much more out than he brought in. Career soldiers and freedom fighters had little opportunity to accumulate much capital. And yet there was no indication Danielle could find of what had happened in those missing years that changed everything for him.

Danielle was still scanning files when the phone rang. Repeatedly.

"Yes," she answered finally.

"Computer lab, Pakad. We're ready for you."

She cleared her throat, checked her watch. It was almost two o'clock.

She'd been at this for over four hours. . . .

Only then did she realize how much her eyes ached, a deep-rooted pain that seemed to come every time she blinked now.

"Please call Detective Resnick and have him meet

us," she told the technician, gently rubbing her closed lids.

Danielle hung up her phone, making sure to turn off the computer before leaving the room.

I THINK WE found your man," the technician explained as soon as she and Yori Resnick entered his windowless cubicle in the subbasement of National Police headquarters. He was balding, with slender wisps of hair hanging down both sides of his face. He squinted as he gazed at the screen, neglecting the eyeglasses held in a case clipped to the pocket of his lab coat. "The print match was ninety-five percent."

Danielle noticed a file scrawling slowly across the screen. "Who is he?"

The technician hit a key and the scrawling stopped. "His name is Ibrahim Mudhil: in a nutshell, one nasty son of a bitch."

He turned back to the screen, continued to speak without reading from it.

"Mudhil spent two separate stretches in our Ansar 3 detention camp between 1983 and 1991. Since then he's been incarcerated three times. Once by us—he was let out after the Oslo Accords. And twice, for briefer periods, by the Palestinians."

"For smuggling?"

"No. Not yet anyway."

Danielle nodded, impressed. "How long has he been out?"

The technician gestured offhandedly toward the screen. "According to this, over two years, but it's hard to tell since much of our intelligence-sharing apparatus broke down during that period."

"I'll need a picture."

The technician reached across the desk. "I have one for you right here."

"And the most recent address you have."

"Hebron," he said, handing her the picture.

"*Hebron?*" Yori Resnick raised grimly. "The one place we'll never be able to operate without Palestinian co-operation."

Danielle was still gazing intently at Ibrahim Mudhil's picture. "Actually, Yori, I think they'll be happy to help." She handed the picture to him. "More than happy."

CHAPTER 29

BEN APPROACHED THE butcher shop just before eleven o'clock that night to learn what the suddenly reluctant and tentative Nazir Jalabad had discovered. He had come straight from Zaid Jabral's apartment, having viewed the tape the journalist had left atop his television again and again.

The first time he pushed PLAY, Ben had half expected Jabral himself to appear on the brightening screen and explain what he had discovered, why he had been killed. A witness to his own murder.

Instead, though, a shaky, blurred picture of two men seated in chairs across from each other took shape. Disappointed, Ben was half ready to turn the television off until the focus sharpened and he made out Jabral seated directly across from Ari Bar-Rosen, Israel's newly elected prime minister. The interview had been conducted outside in a hotly disputed area of the West Bank, where a Palestinian settlement lay unfinished in the shadow of an Israeli one where construction was proceeding furiously. It had to, since Ari Bar-Rosen had promised to shut construction down as one of his first acts upon officially taking office in less than a week's time now.

"*What can the Palestinian people expect from you?*" Jabral started.

"*Fairness and truth.*"

"*I notice you did not say a homeland.*"

"*Because that is not a decision one man can make. I pledged to work toward the formation of a Palestinian state and I intend to keep that pledge. But it would be naive to expect to encounter no obstacles along the way.*"

"*By obstacles, you mean the outgoing administration.*"

The wind picked up and blew Bar-Rosen's still-thick salt-and-pepper hair about. He was fifty but looked ten years younger, a robustly healthy man with hypnotic gray eyes. He smiled frequently, but only when he meant it. He had succeeded first to control of the Labor Party and then to a sweeping victory in the special election on a forceful, uncompromising, and unapologetic platform.

He wiped something from his eye. "*I mean the mentality that administration created. A mentality of punitive actions dispensed toward no achievable goal. My predecessor came into office promising peace with security and gave Israel neither.*"

"*Is that the primary reason for the two-to-one deficit he ran in the polls?*"

"*Common sense accounts for that. What Hamas fears more than anything is mutual acceptance of our two peoples, because that would destroy their reason for being. Peace is the weapon that can most effectively destroy them. So they lashed out, sent their suicide bombers into Jerusalem to create one scene of horror after another. And when each act of terror brought us further from the Oslo Accords and a chance at peace, they continued to perpetuate those acts. The outgoing administration refused to fight them with the greatest weapon at its disposal: the pursuit of peace no matter what.*

"*My predecessor closed the borders and angered millions for the actions of tens. But closing the borders didn't help, and the vindictive measures served only to motivate those with a mentality capable of strapping explosives to their own bodies and yanking the fuse. The only way Israel can ever be truly safe is to destroy terrorism's reason for being. And that lies in the formation of a Palestinian state."*

"You have also pledged hundreds of millions of dollars to Palestinian housing and infrastructure."

"Actually," Bar-Rosen corrected, "I have pledged a figure equal to whatever we invest in settlements completed or expanded on disputed land. The funds will be turned over to the Palestinian Authority to be rationed however it sees fit."

"Disputed land like where we are sitting now?"

"More or less."

"But you have promised to shut down construction on the settlement going up on your right."

Bar-Rosen smiled and laced his thick workman's hands together before him. "That is because the outgoing administration strategically chose this location after giving the Palestinians permission to build a road, so long as no Israeli settlement was inconvenienced. The road was designed to go straight through where we are sitting now that way"—here, Bar-Rosen extended a finger toward the Israeli construction site—"where a settlement will soon lie."

"Meaning no road."

"Exactly."

"So no settlement."

"No Israeli lives there or had signed up to live there. The decision would not displace anyone."

"But do you really think peace is possible?"

Bar-Rosen thought briefly before responding. His olive skin glowed beneath the sun and he swiped at his forehead with his sleeve the way a man used to working in the fields might. "I was born on a kibbutz not far from a Palestinian town that had managed to stay intact. As a child growing up in the fifties, I remember the Palestinian children coming to pick oranges with us. We were too young to understand we were supposed to hate each other. We got along, and that is what peace means to our peoples: getting along. Coexisting with open borders, open trade, and open societies no longer mired in mistrust. It may take generations before our cultures grow together, if they ever do. But that doesn't mean they have to continue to grow apart. Enough people have died. The alternative hasn't worked for either of us. So I'm saying to you what I said to the Israeli people during my campaign:

"Let's give something else a chance. . . ."

Jabral's interview with Ari Bar-Rosen had been published well before his article on Ramira Taji had run, and almost certainly bore no connection to his pursuit of the story that had led to his death. Still, Ben had watched the tape hoping there might be some clue there, something even Jabral himself hadn't realized right away. But if there was, he couldn't find it.

As a result, he had lingered in Jabral's apartment much longer than planned and then rushed to get to the butcher shop in time. The back door was unlocked, and Ben opened it and entered.

The room was almost totally dark, and the forty-degree temperatures, in such contrast to the warm night air, chilled him immediately.

"Nazir," he called softly, his breath clouding before him. "Nazir?"

Ben felt blindly across the wall, having no idea where the light switch was located. He gave up and drew the small flashlight from his pocket instead. The beam struck the cold mist gathering in the air and made it look like fog.

"Nazir," Ben called again, continuing to sweep the small beam past the slabs of hanging beef.

He stopped his light on a side of beef that looked all wrong and quickly saw why. It wasn't beef hanging from this particular hook, it was a man.

Nazir Jalabad.

CHAPTER 30

JALABAD HAD BEEN stripped naked before someone had impaled him on the hook amid the rest of the stripped carcasses. The rising stench of his corpse, mixed with the sour scents of the various meats, made Ben quiver and force a surge of bile back down his throat. He bent over at the waist, wretching, and found himself staring at the blood that had pooled beneath the dead man's body.

But that was not all, Ben realized, shuddering.

Jalabad's right hand was missing, just a jagged bone layered with strips of flesh where it had been. His right foot was gone too, but Ben could see the white of the bone, the cut looking perfectly clean. Nazir's tongue hung obscenely from his mouth. And his eyes . . .

His eyes had been gouged out.

Punishment for crossing Hamas, Ben thought, an instant before the lights in the back room switched on, and Ben blinked in the sudden glare. At least a dozen figures wearing black masks appeared from every side, all wielding pistols. Hamas.

"Drop your gun," one of the masked men ordered.

Ben slid it from his holster and let it drop to the floor without protest. A hand grabbed his head and spun him around, back toward Nazir Jalabad's corpse.

"This is what happens when you see something you're not supposed to," the same voice accused. "Talk and it will be easier for you than it was for him."

"I don't know what—"

The hands grasping him shook him viciously. Then Ben felt a blade pressed against his throat.

"Who else have you told about your investigation?"

Ben recognized the knife as a *jambiya,* an Arabian dagger with a dual-edged, curved blade. "What investiga—"

"The missing children!" the voice blared, and the hands slammed his head into the wall.

Ben's eyes watered. Blood dribbled out from both his nostrils.

"You will tell us what you have learned!"

"Nothing."

"You will tell us who you have told."

"No one."

The powerful hands spun Ben and slammed him face-first into the wall this time. "I will ask you again: who else knows about the missing children?"

"There's nothing to know. I don't know anything myself. And why would Hamas care?"

"You think we are Hamas?"

"You mean you're—"

"What else did your dead friend learn? What else did he tell you?"

"Nothing," Ben replied, more scared now that the identity of his assailants, and Nazir Jalabad's murderers, was a mystery. If they weren't Hamas, then who were they?

"Liar!"

Ben's forehead hit first this time. "His niece was one

of the victims. He said there had been others, gave me some names. That's all." '

"Who else was aware of these names?"

"I shared them with no one."

"And your conclusions?"

"I haven't reached any yet."

The man spun Ben around again and pushed him toward a bulk meat slicer that looked like a mounted circular saw. "Since your friend died before he became cooperative, we are forced to rely on you."

Another black-hooded figure switched the slicer on. The blade began to whirl, blowing away the cold mist that had settled around it. Ben felt himself shoved right up against the long table into which the slicer was built. Only one side of the blade was visible, the rest covered by a housing splattered with still-moist blood. Ben recalled the stubs where Nazir Jalabad's missing hand and foot had been and nearly gagged.

"Who was your friend working for?"

"No one. He used to be Hamas, but claimed he was out."

"Hamas?"

"His story checked out."

A pair of men now jammed Ben down against the steel table. He could smell the heat of the blade. They turned him on his back, so he was looking up at the black masks.

"You have been to see the Israelis. Have you discussed the missing children with them?"

Danielle, Ben realized. *She would be their next stop. . . .*

"There was no reason to." '

"You went to them for help. What did they tell you?"

When Ben didn't respond fast enough, one of the hooded men grabbed his arm and yanked it sideways. Outstretched, it was almost close enough to touch the furiously spinning blade. The other man jerked Ben onto the table so his hand could reach.

"First a hand, and then a foot. That's all we could get from Jalabad before shock claimed him. But I think you, Bayan Kamal, will hold out much longer. We'll be able to get much more off you, unless you tell us what you told the Israelis and what they told you."

"Why do you care about the Israelis?"

The back of a hand slammed the side of Ben's face and grazed his nose. He could taste blood in his mouth.

"I don't know anything!" Ben insisted, and felt his hand dragged closer to the slicing blade.

Suddenly the blade whirred to a halt. The lights flickered and died.

"Find the light switch!" someone ordered.

But it was more than the lights, Ben realized before his captors, it was the power. The hands that held him had relaxed their grip just slightly. He twisted his arms free at the same time he whipped his feet around like a propeller. Both his heels slammed into a flabby mid-section, and Ben lurched off the table in that direction, feeling for the figure in the darkness.

Ben made contact just as the man was freeing his pistol again. He twisted the man in close and spun him around hard, slamming his back into the hard edge of one of the carving tables.

"*Over there! Over there!*" a new voice cried out, and Ben felt certain he had been spotted.

He managed to pull the pistol from the man's grasp in the next instant and dove to the floor. He had started to crawl for the door when a series of softly muffled sounds froze him.

The silenced gunshots were accompanied by muzzle flashes that seemed everywhere at once. He heard a pair of thuds, and a high-pitched wail that ended as quickly as it had come.

Someone was shooting his captors! Someone was rescuing him!

Ben started crawling again, toward the source of the silenced gunshots.

Muzzle flashes began bursting all around the room, his captors shooting desperately at the unseen gunman. More silenced shots answered the fire, followed by thuds as more of the enemy were dropped.

A door burst open suddenly, bathing the room in a thin wash of light. Ben rose into a crouch and scampered across the floor toward it.

"There! I see him!"

Ben dropped to the floor again and fired the unfamiliar pistol beneath the table at a pair of black-clad legs. The man attached to them went down hard, felled like a tree, his shots pouring into the ceiling. Rising only to his knees, Ben scrambled for the open door.

Just then, a lithe figure spun through it ahead of him, fleeing. The figure seemed to be moving slowly, but was out the door before any of the gunmen could recover.

Ben surged into the corridor and shouldered the door closed. There was a dead bolt just over the knob and he twisted it before his surviving captors could follow him out.

He swung toward the front of the store just as the front door rattled closed. Ben rushed to throw it open and saw the gazellelike figure sprinting away with long, loping strides.

"Hey!" he called, racing after it.

The figure swung left down an alley and Ben followed, holding his own.

"Stop!" he yelled at the end of the alley.

But the shape bolted down the new street and turned rapidly onto a narrow cross-through. Ben was just swinging to follow when he saw the shadow stretching toward him. He ducked, and the garbage-can lid smashed stone instead of his face. He kept his shoulder low and launched himself at the figure, feeling a lean and rock hard midsection as he slammed it into a building. Dust blew out into both of them, and the impact drew a grunt of pain from the person who had saved his life.

A grunt that sounded like—

A knee cracked into Ben's chin before he could complete the thought. His teeth rattled. His lower jaw felt like someone had twisted it all the way around. He lurched backward.

The figure caught him with another blow, across the face this time. Ben felt something crinkle in his neck, realized he could smell and taste the mortar of ancient bricks. His legs lost all feeling and gave out. He felt his eyes fading and looked up one last time as the shape moved away from him into the meager light of the street, face faintly illuminated by a cracked streetlamp.

A *woman!* Ben realized, before he finally passed out.

CHAPTER 31

"WHAT HAPPENED NEXT, Papa? You *have* to tell me!"

David Wolfe finished tucking his granddaughter in. "Tomorrow, Tali."

She pouted and crossed her arms dramatically over the covers. "Always tomorrow."

He pinched her cheek. "Don't make that face."

"I'll stop if I can have two questions."

"One."

"Two!"

"One, and that's my final offer."

"When was Revkah Rossovitch's baby born?"

"A few months later."

"A few months after Jacob Rossovitch was killed and his friends got their revenge . . ."

"That's right."

"Did the friends come back and take care of the baby like they promised?"

David Wolfe raised a pair of fingers in the air. "That's two questions, Tali."

"You still haven't told me the secret yet."

"No, I haven't."

"You promised!"

"I said I'd think about it."

"I'm old enough to hear the secret now, you know."

He stroked his granddaughter's forehead, felt her latch a hand onto his wrist when he started to move away from the bed.

"Papa?"

"We'll see."

Tali's eyes followed him as he headed from her room into the hall, leaving the door open a crack behind him. Wolfe realized his wrist throbbed a little where his granddaughter had grabbed it, another sign of age and the arthritis that was eating its way through his body. He had never cataloged all the various injuries suffered during his youth, but now age was doing it for him. And the funny thing was that every time he felt a twinge, his mind flashed back to its original cause—the time, the place, and the circumstances.

Maybe not so funny.

David Wolfe had not a single medal in his possession. He had scars instead, more than he could count and plenty that would slip from his memory until a rainy day or misplaced step brought them back.

Stairs had become especially difficult for him lately, and he found himself clutching the banister harder and harder. He was glad the men downstairs were waiting for him in the study since it would keep them from seeing his slow, stiff-legged descent.

The worst thing was that David Wolfe didn't feel old, not really. His body seemed to be cheating him, getting even for all he had done to it in another lifetime as David Wollchensky. He would have gladly made peace, but it was too late.

The three men waiting for him in the book-lined study of his Greenwich, Connecticut, home looked uniformly grave. Wolfe closed the cherrywood double doors behind him and shuffled toward the arrangement of leather chesterfield chairs and couches set before the fireplace.

"Sorry to keep you gentlemen waiting." They rose politely and Wolfe waved them back down. "I know you wouldn't have come out here if it wasn't important. You know how I feel about conducting business at home."

"A serious problem has come up," started Joshua Davies. At thirty-five he was the youngest of the three; a sabra and the son of a friend of Wolfe's in Israel, he had gone to college in the United States at Harvard and then stayed to join Wolfe Enterprises.

The other two men, Marcus Stern and Abraham Belfidi, were both in their fifties and had been with Wolfe for years, dating back to their days serving under him in Israel. They had come to America shortly after Wolfe in 1978, the only two people privy to all his secrets.

"Is this problem the reason I notice someone has posted guards on my property?" Wolfe asked, stopping before Davies with hands clasped behind his back.

The younger man nodded. "I'm afraid so: an Israeli police inspector has established a link between the murder of Hyram Levy and the bombing in Atarim Square. She was with Max Pearlman when the failed attack occurred." He paused. "And, earlier today, she called your private office line and asked for you."

"She *what?*"

"The call was placed from National Police Headquarters. We have her voice on tape."

"What is her name, this police inspector?"

"Danielle Barnea," said Davies.

"Barnea . . ." He turned toward Stern and Belfidi, who were seated together on a couch. "My God, I knew her father. I'm sure I did. But how could she possibly have . . ."

"We don't know yet," the younger man told him.

"Clearly, though, she has made the connection between you and the others."

Wolfe scoffed at his comment. "We were virtually inseparable for the better part of thirty years. Not a very difficult feat to manage, establishing this link." Across from him, Davies looked no less resolute. "You think I'm in danger then."

"I think we need to play things safe, that's all for now."

"What about later?"

"If this police inspector knows you're Wollchensky, she will try and warn you," proposed Stern. "You're the fourth friend, after all."

"She's trying to keep me alive, that's what you're saying."

Stern nodded. "But if Barnea's good enough to have made that connection, she's good enough to uncover the others."

"Then she's trying to save my life."

"At the same time she learns why it's being threatened."

"Something we cannot afford to have her find out," added Belfidi grimly. "It seems she has left us with no choice."

Wolfe scowled. "I told you, I knew her father."

"I don't see what that has to do with anything."

"But I do. You want we should become murderers, Abraham? Killing innocent people in the performance of their jobs?"

"You used to tell me no one was innocent."

"I also told you there were lines we didn't cross, that those lines are what separate us from our enemies. You want me to change that now?" Wolfe chuckled dryly, shook his head. "If we intend to kill everyone who gets anywhere near the truth, we will need a lot of bullets, my friends."

"We only need one," persisted Stern.

Wolfe stood up and shuffled over until he was directly in front of the man. "Then use it on me."

Stern leaned backward instead. "So we sit here and hope Danielle Barnea does not uncover the truth."

"No," said Wolfe, "we hope she doesn't believe it, even if she does."

DAY FOUR

CHAPTER 32

"A WOMAN, YOU say?" Colonel Nabril al-Asi said at the conclusion of Ben Kamal's story the next morning.

"I'm positive," Ben reiterated. "Just not like any other woman I've ever seen."

Ben shifted uncomfortably in his chair. Everything physical had been uncomfortable for him since last night. His entire body ached and bore the signs of several deep bruises. His nose was swollen and he could barely move his jaw. He had managed to sleep only with the help of some painkillers he had found in his medicine cabinet.

Al-Asi caught the hard stare in Ben's eyes. "You don't think she's one of mine, do you?" He sounded genuinely hurt, insulted. "The Protective Security Service does not employ women."

"Precisely why I thought she might be one of yours, Colonel."

Al-Asi smiled. "So I had her follow you, then save your life, and now I'm denying it. If that were the case,

Inspector, you would owe me an entire suit, not just a tie." He leaned forward. "I believe in the meantime we should focus our attention on your attackers. You are certain they were not Hamas?"

"Yes."

"Just as I am as certain as I can be that neither were they part of one of our overlapping security agencies."

"What about the butcher shop?"

Al-Asi regarded him ruefully. "Do you really need to ask?"

"You found nothing, then . . ."

"We found blood, just what you would expect from such a place."

"Not human blood."

"We're analyzing the samples. Without bodies to go along with it, though, I wouldn't expect much, no matter what our analysis determines."

"What does that leave us with, Colonel?"

"My question exactly."

BEN CLIMBED BACK into his car outside Palestinian Authority headquarters. The day had barely begun and already he was exhausted, his sleep the night before turned restless by tortuous dreams, thanks to the painkillers he had downed before nodding off. In one dream he woke to find Zaid Jabral seated in the chair set in the corner of his bedroom. It wasn't a rocking chair, but in the dream Jabral was rocking slowly.

"What are you doing here?" Ben asked him.

"We need to talk."

In the dream Ben saw that Jabral's face was burned away, exposing bone and pulp. His lips had shrunk like charred paper, his teeth left in a perpetual grin. His clothes were tattered and still smoldering. Ben smelled smoke, but he wasn't scared.

Jabral rose from the chair and hopped a little on his bad leg. "See, it works again. No cane. Did you find the videotape

I left for you in my apartment interesting, my interview with Israel's new prime minister?"

"Yes."

"Anything else?"

"I don't know what you mean."

"Come on, Inspector. It's all there."

"What is?"

"The reason why I'm dead, why they killed me."

"Who?"

Jabral sat back down and shook his head. "Haven't you figured that out yet?"

"No."

"It's all in the tape, everything you need to know."

"Why are you toying with me?"

"I don't have much else to do." Jabral winked, and more of his face seemed to slide away, the grin widening. "Maybe things really aren't clear until you die. That's one of the advantages. It would make a great story. I think I'll go and write it. . . ."

Jabral started to drift into darkness, like viewing a screen fading to black. Ben could see right through him.

"Wait!"

"I've got to go. Sorry."

"Tell me what I'm missing! Tell me what's on the tape!"

But Jabral's ghost disappeared, his perpetual smile the last of him to fade away.

Ben woke up with a start, the dream fresh in his mind and his eyes drawn to the corner where Jabral had been sitting. He lumbered out of bed and moved to the chair, half expecting to find blood and strips of blackened flesh staining the upholstery.

The old wing chair showed nothing but wear, though, leaving Ben to wonder if there was anything to what the ghost had told him as he pushed the chair with his hand to see if he could make it rock. Then he stood in the shower and replayed Jabral's interview with Ari Bar-Rosen in his mind over and over again in search of some clue he had neglected, without success.

After his meeting with al-Asi at Palestinian Authority headquarters, he drove to the rooming house in Bethlehem where Ramira Taji lived. The building was originally planned as a residential care facility for seniors on a Jewish settlement that was abandoned halfway through construction. So it was enclosed today by the shells of structures the Palestinian Authority intended to complete but hadn't quite gotten around to yet.

Ben planned to ask the old woman to repeat for him exactly what she had told Jabral about the child that had been stolen from her in the refugee camp all those years before. He would tell her the story had caught his eye, that he was willing to help her in his capacity as a police officer.

It wasn't a lie.

He found the landlady, an old woman with leathery skin missing her front teeth, tending to a small garden in front of the house. Taking geraniums from their pots and replanting them in the ground.

"Does Ramira Taji live here?"

The landlady barely looked up from her work. "She did."

"Did?"

"She died."

"When?"

"Let me see . . . Five days ago."

Just a few days before Jabral was murdered, Ben noted.

The landlady pushed herself to her feet. Her dress was dark with dirt around the knees. "Are you a relative? Because she owes me two weeks' rent if you are."

"I'm a policeman. How did she die?"

"In her sleep, peacefully. *Haududallah.* First time I ever saw her look happy. Maybe because she died owing me money."

"Did the doctors say anything else about what caused her death?"

"Doctors? The attendants came and took her away when I called. Why would a doctor need to see her?"

"Of course," Ben said, certain he would get nowhere with the landlady. "My mistake."

BEN FOUND DANIELLE Barnea waiting when he got back to his office at police headquarters in Jericho.

"Looks familiar," she greeted, moving her eyes about the room. "I'd have thought once you became a hero you would have rated a bigger office."

"I decided to stay. I like the view."

Danielle noted the absence of any windows. "There isn't any view."

"That's what I like about it."

Ben kissed her lightly on the cheek, feeling her lips brush politely against him.

"Your face is swollen," Danielle realized. "Reminds me of the last time we worked together."

"It's always nice to relive happier times."

"I brought something with me that should make you happy again," Danielle said, and she extracted an envelope from her shoulder bag. "One of the names on that list of suspected Palestinian smugglers you gave me matched up with a set of fingerprints lifted from Levy's shop: Ibrahim Mudhil."

"Do I know this man?"

"As a matter of fact, you do," Danielle said, pulling the smuggler's picture from the envelope and handing it to Ben. "He's the man who kidnapped Leila Fatuk."

CHAPTER 33

BEN RECOGNIZED THE scarred-over, empty eye socket instantly. His gaze drifted to his bulletin board and the picture Israeli computers had enhanced yesterday of Leila Fatuk's kidnapper: Ibrahim Mudhil.

"So a man who abducts children in the West Bank," Ben said, "is now a murder suspect in Israel."

"We have no proof that he's a murderer, only that he was inside Hyram Levy's shop the day he was killed."

"So what's our next step?"

"We join forces again. Mudhil lives in Hebron, strictly off-limits to us in a situation like this."

"It never stopped you before."

"Before, it was the military. This is a police matter."

"What's the difference?"

"I'm in charge, for one thing. The fact that a man like Mudhil would smell an Israeli coming from the border, for another. We need to work this together . . . for both our benefits."

"A joint effort."

"Yes."

"A joint interrogation as well, Pakad?"

"He has two hands. More than enough fingers for both of us to break."

WHAT EXACTLY ARE you proposing?" Captain Wallid asked after Ben had finished explaining Ibrahim Mudhil's involvement in both investigations.

"A joint operation by us and Pakad Barnea's people to bring Mudhil into custody."

Wallid continued to rotate his gaze regularly toward Danielle, even though she hadn't spoken since their brief introduction. "An operation like that would take considerable time to coordinate. The channels, the approvals—who knows where Mudhil will be once you are ready to proceed?"

"We're ready now, *sidi*," Ben told him.

Wallid thought briefly, eyeing Danielle again. "Not without official approval, we're not, and that would mean acknowledging your involvement, Inspector."

"We've had some experience in these matters before," Danielle said before Ben could warn her off with his eyes.

"Things were different before, Chief Inspector Barnea. I'm afraid we cannot rely on the spirit of cooperation to be of assistance this time."

"Unless a different department handled the operation on our behalf," Ben interjected. "Say a department beyond reproach."

"You're speaking of Mukhabarat."

"Intelligence," Ben said to Danielle.

Captain Wallid nodded, liking the prospects. "They would, of course, understand that we have called them in for assistance because of security and jurisdictional concerns, and that the responsibility for failure lies squarely with them."

"Some departments have no fear of failure."

"Your friend Colonel al-Asi's, for example."

"I think he would be open to assisting us, yes."

Wallid's stare grew a little deeper. "Let me give the colonel a call myself."

CHAPTER 34

THAT'S HIS HOUSE on the corner," Nabril al-Asi said as his driver pulled the Mercedes sedan up to the curb. A few people passing by tried to peer inside through its darkened windows. "According to our sources, Ibrahim Mudhil returned home just after midnight with a woman and has remained there ever since."

"So what happens now?"

Al-Asi checked his watch. "In less than three minutes, my men will pay him an unannounced visit. Then we will have a talk with him." The colonel's eyes lingered on Danielle. "All of us. By the way, it is good to see you again, Pakad Barnea."

"I don't think we've ever met before."

"We haven't, but I have seen you all the same."

Danielle turned to Ben, unsure how to take al-Asi's remark until Ben smiled.

"Two minutes," al-Asi announced.

No city better illustrated the tenuous and difficult peace than Hebron, Ben reflected, a city where

130,000 Palestinians lived side by side with 450 Jewish settlers and three times that many Israeli soldiers there to protect them. In years past those soldiers had dominated life in Hebron, securing a peaceful existence for the settlers no matter what the cost to the vast Palestinian majority.

Although much had changed since the city was turned over to Palestinian Authority control, some things remained the same. A security fence still enclosed the Jewish enclave of Eli, but it was patrolled by even more soldiers. Palestinians were finally able to drive vehicles, not just donkeys, down the city's main thoroughfare, Al-Shohada, although the north end was blocked by an Israeli checkpoint to protect the Jewish settlement. So, too, the Palestinians were now allowed to use the pay phones installed years before on the street; but, strangely, they seldom worked since the Israelis had ceded control. The settlers used to buy fresh fruits and vegetables from Palestinian marketplaces. Following the change in control, the army had banned them from the city for security reasons.

The stone houses that lined Ibrahim Mudhil's street looked faded and bleached, narrow in the front with a greater depth stretching to the rear. Spaced very close together, with paltry yards, they were indicative of the city's predominantly working-class population. Al-Asi knew those homes well from a number of sweeps his men had conducted here in search of weapons which might have been used in attacks against the settlers if they had not been confiscated.

"It's time," the colonel said, and looked up from his watch.

In eerie synchronization a team of his plainclothes operatives, dressed to blend perfectly with the residents, appeared from a variety of directions and approached Mudhil's home. Ben noticed several of them holding their hands close to their faces.

"Formerly state-of-the-art communications equipment," al-Asi explained, fitting an earpiece into place. "The Israelis were kind enough to pass on to us what the American Secret Service passed on after they no longer needed them." He touched his earpiece. "My men are at both doors now."

Ben and Danielle watched through the rear window as a pair of the colonel's men broke through the front, imagining a similar scene taking place in the back.

"They're in," al-Asi narrated. "Checking both floors for our friend. Entering the bedroom . . . *now!*"

Al-Asi's features sank. He yanked the earpiece from his ear and stuffed it in his pocket.

"What's wrong?" Ben asked.

"They found the woman," al-Asi said, throwing open his door. "Ibrahim Mudhil is gone."

THE STONE HOUSE smelled hot, baked by the early-afternoon sun. The inside felt like an oven. Ben could feel the sweat running down his brow and see dabs of it soaking through Danielle's light blouse. Only al-Asi seemed impervious, striding up the steps in a carefully pressed Canali suit, unruffled except for a matching handkerchief held in his hand.

The woman his men had found was sitting on the edge of the bed when he entered the larger of two bedrooms. She looked to be in her late twenties: rumpled hair, a dark complexion, and eyes that couldn't decide between scared and angry.

"You know who I am?" the colonel asked her.

"The police?"

Al-Asi shook his head. "This is your lucky day. They would just beat you and throw you in jail. I, on the other hand, will give you a chance to avoid both those fates."

"I have done nothing!"

"No one ever does. Makes my job simple. Do you know why?"

The woman shook her head.

"Since no one, it seems, ever does anything, it allows me the luxury of embellishing events as I see fit. Do you understand?"

The woman nodded, even though she didn't look like she understood at all.

"I can do this to the benefit or detriment of anyone I choose, the decision for which is ultimately left to them." Al-Asi came right up to her and cupped her chin gently in his hand. He raised her head slowly, turned it from side to side as if inspecting her. "You, for example, could be a good woman or a prostitute."

"I am not a prostitute!"

"That makes you a good woman."

"Yes!"

"Where is Ibrahim Mudhil?"

"I don't know."

"That makes you a prostitute."

The woman didn't hesitate. "He left early this morning through a tunnel to the house immediately behind this one."

Al-Asi nodded to a pair of his men, who exited the room in search of it. "I see," he said, walking deliberately through the room, letting his eyes wander. "Where did he go?"

"To work."

"And what is he stealing or smuggling today?"

The woman pushed some air through her lips.

Al-Asi stopped at a worn, antique bureau, atop which rested a circular chunk of marble that had been turned into an ashtray. He dumped the ashes and cigarette butts onto the floor and wiped the residue with his handkerchief. Then he brought it with him to bed, holding it gently as he sat down next to the woman on the bed. She stiffened, no place to go.

"A nice ornament," said the colonel, "although I believe this is actually the bottom of a bowl that has been evened out around the edges. A shame really, because it will now be impossible to match up the rest of the real piece." He turned his eyes from the marble back to the woman. "Are you aware of the penalty for smuggling antiquities?"

"That's an—"

"They're rather severe, let me assure you."

"I didn't know—"

"I'm sure you didn't, but you will find our government most unforgiving when it comes to removing artifacts from land we have just recently been able to call our own. The Jordanians and Israelis are even less forgiving, and I believe this piece more likely came from one of their sites." Al-Asi stood back up. "I don't think you want to find this out for yourself."

"It's not mine, I swear!"

The colonel walked over to the floor where he had dumped the ashes and leaned over. He found a cigarette butt and held it so the woman could see.

"Magenta lipstick. The same shade, I believe, you are wearing now. You used an ancient artifact as an ashtray. I'd say that makes it yours."

"I didn't steal it."

"Mudhil did."

"He brought it home."

Al-Asi held his finger up dramatically, as if to stop time. "Now, listen to me. You are very close to being able to go free now. You are also very close to being turned over to either the Israelis, who will detain you without a trial, or the Jordanians, who will sentence you no matter how the trial comes out."

"Petra!" the woman screeched, bouncing off the bed to her feet. "Ibrahim Mudhil's been going to Petra! I'm telling the truth, I'll prove it!"

The woman began to move madly about the walls, feeling for Ibrahim Mudhil's secret stash. "It's here, I'm telling you! I've seen him open it when he thinks I'm asleep!"

Al-Asi was standing close to another part of the wall,

not leaning against it lest his suit pick up some of the grit shed from the white stone.

"You've got to believe me!" the woman pleaded. "It's here!"

The colonel turned from her and effortlessly pulled a hinged section of the stone wall away to reveal a secret compartment he must have noticed before. "You mean this?"

I'M IMPRESSED, COLONEL," Danielle complimented al-Asi after the woman had been escorted from the room. "I truly am. I admire your tactics."

"You should, Chief Inspector Barnea. After all, I learned them from your people."

"Can we get into Petra?" Ben asked as Danielle and al-Asi continued to look at each other respectfully.

"It is complicated," the colonel said. "I'll have to call the Jordanians and inform them. They insist on such courtesies, you understand."

"But will they cooperate?"

"Most certainly. After all," al-Asi said, holding a hand out to indicate the cache he had found in the wall, "we have some items to return to them."

CHAPTER 35

I'VE ALWAYS WANTED to see Petra," Danielle said when they were back inside al-Asi's Mercedes.

Ben closed the door behind him. "It looks like you're going to get your wish."

"Are you a student of archaeology, Chief Inspector?" al-Asi asked from the front seat.

"I've lived in the Middle East all my life. It's difficult not to be an admirer of it at the very least."

"I understand," al-Asi said as the Mercedes' engine turned over and a burst of cool conditioned air filled the cab. "You will be especially impressed with Petra. You will see why that means 'City of Rock' when we get there later today, if the Jordanians are willing."

He had stowed the now carefully wrapped and cushioned antiquities removed from Ibrahim Mudhil's wall in a leather tote bag resting next to him on the front seat. The bag shifted slightly as the Mercedes pulled away, and Al-Asi latched a hand onto it to keep the contents from being jarred.

"It was a fortress at one time, wasn't it?" Ben asked.

"Impregnable and virtually unreachable, thanks to a single approach through what amounts to a narrow ravine."

"Many an army stopped in its tracks, no doubt," said Danielle, remembering pictures of the gorge the colonel was referring to.

"But I seem to recall Petra itself came to a bad end," Ben said to al-Asi.

"Indeed. Consider the location: equidistant from the Dead Sea and the Gulf of Aqaba near the intersection of the great caravan routes from Gaza on the Mediterranean, Damascus, Elat on the Red Sea, and from the Persian Gulf."

"So what happened?" asked Danielle.

"A rival city, Palmyra, stole its trade. Petra was finally conquered by the Muslims and then captured by the Crusaders. Eventually, without trade, it crumbled and fell into history."

"How quickly can you arrange for us to get in there?" Ben asked.

"Late this afternoon at the earliest. I must reach my counterpart in Jordanian intelligence to smooth the process. We don't want to make a fuss about this, do we?"

"No," Ben and Danielle said together.

THAT AFTERNOON AL-ASI'S Mercedes and a pair of Protective Security Service cars drove past the banana and date groves beyond Jericho for the Allenby Bridge. The air was dry and dusty, leaving a film on the windshield of the Mercedes that reappeared as quickly as the driver cleared it with the wipers. Ben wondered how so much vegetation could flourish here. Another paradox of Palestine.

They crossed the quarter-mile length of the bridge into southern Jordan, where the irregularly shaped

Shara Mountains, colored gray and ash, rose ominously before them. They were met on the Jordanian side of the bridge by a single all-terrain jeep. A man in a kaffiyeh stepped out and embraced al-Asi as soon as the colonel emerged.

"It is good to see you, my brother," the Jordanian said, squeezing himself against al-Asi's Canali suit.

"I have brought you a present, my brother," the colonel said, and handed him the small paper bag he had brought with him in the car.

Ben watched as the Jordanian intelligence officer opened it and removed the Zegna tie Ben had brought back for al-Asi from Jerusalem. The Jordanian's eyes bulged happily. He embraced al-Asi again, even tighter.

"Thank you, thank you, my brother!"

"A token of our appreciation, Major Marash," the colonel said, gesturing subtly toward Ben and Danielle. "And . . ." He signaled for his driver to approach with the leather bag of smuggled antiquities in hand. He took the bag and handed it to the Jordanian.

Marash returned the tie to al-Asi long enough to unzip the bag and inspect its contents. His eyes bulged again.

"Allah be praised! You have done a wonderful thing for my country, my friend. We are in your debt. Ask of me what you want."

"The man who did this, once we find him."

Marash's expression changed from grateful and friendly to stern. "We go to Petra. You will follow me."

FROM THE ALLENBY Bridge they had to take a wide sweep around the mountains and approach Petra from the east. After they passed a guardhouse at the edge of a cultivated valley, the road began to narrow, shrinking finally to a thin gorge enclosed on both sides by menacing walls of jagged sandstone. Here they abandoned their vehicles in favor of donkeys before entering the famed passage called as-Sik, which led into Petra.

The gorge swept circuitously through the imposing pinkish stone for over a mile, twenty minutes by foot or donkey.

"I've heard it told," al-Asi said, riding between Ben and Danielle, "that the rocks on either side of this chasm are so high and the passage so narrow that a mere ten men could easily hold advancing armies at bay."

"Comforting thought," Ben noted, peering up at the sandstone walls rising two hundred feet above them.

The gorge remained a dozen feet wide at its narrowest point. Sturdy vehicles were capable of passing, but were forbidden to enter in all but emergency situations out of fear of pollution and damage.

It was late afternoon by the time they caught their first glimpse of the temple from the gorge, the sky beyond the sandstone monoliths darkening not only with the coming dusk, but also with the clouds of a rare storm approaching. Ben could smell it on the wind amid the dust his donkey kicked up as it thumped atop the hard-packed earth.

"There are several teams working in Petra at any given time," Major Marash explained when they were grouped tightly again. "But the antiquities you were so gracious to return came from the Khaznet Firaoun, which means 'Treasury of the Pharaohs.' According to legend, the Romans hid vast treasures in catacombs beneath its temple that neither the Muslims nor the Crusaders after them ever found. But a few months ago, an American archaeological team unearthed a network of tunnels that may be those catacombs under the Khaznet's central hall and rear chamber. No priceless treasures have been uncovered so far, but someday . . ." The Jordanian completed his remarks with a shrug.

"Then if Ibrahim Mudhil is here," al-Asi said, "we've got a very good idea where to find him."

"Yes, I think we do."

BEN AND DANIELLE were riding next to each other when they reached the entrance to the Khaznet Firaoun. The structure was hewn out of solid rock, literally carved out of the mountain starting with a magnificent pillared facade, colored a rosy pink and adorned with statues and carvings.

Major Marash was the first to climb off his donkey, and the others followed. A pair of Marash's men had arrived ahead of them, easily distinguishable from the American students and local bedouins from the Bedul tribe even before they started forward. Marash met them halfway to the broad portico housing the massive entrance to the Khaznet—twenty-six feet in height, built as if to accommodate giants.

Ben walked up alongside Nabril al-Asi as Marash conferred with his men.

"How are we going to handle this, Colonel?"

"Whatever way he tells us, Inspector."

Ben watched as Marash touched the shoulders of his men affectionately and returned to the group. "My men have quietly been circulating among the Americans and bedouins through the afternoon, showing them Mudhil's picture. Apparently, a one-eyed man has been passing himself off as a Jordanian government liaison for days. He is inside the catacombs now. Do you have reason to believe this man is dangerous?" Marash asked al-Asi.

"Enough to advise caution when approaching him, my friend."

Marash looked a bit grim. "I ask because he may have American students around him. My primary concern must be for their safety. We don't want any incidents."

"Your suggestion?"

"Wait for him to emerge."

"How long?"

"Nightfall. Perhaps a little before."

Ben and Danielle exchanged a glance, each thinking of the ease with which Ibrahim Mudhil had already slipped out of their grasp once today.

"And there's no other way out of the temple," Ben raised, "through these catacombs maybe?"

"Not that the archaeologists have found, Inspector."

"Which doesn't mean Mudhil hasn't found it."

Marash didn't look very worried. "Petra means 'City of Rock' for good reason. If there were any secret exits, they would have been discovered long ago."

Ben gazed up at the threatening sky. The breeze had begun to blow noticeably cooler.

"The storm's drawing closer," said Danielle.

Marash didn't disagree. "That might work to our advantage, by forcing those inside the temple out earlier than they had planned. You don't want to be underground around here when a storm comes. The flooding is dangerous."

"So we wait," al-Asi agreed, moving off to brief the four agents of the Protective Security Service he had selected to come along.

The first wave of rain, a light sprinkle, began, and one of al-Asi's men rushed over with a huge umbrella he opened right away. Within minutes the rain was coming down much harder, and the sky had blackened with the promise of thunder and lightning to follow.

The group gathered under the cover of the portico while the students hurried to shield their work in progress on the ground in front of the facade with plastic drop cloths. The wind picked up before many of the cloths could be nailed down, and students ran to each other's rescue, battling the elements and racing the storm.

"I think I hear some people coming," Marash said a

few minutes later, peering into the darkness beyond the facade. His operatives shadowed him like bookends as flashlight beams swept toward the entrance from within the temple.

Both Ben and Danielle tensed. Al-Asi's men moved their hands toward their pistols. The colonel remained under his umbrella even though only a light spray of rain managed to penetrate the cover of the portico.

A pair of gunshots rang out. Screams sounded from inside the temple. The flashlight beams crisscrossed madly, then extinguished.

Marash and his men surged through the facade, followed closely by al-Asi's.

The colonel dropped his umbrella.

"No!"

The shout came from Ben, Danielle, and al-Asi almost at once, but it was too late. More gunshots echoed within the Khaznet. Men shouted, screamed. Return fire blared. Briefly. Then more shots, more screams. The other students who had taken shelter beneath the portico pressed against the facade or dove for cover beyond the columns.

Ibrahim Mudhil had sprung his trap, baited with his gunshots, luring the men into darkness his eyes had grown accustomed to. At that point, he must have cut them down easily.

Marash staggered out, clutching his bloody shoulder. "My men," he moaned. "My men . . ."

He started to collapse against the facade, and al-Asi rushed to cushion his fall. Blood stained his pristine Canali suit jacket as the colonel eased his friend down.

"He's in there!" Marash screeched. "The bastard's in there!"

Ben and Danielle had their pistols drawn now, eyeing each other from opposite sides of the entrance. Al-Asi took Marash's side arm, which had not even left its holster.

"Get him!" the Jordanian pleaded, clutching al-Asi's lapel with a trembling hand. *"Get him!"*

Before the colonel, Ben, or Danielle could move, a horde of footsteps thudded toward the huge door from within. Terrifed students charged past them into the pelting rain, tools and finds abandoned back in the temple.

Ben and Danielle stood on either side of the on-rushing pack, searching for a face that resembled Mudhil's or a figure stooped to keep his face from being seen at all. The last of the students filtered out with no sign of Mudhil among them.

"What's he doing? He should have tried to use the American students to escape," Ben said from his stance just to the right of the entrance.

"No, he doesn't need them. He's reduced our numbers," Danielle reminded him. "Changed the odds to his favor."

Ben peered into the darkness, where the painful moans of wounded men continued to sound sporadically. "We've got to go in there after him."

She nodded, steadying her breathing. "The wounded first."

"No," al-Asi said in what sounded like an order. He was crouched next to Marash, his handkerchief pressed against the Jordanian's shoulder. "I'll get the wounded. The two of you go get your man."

Ben gazed at the colonel, the blood darkening on his suit. "If he gets by us . . ."

Al-Asi was still holding Marash's pistol. "I'll be waiting."

Danielle snatched a pair of soaked, discarded flashlights from the ground nearby and handed one to Ben.

"Don't turn it on until I tell you," she instructed.

"Ready?" Ben asked her.

Danielle nodded, and they spun together through the entrance of the Khaznet Firaoun.

CHAPTER 36

DANIELLE MOTIONED BEN behind her and they crossed into the semidarkness. The interior of the Khaznet was utterly plain, in striking contrast to the ornate exterior of the facade. They advanced farther into the central hall, the moans and cries of the wounded covering the sound of their footsteps.

Ben felt Danielle stop short and just missed smacking into her. Her gun hand pressed against his chest signaled him to remain silent and still. Ben heard the click of her flashlight being switched on, the lens pressed against her body to hide the beam until she tossed it forward and to the right.

As soon as the beam pierced the temple's interior, a quick series of shots aimed at where the flashlight had landed rang out, muzzle flashes like eruptions of color in the dark. Danielle snapped into a shooter's crouch, but Ben grasped her shoulder before she could fire.

"We need Mudhil alive, Pakad," he whispered.

"Pity."

They headed on cautiously for thirty feet, where they found a ladder that descended into the start of the ancient catacombs extending beneath the central hall. Keeping a safe distance with gun ready, Ben shined their remaining flashlight into the hole.

"Well?"

"I'll go first," Danielle said, and began to lower herself onto the ladder.

The ladder led down into a circular pit that had obviously been excavated with great care and attention. Whoever had done the digging probably hadn't expected to unearth the opening to a legendary labyrinth of tunnels. Ben ducked under an archway, Danielle at his side.

The catacombs reminded Ben of an old mine, right down to the lights recently strung from the ceiling to illuminate the students' work. According to legend, the catacombs had been constructed with a number of "vaults" running off a mazelike network of passageways. It was these vaults that contained the Romans' treasure, and evidence of persistent efforts by archaeological teams to find them could be glimpsed in the neat chiseling away at various sections of the walls.

Danielle started to lead the way.

"Uh-uh," Ben said, cutting in front of her. "My turn to go first."

He kept his gun raised and ready, trying to anticipate any turns that came up in this tunnel so Mudhil wouldn't be able to surprise them.

"We're playing right into his hands," Danielle suggested, "you know that. This is what he wants."

"I don't think so. How's the ground feel?"

"Soft. Muddy."

"That's because it's wet. Water from that storm outside is rushing in from somewhere up ahead."

"How far?"

"That I can't tell yet, Pakad. But it's starting to look

like Mudhil has found himself another way out."

They picked up their pace, sacrificing some caution for speed. Suddenly Ben leaned over and felt the ground.

"Any tracks?" Danielle asked him.

"The water's pooling too fast."

Both of them could hear it running down the walls now, making them feel even more closed in.

"Mudhil has to be up ahead somewhere close," said Danielle as they started to advance again.

"He knows every crevice and alcove, every possible hiding place."

"He should have tried to get out with the rush back upstairs. He should have tried to run."

"What's your point?"

"Why didn't he? There's got to be a reason."

They ventured another hundred feet or so along the ancient catacombs before the line of lights strung above them ended. They continued on until the beam of their single flashlight illuminated a moist, dark wall directly in their path.

Ben sloshed forward, the water covering his feet now, and checked the wall. "This is as far as we go," he said to Danielle.

She backtracked slightly. "Where the hell is he?"

"Maybe he doubled back, hid somehow."

"No, no. We would have seen or heard *something*." She followed the flashlight beam to a section of the near wall. "Someone's been digging here . . ."

She crouched down near a neat section of wall that had been chipped away at floor level. She could see the water pooling its way through, leaned close to peer inside, and caught a smell like that of spoiled meat.

"There's something in here," Danielle said, and pushed her hands through the mud to widen the opening.

Ben had just moved to her side when a flash of movement made him turn. A dark mass loomed to his

right. His first thought was that the side wall was collapsing. Then he saw a pistol coming upward, and he
locked a hand on the wrist over it as a mud-covered
Ibrahim Mudhil slammed into him.

Impact sent both of them smashing backward hard
into a stunned Danielle and through the wall she had
been working on. The wall collapsed instantly, tumbling Ben and Mudhil into a chamber hidden from
sight for almost 1,500 years. The stench of dead, stale
air flooded Ben's nostrils as Mudhil's pistol flared
twice, echoing loudly in the enclosed space. Danielle's
flashlight was rolling back and forth on the tunnel
floor beyond, its beam catching what looked like
suitcase-sized stone chests stowed neatly through the
chamber.

Part of the legendary treasure! Ben realized. *No wonder
Mudhil wasn't so quick to take his chances with escape. He
couldn't leave the remarkable find behind. . . .*

Ben was still struggling to hold Mudhil at bay when
the rolling flashlight beam caught Danielle surging
into the chamber, gun rising in her hand. Before she
could strike Mudhil with it, he lashed his free hand
backward and caught her in the face. Her head whip-
lashed sideways into a wall and she disappeared into
the darkness. Ben glimpsed her frame in the shadows
as she slumped toward the oozing ground.

He kicked hard with both legs, managing to extract
himself from Mudhil, and rolled when the smuggler
clacked off four quick, wild shots from his pistol. Ben
drew his own gun as Mudhil lurched out from the
chamber and fired one last errant bullet before has-
tening away.

Ben tried to regain his feet, but the soggy ground
afforded no purchase. He ended up half staggering
and half crawling back into the catacombs, steadying
his pistol before him. He opened fire, aiming not for
Ibrahim Mudhil, but high and ahead of the smuggler.

Mudhil was looking back, reaiming his gun on the

run, when the tenuous ceiling above him began to collapse in a wet blanket of black. Ben's bullets had loosened the precarious earth and rock. Mudhil tried to keep going, but he was finally buried beneath the weight of the crumbling ceiling.

"Let's go!" Ben said, making sure Danielle had recovered enough to move on her own.

When he slowed, she rushed ahead of him, the water up to her ankles now. She reached the irregular pile of stone and dirt that had nearly buried Mudhil alive and drew him upward. He was still breathing, but limp, and it took both her efforts and Ben's to drag him all the way out of the muck.

Around them the walls themselves were starting to shed pockets of hard-packed dirt, the fragile integrity of the ancient catacombs compromised. The dim lightbulbs overhead popped dead in rapid succession as Ben hoisted the dirt-encrusted Mudhil over his shoulder.

"Hurry!" Danielle yelled.

They ran together along the crumbling tunnel, narrowly skirting the heaps of dirt and rock left by the collapsing walls and ceiling. They reached the ladder to the rumbling accompaniment of a shaking that seemed to encompass the entire temple. The ladder vibrated beneath their grasp, shifting sideways and threatening to spill them off.

Danielle climbed quickly to the top and leaned over to take Mudhil from Ben. He pushed while she pulled the smuggler over the edge, then reached for the last rungs himself.

The ladder listed away from the rim of the pit. Danielle swung back and grabbed Ben's outstretched hand an instant before he would have been out of reach. She joined her second hand to his wrist and yanked him up off the ladder as it tumbled sideways into the pit, which was now filling rapidly with mud and water.

"Grab one of his arms!" Ben told Danielle when he was safely on the surface.

Danielle reached down for a hold on Mudhil, and the smuggler's right hand shot up and grabbed her by the throat. Ben lunged to help her, and Mudhil lashed at him with a knife he must have had hidden. Danielle snapped her foot against Mudhil's wrist, and the blade went flying before the smuggler could manage a second swipe. Then she kicked him hard in the head. The smuggler's eyes turned glassy and he let go of her throat, slumping.

Ben and Danielle latched onto Mudhil and dragged his limp form back toward the portico, where Nabril al-Asi was waiting for them just outside the entrance.

"What took you so long?" the colonel asked, as the storm raged beyond.

CHAPTER 37

AL-ASI STOOD AMID the wounded men he had dragged from the temple himself. His clothes were soaked, filthy with caked blood and dirt. He had spread his suit jacket over his friend Marash's trembling form. The archaeological students, to remain shielded from the storm, had clustered in one of two nearly twin chambers located to the left and right of the portico.

"Let's tie this one up," the colonel said, looking at Marash, "so we can tend to the others. More help is coming."

It was another hour, though, before that help reached them, the nature of the emergency reason enough for Jordanian police and rescue vehicles to traverse the gorge, startling the donkeys when they screeched to a halt in front of the temple. The rains had turned torrential by then and the winds strong enough to stagger Ben, Danielle, and al-Asi as they stood vigil on the portico.

There were four dead in all: both of Marash's men

and two of the four who had accompanied al-Asi. The dead were covered tightly in the same plastic drop cloths used to protect exposed dig areas overnight. The colonel's three wounded men, including his driver, and a half dozen injured students crowded into the three ambulances to be taken to a hospital in Amman. Marash refused to be taken anywhere and insisted on being treated at the scene. Jordanian emergency personnel did the best they could dressing his shoulder and then immobilizing his arm in a tight sling, but he was clearly in considerable pain.

"I don't care that I'm hurt," he said, grimacing, when al-Asi tried to get him onto an ambulance one last time. "You think I'm stupid? You think I am just going to hand this animal over to you now?"

"This animal is what brought us here."

"That was before he killed two of my men. The situation has changed substantially. He will be tried in Jordan. We will be glad to provide you with his corpse."

"Two of my men are dead too, my friend."

"And I mourn for them as well, my friend. But we are in Jordan now."

"This man is a witness in two investigations, both in Israel and Jericho," al-Asi reminded.

"And now he is a murderer in Jordan."

Al-Asi nodded; Ben recognized the silky calm expression that appeared on his face like a mask. "Of course, your superiors knew of the precariousness of the mission you were undertaking."

Marash said nothing.

"You did inform them, didn't you?"

"I was doing you a service," Marash said, eyes widening.

"A benevolent gesture between friends and colleagues, but difficult to explain, all the same. Open to a number of different interpretations."

Marash mulled the thought over.

"This is the way I recall it happening," al-Asi continued. "We entered Jordan without authorization to retrieve the prisoner and encountered resistance when we tried to apprehend him. You and your men arrived in the midst of the battle, summoned to the area by the archaeologists. You saved our lives and captured a criminal wanted by the Palestinian Authority on our behalf and returned him to us after securing a promise from me that he will face charges in Jordan first, but only after undergoing interrogation in Jericho. Can you live with that?"

Marash turned toward Ibrahim Mudhil before responding. The smuggler's wrists were cuffed and his legs were chained together. Up close, his scarred and sunken eye socket looked even worse than it had in the photo.

"I can live with that, my friend."

The weather continued to deteriorate after nightfall, and Marash summoned vehicles to take all of them back to the border while the roads were still passable. Clearly the deaths of four intelligence officers, two of them Palestinian, would require the most delicate of diplomatic channels to deal with, but for now those channels would have to wait.

Al-Asi was wearing a rain poncho provided by one of the Jordanian emergency medical workers when he approached Ben and Danielle. His hair was soaked, his suit pants sodden with water. A somewhat surprising sight for Ben, who had never seen the colonel anything but perfectly coiffed and elegantly attired.

"Our transportation has arrived," he informed them. "We are ready to depart. Get your prisoner ready to travel."

The ride through the mountains back toward the border and the Allenby Bridge was as nerve-racking as any of them could remember. Marash rode in the lead vehicle with a trio of Jordanian royal police. The second vehicle held Ben and Danielle in the rear, sandwiched around a shackled Ibrahim Mudhil, while al-Asi rode up front with their Jordanian driver. Their pace was painfully slow, headlights forging hardly a dent in the storm and the windshield wipers unable to keep pace with the pelting rain. Their tires churned fitfully through the water that had pooled high on the rut-filled roads.

They were still ten minutes from the Allenby Bridge when a Jordanian army patrol jeep loomed before them, parked horizontally across the road. A uniformed officer emerged from the jeep and addressed Major Marash through a window of the lead vehicle. Once the officer took his leave, the passenger door opened and Marash climbed awkwardly out into the storm. He was flanked instantly by two Jordanian police, each opening umbrellas. He traipsed toward the second car, where al-Asi opened his window a third of the way.

"I am told the storm has washed the bridge out!" Marash said over the sounds of the rain slamming down everywhere. "We can't get across!"

"I need to get this man to Jericho tonight!" al-Asi insisted.

"*No one* is getting to Jericho tonight, my friend, at least not for a while." Marash pointed a finger back down the road. "There is a guard post a few miles back at the entrance to the valley. No longer in use but still functional enough for us to hole up until the bridge reopens."

"We will leave our people there. Then you and I will come back and check the bridge ourselves."

"Colonel, I—"

But al-Asi slid the window up again before Marash could complete his protest. The Jordanian knocked on the glass twice before storming angrily back to his vehicle.

With the road badly flooded on both sides, managing the swing back around the other way was no easy task. It took several maddening thrusts forward and backward before both vehicles finally headed off again in the opposite direction. The Shara Mountains around them seemed even more ominous in the storm, regularly shedding rocks and debris down into the road their jeep had to thump over.

It was the sudden smoothing of the road, as much as anything, that told Ben they had reached the head of the valley just before they came to the guard post he remembered passing on their way into Petra. The post was a white stone structure that from the outside looked little larger than a shack.

Ibrahim Mudhil, meanwhile, sat stoically between Ben and Danielle, treating the entire day's events impassively, as if he didn't realize the penalties he faced for the murder of four security officers. Regardless of what al-Asi had promised, the greatest struggle would still be between the Palestinian Authority and the Jordanian government to see who got to execute him first.

The door to the post was locked, and Marash ordered one of the royal policemen to shoot it open. Then Ben and Danielle escorted their bound prisoner inside with Colonel al-Asi leading the way.

The lights in the post still worked, as Marash found when he tried the switch with his good hand. The interior smelled moldy and damp with disuse. Just a single open room with an enclosed office cubicle on one side and a cramped bathroom containing a sink and toilet on the other. There was an empty desk, a long table, and a shorter one upon which rested an ancient shortwave radio the guard post must have used in its operating days to stay in contact with headquarters. Dust and cobwebs covered the corners of the walls and much of the ceiling. Several of the windows had cracked in a spiderweb pattern but hadn't shattered yet, even with the rain slamming into them.

Al-Asi drew Ben and Danielle aside as Marash issued orders to the driver and royal policemen who would be remaining behind. "I suggest you both interrogate your witness now," he said softly.

"Here?" Danielle asked.

The colonel shrugged. "There may be no other place, no other opportunity. Even if the bridge is crossable by morning, the Jordanians will never let us leave their country with Mudhil."

Ben's eyes fell on the small enclosed office. "We'll take him in there," he said to Danielle.

Al-Asi had already walked over to Marash. "We will check the bridge now."

"You heard what they said at the checkpoint. This is foolish."

"I have learned only to accept what I can see for myself, my friend. Let's go."

Marash looked between Danielle and Ben, and two royal policemen armed with pistols. "These men will protect you until we get back," he said simply, casting a brief glance at the remaining driver.

"You have more weapons in the trucks?" al-Asi asked him.

"Yes," Marash said, instantly regretting it. "A pair of rifles in each."

Al-Asi turned to Ben. "Accompany us to the trucks and bring two back inside with you." Then, to Marash, "For added protection. Just in case."

Accompanied by a single driver, al-Asi held an umbrella over Marash and guided him through the rain. Ben kept pace with them and accepted the pair of automatic rifles gratefully. He rushed back through the storm, slammed and bolted the guard post's door behind him.

Then, much to Danielle's surprise, he gave one rifle to each of the Jordanian royal policemen. The men smiled at him and tested their weight as Ben moved back to Danielle, who was hovering over the now seated Mudhil.

Outside the front windows they could all see al-Asi

and Marash drive off in the second vehicle.

"Why'd you do that?" she asked Ben.

"Do what?"

"Give them the rifles."

"To show we trusted them."

"Al-Asi wanted us to have the rifles."

"The colonel also suggested we interrogate our prisoner as quickly as possible. We can't do that if our Jordanian friends don't let us."

Without missing a beat, Ben hoisted Mudhil up from his chair behind the long table and led him into the office-sized cubicle. Danielle followed. The Jordanians paid no attention at all, content to guard the post.

The windowless cubicle had a small cot squeezed against one wall for the nights when things were slow. Ben guessed the long shifts always comprised two men who must have rotated their sleeping in here. Beside the tattered and moth-eaten mattress, there was a single chair. Nothing else.

Ben plopped Mudhil down atop the mattress and looked into his eyes. "What do you say we get started?"

CHAPTER 38

I WOULD LIKE a cigarette," the smuggler requested.

"Sorry, neither of us smokes."

"At least take my handcuffs off."

"And why should we do that?" Danielle snapped.

"Because you want me to answer your questions." Mudhil smiled, leaning back as much as his chains would allow.

As Danielle looked on disapprovingly, Ben slipped behind Mudhil and uncuffed his wrists.

"I'm told you're a dangerous man," Ben said.

"I've been accused of that," Mudhil said, stretching his arms.

"Please don't give us a reason to prove your reputation wrong."

Mudhil settled back comfortably, his single eye rotating between Ben and Danielle. "I'll be glad to answer your questions now."

"You're not worried the answers might get you in trouble?"

Mudhil turned toward Ben, smirking. "When the Jordanians realize how much more they are missing, they will gladly make a deal in exchange for its return."

"What about us?"

"Your government will do the same when they learn how much I possess that belongs to them," Mudhil said confidently. Then his expression changed, coming up just short of a wink. "That is, unless we go back and share the treasure ourselves."

"Steal it from the catacombs, in other words."

"There's plenty to go around."

Ben dragged the chair close to the prisoner and sat down facing him. "You think this is about smuggling?"

"I got careless. You caught me." Mudhil sounded nonchalant now. "What else could it be about?"

Ben shoved his chair a little closer. "We don't care about whatever artifacts and antiquities you've stockpiled. This isn't about smuggling. Tell him why you're here, Pakad."

"Your fingerprints were found in the Jerusalem shop of Hyram Levy. He was murdered four days ago. We believe you were there with him very close to the time he was killed."

The confidence drained from Mudhil's expression. "Levy?"

"You smuggled goods for him, didn't you?" Danielle demanded. "Did you fill orders or bring items to him on your own? What happened, Ibrahim? He caught you moving fakes and wanted his money back? You ripped him off and then you killed him, is that it?"

Mudhil seemed not to hear her. "Levy," was all he said, more of a mutter, the cockiness in his tone gone.

"Inspector," Danielle said, "why don't you tell him what you're doing here?"

Ben looked into Mudhil's single eye. "I have a picture of you in the process of kidnapping a girl named Leila Fatuk in Jericho last week." He looked toward

Danielle. "A pity we'll probably have to fight the Jordanians for him now."

"He would be best off cooperating with us."

"A man who kills two Jordanian intelligence officers might not find this country's courts very sympathethic. . . ."

"What do you want?" Mudhil's tone sounded suddenly desperate. His single eye blinked rapidly.

"I think we've got your attention now, don't we, Ibrahim?" Ben pulled back a little. "The chief inspector here would like to know if you killed Hyram Levy. I, on the other hand, am much more interested in the whereabouts of Leila Fatuk."

"I can't tell you!"

"Tell us what?" Danielle asked him.

"Anything. About the children. For all our sakes. *Please!* You *must* believe me!"

"Children," Ben repeated. "It wasn't just the Fatuk girl, then. There have been others."

"If I tell you anything about the children, I will die. He will kill me for sure. He will kill all of us."

Ben leaned forward again. "Who? Who are you talking a—"

"Listen to me—it may already be too late," Mudhil said fearfully, twisting his eye desperately about. "He's probably already on his way! We've got to get away! Do you hear me? *We've got to get out of here!*"

"Just as soon as the bridge is passable," Ben told him.

"No, that will be too late. He's coming, I tell you! You don't know what you've done!"

"Why don't you tell us?"

But Mudhil's single eye continued to bulge furiously. "*B'id ash sharr,* we're *trapped* here!"

"Who is this person you're so frightened of?" Danielle broke in.

Mudhil took a deep breath, needing every bit of it to steady himself. "Al Safah."

Danielle shook her head uncertainly. "What does that—"

"It means 'the Butcher,' Pakad," Ben said, feeling a cold shudder course through his body.

"You see why I can't tell you anything!" Mudhil roared. "You see why we must get out of here!"

"What is he talking about?" Danielle demanded of Ben. "Who is this Al Safah?"

"Not a who, Pakad: a what. A thing, a monster, a spook story I thought I had forgotten." Ben's voice grew slightly distant. "When I was a small boy and misbehaved, my mother would say I had better be good or Al Safah would come and take me, as he took many children and made them disappear."

Mudhil came forward off the cot until Ben restrained him by the shoulders. "He's not a spook story; *he's real, I'm telling you!*"

"And how do you know this, Ibrahim?"

"Because I work for him."

Ben eyed Danielle before responding. "You kidnapped Leila Fatuk because Al Safah told you to?"

"He'll kill me if I talk!"

"And the Jordanians will kill you if you don't," Danielle reminded.

Mudhil fixed his one eye upon her. "They will never get the chance unless we get away *now!* Listen to me!" He touched his empty eye socket with a trembling hand. "I know."

With a chill, Ben recalled Nazir Jalabad's corpse hanging from a spike in the back of the butcher shop, his eyes gouged out. "Al Safah did that to you?"

"He had it done. Punishment for making a mistake, slipping up. The last thing I saw with this eye was a hot poker coming toward it."

Danielle cringed. "What does this Al Safah look like?"

"I've never met him. Nobody ever meets him." Terror continued to claim Mudhil's expression. "Listen to me. He'll know that you're onto him. It's not just *me* he'll be coming for!"

Ben recalled the interrogation he had endured in the rear of Nazir Jalabad's butcher shop by men determined not only to find out what he knew, but who else he had told. Jalabad had paid with his life for telling him about the disappearing girls, had hinted he had uncovered even more before he was killed. And Ben would have paid that same price if the mystery woman had not intervened. He had assumed incorrectly at first that his inquisitors were Hamas. Now he understood who had really sent them:

Al Safah.

Ben burst out of his chair. It tipped over as he pressed himself right into Mudhil's face. "How many children did you steal for Al Safah?"

"*I . . .*"

"What did you do with them all?"

"*. . . can't . . .*"

"Where is Leila Fatuk?"

"*. . . tell you!*"

"But you know, don't you? You know exactly where she is. You can tell me right now where I can find her."

Outside the rain slapped against the windows and crackled against the hard roof surface.

"Perhaps he'd rather tell me if he killed Hyram Levy," Danielle interjected.

"No, that wasn't me! I swear!"

"You were in his shop?"

"Not to kill him! Not to kill him!"

"You did business with him."

"Yes!"

"And then something happened and you killed him."

"No!" Mudhil coiled fearfully against the wall. "I've already said too much. *Haududallah*, I've said too much. . . ."

"Then you might as well tell us the rest," Ben urged. "Let us protect you."

Mudhil tried to laugh, and something like a rasp emerged behind his spittle. "Protect me from Al Safah? You won't even be able to protect yourselves. We're all going to die tonight."

"No one's going to die," said Danielle.

A window shattered in the room beyond. One of the Jordanian guards screamed.

"He's here," Mudhil muttered.

CHAPTER 39

I TOLD THEM *noth—*"

Ben clamped a hand over Mudhil's mouth and drove him back to the mattress. "Stay down! On the floor, under the cot. *Now!*"

Mudhil fearfully did as he was told. Danielle kicked open the door leading back into the main area of the guard post, pistol held high near the shoulder. Ben joined her on the other side of the door. They nodded and spun out together in a crouch, guns leading.

One of the Jordanian policemen lay on his side in a spreading pool of blood. He had been shot in the face and had fallen on the rifle Ben had allotted him. The driver and the second policeman crouched beneath windows on either side of the guard post's interior. The window near the driver had been blown out by bullets, allowing the storm to wash into the room.

Ben and Danielle started forward, still crouched down. The side windows shattered almost simultaneously behind twin barrages of automatic fire, and they hit the floor. More glass popped inward, spraying them with shards and fragments.

Danielle crawled over the glass toward one of the blown-out windows. Cold air and rain flooded the post, the wind whipping her hair wildly about. She finally pressed herself against the wall beneath the sill and signaled Ben to do the same as she steadied her gun.

He reached the window on the other side of the room as multiple footsteps sloshed through the muddy ground beyond. He watched Danielle slide over to the side of the window and did likewise, ready when one of the attackers crashed his upper body through what was left of the glass.

Ben spun away from the wall firing, enough nine-millimeter bullets pounding the man to catapult him back outside. Across the floor, Danielle's first shot had snapped a second attacker's head back. When he crumpled, his arms stayed perched on the drenched windowsill. Danielle hunkered low and pried the submachine gun from his hands, sliding it toward the center of the floor.

"Scouts," she said to Ben, tightly wedged against the wall. "Sacrifices."

"How many more?"

The Jordanian royal policeman still crouched beneath a front window tried to peer out and was greeted by a hail of fire that coughed yet more glass into the room.

"Tell him you know nothing!" Mudhil screamed from the doorway of the cubicle. "Tell him I told you nothing!"

"Get back inside and *stay down!*" Ben yelled at him.

His eyes flashed around the room and came to rest against the two tables. "Pakad," he said, gesturing with his stare.

She nodded.

"Which windows?" Ben asked.

"Both sides. So we can concentrate on the front." She turned to the driver and the policeman. "Cover us."

The two men rose on either side of their windows and tried to peer out from a safe angle.

Ben and Danielle crawled for the larger table, which was long enough to cover the entire window. Then, staying low, they dragged it to the nearer of the side windows and turned the table sideways before sliding it over the shattered panes.

The radio tumbled from the shorter table and crashed to the floor as they dragged it to the other side of the room. Tilted upright, it covered the window almost to the top of the frame. Neither of the tables would stop an assault, but they would stop bullets and, just as importantly, keep the force outside from seeing in through the guard post's flanks, substantially reducing the enemy's effective field of vision.

Ben crawled across the floor and yanked the automatic rifle from beneath the dead royal policeman's body.

"What are you doing?" Danielle asked, crawling up to join him.

"One of us has to go outside."

"You've never used a gun like that before, not for real."

"I'm a fast learner."

"Bad time for class. You won't stand a chance."

"Against Al Safah?"

"Against whoever's out there. At night, in a storm. With a rifle you're not familiar with." Danielle slid the submachine gun toward Ben and reached for the automatic rifle; a Kalashnikov AK-47, she recognized. "I'll go."

Ben grasped the submachine gun and tried to get the feel of it. "What do we wait for?"

"The next barrage," Danielle said, and turned back to the two men in the front of the room. "When it comes, I want you to return the fire this time. Even if you can't see what you're shooting at. Even if you feel like you're wasting bullets."

The barrage came seconds later. More glass filled the air and the door thumped inward with repeated hits. The driver and the policeman opened fire as bullets continued to slam into the stone structure.

The post itself seemed to be shaking when Ben and Danielle moved together for the smaller of the two tables. Ben drew it aside enough for Danielle to pitch herself through the shattered glass and roll once she hit the ground. Ben held his breath the whole time, submachine gun ready in case one of the enemy was lying in wait. When Danielle was no longer visible, he replaced the table and turned his attention to the front of the post, where more fire surged in, cracking apart the post's interior and sending fragments of stone cascading inward.

The driver was caught in the face with flying glass. He raised his hands desperately and a bullet took him in the stomach, spinning him around for a burst that stitched across his back. He twisted into the wall, bounced off, and fell face first to the floor.

Ben replaced him by the window, firing out at shapes that were no more than blips of movement in the dark.

Who were these men? Who had sent them?

Ben thought of Ibrahim Mudhil cowering in the cubicle certain he was about to be taken by a spook story, a legend.

Al Safah . . .

Ben opened fired on some darting shapes, shattering remnants of the window glass. He heard something rattle on the roof, thinking it was footsteps until an explosion sounded and a burst of stone poured downward.

DANIELLE SNAPPED OFF two shots from the brush and killed the man who had hurled the grenade. She moved low amid the foliage that enclosed the previously abandoned guard post. The untended bushes, shrubs, and plants grew wild and untamed, offering her sufficient cover if she kept to a crouch.

She wiped the pelting rain from her eyes and glimpsed a trio of gunmen converging on the front of the post while a pair trailed slightly behind them, more grenades held stiffly in their hands. Danielle sprang, but not before they had lobbed their grenades upward.

She aimed for the rifle-wielding attackers first, then instantly turned her fire on the grenade throwers. She thought she had managed hits on all five, but her triumph lasted only until fresh fire poured her way from behind her. She swung fast and used the muzzle flashes to direct her return shots, her ears stung by the gun bursts and thunder, the night alive with the pounding of feet everywhere.

But she couldn't hold them forever, or even much longer with her remaining bullets. Danielle dove into the mud and pressed herself against the ground, in clear view of the four-wheel-drive vehicle that had brought her and Ben here. It was only a dash away, and she was weighing her chances of reaching it when the guard post erupted behind her.

THE POST'S FLAT stone roof coughed rubble into the air. Ben gazed up from the floor and realized he could see the night as chunks of the roof crashed to the floor. Part of the side wall gave way with it and utterly entombed the second royal policeman.

Ben scampered through the crumbling mass of stone for the cubicle where Mudhil was stowed. He felt the rain pour over him, mixing with the dusty stone to create a sour, spoiled smell like mud baked by a scalding sun. He was crawling now, feeling flecks of rock and rain hit him.

The cubicle's door was missing, and inside he could see Mudhil pinned by the debris.

"Give me your hand!"

Mudhil obliged weakly, his flesh powdered by the dirt and dust. Ben steadied his submachine gun in one hand and with the other pulled Mudhil back into the center of the post. All that remained reasonably whole were the walls, and of these the front one looked as if it could tumble at any time.

Ben saw a series of figures rushing for what remained of the post's entry. He shoved Mudhil behind him, steadying his submachine gun in one hand, pistol in the other.

As he readied to fire, a roar like thunder sounded just before the back end of a jeep crashed through the remnants of the front wall.

DANIELLE STARTED SHOOTING from inside the jeep the moment it screeched to a halt with all four tires perched atop splintered stone inside the post.

Ben leaped up from behind the jeep, blasting away with his submachine gun until it clicked empty.

"Get in!" Danielle screamed at him.

She looked back to see him hoisting Ibrahim Mudhil through the jeep's shattered rear window. Danielle discarded her empty AK-47 and opened fire with her pistol in its place, feeling the vehicle rock as Ben joined Mudhil inside.

"Drive!" he yelled.

Danielle floored the jeep and it slammed through what was left of the wall and rattled to the ground. The hood flew open and then snapped down again. The headlight on the passenger side fluttered and died.

The windshield exploded under a burst fired from straight ahead. Danielle ducked and floored the accelerator pedal. The jeep zoomed forward and struck a gunman dead on. Part of the loosened bumper separated at impact and ground along the ground. The jeep thumped up onto the road and shed it altogether.

Danielle kept her eyes trained on the rearview mirror until she was satisfied no one was following.

"You're going to talk to us now, aren't you?" Danielle said, turning her gaze on Ibrahim Mudhil. "You're going to tell us *everything!*"

CHAPTER 40

I DON'T HEAR you speaking," Danielle continued, her eyes riveted on Mudhil in the rearview mirror.

She braked the jeep into a spinning, screeching halt diagonally across the flooded road. Its one remaining headlight flickered briefly, catching the mountains that rose again before them in its spill, as she spun around and faced Mudhil.

"We'll wait for them here, I don't give a shit! We'll wait for Al Safah himself until you talk!"

"Drive, please!"

"Talk!"

Mudhil flapped his hands in concession. "All right, all right . . . Yes, yes, but keep driving. Please!" He peered frantically out the window.

Danielle righted the car and started it forward again.

"Faster!" Mudhil urged, from low in his seat.

"If I stop again, I'm tossing you out! No more chances. We ask a question, you answer it. Clear?"

"Anything! Anything!"

"Ben," Danielle said, and drove onward through the storm.

"Leila Fatuk wasn't the only girl you kidnapped, was she?" Ben asked Mudhil.

"No, there were many. Mostly girls, some boys. All ages."

"And what did you do with these children?" he asked, almost fearing the answer.

"Delivered them. Different checkpoints, different contacts."

"And what did your contacts do with the children?"

"I don't know."

"He asked you a question!" Danielle wailed from behind the wheel.

"I don't know!"

She screeched the jeep to a halt once more. "We'll leave you here if you don't talk."

"I'm telling you, I don't know *what* happens after I deliver them!"

"You deliver them to Al Safah. That's what you're saying."

Mudhil trembled visibly. "I told you before, I've never met him, never *seen* him."

"But these men—your contacts," Ben picked up, as Danielle once again edged the jeep forward through the storm.

"None of them had ever seen Al Safah either. Like me, except . . ."

"Except *what?*"

Mudhil glanced up fearfully at Danielle in the front seat.

"They were all Israelis."

"Your contacts?" Danielle demanded, shaken.

"Don't stop! Please! I am telling the truth."

"And these Israelis," she resumed, "they were the ones who gave you your assignments, selected your targets for you?"

"No, that was someone else."

"Who?"

Mudhil said nothing.

Danielle's foot teased the brake. *"Who?"*

"Hyram Levy."

The jeep thundered through the storm.

Y OU KILLED LEVY, didn't you?" Danielle raged.

"I didn't kill him! I swear!"

"But you know who did. You must."

"No! I know nothing about that!"

Danielle thought of something. "Hand me my bag."

"Your . . ."

"My bag. It's back there somewhere. Check the floor."

Mudhil found her bag there and handed it over the seat.

Danielle fished wildly through it until she located a copy of the picture constructed by Moshe Goldblatt. A picture of the man last seen with Hyram Levy, the man who had visited her in the hospital.

I can help you. . . .

She held it out behind her over the seat. "Take this. Tell me if you've ever seen this man before."

Mudhil took the picture in his trembling hands. He gasped. His single eye gaped in terror.

"Who is he?"

Mudhil crushed the edges of the picture together. When he spoke, his voice was weak but flat. "The man who took my eye out with that hot poker."

D ANIELLE DROVE ON through the mountains, her head starting to pound. The information was coming too fast for her to process, and what she did process made no sense.

Two men had been positively identified as being in

Hyram Levy's shop the day he was murdered, two men connected by an abduction ring that the Engineer himself was ostensibly involved in through a phantom named Al Safah. One of those men had paid an unannounced visit to Danielle in the hospital, sent by Levy as a favor to Commissioner Hershel Giott of the National Police. What could the man have wanted of her?

Everything was connected.

But nothing made sense.

"What's his name?" she asked finally. "This man who took your eye out."

"I don't know. I never knew."

"How were you paid?"

"In cash. On delivery."

In the backseat, Ben kept glancing over his shoulder out into the stormy night. "What happened to the children after you dropped them off with your contacts?" he demanded.

"I told you, I don't know."

"Let me phrase it a different way: Where were they taken?"

"I never asked, didn't care."

"None of these children were ever seen by their parents again."

"No."

"Never a ransom demand . . ."

"Not from me."

". . . and nothing to do with revenge."

"I don't know the motive. I did what I was paid to do. They told me the kinds of children they were looking for. The rest was up to me."

"Random selections?"

"Mostly."

"For how many years?"

"A few. Several. Five or six, anyway."

"You have been kidnapping children for five or six years?" Ben demanded, disbelievingly. "How many have you taken? How many families have you destroyed?"

"I don't count."

"Give me an estimate."

"Between twenty and twenty-five."

Ben could feel himself starting to quiver with rage and tried to calm himself with some deep breaths. "I'm going to ask you a few more questions, Mudhil. Your answers will determine whether I kill you or not."

"I am dead anyway. Wherever I go, Al Safah will find me."

"Did a parent ever give you a child willingly?" Ben asked, remembering the woman who denied her missing daughter had ever existed.

"For money, yes."

"So you bought children as well," Ben said, revolted.

"Sometimes, so long as they fit the specifications."

"What about runaways from refugee camps who went with you of their own accord?"

"The least complicated operations of all."

"Because they didn't know what they were getting into. Because—"

Headlights pierced the heavy rain ahead of them, streaming through the jeep's shattered windshield. Danielle twisted the wheel and felt for her pistol at the same time. Ben shoved Ibrahim Mudhil down to the floor and tried to steady his gun over the seat back.

The tires couldn't hold the road through the rain and mud. The jeep skidded sideways across the road, headlights bearing down on it in the last instant before impact.

CHAPTER 41

THE ONRUSHING VEHICLE screeched to a halt, tires acting like skates the last stretch of the way but stopping a yard from the jeep's side. A passenger door flew open and Colonel Nabril al-Asi lunged out.

"What's going on?" he asked, shielding his eyes from the rain. "What are you doing?"

Ben opened his window and leaned out. "We were attacked!" he shouted over a sudden burst of thunder. "Everyone else at the post is dead!"

Al-Asi stiffened. *"Hal 'arsat,"* he sneered. "The bastards . . ."

"The bridge, Colonel, can we cross it?"

"It's still impassable."

"But can we *cross it?* They could be coming!"

Al-Asi and Ben gazed back down into Jordan. "We can try," the colonel said. "Leave your jeep here, just like this. We'll crowd into mine."

"What's happened? Where are my men?" Marash called out, sliding through the muck, his wounded arm pinned up in a makeshift sling.

"Get back inside, my friend," al-Asi advised him.

Marash noticed the jeep's condition. *"Barrak Allah Feik . . ."*

Danielle and Ben hustled Ibrahim Mudhil into the other jeep. Marash squeezed up front with al-Asi and the Jordanian driver.

"How far are we from the bridge?" Ben asked.

"Twenty minutes in these conditions." Al-Asi twisted sideways. "What happened back there? Who was it?"

"Mudhil claims it was someone called Al Safah."

"Who?"

"Al Safah?" muttered Marash.

"I see you've heard of him."

"My children still love to hear me tell the story my own father told me. The problem is that's all Al Safah is—a story."

"Let's hope so," Ben said, and left it at that.

AL-ASI HELPED MARASH out of their jeep at the final checkpoint just before the Allenby Bridge.

"I expect you to return my vehicle tomorrow, my friend," Marash said to him.

"You have my Mercedes as collateral."

They embraced in the pouring rain before al-Asi rushed back to the jeep.

"You drive," he told Danielle. Then, to both of them, "I have men waiting on the other side."

"How did you know when we'd be crossing?" Ben asked.

"They've been waiting for hours now."

"Someone you trust, obviously."

"Your Captain Wallid," al-Asi said noncommittally.

IT WAS A maddening drive, the wind forever on the verge of tipping the jeep over the side. The quarter-mile length was covered often in inches amid frantic stops and starts. The sway was terrifying, and the water that cascaded in sheets over them felt like ocean waves at high tide. The headlights and windshield wipers were for the most part useless.

Danielle leaned over the wheel, squinting to see well enough to keep them on the bridge roadway. Visibility worsened the closer they got to the center of the bridge to the point that she was driving almost purely on instinct. The West Bank was nothing more than a huge dark void on the other side. All Danielle could do was hold the wheel straight and steady against the determined efforts of the wind and water to twist them about.

Finally, a pair of high beams threw shafts of lights onto the bridge, illuminating the final stretch to the other side. Danielle headed the jeep directly at them, trying to keep her lights pointed into those facing her to hold the jeep on track.

The man behind the wheel of the car waiting for them outside the guard post on the West Bank side of the bridge backed up when she drew close, opening a path for Danielle to use. She slid to a stop, barely able to pry her fingers from the steering wheel because she had been squeezing it so hard.

"We must make all this worth it," Colonel al-Asi said sharply before he stepped back out into the storm.

"That shouldn't be too hard," Ben assured him.

CAPTAIN WALLID TOOK Ibrahim Mudhil into custody, promising around-the-clock surveillance on his holding cell. As politely as possible, Ben made it plain that Mudhil was being protected more than guarded.

"It's after midnight," al-Asi said to Danielle when it was just the three of them. "How are we to get you back to Jerusalem?"

"She'll be staying with me tonight," Ben offered. "It makes the most sense."

"Very well," the colonel said. "Let me drop you."

CHAPTER 42

"YOU SHOULD HAVE asked me first," Danielle said, sipping a piping hot instant coffee in Ben's apartment.

"I knew what your answer would be."

"How?"

"How often have you slept at home lately?"

"What makes you such an expert on my nighttime habits?"

"I was in your office, remember? It wasn't too hard to figure out where you'd been sleeping. I am a detective, after all."

The storm had let up, just a soft pattering against the windows now. Ben had turned on only a single light and the ceiling fan spun lazily overhead, casting long, rain-spotted shadows across the room.

They had both showered and changed, Danielle into Ben's bathrobe while he washed her clothes in the ancient machine housed in the building's basement. Ben kept checking his watch to see when he had to go down and flip her clothes into the dryer. In the meantime, he sat across from her in his chair, smelling the sweet scent of shampoo rising off her hair and trying not to let his stare linger too long on the healthy sheen the bath oil had given her skin. He would have been content to sit like this all night; if she fell asleep, he doubted he would move, would just watch over her until sunrise.

"There's something I need to tell you," she said suddenly.

"You don't have to tell me anything."

"This is business—I think it might be anyway."

"Then by all means, go ahead, Pakad."

"It goes back to when I was in the hospital, after I lost the baby. A man I didn't know came to my room and said there was a way he could help me. I was pretty groggy and didn't pay much attention, but it seemed so strange I never really forgot about it."

"What changed?"

"The man was identified as being with Hyram Levy the day he was murdered."

Ben felt static rush up his spine. Gooseflesh prickled the hair on his arms.

"It was the same man who took Ibrahim Mudhil's eye," Danielle resumed.

Ben recalled the glimpse he'd gotten of the drawing. He moved to her on the couch but stopped short of reaching out, holding his ground as if a barrier had risen between them.

"Levy sent him after receiving a call from Commissioner Giott of the National Police."

"Are you saying *your superior* is connected to Mudhil?"

"I don't know. I don't understand—that's what I'm saying."

Danielle sipped some more of her coffee. She tried to imagine what it would be like now to be back in her apartment alone with the sounds she had come to dread and hate. The mere thought of it made her shudder. In spite of her exhaustion she knew she'd never have been able to sleep. She probably would have returned to her office instead, if Ben hadn't extended his offer.

"Thanks for inviting me to stay," she said finally.

"Don't mention it." But he was glad she had.

"It's just that I haven't liked being in my apartment for a while now. I didn't realize how much until this case gave me an excuse to live out of my office."

"No way to live."

"The thing is I used to love living alone, being alone. Now it frightens me."

"Since the hospital?"

"Yes."

"Makes sense."

"How?"

Ben wondered if he had already said too much, but it was too late. "You weren't expecting to be alone anymore."

Danielle's features sank. "I guess I knew that. Do you know I haven't looked at my mail in over a week? I haven't paid my bills. They keep calling me from the post office to pick up some parcels. The more I get into this case, the easier it gets to push everything else aside. Almost like I don't care."

"Sounds familiar."

"Your family?"

Ben nodded. "For months after they were killed. I lost track of the little things, just like you. I didn't care anymore and there was no 'almost' about it. It didn't matter if I was alone or not. I wasn't really there when someone else was with me anyway."

"That's why you came back to Palestine."

"When in doubt, go back home. And now I'm thinking about returning to the U.S."

"Why?"

Ben hesitated. "There's nothing here for me anymore. Things didn't work out like I planned."

"They seldom do."

"I feel cheated. It's gotten so I often forget why I came back in the first place."

"You're lucky to have a choice, somewhere else to go."

"Not unless things prove different in Detroit."

"Where do you think I should go?"

Here, Ben thought, but said, "You should have called me."

"Some things you've got to bear alone."

"Some things you *can't* bear alone."

"I wish you had come to see me."

"I wish I had too. But I was angry, jealous."

"I'm sorry."

"You have nothing to be sorry about," Ben told her. "And neither do I. Unless you count living through history at the same time. After everything we did, everything we went through, I couldn't go to a hospital in Jerusalem without a special pass."

"Pointless," Danielle agreed.

"It made me more than angry; it made me bitter. This world made it impossible for us to stay together because of who we were, even though we wanted to." Ben hesitated. "You did want to, didn't you?"

"Yes." She nodded.

"We had each other only as long as it suited the needs of our superiors, as long as we were working together to serve them."

"We knew that when we started."

"But then they lied to us, didn't they? The peace process we had saved broke down. Things deteriorated, regressed. Makes me wonder why we bothered."

She slid closer to him on the couch. "We're both angry, Ben."

He stared deeply into her eyes. "I'm angry because I didn't know enough to say screw them and stay with you. Whatever it took."

"I would've had to make sacrifices too. I'm not sure

I was ready to do that. Even if we left this part of the world, nothing would change."

"What about America?" Ben said, asking the question he had meant to ask eighteen months before. "For both of us."

"Come on, neither of us was about to give up who we were to be together, and that's what we would have had to do in the end. Our deepest dedications lie outside each other, always have, and once we were confronted by that again, we couldn't make it work." Her voice softened, quieted. "It isn't just about being a Palestinian or an Israeli; it's about how you and I defined ourselves, and those definitions are all wrapped up in the cultures we were born into."

"Then why did it work for as long as it did?"

"Because for a while, with peace appearing to be a reality, the definitions we had lived by didn't matter as much. When peace broke down, we were back where we started."

"That I could have accepted," Ben told her. "I had gotten used to living with sadness. But you showed me how to be happy again. You made me remember. And when you left, that made the return of the sadness almost impossible to bear."

"When *I* left? I didn't leave, Ben, and neither did you. Both of us just stayed where we were—that's what I've been trying to tell you. You talk about what this has done to you. Have you thought about what it has done to me?"

"Maybe my child would have lived," Ben said, instantly regretting it.

"And what would we have brought him up as? What if we had had him and *then* parted? My God, what if one of us died? Could the survivor have sufficiently filled the other half of his being?"

"We loved each other!"

"I think we did. Maybe we still do. And that's why we ended things, because we could see where they were going and it wasn't someplace good."

Ben reached out and touched her hair. "So look where we ended up."

Danielle smiled sadly. "At least we're together again."

"Until we solve this case."

"It could take a while."

"I hope so," Ben said, holding her at arm's length and knowing that was as close as they could be.

CHAPTER 43

"WHY ARE YOU crying?" David Wolfe asked his granddaughter as he stroked her hair.

Tali looked up at him from her pillows and dabbed at her eyes. "That part of the story is so sad. I hate it. Poor Revkah Rossovitch . . ." Her large brown eyes brightened a little. "Can't you change that part of the story, Papa?"

"Then it wouldn't be true anymore, would it? Then you wouldn't enjoy the part when I pick up the story next time."

The little girl propped herself up on her elbows. "Can you tell me that part now? Can you tell me what the friends did to, ah, how do you say it? . . ."

"Make things right."

". . . make things right." She grabbed his hand and wouldn't let go, David Wolfe trying not to show how much it hurt. "Please, please, please!"

"Then you would have nothing to look forward to tomorrow." He finally extracted himself from his granddaughter's determined grasp. "Besides, you know my friends are waiting downstairs."

"What about the secret?"

"We haven't come to it yet."

"But you'll tell me," Tali implored. "You promised you'd tell me!"

Wolfe moved for the door. "You enjoy the ending so much the way I've always told it."

"Does the secret the friends kept change the ending?"

"I'm not sure yet," David Wolfe said, and flipped off the light.

WOLFE INSISTED ON pouring the three men snifters of imported Israeli brandy before the meeting got under way in his book-lined study.

"I would like to propose a toast," he said, passing the glasses out. He raised his own into the air. "To the great fortune that caused the attempt on Max Pearlman's life to fail."

Stern, Belfidi, and Davies looked at each other.

"Come now," Wolfe resumed, "did you think I wouldn't hear of the measures resorted to?" His face wrinkled in disgust. "Suicide bombers in Atarim Square?"

"The operatives retained never submitted their plan for approval," said Marcus Stern.

"That is supposed to pacify me?"

"We trusted their judgment."

"Then you are all fools. All those innocent lives almost lost. My God, how could we ever have lived with ourselves. . . ."

"Don't forget, time was of the essence," Abraham Belfidi reminded.

"So in the interest of time, we sacrifice sound judgment. Is that it?"

Belfidi and Stern looked at each other. "From the beginning," Stern said, "you were the one who stressed the magnitude of the stakes involved here."

"At least," picked up Joshua Davies, "we succeeded in forcing Max Pearlman into hiding."

"You succeeded in nothing. Max will try to finish what he and Levy started from wherever he is."

"Perhaps," said Stern, rising from his chair, "we should let him."

David Wolfe swung his way in a motion that surprised both of them. Some of his brandy spilled over the rim of his glass. "No! I swore an oath, do you hear me?"

"All three of you swore an oath," said Belfidi.

"And the other two decided to play God."

"You *all* decided to play God," reminded Belfidi. "That was how all this started, David."

"You don't need to remind me. I tried to talk them out of it," Wolfe said distantly. "God knows I tried."

"Only their convictions were as strong as yours."

Wolfe gazed wearily at Stern. "Tell me something, Marcus: Whose side are you on?"

"Yours."

"And whom do you agree with?"

"Them."

"Abraham?"

Belfidi nodded.

Wolfe turned to Joshua Davies. "Joshua."

The younger man's eyes gave his answer.

"You all think I'm wrong." Wolfe sighed. "Maybe you're correct. But this isn't about right and wrong, it's about duty and obligation, commitment. And I am committed to keeping a promise I made almost fifty years ago."

"Regardless of cost?" Stern wondered.

"That's right."

"And where does that leave Israel, David?"

"She has seen her way through a half dozen wars," Wolfe responded. "She'll see her way through this, too."

"With your help," Belfidi added.

"You keep saying that, all of you, but it's not true. I told Pearlman and Levy to do *nothing*, to leave things alone."

"A risk they could not accept."

"So they chose to try to play God a second time," said Wolfe. "And I chose to stop them."

"But what if you haven't?" Marcus Stern asked solemnly. "There are only four days left, and we have another problem confronting us now." Stern looked toward Davies. "Joshua, tell him."

"Yesterday, Chief Inspector Barnea followed the trail of one of Levy's smugglers into Jordan, a man named Ibrahim Mudhil."

"What do Levy's smugglers have to do with me?"

"She is piecing things together, that's what," Stern snapped. "She is following a trail to the truth, and that means to you and the others—everything!"

"Danielle Barnea's investigation could eventually expose the same truth Levy and Pearlman wanted to erase and you sought to protect," Belfidi elaborated.

Wolfe sipped some more of his brandy, reluctant to meet any of his guests' eyes. "How close is she?"

Stern and Belfidi again looked toward Joshua Davies, who took his cue. "Our information indicates she has uncovered a link between her investigation of Levy's murder and an investigation being conducted by a Palestinian detective named Ben Kamal, the same one she was partnered with two years ago. We believe they were in Jordan together last night."

"That's not what I asked."

"Kamal's investigation concerns the search for missing Palestinian children."

Wolfe moved to the bookshelves and turned away from his guests.

Stern's voice followed him. "If we stop Pearlman and Levy's plan, we win. If we fail, we still do not lose. Only if the truth is exposed do we lose, does *everyone* lose."

Wolfe heaved a deep sigh, his shoulders slumped.

"There was a time, my friends, when truth was not something to be feared. When it was all we had."

"It still is all we have, David," said Belfidi. "It's merely a different truth. Just like you use a different name."

"But I'm the same man, Abraham."

"And you face losing everything you have worked for. The dreams you fought for, the world you helped to build, unless we put an end to these investigations. Through whatever means are necessary."

"We don't have any other choice," Stern agreed.

"There may be one," Wolfe persisted.

"For God's sake, David, *what?*"

"The truth, my friends," Wolfe said, straightening his shoulders and turning back around. "We use the truth."

DAY FIVE

CHAPTER 44

DANIELLE DROVE HER car back to Jerusalem first thing the next morning, having woken stiff on the couch after a sleep that started by being blissfully restful but was soon haunted by dreams. She hadn't told Ben about the dreams that had plagued her since her stay in the hospital, and last night they had seemed the most vivid and unsettling yet.

Her baby was always in them; alive, well, and with her. In the dream she found the security and love that reality had denied her. She basked in the glory of not just a new mother, but an Israeli mother doing her biblical duty to sustain the race. Every woman in Israel bore children. It wasn't like the United States, where so many more choices were open and available. In Israel it wasn't a choice so much as an obligation all women willingly, and lovingly, took on. To not bear children was a betrayal of sorts. To be unable to bear children was a tragedy. She wanted so much to try to have a child again, yet the doctors weren't sure if she would be able until she tried.

Ben was still sleeping when she left, and Danielle was careful not to disturb him. He could have taken her last night. She wouldn't have resisted; a part of her was hoping he would. He had shown how much he cared by not trying; how well he knew her.

Strange. The man she had conceived a child with didn't know her, her father was dead, and Hershel Giott had become a man shrouded in mystery. That left Ben Kamal, a Palestinian, as the man who knew her best. A part of her had wanted to stay with him. A part of her had wanted to climb into bed alongside Ben and couldn't explain what had stopped her in the end.

Back in Jerusalem, Danielle stopped at her apartment long enough to sort through the hefty pile of mail, dividing it into three separate piles to be further scrutinized later. She didn't open any of the envelopes, but felt better all the same just to have tackled the job. She stuffed into her bag the two postcards alerting her that parcels were waiting to be picked up at the local postal branch. The oldest had been there for exactly a week.

She did some quick cleaning and emptied the dishwasher she had run a week before too. Then she took a long, hot shower and changed into fresh clothes from the ones Ben had washed for her the night before. She thought she could still smell the scent of his home on her blouse and hung it in the closet apart from the others.

Finally she went back to the book filled with names of those who had attended her father's funeral or one of the shivah sittings, trying to remember who had been there and what exactly they had said.

If you ever need anything . . .

Everyone says it a lot, but few really mean it. Danielle needed to find someone who really did.

Perusing the book, she came across the name of Harry Walls, a man a little older than she who had gone through training for the Sayaret, the Israeli Special Forces, at the same time she had. His brother had been critically wounded at Entebbe, and although she and Harry had served in different branches of the Sayaret, they had kept in touch from time to time afterward. After his name in her father's memorial book, Harry Walls had written his phone number and underlined it twice. Danielle picked up the phone and dialed.

She wasn't disappointed: it rang twice, was answered, then there was a beep.

"Danielle Barnea, Harry. Could you call me, please."

She didn't leave her number; if she was right about Harry, she didn't have to.

Sure enough, her phone rang less than two minutes later.

"Harry?"

"Hello, Danielle."

She pressed the receiver tighter to her ear. Harry Walls had given her a special number rigged into a network reserved for intelligence operatives.

Operatives of the elite Mossad.

"It's been a long time," Walls continued.

"My father's funeral. You said if I ever needed anything I could call you."

"Name it."

"I need an ID on a photo."

"I was hoping it was a date," Walls said, sounding disappointed, and Danielle remembered hearing something about a divorce.

"Not this time."

"National Police data banks come up empty for you?"

"I see you heard I came back."

"I told you I'd be checking up from time to time."

"And I'm sure you know the National Police data banks are not, how should I say it, as thorough as yours."

"True enough."

"How can I get the photo to you?"

"Do you have a fax?"

"Yes, but sending a picture, the quality . . ."

"Don't worry about the quality." Danielle could almost see Harry Walls smiling smugly on the other end. "Our machine will take care of that. Here's the number . . ."

"I'll send it through now," Danielle said after jotting the exchange down. "When can I expect to hear from you?"

"Later today."

"I don't know where I'll be."

"Don't worry," Walls told her. "I'll find you."

CHAPTER 45

IN SPITE OF being exhausted, Ben had slept fitfully through the night. Thoughts of Danielle sleeping in the next room were too disturbing and he kept being awoken by intense dreams, one after the other. In some, he went to her. In others, she came to him. In all, they found each other and the result was a bliss he hadn't known since they had parted eighteen months before. But each time the dream ended he was still alone, his sleep growing more and more choppy as the night wore on. Worst of all, Ben knew in the morning she would be gone, back to Israel, and he wanted her near him, even on these terms—on *any* terms.

When he finally woke up, or thought he did, the ghost of Zaid Jabral was back in the corner chair. The creaking noise the chair made as the ghost rocked itself sounded strangely peaceful and soothing. Finally Jabral stopped and sat still. Part of his smoldering suit fell away and his exposed flesh squished against the chair's fabric.

"You still haven't figured it out, have you, Inspector?"

"No. I've tried, but I can't."

"You haven't tried hard enough. I'm beginning to think my faith in you was mislaid, since I made you a national hero."

"After you made me an outcast."

"Both were called for. Just doing my job. And if you would do yours, you could clean up this mess. Finish the work I started."

"Tell me how."

"I just did."

"I must not have been listening."

"It's right in front of you."

"Do all ghosts speak in riddles?"

Jabral's bulging eyes, like cue balls stuck in his patchwork face, flicked toward the living room, where Danielle was sleeping.

Ben sat up straigher in bed. "What does she have to do with it, Jabral?"

"We're all connected, the three of us. And if you don't start thinking, you'll both be joining me."

"Ramira Taji is dead."

"I know."

"She was murdered, wasn't she?"

"What do you think, Inspector?"

"I think she was murdered by the same people who had you killed."

"So do I."

"You could be a little bit more help than that."

"Sorry. They make us play by the rules here. Go back to my apartment, Inspector. Try again." And he started to fade out, just as he had the last time.

"Wait, Jabral, wait!"

What was left of him held thinly to the darkness. "Make it fast."

"Does Al Safah really exist?"

"How should I know?"

"I just thought that maybe . . ."

"He wouldn't be with me, Inspector. He'd be somewhere else entirely."

And then the rest of him faded away.

When Ben finally woke up hours later, Danielle was gone. He went into the bathroom, cupped his hands, and drank water until he felt he might burst. Twenty minutes later his mouth was dry again, and he tried a piece of fruit.

Go back to my apartment, Inspector.

Advice Jabral's ghost had given him. What had he missed or failed to give sufficient weight to? By now, though, the apartment would have been ransacked by his fellow policemen. Once again, Ben reran the taped interview with Ari Bar-Rosen in his mind, searching for a clue that wasn't there. Then he went over everything he had done, step by step, searching for something he had found and brushed aside.

A chill suddenly passed through him. *The summons!* Jabral had been detained briefly in Israel by the IDF last week.

It's right in front of you.

And it had been. The summons lying on the floor beneath Jabral's desk.

Ben grabbed two more pieces of fruit for the road and rushed for his car.

NOT ALL ROUTES into Israel were monitored by checkpoints. An estimated ten to fifteen thousand Palestinian workers used back roads and even old goat paths to get to their jobs whenever Israel shut her borders. The odds of getting through were very good. But for those who didn't make it the penalties were severe, months of administrative detention with no charges filed, at the least. A stretch in Megiddo Prison on a trumped-up charge, at the worst.

That morning Ben decided to take his chances. The road he chose he knew for a fact was a favorite among those who sneaked their way into Israel to keep food on their tables. His heart was pounding as he neared the border, out of worry as well as expectation over what might be waiting for him in the area Zaid Jabral had obviously been investigating.

Ben veered off Jaffa Road, connecting Jericho and Jerusalem, and crossed the border without incident. He continued on toward the Arab town of Abu Ghosh, outside of which Jabral had been issued his summons. The hills beyond Abu Ghosh, west of Jerusalem, contained a number of kibbutzim established following the 1967 Six-Day War as defensive fortifications when Israel took Jerusalem. Most were open to tourists and advertised this fact from the highway, a fact certain to facilitate Ben's entrance and minimize undue scrutiny given him. But which kibbutz, if any, had Jabral stopped at? And what was he looking for there?

Ben decided to take them in order. It was not an altogether unpleasant task, especially given the comfortable temperature and cooling breezes that made the hot dusty air of Jericho seem much farther away than it really was. He made sure to park his car out of sight from the entrances, so no one would notice his white Palestinian license plates, and then walked on to the communes innocently, flashing his badge to the first residents to accost him. His English proved a godsend since he spoke no Hebrew at all, and the vast majority of Israeli adults and older children spoke English.

At each kibbutz, he described Jabral in order to learn if the journalist had been there. If the answer was no, there was no reason to continue. The first three yielded nothing, but a fourth, which did not cater to tourists at all, proved considerably different.

"Walked with a limp?" asked an older Israeli to whom Ben had been introduced.

"And a cane, yes."

The old man nodded, gazing out over the freshly

watered fields and groves. "The journalist. I remember him now. He was here last week, or maybe the week before."

Ben tried not to look too excited. "What was he looking for?"

The old man suddenly turned suspicious. "Why are you asking?"

Ben opted for the truth. "Because he was murdered two days ago. His name was Zaid Jabral. He was my friend, and I think something he learned here may be connected to his death."

"You're Palestinian, aren't you?"

"Palestinian-American."

The old man gave him a longer, tougher look. "I'm certain your friend didn't learn anything here at all."

"What do you mean?"

"He asked very specific questions, as I recall, about weddings and deaths and births. Especially births; he asked about them twice. He wanted to see our records. But they were all lost when we relocated here in 1967."

"Relocated?"

The old man nodded. "After the Six-Day War, when Jerusalem was ours again, we were the first kibbutz to move to the city's outskirts."

"From where?"

"Halfway to Tel Aviv, near Sefir. I told your friend that and he became agitated. Asked me about the lost records again."

Ben wondered what had so sparked Jabral's interest. "And he wasn't interested in any records other than the ones that were burned?"

"He didn't ask to see any of the ones we had, so I guess he wasn't."

"Did he ask about any year in particular?"

The old man stroked his chin. "Late nineteen forties, maybe early fifties. I forget which. He stayed for lunch. Took a lot of notes. Asked if he could come back another time to do a more in-depth story on our way of life for the Arab press." The old man's face drooped a little. "I would have liked to have talked with him again."

"I would have, too."

The old man walked Ben back to the gate and saw him off. He hadn't learned what he had come here after, but he had learned something:

Zaid Jabral had stopped at this kibbutz and no other. That meant he knew the information he was seeking was contained in the records that had been lost over thirty years before, records from somewhere in the late 1940s or early 1950s.

So Jabral hadn't come here on a flier, hadn't come here on a hunch. He had known exactly what he was after and where to find it.

What am I missing, you damn ghost, what am I missing?

CHAPTER 46

I HAVE TAKEN the liberty of filling out a report on the joint operation I approved between us, the Israelis, and the Jordanian police yesterday," Captain Wallid greeted as soon as Ben returned late that morning from his surreptitious visit to Israel. "Your signature is required before I file it."

Wallid slid the neatly typed two pages across the desk, complete with a pen clipped to the top. Ben signed the bottom of the second page without reading it.

"I'd like to see Mudhil again as soon as possible," Ben said, sliding the papers back across the desk.

"I have unfortuante news concerning that, Inspector. Another agency with an interest in him learned of his incarceration last night. They picked him up right after sunrise."

"What agency?"

"I assure you their papers and requisitions were in order."

"In other words, Arafat's secret police: Force 17."

Of all the competing and often redundant Palestinian security agencies, Force 17 enjoyed the freest mandate. Since its primary responsibility was the safety of President Arafat and his closest advisers, its personnel went to any lengths to assure his administration remained secure from both the inside and the out. In some respects, Force 17 was the next step beyond al-Asi's Protective Security Service. In others, the organization was a world unto itself, its sole objective being to remove anyone who posed a threat to President Arafat, and it defined "threat" in the broadest sense of the word. Force 17 seldom shared information. Its personnel never worked cooperatively. They protected the president and did what he told them. That was all.

"It is not wise to refer to them as the secret police, Inspector," Wallid said, his tone flat as always.

"What could they possibly want with Mudhil?"

"I wasn't here at the time, and I would not have asked if I had been. The duty officer called me at home. I tried to delay the transfer, but agents of Force 17 are not known for their patience."

Ben felt himself growing hot. "Does Colonel al-Asi know?"

"I spoke with him first thing this morning."

"How do you suppose they found out we had Mudhil in custody, Captain?"

"I suggest you ask your friend Colonel al-Asi that question."

Ben stood up.

"You don't have to go far, Inspector," Wallid said. "He's waiting in your office."

BY THE TIME he reached his office to find Colonel al-Asi sitting behind his desk, Ben's mouth tasted like paste again.

"I hope my friend Marash liked the tie I gave him,"

the colonel said, "because he won't be getting the prisoner he expects from me."

"I wouldn't worry," Ben told him. "You have wonderful taste."

"I was hoping you would stop in here before going to see your captain."

"He told me about Mudhil, about Force 17 taking him into their custody."

Al-Asi shook his head regretfully, hair returned to its perfect coiffure. But his eyes looked tired, evidence the colonel had probably not slept well last night either. "That's what he told you because that's what I told him. When I learned Mudhil had been removed from our custody, I thought the Jordanians had acted quicker than I expected. Then I received a call from Marash's superior insisting that we turn Mudhil over to them."

"So if it wasn't us and it wasn't the Jordanians . . ."

Al-Asi's eyes grew interested. "Are you thinking of Al Safah, Inspector?"

"Aren't you, under the circumstances?"

Al-Asi rose and moved out from behind Ben's desk. "There is someone waiting in my car who most certainly is. Care to join me?"

Ben nodded, aware he had no choice. Outside, the colonel's Mercedes, back from Jordan and freshly washed, was parked in front of police headquarters, illegally as always. A tall, lithe figure with short black hair leaned against an open door smoking a cigarette.

"Superintendent Faustin," al-Asi called, "may I present Inspector Bayan Kamal of the Palestinian police."

The figure stamped out the cigarette beneath a scuffed black boot and turned slowly around.

"Inspector," the colonel continued, "Superintendent Faustin is with Interpol. I believe she can lend some important insight to your investigation."

She? Ben thought in the last instant before he saw her face.

"We meet again, Inspector," Faustin greeted.

It was the woman who had saved his life in the butcher shop four nights before!

CHAPTER 47

DANIELLE CALLED HER office voice mail from her apartment. There was a message from Hershel Giott requesting that she contact him immediately, several from Yori Resnick, and several more from her direct superior, the chief of detectives, who sounded more perturbed with each successive call.

Instead of facing any of them, she headed for Haifa, hoping that the drive would clear her mind, and that the hunch she was playing might pay off. The key to finding Hyram Levy's killer, she told herself, was following the trail Ibrahim Mudhil had set her upon. That meant tracking down the shadowy figure she recalled from her own hospital stay—the man she had come to see as her number one suspect. Assuming Harry Walls failed to identify him for her, though, she had to have another strategy prepared. She proceeded on the assumption that the children, once delivered by Mudhil to his various contacts, were taken out of the country, and she considered the most likely options he had available to him. Danielle felt certain that security at Ben-Gurion Airport would have ruled out travel by air, which left travel by sea as the most probable choice. And travel by sea almost invariably meant departing out of Haifa.

Haifa was a major Mediterranean port city, lined with harbors that featured a constant flow of boating traffic, both large and small. From fishing boats, to pleasure craft, to expensive yachts, to freighters hauling merchandise in and out of Israel, Haifa's port was home to some, a way station for many, and a quick stopover for still more. Its strategic Mediterranean location made it conducive to trade for virtually any European commerical center and convenient for virtually any seaworthy pilot.

The sound of boat horns and the smoky bellows of incoming freighters battled the noise of traffic inching its way along the city's busy portside streets. All of Haifa was enveloped by a sense of having to get somewhere fast, noticeable from the rush of tourists to snap their pictures to the sulfur smell of steaming car engines mixing with the salty sea air.

The city itself was built into a hillside layered into three separate tiers. But Danielle was concerned only with Haifa's lowest tier, or port level, containing the harbor and central to all businesses connected with shipping.

She drove around for some time in search of a parking space, finally managing to squeeze into a spot not far from the Kikar Paris. Paris Square was the center of the port district, a gathering point for any and all who had business in Haifa. Though lunchtime was still over an hour away, she walked toward the Banker's Tavern restaurant located on Habankim Street, keeping the Mediterranean on her right the whole time.

Banker's Tavern was laid out in the rich dark hues and paneled walls of a traditional English pub. It was known for a varied menu, a packed crowd every day for lunch except Saturday, and, to a lesser extent, its most regular customer.

Danielle had come to Banker's Tavern to seek out a man who held office hours there every day in a corner booth. She knew him only as Sabi, although his bulbous frame and hoarse, cigarette-stained voice led many to refer to him as "Jabba" after the sluglike crime boss in the third *Star Wars* installment.

The likeness was accurate in more than one way, since Sabi was as close to a crime boss as Israel had. A smuggler as well as an Israeli Arab, Sabi was one of the few people who got along with everyone. Palestinians welcomed him because of the constant flow of merchandise he expedited, free of Israeli duties and taxes, into the West Bank and Gaza. And Israeli officials looked the other way for the most part, because Sabi's shipping contacts in Alexandria, Port Said, Turkey, and elsewhere were crucial to the nation's trade. The National Police, meanwhile, left him alone because he kept control of the unsavory characters who came and went from Haifa much better than they could ever hope to. He could play both sides against the middle and never seemed to lose. He practiced his trade openly and was willing to give audience to anyone with a business proposition.

Danielle had never met Sabi before, and as soon as she entered the Banker's Tavern, she was amazed by the degree to which he resembled exactly what she had been expecting. He sat in his corner booth, occupying most of one side by himself. His huge jowls hung like slabs of meat from his face. He had a triple chin and a roundish, basketball-sized head that seemed to grow directly out of his neck. A pair of men sat opposite him in the booth. Sabi was drinking a tall glass of tea swimming with mint leaves. The men drank nothing, their eyes riveted on Danielle from the moment she entered the restaurant. She waited near the door patiently until a third man approached her.

"May I help you?"

"I'm here to see him," Danielle replied, tilting her head toward Sabi, who seemed to look at her for the first time.

"Do you have an appointment?"

"No, just this," she said, and produced her badge and identification.

"Follow me." The man led her politely toward Sabi. "Can I get you something?" he asked on the way.

"No. Thank you."

"Very well." He stopped slightly ahead of her when they reached Sabi's booth. "Pakad Danielle Barnea of the National Police to see you, sir."

Sabi lit a cigar and puffed it to life as he waved the men across from him out of the booth. They left and took up a vigil out of earshot several yards away. Danielle slid in across from Sabi in their place. The booth offered an excellent view of the harbor, Sabi's domain.

"Something to eat?" Sabi asked her in a grating voice that sounded as if his vocal cords were coated in steel wool.

He gestured toward the table where a generous assortment of foods had been laid out. Danielle recognzed tabbouleh, a bulgur wheat salad, along with a spinachlike soup called *melukkhiya,* an assortment of breads and spreads, and a variety of pastries.

"Help yourself. *Min fadlak.* Please. There is plenty."

There was indeed, Danielle thought, too much even for a man of Sabi's bulk. Obviously he was always prepared for guests.

"No, thank you," she said.

"Cigar?" he asked, holding a fresh one out toward her.

"Not right now."

"Lots of women smoke them these days. I get these from Cuba, by way of Madrid." He puffed some more, the fragrant smoke wafting across the table. His jowls flexed in and out like a fish drinking air. "It's the way of the world these days, eh, Pakad Danielle Barnea? Nothing gets anywhere directly."

"True enough."

"That's what keeps me in business."

"There is one exception."

"What's that?"

"Information."

"That is what you want, Pakad Danielle Barnea?"

"Yes."

"What kind of information?"

"Smuggling."

"Then you've come to the right place." He pulled another of Havana's best from a suit jacket that looked like a linen sheet with arms. "But try a cigar first. It's a Cohiba Siglio. Perfectly aged and very mellow."

Danielle eased the end into her mouth, let Sabi light it for her. Puffed a few times.

"Not bad, eh, Pakad Danielle Barnea?"

"I don't have much to compare it to."

"Then you'll have to trust me, won't you? Shouldn't be a problem since here we are, two new friends sharing a smoke."

"My business here doesn't concern you."

"If it involves Haifa, it concerns me."

"Not directly," Danielle said pointedly.

Sabi smiled, looking as though he had swallowed a football and now had laces for teeth. "Very good. I like you, Pakad Danielle Barnea. Especially if we have no trouble between us."

"We have none."

"That is good." Sabi leaned as far forward as his bulk allowed. "Now, what kind of smuggling are you interested in?"

"Children."

Sabi stopped puffing and eyed her questioningly.

"Palestinian children are being kidnapped and handed over to Israeli middlemen. I believe those middlemen are then smuggling them out of the country."

"Via Haifa?"

"Is there anywhere else?"

"Not really. We are two professionals sitting here sharing more than an ashtray, eh, Pakad Danielle Barnea? We must keep everything between us in the open. For instance, I trust you are not accusing me of having something to do with such an operation."

"Not at all. I assured you of that before."

"That is good. I'm a father, you know. Many children, both Jew and Palestinian . . . A few Turkish, one Egyptian I believe, even an American. I would hate for someone to think that badly of me."

Danielle puffed her cigar, recalling the day her father finally let her smoke one of his as a teenager, after having let his sons do the same. Finally she spoke. "I thought you might share my concern."

"My concern, Pakad Danielle Barnea, is that you are describing something I have never heard of."

"I think a rival of yours may be involved."

"I have no rival."

"What about Al Safah?"

Sabi reared his head back for a throaty laugh that made the flesh of his midsection ripple and quiver. "You have not come to Haifa looking for him, I hope. You wouldn't be the first, you know. People have been hunting Al Safah for years. Many of them stop here. I send them different places, pretend I am terrified by the mere mention of his name. And when they get there, someone I have waiting sends them somewhere else. We have a good time. Once we kept a writer looking for six months."

"I take it you don't believe Al Safah exists."

"And I take it you believe he is the one behind your missing children."

"I'm considering the possibility."

"I always heard he ate his victims, left their bones behind in their beds."

"We haven't found any bones left."

"Perhaps Al Safah's appetite has grown over the years, eh, Pakad Danielle Barnea?" Sabi laughed heartily again at his own joke. "What's the matter? You don't think I'm funny?"

"I don't think missing children are funny."

Sabi sat back in the booth. Danielle could hear the leather creak from the strain as it receded, conforming to his shape. She could see him thinking, trying to size her up. Finally he pointed his smoldering Cohiba Siglio cigar across the booth.

"You know something, Pakad Danielle Barnea?"

"What?"

"I like you. Few people can come in here, sit in this booth, and tell me something I don't already know. In Haifa, I know everything." The tone of his voice changed. "But I don't know anything about children being smuggled out under my nose. This I don't like. So I'm going to look into it. *Mish mushkeleh.* No problem. I'm going to look very hard. I will probably find you are mistaken."

"I hope so."

"But if I find you are not mistaken, I am going to call you. I am going to call you and together we will deal with the bastards behind this. And should we run into Al Safah, we will end his legend once and for all. What do you say to that, Pakad Danielle Barnea?"

Sabi wedged the cigar back into his mouth, and Danielle puffed right along with him.

Chapter 48

DANIELLE HAD JUST unlocked the door to her car parked a block away from the restaurant when a dark sedan pulled up alongside her, stopping. She swung fast, gun whipped from her belt.

"Get in," said Harry Walls from the driver's seat. "Come on, hurry!"

Danielle relocked her car and climbed into the sedan. Walls drove off as soon as she had closed the door behind her, checking the rearview mirror repeatedly. She remembered him fondly from their training in the Sayaret: someone who was always there for her, always with a smile.

But Walls wasn't smiling today.

"What the hell is going on?" he demanded. His taut biceps and forearms flexed against the steering wheel, the lean muscles of his face stiffening to the point where his mouth barely seemed to move when he spoke.

"I don't know what you're talking about."

"If you don't, you're a bigger fool than I am. What are you into here?"

"This is about the man I asked you to identify," she realized.

His eyes blazed at her from the driver's seat. "You're damn right it is, and somebody's going to catch hell for it!"

"What are you—"

"You sent me to check out one of our own men!"

Something heavy sank in Danielle's stomach as she pictured the gaunt man who had jabbed a poker into Ibrahim Mudhil's eye and later visited her in the hospital.

"He's Mossad, gotldamn it! I ran with his file and ended up in our own backyard. And I did it sub rosa. Do you know what that means? Do you have any idea what that means?"

"I didn't know!"

"His name is Esteban Ravel, a South American Jew who immigrated in 1985. Formerly of the Paraguayan secret police. Strictly a black bag operator. Likes to get his hands dirty. In Paraguay, he was the man they sent when someone was getting out of hand. *Nothing* was beneath him: women, children, torture. Would you like to hear why he left Paraguay?"

Danielle didn't say yes, but Walls continued anyway.

"A general, a rival to the country's president, was allegedly planning a coup. He was guarded twenty-four hours a day by dozens of soldiers. No one outside of his own people had even seen him for weeks." Walls stopped and swallowed hard. "They found the general in bed one morning with his throat cut. Nobody knows how Ravel got in. Nobody knows how he got out. Even the security cameras didn't pick up a thing."

Walls screeched around a corner, eyes still darting back and forth from the rearview mirror.

"This guy's a fucking ghost, Danielle. You can't mess around with somebody like this. How in the hell did you even obtain his picture?"

"My God . . ."

"Talk to me!"

"Stop the car."

"Danielle—"

"Let me out!"

Walls screeched to a halt on a side street running uphill, pinning Danielle's door too close to a parked car to open. "Not until you tell me what the hell's going on!"

"I've already told you too much."

"Listen to me, you can't fuck with this guy. Whatever Ravel's done, whatever you're investigating him for, there are ways we can handle it. Channels."

"Forget channels. We're way past that."

"Ravel's a stone killer! If he finds out somebody's—"

"Ravel's a lot more than a killer. Check that black bag of his, Harry; he's got plenty of surprises inside."

"That's what I'm talking about."

"Pull up and let me out."

Walls didn't move. "You don't go after a man like this, whatever he's done, especially by yourself. We need to handle this in-house. I need to bring you in."

"To Mossad?"

"To people who can help. Ravel's not one of our regulars. He's a specialist they might be willing to pull, if you tell what you know."

Danielle slammed open her door and tried to squeeze herself through. Walls lunged over, grabbing her arm. Danielle latched a hand onto his wrist and twisted, felt something give. Walls grunted in agony and pulled the hand away.

Danielle smashed the window with her elbow. "I don't know *anything!* That's the problem. Maybe I will soon, but I don't now."

Walls was cradling his now trembling hand. "Just let me help you."

Danielle hit the window again and the glass broke away along the fracture lines left by her first strike. "You want to help me? Then listen: Ravel is connected to something that may go back fifty years. Back to men who have been heroes in this country longer than we've been alive, back to the time of our fathers. And now, for some reason, somebody wants them dead. You want to help me? Go back to your files and dig up everything you can on Al Safah."

"Al Safah?"

"It means 'the Butcher.' "

"What else does it mean?"

Danielle started to ease herself out backward through the window, knocking the stubborn remnants aside. "That's what I need to find out."

And then she was gone.

CHAPTER 49

I WASN'T AWARE that Interpol conducted criminal investigations, Superintendent Faustin," Ben said, after al-Asi had ushered the two of them into his office at the Palestinian Authority building. Neither had taken a chair. "I was under the impression it was no more than a records clearinghouse that collates and communicates information from one country's police to another's."

"There you have it then," Faustin told him. "I have come to the West Bank to gather records for future collating and communicating."

"You shoot and fight pretty well for a clerk."

"Gathering records can be more dangerous than most realize," Faustin said, not varying her tone at all. Standing, she was almost as tall as Ben was: five foot ten, at least. Bands of lean, sinewy muscle were clearly visible beneath her tight-fitting black slacks and shirt. Her hair was ink black too, cut and layered so short that it made her look even taller. Faustin's complexion was a combination of tones, not quite dark enough to make her Semitic, but too dark to be simply European. Her cheekbones were high and sharply defined. Her small, tight mouth looked as though it were a stranger to smiling. "It pays to be cautious."

"Deadly would be the way I'd describe it."

"When you're in the business of gathering records some don't want you to have, things tend to get dangerous."

"Records on what?"

"Records on *whom*, actually, in this case: Al Safah."

Ben and Colonel al-Asi exchanged a wary glance.

"Then," Ben started, "*what* would indeed be closer to the truth."

"Make no mistake about it, Inspector. Al Safah is a man."

"If he really exists."

"Oh, he exists all right," Faustin said, her voice chilling in its certainty and matter-of-factness. Her accent defied easy recognition. Ben thought at first there was a French base to it, then changed his mind to German before finally settling on English learned young outside the United States and England. "And not just in Palestine either. He exists in dozens of other countries. Always the same man, always the same deeds, the same methods; only the name is different."

"I get the point, Superintendent."

"Do you? Few others have over the years. Even my superiors continue to doubt Al Safah's existence despite the 'records' I have already accumulated for them."

"So you came to Palestine."

"To obtain indisputable proof."

"And what would that be?"

"Al Safah himself: he's here. At least he has left the warmest trail I've been lucky enough to find. I'm going to trace it back to him. And I'm going to get him."

There was a resolve in Faustin's voice that Ben found eerie and unnerving. He had known plenty of deter-

mined people before. He had known plenty of single-
minded people. But this woman was operating on a
level so intense Ben felt uncomfortable being around
her.

The intensity showed foremost in her eyes, which
were as black as her clothes and hair. They were wide
and deep-set and never seemed to blink, as if afraid to
lose their focus. Distrustful eyes. The eyes of someone
who wanted no one looking in.

"Al Safah would not have remained a legend this
long if he left any trail at all," Ben said finally.

"I know that better than anyone. There's never
anything direct. But I've uncovered pieces that seem
especially pronounced right in your backyard, Inspector."

"The missing Palestinian children," Ben realized.

"His approach here is especially bold. I would venture to say he has little faith in your investigative ca-
pabilities."

"Then he's in for a surprise, isn't he?"

Faustin shrugged, yet seemed to accept Ben's words.
"In the past five days, you've gotten closer to Al Safah
than any other local authority I have ever encountered."

"And you know that, of course, because you've been
following me."

Faustin nodded. "Colonel al-Asi has been gracious
enough to keep me updated on your progress."

Al-Asi shrugged. "The superintendent came to see
me the morning after the incident in the butcher shop.
She requested that I not say anything until she was
ready to approach you."

"What took you so long?" Ben asked her.

"I've gotten close myself, but Al Safah and his henchmen always pull back before I can make my move. I
figured I'd take my chances with you."

"Assuming I wouldn't concern them enough to pull
back."

"You and the entire Palestinian investigative apparatus. Al Safah has staked his claim here in Palestine for the time being. That is how he operates, Inspector," Faustin continued, almost emotionlessly, as if these were words she had spoken too often before. "That is how he avoids detection and hides behind the myth of a legend. Here for a while, then he will move into another country. Always varying the pattern. Resisting any of our attempts to outmaneuver him. I honestly don't think he knows what his next step is going to be until he takes it, so how can we?"

"But it's always children, mostly young girls, isn't it?"

"Yes and no."

"What do you mean?"

"It doesn't matter. What matters is that Al Safah is known for what he wishes to be known as: a monster who steals children in the night. The name they gave him in France translates to 'Taker of Young Souls.' In Russia they call him *Maniak,* which means 'monster.' It's pretty much the same everywhere else. Fear keeps anyone from looking any deeper, fear and ignorance."

"And what would they find if they did look deeper?"

"The same thing I have, I imagine."

"I don't suppose you want to tell the colonel and me what that is, do you?"

Faustin took one step toward him. "I'd rather show it to you, Inspector. Tonight."

CHAPTER 50

A SECURITY GUARD stopped Danielle as soon as she signed in upon entering National Police headquarters.

"I have orders to escort you upstairs to the Rav Nitzav's office the moment you arrived, Pakad."

"That's not necessary."

"I'm afraid it is," he retorted stiffly.

They rode the elevator alone to the sixth floor. The uniformed guard accompanied her every step of the way to Hershel Giott's office, making sure she went inside.

Giott was already standing when she entered, obviously having been forewarned she was on her way. Three other men, two in formal dress uniforms, sat in a ring of chairs before his desk. She recognized them as her three immediate superiors, including her captain, the chief of detectives, and the deputy commissioner. The way they were seated, in deference to Giott, indicated they were going to be silent participants in whatever transpired.

"Close the door, Pakad," Giott said, leaning his knuckles against his desktop.

Danielle closed the door and approached slowly. The commissioner of the National Police waited until she was standing in front of his desk, the eyes of her other superiors burning into her from behind, before he continued.

"I regret that this meeting has become necessary. But we all feel your performance in recent days has left us no choice. This especially pains me because I feel I was in error in reinstating you to your former position in the National Police."

Giott's expression became even more grim.

"Pakad Barnea, we have serious concerns about the manner in which you have proceeded with your investigation into the murder of Hyram Levy. We are aware, for example, of your unauthorized visit into Jordan yesterday."

"I was following up a crucial lead, sir." Danielle knew she shouldn't have spoken until specifically asked to, but she couldn't help it.

"Without obtaining the proper authorization or diplomatic credentials."

"It was a cooperative effort. An exchange of information, that's all."

"You mean, that's what it was supposed to be, Pakad. We understand things became quite dangerous, violent and potentially embarrassing to the State of Israel. A diplomatic nightmare, in fact."

Giott stopped to give Danielle a chance to respond, then continued when she remained silent.

"Pakad Barnea, the status you attained as a result of your heroics two years ago was enough to warrant an exception being made regarding reinstatement at your previous rank and level. But that same status does not allow for your repeatedly going against established procedures and"—here Giott looked almost hurt—"not being totally forthcoming even when questioned directly. I refer to the matter of me asking you if a second copy of Hyram Levy's phone records existed."

"I told you it didn't."

"And was that correct?"

"As far as I knew at the time you asked me. Before the original copy disappeared. It turned out I had an extra," she said, eager to protect Yori Resnick and hide his complicity.

"You also utilized National Police resources, providing unauthorized material to aid in a concurrent Palestinian investigation into another matter, did you not?"

"It was an even exchange. And the Palestinian investigation you're referring to may not be an altogether different matter at all. The cases are connected."

"You have proof of this, Pakad Barnea?"

Danielle looked down. "Not firm proof; not yet, sir," she admitted, and she could almost feel the scalding stares of her superiors blazing into her from behind.

"And yet you are convinced that Palestinian assistance is vital to your pursuit of Hyram Levy's killer."

"I didn't think so at first. I do now."

Giott's eyes continued to narrow. "Let me get to the point: the Palestinian detective you are working with, he is familiar to you, isn't he?"

"He's the same one I liaised with on the serial killer case two years ago."

"On a sanctioned basis at that time."

"Yes."

"And you continued to see him after your investigation was concluded."

"Not professionally."

Giott didn't respond right away. "No, I suspect not." He gazed beyond her at the three men, who had not been invited to say a word. "Pakad Barnea, it is wrong to confuse personal feelings with professional duty. I know this because I made the same error with regard to your reinstatement. Not only did I return you to an investigatory position, I assigned you a high-profile case when it should have been clear to me the recent trauma you had suffered left you in no condition to handle it."

Danielle bit her lip to keep from shouting out in protest.

"Because a portion of the onus for these events falls on me, we will not be asking for your resignation. You will be suspended for one month, after which you will be free to return to the National Police in a position to be determined later. Is that clear?"

Danielle wondered what would happen if she confronted Giott right now with the truth about the man Hyram Levy had sent to her hospital room on his behalf. Esteban Ravel formed an inescapable link between Giott and whatever had led to Levy's murder. In fact, under different circumstances, she would consider the man who had just suspended her to be a crucial, if not material, witness. Now, though, she had been so discredited that any questions she posed, based on information obtained from Harry Walls in Haifa a short time before, would be inalterably tainted. Giott had successfully managed to cut the link.

"Is that *clear?*" Giott repeated, louder.

"I'm sorry. Yes."

He no longer even bothered to regard the three police officials who sat behind her. "You will leave your identification cards, access strips, and all other materials belonging to the National Police with me for the duration of your suspension, Pakad Barnea. You will not enter this building for any reason. You will not establish contact with any members of your investigation team, and you will immediately cease all ongoing cooperative efforts with the Palestinian. To disobey any of these orders will be grounds for immediate dismissal and could lead to formal charges being levied against you by this department. Is that also clear?"

"Very."

What was clear was that Hershel Giott, a man she trusted and who had been like a second father to her, had destroyed her career to keep her from getting at the truth he likely had knowledge of. He had preempted her efforts to uncover not only Hyram Levy's killer, but also the reason behind his murder, thereby protecting some greater secrets that would remain veiled now as a result. She believed more fimly than ever that the abortive bombing in Atarim Square was designed specifically to assassinate Max Pearlman. And she was certain Giott knew this as well.

"Very well," he said dismissively, "I believe we are finished here."

THE WORST THING about her suspension was having to go home and stay there. And if being alone wasn't bad enough in itself, she was alone with the knowledge that a killer named Esteban Ravel was at large. Should he learn of her interest, he would come for her. A top-notch black bag, deep-cover man. A specialist, Harry Walls had called him, who obviously frightened even his fellow Mossad agents.

Danielle would have to prepare herself. But she sat on her couch through the afternoon and well into the evening doing anything but, turning the facts over and over in her mind. When darkness fell, she switched on only the table lamp she could reach, lacking the motivation to move from her seat. She knew the feeling of depression well enough to sense herself falling into it again. Just like when she had returned from the hospital, her child lost then. Her career lost now.

The phone rang, jarring her, and she snatched it clumsily to her ear.

"Hello."

"Pakad Danielle Barnea?"

"Sabi?"

"How quickly can you get to Haifa? There is something I think you should see."

CHAPTER 51

WHEN ARE YOU going to tell me what exactly is going on?"

"After you've seen it for yourself," Faustin replied.

Ben had parked his car in clear view of the entrance to the Einessultan refugee camp half a block away. The camp was located on the outskirts of Jericho, at the very edge of the oasis that exists amid the vast desert plain. To the south lay a grove of orange trees, to the north rolling hills of desolation. An abandoned Israeli military encampment was visible from the camp's entrance to the east.

It was past midnight, and traffic, both pedestrian and vehicular, was thin, almost nonexistent. Whatever they were looking for within the endless cluttered rows of stone houses built on a slight upward grade, Faustin obviously hadn't seen yet.

"How about your first name?" Ben resumed. "Can you tell me that, Superintendent?"

"Mathilde."

"French?"

"It's not my real name," she said noncommittally, "just the one I was given. I keep it as a memory."

Ben decided not to press her, knowing her answers would continue to be as evasive as they had been since they had first met earlier in the day.

"You've taken a personal interest in this case," Faustin continued. "I can tell."

"And if it hadn't been for you, that personal interest would have got me killed."

"At least you tried. Missing persons cases, especially children, receive very little attention." Ben thought he almost saw Faustin smile. Her mouth looked uncomfortable with the effort. "That's why there are so few records at Interpol to be communicated between one country and another, if there were any countries interested, that is."

"You sound bitter."

"I have my reasons."

"Personal as well as professional, it sounds like."

"You have a good ear."

"Care to share them, Superintendent?"

"No."

"It's just that I've had some experience with bitterness, too."

"I know."

Ben looked at her again. Faustin's stare was fixed outside the windshield, riveted on the refugee camp entrance as if in search of prey. "From al-Asi?" he asked.

"Before. The records of your exploits *were* available from Interpol."

"In Detroit or Palestine?"

"Both."

"So you know pretty much all there is to know about me."

"Yes."

"While I know virtually nothing about you."

"That's right."

"And it will be difficult to learn any more if you keep your answers to one or two words."

"True."

"Why were you following me, Superintendent? I expect you can tell me that much?"

Faustin glanced back at Ben again, looking slightly annoyed. "You sent a request to Interpol for records on similarly patterned disappearances or abductions."

Ben nodded. "And you came to Jericho to deliver them personally."

"I was already here."

"Because of the elusive Al Safah."

"On his trail, yes. You don't believe in him, do you?"

"No," Ben replied, half-lying.

"Do you know how long the file on him at Interpol is?"

Ben shook his head.

"Just over a page, enough to list the inference and innuendo that surrounds him, no more."

"What do you expect? You're talking about a man who reportedly has never been seen, can't be identified."

"I'm talking about a criminal mastermind who hides behind the greatest disguise there is: an international legend."

"Or a spook story, a ghost."

Faustin continued to fix her gaze out the windshield. "A ghost who was in this country in the past month. That's why I'm here."

"And how did you learn that?"

"A tip."

"A tip about a man no one knows . . ."

"This person knew Al Safah, knew him from the very beginning."

"I don't suppose you can introduce me."

Faustin's unchanging voice slowed a little. "Not anymore: the source is dead. I never met her myself. There was one phone call, that's all."

"A woman?"

"What's the difference?"

"None, I suppose. Except that Colonel al-Asi has now been in touch with your superiors."

"I would have expected as much."

"You've been on indefinite leave from Interpol for six months."

Faustin did not turn from the windshield.

"Up to that point your superiors had only good things to say. They did not say, though, how you mastered the skills I witnessed the other night in the butcher shop."

"I saved your life."

"Yes, you did."

"I'd say you owe me something in return."

"Name it."

"Stop asking me questions."

"Just one more, Superintendent. Why'd you bother?"

"I already told you: I thought you might be getting close to Al Safah."

"Meaning you believe he is still in the area."

"Even if he's gone, I've got a hard trail to follow for the first time. All the years, all the disappointments. Even Al Safah had to get careless sooner or later."

Ben settled back in his seat. "When I was a boy I heard he cooked and ate children. Is that true?"

"No, but he cuts out the eyes of those who get too close, so even after they're dead they won't be able to identify him."

Ben shivered, thinking of Nazir Jalabad's eyeless corpse and the hot poker that had mutilated Ibrahim Mudhil.

Faustin looked at him as though she could read his mind. "I think you can see, Inspector, why no one can identify this man the world calls a ghost."

Faustin stopped when an approaching car's headlights caught her attention. She tensed and slumped lower in the passenger seat.

The car parked across the street from the entrance to the refugee camp and turned off its lights. An old sedan—a Volvo, Ben thought.

"Can you make out the license plates?" Faustin asked him.

He raised the small binoculars to his eyes. "White."

"Palestinian . . . Just as I thought."

"What's happening?"

"Watch! Don't let them see you! . . . There! *Look!*"

Ben's eyes followed hers to the camp entrance. A girl was heading toward it from the inside in the company of a man who looked to be in his twenties. He was overweight and wore a dark shirt that hung out over his belt.

Ben raised the binoculars again.

"Careful! They might see you!"

He ducked his head lower beneath the cover of the dashboard and focused the binoculars on the steadily advancing girl. On closer inspection she looked to be about twelve or thirteen, the same age as the Shabaz girl who had disappeared from the Deheisha camp he had visited. She wore jeans and a print shirt. The jeans were frayed and tattered. The print on the shirt had faded. In most other places the style would have been called fashionable; here it was impoverished.

Ben peered through the binoculars. The girl definitely seemed to know the man walking by her side, or at least felt comfortable with him. He led her off the camp grounds toward the waiting car, reached the back door just ahead of her, and opened it.

In the few brief seconds the light stayed on, before he closed it behind the girl, Ben glimpsed another young face on the other side of the backseat.

"There's a second girl in the car," he told Faustin.

She didn't look surprised at all. "When they drive off, follow them."

"We should have a second car for this."

"They won't be expecting a tail, don't worry."

The Volvo's headlights came back on. Ben started his car as the Volvo came forward and slipped past them. Not rushing, he waited until it was safely ahead before pulling around to follow.

It had been a long time since Ben had been on a moving stakeout; he couldn't even remember when exactly, although it was well before he took up pursuit of the Sandman back in his days as a Detroit detective. He quickly recalled the basic tricks to it, and, as Faustin had suggested, the Volvo's driver obviously wasn't expecting a tail.

"Don't lose him!" she warned, leaning stiffly toward the dashboard, eyes held wider than Ben had seen them yet, perhaps afraid the Volvo might vanish from her view otherwise.

"Relax, Superintendent."

"I've never been this close to Al Safah before!"

"I hope you don't expect to find him in that car."

"No, but that car is going to him, one way or another."

Ben maintained a safe distance, the Volvo lapsing from sight only around bends and curves in the road, each one of which left Faustin breathing a little faster.

"You think I'm ready to hear what this is really about now?"

"No, but I'll tell you anyway: those girls belong to Al Safah now . . . just as I once did."

Ben turned toward Faustin, saw that her expression seemed to have lost its focus, becoming glazed and distant.

"You want to know why I joined Interpol? You want to know why I spent years mastering the skills that saved your life three nights ago? . . . Because I was once much like those girls are now." Her voice sank, drifted. "Because someday I knew I would get my chance to destroy Al Safah. You know all about vengeance, don't you, Inspector?"

"Yes."

"When you shot the man who had murdered your family, what did it feel like?"

Ben recalled that night back in Detroit when he had come home on the verge of a major break in pursuit of a killer who preyed on entire families as they slept.

"I didn't want him to die, so I could keep killing him."

Halfway to the steps, he had seen the front door was cracked open. He remembered how hard it had been to breathe as he drew his Glock nine-millimeter pistol and charged up the stairs, screaming his wife's name.

He smelled the blood when he reached the top, just before a blur whirled at him in the darkness wielding a blade that glinted in the naked light emanating from the open door downstairs. The Sandman held the knife overhead as he charged, and Ben started firing.

It took a whole clip to bring him down, the final bullet blowing away the top of the killer's head. Ben then checked the rooms slowly, without turning on the lights; he didn't need to see death to know it.

It was a while before he broke down, weeks that were numbed by the pain. Time had stopped passing and didn't start again until he returned to his homeland. Then it had seemed to stop again when he lost Danielle eighteen months before.

"You do know how I feel," Faustin was saying. "I can see it in your eyes."

"What I don't know is why."

"You know enough." Her eyes returned to the windshield.

"We're in this together now. I want to hear everything."

Faustin kept her eyes fixed on the lights before them. "You asked if I was French."

"You didn't answer me; not directly, anyway."

"I didn't answer you because I can't. I don't know what I am, Inspector. Oh, I've developed some ideas over the years, but none of that matters. I don't remember where I was born. I don't remember my parents. I don't even remember my real name."

She finally turned toward Ben from the passenger seat and their eyes met.

"You see, I was stolen."

CHAPTER 52

"WHITE SLAVERY," FAUSTIN continued.

Ben felt as though a cold blast of air had struck him.
He shivered slightly.

"That's what happened to the young girls you're
looking for, just as it happened to me. . . ."

Faustin went on to explain that she did have some
memories of her "original" childhood, as she called it,
but they were vague and muted. So much like dreams
that she could not honestly distinguish any concrete
reality. Her earliest continuous memories were of a
great house and grounds she was never allowed to
leave. There were other children there too, all of them
girls of varying ages. She was well fed, clothed and
schooled; looked after and raised by the people she
would later realize were her captors.

"You were kidnapped," Ben said, shaking off his
shock, "just like Leila Fatuk."

"I hope I was kidnapped."

"What do you mean?"

"The fact is that a great number of children involved in the white-slave trade are actually *sold* to traffickers by their parents."

Ben swallowed hard, thinking of the woman in Nablus, Arra Rensi, who he felt quite certain had sold her daughter to a man like Ibrahim Mudhil.

"You thought such a practice was limited to places like Nepal, Bangkok, the Third World."

"I used to. Not anymore."

"Actually, forcible abduction accounts for a relatively small percentage of trafficking. The girls who aren't sold into the trade often volunteer. Procurers, recruiters more or less, seek out the poor with promises of better lives for the children away from their homes. These are children and young women who have nothing, so it can be difficult for them to resist such overtures."

"The girls from the refugee camps," Ben realized.

Faustin didn't bother to nod. "Once they agree, they become totally dependent on these procurers for their very survival. By the time the girls realize the truth, it's too late. They're prisoners."

"Like you."

"I was too young to realize it. At first."

"Go on," Ben urged.

Faustin didn't mince words. "By the time I was in my early teens, I could speak four languages fluently and was ready to be taught the trade they had stolen me for."

"Prostitution."

"But I was one of the lucky ones," she said, a trace of irony creeping into her voice. "Most girls and women who become part of the white-slave trade end up in cheap brothels or whorehouses where they are literally chained to the bed to make sure they don't escape. As for the few that manage to escape and then go to the police, their efforts are rewarded with a ride back and a beating, because the police almost invariably have been paid off."

Ben felt a heaviness building in his throat. "Here? In the West Bank?"

Faustin didn't answer, which was answer enough.

"What about the Israelis?"

Faustin flirted with a smile. "Israeli traffickers have become rather adept at importing Slavic women solely for the purposes of prostitution. The women are desperate. By they time they reach Tel Aviv they have no money, no place to live, and no choice."

"We were talking about Palestinian children, not Slavic women."

"Do you know something, Inspector?" Faustin asked, instead of responding. "In some countries, including Israel, there is not even a specific law against the sale of human beings. It goes on right in front of the authorities. Even the thousands they manage to deport every year are swiftly replaced."

"Two of the Palestinian girls who disappeared were both enrolled in a student exchange program with Israel," Ben persisted. "Someone there could have sold the enrollment files."

Faustin kept her eyes focused on the car ahead of them, but Ben could tell her focus had changed. To the pain and heartache which, more than anything, had drawn her to Palestine in the first place. "Yes, they could have."

"You don't care."

"I care about Al Safah."

"And Ibrahim Mudhil is linked to him as a trafficker."

"The lowest man on the ladder. Little more than a delivery boy. Each time a connection is made, we climb another rung."

"And at the top?"

"Al Safah."

"You're saying he's in charge *everywhere* across the

world? One man running the entire white-slave trade?"

Mathilde Faustin hesitated. "I haven't been able to prove that to anyone's satisfaction at Interpol yet."

"It's no wonder. That's a lot of countries, and brothels, to keep under control."

"I believe that he *seized* control of the trade in those countries, and the white-slave trade has gone way beyond brothels in modern times. Interpol estimates two hundred million people are currently victims of contemporary forms of white slavery and most have nothing to do with prostitution. They could be deaf Mexicans selling pencils in New York City, or children in Indonesian sweatshops, or Nepalese children begging on the streets of Paris and London, or Chinese peasants being exported by the thousands to work in slave labor camps without anyone knowing, or Guatemalan babies stolen from their mothers, or beautiful women who answer ads from Third World countries that sound too good to be true because they are— women who are later drugged, imprisoned, forced into prostitution, and often never seen again. I have files on these things and more. It happens in civilized countries, often among respectable people. The trade could never have reached the level it has *unless* one force was responsible for it all."

Ben considered Faustin's assertions, wished he could refute them. Undeniably, though, she was providing an explanation for exactly what his investigation had turned up in Palestine:

Two girls kidnapped.

A third runs away from a refugee camp and is never seen again.

The existence of a fourth is denied by a mother who may have sold her so she could afford a better house.

"And Al Safah is here now," Ben said finally. "You're sure of that."

"I'm sure he *was*. I'm sure I'm closer to him than anyone's ever been before. I'm sure . . ."

Ben listened to Faustin's voice tail off. "What?"

She wouldn't look at him. "Nothing."

"How did you get away from him, Superintendent?"

Mathilde Faustin turned toward him again tentatively and began to speak.

CHAPTER 53

BY THE AGE of fifteen, she related, she had been placed in an exclusive Paris bordello that discreetly served a wealthy clientele. She knew little of what went on in the rooms other than her own, but sometimes when she lay quietly she heard sounds that terrified her. She had been introduced to sex at an age and in a way that reduced it purely to the base act she was practicing. Her skills were undeniable, but performed without any passion. "Servicing" was all she knew, and while she could contemplate escape, the unknown world beyond frightened her much more than the Paris house or the others she would come to know.

Still, the muffled screams she often heard, and the girls who appeared the next morning beaten (and occasionally did not appear at all) forewarned her enough of what was coming. She tried to escape three times, succeeding in her third attempt only to be brought back to a house in Geneva by the police. Her punishment was being relocated to a Hamburg, Germany, brothel where the furnishings were equally nice but the clientele considerably less subtle. One of these tied her to the bed, gagged her, and then beat and whipped her for hours. She was taken from the bordello and left half-dead along Hamburg's notorious Reeperbahn where she had plenty of company in the gutter.

Mathilde Faustin was lucky enough to be brought to a hospital where they saved her life and then turned her back to the street, as was the usual practice. But she was determined not to stay there. Fueled by rage, Faustin returned to the Hamburg brothel and set fire to the basement. The entire house burned while she watched the girls, who were as helpless as she had once been, rushing out into the night.

Her teachers had done an extraordinary job of breeding emotion out of her. But they had forgotten about rage, and that was going to cost them.

"You kept the name they gave you, didn't you?" Ben asked her, inadvertently squeezing the steering wheel a little tighter.

"Because it would stop me from forgetting. Ever. I didn't want to forget. From that night I burned the house in Hamburg, I saw what I had to do."

"Did they know it was you?"

"Not that time, no."

"Other houses . . ."

"*All* of them, all the ones in which they placed me."

"But you had no passport, no money, you had *nothing.*"

"I had my rage; it was more than enough. In Hamburg it wasn't difficult to buy a fake passport."

"It is without funds."

"But I had skills, didn't I? And this time when I put them to use, I did it for me. The whole time I was listening, learning, accumulating a list of who I could contact in other cities for similar favors."

"That doesn't explain how you learned to shoot, to fight."

"Anything can be bought if you're willing to pay, Inspector, including those types of skills, especially when one is willing to work for them." Her voice drifted briefly, was not quite as sharp when she resumed. "I saved Paris for last. Would you like to know how I did it?"

Ben swallowed hard.

"I came in the guise of a prospective client! They didn't even recognize me; I had to remind four of my former watchers who I was before I killed them. Up close this time, which was infinitely more satisfying."

"But it wasn't enough," Ben said, and suddenly realized what had been bothering him about Faustin's eyes. He had seen that vacant, resigned, mad look once before: in his house, the night his family had been killed, when his gaze locked briefly with the Sandman's.

"I got the girls and their customers out," Faustin said as an afterthought. "Then I burned that house too."

"I was talking about after."

Faustin nodded. "No, it wasn't enough, and it won't be until what happened to me can't happen to another child. I was barely twenty years old, fifteen years ago. And I have spent those fifteen years following every lead, collecting and collating information. That's why I joined Interpol. That's how I first became aware of Al Safah."

"He knows you're here, doesn't he?"

"I'm counting on that, Inspector."

"That's why his operation continues: he wants you to follow him, so he can trap you."

"I'm counting on that, too."

"Then if he does exist, you're a fool for playing right into his hands."

"And what does that make you, sitting in the same car as I, on the same trail?" Faustin didn't give Ben long enough to answer, even if he had meant to. "I am going to follow the girls in that car, wherever they are taken, until I find someone who can lead me to Al Safah. Don't go outside or Al Safah will eat you—that's what children are told every day all over the world. Well, I am going to make it safe for them to go outside again." She paused longer this time. "You still don't believe me, do you?"

"I believe by looking for a single man, it will be impossible for you to ever find what you seek. I believe you have already fallen into their trap."

"And Al Safah?"

"A spook story. A distraction that works as a net to catch all those who venture too close," Ben said, and looked across the seat at Faustin.

"Well, it looks like we're getting close now, Inspector," Faustin said, tensing a little. "Look."

Before them, the Volvo had pulled off the road and halted near a black Mercedes. A single man emerged from each car and they conversed briefly. Then the two teenage girls were escorted from one backseat to another.

"All this because a woman called Interpol and claimed she had recognized Al Safah," Ben said, focusing on the Mercedes now.

"A Palestinian woman, who called the Israeli and Palestinian police actually, to claim she had seen Al Safah in Jerusalem. But they wouldn't listen, not even when she told them he had stolen her baby fifty years ago. And for her efforts, she was killed."

Ben's breath caught in his throat. "The woman who recognized Al Safah," he stammered. "What was her name?"

"Taji," Faustin replied, without missing a beat. "Ramira Taji."

CHAPTER 54

SABI WAS WAITING at the harbor when Danielle arrived in Haifa. It was a misty night and the docks were covered in a blanket of gray that left a wet sheen on the walkways.

As Danielle approached, she counted five men around the bulky figure of Sabi. She recognized two of them from the restaurant that afternoon. She had never seen the other three before, but they stiffened at her approach, hands creeping inside their jackets.

Sabi edged away from them when she drew close and spoke quietly. "I'm glad you could make it, Pakad Danielle Barnea."

"I'm glad you called," Danielle said, taking a closer look at the three men, who had not stopped studying her.

Sabi didn't waste time. "A freighter has been docked in Haifa for two days now, presumably laid up for repairs. It is of Liberian registry and is called the *Lucretia Maru.*"

"What else?"

"They have ordered no parts, commissioned no re-pairs. The crew never leaves the ship. I have made some discreet inquiries and learned that the *Lucretia Maru* sank three years ago off the coast of Algiers. Her owners were most surprised when I informed them their ship was docked in my harbor, especially when her description did not match that of the freighter they had lost."

"Have you boarded her?"

"I wanted to speak to you first, in case you wanted this handled by more traditional authorities."

"I don't."

Sabi smiled thinly, further inflating the size of his jowls. "I didn't think so. Otherwise you wouldn't have come to me in the first place."

"Where is she?" Danielle asked, gazing over the myriad of ships lining the port of Haifa.

"There is something else you should know first, Pakad Danielle Barnea: I have been told that strange sounds have been heard on the ship in the night."

"Then let's you and I go find out where they're coming from."

BEN SNAILED HIS car down Habankim Street along the dockside of the port of Haifa, keeping a few blocks behind the Mercedes.

"He's turning in there," Mathilde Faustin said from the passenger seat. "I think he's parking."

Ben drove on.

"They always work in teams," Faustin had explained after the girls had been led out of the Volvo and ush-ered into the Mercedes back in the West Bank. "Elim-inates uncertainty and reduces the chances of betrayal, especially when different cultures are involved."

"The men in the Mercedes are Israelis?" Ben had asked, focusing his binoculars on the license plates. The plates were yellow, indeed Israeli.

"Definitely. They're the next rung up the ladder, Inspector."

"What happens now?"

"They get the girls out of the country, possibly direct to a city but more likely to a central distribution point."

Ben looked at Faustin questioningly.

"Everything I've uncovered points to the fact that Al Safah has a facility where he keeps the children until they can be permanently settled," she explained. "Some of the victims I've interrogated have tried to describe it, but many were either drugged or terrified the whole time they were there, so their memories are clouded and unreliable. The one thing they all seem to agree on was that it was an island."

"Even if they went along willingly like the two we're following?"

Faustin's stare hardened. "They did not willingly give themselves up to slavery. They were promised something else entirely. A better life at the very least, a job or even a career, and when they realize they were lied to and are no better than slaves, their terror can be as bad as that experienced by the victims procured by kidnapping or sold into the trade by their families."

Ben shook his head, sighing deeply.

"Selling children is nothing new in this part of the world, Inspector. Instances of it in Persian and Arab cultures have been recorded for thousands of years. History has been kinder to the practice, explaining it off as a means of keeping peace, or establishing trade, or—"

"That doesn't make it any less barbaric."

"What's truly barbaric is that one force has taken over the entire trade, giving it a kind of clandestine legitimacy like selling drugs or moving arms."

In the dead quiet of the night, Ben had followed the Mercedes to a border crossing into Israel beyond Nablus, lagging back as it was swiftly passed through.

"What are you doing?" Faustin demanded.

"We can't go into Israel."

"We can!"

"I'm not cleared."

"I am! Forget about your license plates and drive up there before we lose them!"

Ben had done as she instructed, then stopped and rolled down his window for the approaching Israeli soldier. Before Ben could say a word, Faustin had thrust her identification and a letter folded into quarters across him. The soldier inspected the ID, then read the letter. His eyes lingered on Faustin after he finished. Then he passed them through.

"Well done, Superintendent."

"The Mercedes made it through even faster."

"Even with two girls without any papers sitting in the backseat."

"I'm glad you noticed."

"You're saying the soldiers were bribed?"

She shook her head. "Only that the IDs presented stopped them from checking any further."

"Like yours."

"Even better."

DANIELLE STOOD WITH Sabi and his henchmen behind a supply hut that overlooked the *Lucretia Maru's* berth against the pier from two hundred feet away, camouflaged by the fog that continued to roll in.

"She's seen better days," he said softly, both to Danielle and to the five men who had accompanied him to the harbor.

The men shrugged, readying their weapons. The three Danielle had never seen no longer bothered to hide the Uzis tucked under their coats.

"Israeli military surplus," Sabi explained. "I got a good buy."

Danielle returned her gaze to the *Lucretia Maru.* With binoculars, she could see the freighter wobbling in her berth amid the currents, bleeding rust along the hull and looking pale and discolored below the water-line. Her chimneys were decaying, and Danielle could make out slabs of irregularly shaded steel where her deck plate had been repeatedly welded. The two doors on deck in her view stood ajar, swollen beyond the girth of their frames, impossible to close without a total refitting the freighter wasn't going to receive anytime soon.

Danielle couldn't help but remember the story of a similar freighter called the *Gideon*, convinced that was where the origins of this mystery actually lay. More than fifty years earlier, three young men had come aboard the *Gideon* to Palestine, where they were joined by a fourth until tragedy struck. Something had happened in the months or years after Jacob Rossovitch's death that had forever changed the lives of the three surviving friends. Hyram Levy was dead because of it, Max Pearlman had gone into hiding, and David Wollchensky, now Wolfe, was in America. Like the *Gideon* before her, the *Lucretia Maru* held a secret that could kill, had killed. And somehow that secret was connected to something only two men left alive knew.

"What do you expect to find on board, Pakad Danielle Barnea?" Sabi asked her.

"I'm not sure. The reason why a man was murdered, I hope."

"Hyram Levy?"

Danielle couldn't hide her surprise. "You knew him?"

"We did some business from time to time. I also know that until earlier today you were in charge of the investigation to find his killer."

"I congratulate you on your sources."

"A good thing I have them, Pakad Danielle Barnea. Otherwise, you might have been waiting a very long time for my call." Sabi looked back at the *Lucretia*

Maru. "What exactly was my friend the Engineer involved in?"

"Far more than everyone realized, obviously, or he wouldn't have been doing business with you."

Sabi stifled a hearty laugh. "And now *you* are doing business with me. I doubt your friends at the National Police would approve."

"You said it yourself: after today, I have no friends at the National Police."

"Then why are you here?"

"To find out for myself."

"Then what are we waiting for?" Sabi asked, turning to his men.

He had just signaled a pair of his men to lead the way onto the dock holding the *Lucretia Maru* when Danielle froze them with a raised hand.

"Stop!" She swung around and lowered her voice. "Someone's coming!"

CHAPTER 55

BEN AND MATHILDE Faustin waited until the two men from the Mercedes escorted their charges down toward the docks before emerging from the car across the street.

"What now?" Ben asked.

"We find out which ship they board."

"I mean after that."

"Good question," Faustin replied.

"We could call the Israeli authorities."

"And what would we gain from that? A few arrests? A few children returned to their homes?"

Ben thought of taking Leila Fatuk back to her family and almost said yes. "Maybe the answers you're seeking."

"No one on any boat here has those."

"Then what do you suggest?"

Instead of answering his question, Faustin led the way slowly down into the harbor, making sure to keep her distance. "Do you have a gun?" she asked Ben softly.

He was about to say no, accustomed to leaving it behind whenever he entered Israel. Then he remembered the unforeseen and unorthodox entry they had made tonight and said, "Yes. Why?"

"Just in case."

DANIELLE PEERED OUT from behind the cover of the storage shed as the footsteps came closer. Sabi's men had edged farther out into the darkness and fog, guns ready, wary of an attack.

The walkway extended down from the street and then leveled out closer to the docks. It ended about thirty feet from their position, the thickening mist making that distance seem much greater.

"Perhaps they were expecting us," Sabi whispered.

"How?"

"This could be a trap meant for you, Pakad Danielle Barnea."

"No," Danielle insisted halfheartedly.

"You have crossed the wrong people. Bad mistake in Israel. It's a good thing you called me."

"Tell your men not to shoot!"

"They know."

The footsteps sounded louder against the wooden slats of the walkway. Danielle caught a glimpse of four shapes, an odd group of two men and two young women, proceeding in the general direction of the dock accessing the *Lucretia Maru*. No way to tell for sure yet if that was their destination.

Sabi's three gunmen wielding silenced Uzi submachine guns edged closer to the walkway, trying to better their vantage point and angle of fire. Danielle noticed one of the figures slow for a moment, then head on again through the fog.

"Tell your men to back up," she whispered to Sabi.

"What?"

"Call them off! They've been—"

A gunshot sounded in the night, a soft pop dulled by the thick, fetid air. One of Sabi's men twisted sideways, clutching his shoulder as the familiar spitting sound of silenced gunshots burst from his Uzi's barrel. Then the other two of Sabi's henchmen spun away from the fat man, pistols leveled before them.

"No!" Danielle called, but no one heard her.

She saw one of the men up on the walkway go down, followed closely by one of the young women. Danielle spun out from behind the storage shed, and the window immediately over her head exploded.

"Stop!"

It was no use. The second man who had just walked down from the street lunged off the walkway and took cover behind a guard post Sabi's gunmen instantly splintered with bullets. The other young woman panicked and tore off, running back up the walkway for the street. Danielle watched long hair splaying out behind the figure and realized she was more a girl than a woman. Then, through the window of the empty guard post, Danielle saw the man who had escorted the girl toward the docks turn his own gun upon her.

No! Danielle thought, and bolted into the open. Skirting the relentless fire of Sabi's henchmen, though, cost her critical moments. By the time she reached the shed's window on the opposite side, the man fired and the girl's spine arched, standing her straight up.

Danielle watched him steadying his pistol again as she fired hers. The glass popped away from her bullet's path and the man's head snapped sideways. He thudded to the deck and slipped over into the water.

Up the walkway, the girl staggered forward a few more steps, then collapsed. Danielle rushed out, Sabi's gunmen not far behind her.

"Damn!" she screeched in frustration. *"Goddamn it!"*

She heard Sabi chugging up behind her just as a fresh hail of bullets rained down from the top of the walkway. She dove hard to the wet wood and retrained her pistol. Around her two of Sabi's Uzi-wielding henchmen went down in matching heaps. The two with pistols sprayed a wild barrage at an elusive shape that seemed to disappear into the mist, their bullets not even coming close.

Danielle fought for a bead on the shape that moved like a shadow. She had actually begun to wonder if that's what she had seen when the shape emerged directly in line with her unprotected flank. No way she could possibly get a shot off in time, but she twisted around to try, as the shape's pistol steadied on her through the fog.

GODDAMN IT!"

It was Danielle! Ben realized as Faustin rushed ahead of him toward the docks. He recognized her voice, confirming the few earlier glimpses he had caught after the shooting that had claimed both Palestinian girls had started.

Ben charged down the walkway after Faustin. He had cut the gap between them in half when her sudden burst felled two men wielding submachine guns. He watched Faustin turn her attention on Danielle and launched himself into motion, closing to within a lunge of the woman from Interpol when her finger began to close on the trigger.

DANIELLE BROUGHT HER gun up, facing death in the form of a lithe figure in black, a female Grim Reaper. Just as the woman fired, though, a man crashed into her and spilled her to the walkway, sending her bullet errant.

"Don't shoot!" he yelled before Danielle could pull her own trigger.

My God, she thought, *that voice . . . .*

"Danielle, it's me!"

Ben!

Sabi's remaining three men rushed out, one holding an Uzi with one arm while the other arm dangled uselessly by his side. They closed on Ben and the figure he was wrestling with on the walkway.

"Hold your fire!" Danielle screamed, lurching to her feet and throwing herself between Ben and the gunmen. "Hold your fire!"

Only then did she realize she had steadied her pistol on them, would have shot the men had they showed any signs of not following her order.

The three men stopped, unsure, as Sabi lumbered forward. "What is this? What's going on?"

"Get off me!" Faustin rasped at Ben. She twisted the wrist he had fastened around her into a painful hold that made him gasp and let go.

Faustin resteadied her gun.

Sabi's men resteadied theirs.

Danielle lowered her pistol, stiffening as she stood there. Ben struggled to his feet and rushed to her, hand hanging limp by his side.

"Who are you?" Mathilde Faustin demanded, standing with her gun held low but taut, seemingly unfazed by the weapons trained upon her.

"Who are *you?*" Sabi's eyes shifted rapidly from Ben to Faustin.

Sirens wailed in the distance. Danielle moved past a stunned Sabi toward the body of one of the girls she had seen gunned down.

"She's my partner, Superintendent," Ben said.

"What have we done here?" Danielle muttered, kneeling over the body.

"Your Israeli friend, eh?" Faustin asked Ben. "Perhaps one of us should tell her she shot one of her own people."

Danielle spun round. *"What?"*

"The man behind the guardhouse who spilled into the water. The other one, too."

"Israelis?" gasped Sabi.

"Tell her," Faustin urged Ben in disgust. "Tell them both."

"Leave me out of this. I'm getting out of here," Sabi said, already starting back up the walkway under close escort by his henchmen.

Danielle stepped out, coming up just short of blocking his way. "The bodies . . . Your men . . ."

"So long as I'm not around when they are found, things can be squared. Take my advice and leave too, for your own sakes."

"Not until I've seen what's on that ship," Danielle said adamantly.

Ben and Mathilde Faustin looked at each other.

"What ship?" Faustin was the first to ask.

Danielle stood up. "I'm going to board her. You can join me if you want."

Faustin locked a hand on Danielle's elbow when she tried to pass. The two women held stares, neither about to give.

Ben approached as Sabi disappeared into the fog. "The dead men are both Israelis," he told Danielle. "We watched them take delivery of two Palestinian girls who walked out of refugee camps."

"The ship," she realized.

"It's how they must get the missing children out of the country," Ben said. "That's why they brought the girls here."

"And we were following them," Faustin interjected, still having not let go of Danielle's arm. "We *had* them."

Danielle glared into the taller woman's eyes. "The ship is called the *Lucretia Maru*. It's docked at the end of the pier."

CHAPTER 56

YOU'RE WELCOME TO join me on board," Danielle said staunchly, after both she and Ben had repeated the paths that had led them here. She stood eye to eye with Mathilde Faustin, neither about to back off.

"No," Ben argued, maneuvering himself between the two women. "Sabi was right. We should get out of here while we still can."

The *Lucretia Maru* was docked two hundred yards away from where the gunfight had ended just minutes before. The dock was already swarming with Israeli police and army officials, both having arrived at approximately the same time. The harbor was coming alive in the fog, which still provided sufficient camouflage for Danielle, Ben, and Faustin to slip away toward the cover of the ships bobbing in their berths. They had stopped just before the *Lucretia Maru*, hidden from the throngs of police investigating the scene but able to easily keep track of their presence by following the sweep of their flashlights.

Danielle shook her head. "I can't do that. I can't leave until I've seen what's on board that ship."

"You already know what you'll find," Faustin said. "We told you."

"I have to see for myself. I have my reasons, believe me."

"It doesn't matter if I believe you. The gunfight will have already made whoever's on board suspicious. If you're caught, it will compromise my mission."

"I don't give a shit about your mission."

Ben eased himself closer to Danielle. "It's my mission too now, Pakad. We didn't realize it at first, but it all fits. I was looking for missing children; you were after the killer of the man involved in making them disappear."

"You really think that's all there is to this?" Danielle posed.

"Isn't that enough?"

"Maybe, but it's not even close to the whole truth." She looked toward Ben. "Levy's contact, the man in the picture who blinded Ibrahim Mudhil, is Esteban Ravel, a contract killer who's got even his fellow agents in Mossad running scared."

"A Mossad agent was involved in smuggling children?"

"Like I told you," Faustin interjected. "Governments are *always* involved, or at least people well placed within them."

"Ravel was involved through Levy," Danielle said finally, "and he's my number one suspect in Levy's murder. But Hyram Levy wasn't killed because he was smuggling children. He was killed because something terrified him two months ago and somebody wanted to make sure he didn't tell anyone else what it was."

Ben thought of Zaid Jabral's ghost coaxing him to search for more, to put all the facts he had uncovered together. Could whatever Jabral had discovered be the same thing that led to Levy's death?

"Whatever you're looking for, you won't find it on that ship," Faustin insisted.

"Maybe I'll find Al Safah for you."

"Only his work."

"Close enough."

Danielle started to slip away, but Faustin's voice chased her. "They're going to pull your bullets out of the Israeli you shot back there, another rather well-connected man much like this Ravel, unless I miss my guess."

Danielle stopped and turned back toward Faustin.

"You've given them what they need to destroy you," Faustin continued.

Danielle looked briefly from her to Ben. "They've already got more than enough."

DANIELLE WAITED UNTIL there was only one seaman left patrolling the freighter's deck before covering the final stretch through the fog. The *Lucretia Maru* rode high in the water, indicating a light cargo for a ship her size. From what Sabi had been able to tell her, though, the freighter was manned by a skeleton crew at best. That probably accounted for why so few seamen had come topside in the aftermath of the battle, alerted not by the sound of gunshots so much as by the approaching sirens.

The last seaman on deck was no longer visible when she walked up the gangway. Approaching the end of the gangway, she could see the deck guard through the fog, smoking a cigarette. No way she could just walk onto the ship without being seen, so Danielle nimbly hoisted herself over the rail and grabbed hold of the rope truss that extended along the freighter's starboard side. She shinnied sideways until a quick peek over the gunwale revealed that the guard's view of her was blocked from this angle by a decaying chimney, then began to climb the rest of the way.

* * *

COME ON," FAUSTIN urged Ben as Danielle lifted herself over the gunwale onto the deck of the *Lucretia Maru*.

"And leave her?" he returned defiantly, holding his ground.

"It's the ship we can't leave, Inspector."

"What are you talking about?"

"When the freighter departs Haifa, we've got to stay on her trail."

"Follow her at sea?"

Faustin nodded. "First thing in the morning, I'll find a captain to be ready as soon as she pulls out. You don't have to join me."

"Yes, I do. You're after Al Safah, and I'm after the children this all-encompassing network you describe has taken. One way or another, we'll both find what we're looking for in the same place. I'll just have to call in. Speak to my superiors."

Faustin shook her head. "Haven't you learned anything tonight?"

"What are you talking about?"

"Corruption, payoffs, bribes. You call in to report what you're doing, and the *Lucretia Maru* will never reach another port. Al Safah will sink her and then come after us."

"Al-Asi will listen. He might even be able to help us."

Faustin's face had taken on the flat empty expression that tolerated no argument, the face of a person who has seen so much she no longer has patience for those with a normal view. "You want to come with me, Inspector, we leave with the freighter and nobody hears about it."

Ben gazed at the deck of the *Lucretia Maru*, where Danielle had already disappeared from sight. "I'm not going anywhere until Chief Inspector Barnea comes back."

"Suit yourself."

"What's she going to find on board, Superintendent?"

Faustin chose not to answer him.

DANIELLE CREPT TO an open hatch and descended a stairway into the bowels of the ship. The air smelled stale, almost rancid. The coppery scent of baked rust mixed with a stink like that of sour earth. The ship creaked and groaned as the currents moved it slightly on its moorings.

The lower deck felt twenty degrees hotter than above, with the stench of dried sweat and urine added to the others. Danielle listened for a sound to tell her where to head next, but none came. She moved on, sliding her feet to keep her heavy soles from drawing any sound from the steel floor that was peeling layers of paint like sunburned flesh. The walls were moist and sweating warm driplets that rolled to the floor to form more rust someday.

Danielle stopped suddenly, alerted by a faint sound. A moaning, or a whimpering maybe, that seemed to be coming from a hold just ahead. She reached it and pressed her ear against the sweating steel. The moaning was interspersed with whispers passed between what sounded like women. Danielle lowered her hand to the latch and tried to open the hold.

Nothing. It was locked.

She was considering how to break the latch off when a rattling sound from farther down the passageway froze her. Someone was coming, making no effort to be silent.

She needed to get out of sight fast. Knowing she couldn't risk the time it would take to try the latches on the other doors she had already passed, Danielle retreated behind the stairs she had just climbed down.

She ducked beneath them and crouched as low as she could.

A woman was coming straight for her, struggling with a small wooden crate loaded with bottles that jiggled against each other. The woman stopped briefly to better her grip and moved on, without ever looking Danielle's way. Danielle watched her for a moment and caught a glimpse of the bottles.

Not ordinary bottles, but . . .

She told herself she was imagining things, that she hadn't gotten a good enough look to be sure. When she started back down the passageway, though, her stride was quicker, a little more bold. She passed the hatch she had tried to open and followed the passage around to the right.

A black steel door lay directly before her, this one unlatched and open a foot or so. Danielle's heart was racing as she reached the hold and pushed the door open just enough to let her squeeze through sideways.

A shriek pierced the silence and Danielle braced herself against the wall, grazing the door and forcing it further inward. Light splashed inside from the corridor in thin shafts like tiny spotlights. Danielle followed their path, looked down.

Went cold.

Y OU BELIEVE ME now," Mathilde Faustin said after Danielle had described to them what she had seen on board the ship.

"What I believe doesn't matter."

Ben caught the forlorn, beaten tone in Danielle's voice.

"There's something I have to do," she finished. "Someone I have to see."

"Are you going to summon the authorities, Chief Inspector?"

Danielle didn't even look at Faustin. "No, Superintendent, I'm not."

"They're right over there still. I'm sure they'd be most interested to hear what you have to say."

"That's not who I'm going to see."

"The answers we seek are not always pleasant, are they, Chief Inspector?"

Danielle's eyes flared upon her. "Leave me alone."

Faustin planted herself between Danielle and the nearest walkway. "I can't, you see, because if you send anyone else onto that ship, I lose the first chance I've ever had to put an end to this madness."

"I don't think you're up to it."

"I'm going with her, Danielle," Ben said hesitantly.

Danielle cast him a sidelong glance, then looked back at Faustin. "I won't get in your way, either of you. Now, get out of mine."

For a long moment, neither woman moved. Then Ben eased Mathilde Faustin aside.

"Don't go to your authorities, Chief Inspector," Faustin said as Danielle walked stiffly past her. "This is not an Israeli problem."

Danielle stopped and turned back. "That's right. It's my problem now."

DAY SIX

Chapter 57

As always, Hershel Giott, commissioner of the National Police, rose shortly after sunrise. Careful not to disturb his still-sleeping wife, he padded softly into the hall for the stairs and descended to the first floor of the home in the Jerusalem suburb of Har Adar, where he had lived for twenty years.

A lamp switched on in the living room as he reached the foyer. Giott swung fast, feeling his heart skip a beat.

"Good morning, Rav Nitzav," greeted Danielle Barnea from a chair set against the drawn blinds.

Giott reflexively tightened his bathrobe. "I wish I could say the same, Pakad, but it is difficult after finding an intruder in my house."

"It had started to rain outside."

"So you broke in."

"Actually, I picked the lock—a skill not limited to black bag operatives from Mossad."

"And this is how you are spending your suspension?" Giott said regretfully. "I had hoped you would have put your time to better use."

"I have been, believe me."

"I would have also expected you to show greater respect for someone who has always supported you."

"Until yesterday."

"That couldn't be helped."

"And that's why I'm here, Rav Nitzav." Danielle rose and walked slowly forward, stopping halfway between the chair and Giott. "I came to speak to you before I went anywhere else. I want to hear the truth from you."

"What truth?"

"Let's start with my hospital stay."

Giott rolled his small eyes indifferently. "So we are back to that again. . . ."

"It never stopped bothering me. A man who appeared in my room. A man who said he could help me. A man sent by you through Hyram Levy. . . ."

"I warned you that—"

"A man named Ravel who works for Mossad. A former member of the Paraguayan secret police known for his brutality. An assassin who I believe is the man behind Levy's murder. I want Ravel, and I think you can help me get him."

Giott reached out and grasped the railing of the staircase with his right hand for support.

"Ravel has also been identified as part of a ring that smuggled children out of the West Bank. His association with Levy indicates the Engineer was involved, too, at a much higher level." Danielle stopped and swallowed hard. "So what could Ravel have done for me? For what reason had you arranged for him to come to my room?"

Giott bent slightly at the knees.

"I couldn't see the answer, I was *afraid* to see the answer. But I saw something else last night that makes it impossible to turn away." Danielle stepped into the foyer. "*Look at me!* Ravel came to offer me a baby. That's it, isn't it?"

* * *

*T*HEY HAD BEEN lined up in dilapidated cribs in the hold she had entered on board the *Lucretia Maru.* The slivers of stray light sneaking in from the steel hall beyond caught their softly sleeping faces. The occasional whine or whimper rose, but for the most part the children were quiet, having just been fed with the formula bottles Danielle had recognized when the woman walked past her near the stairway.

That woman would be coming back any moment. Danielle knew she had little time.

How much she wanted to pick these babies up and comfort them, tell them everything would be all right. But that would be a lie. The truth, very likely, was they had been stolen or purchased to be sold in other countries to people desperate enough for a child to pay top dollar through any means of procurement available.

People like herself, Danielle realized with a chill.

Accustomed to the darkness now, Danielle edged closer to study the infants' faces. It was difficult to determine nationality without much closer inspection. But any of the children against the right-hand wall could have passed for Israeli, or French, or American, or British—all of whom made up the most likely customers. She had started to move to the left when the sound of approaching footsteps made her shrink back against the wall.

The woman who had passed her lugging a carton of empty formula bottles entered the hold empty-handed, not seeming to notice the door was open more now than when she had left. The cover of that door kept her from noticing Danielle, and when she began a careful round from crib to crib, Danielle slipped back into the corridor.

Danielle's breath came in deep heaves. She had to lean against the fetid bulkhead for support.

Then, while retracing her steps back to the deck, she

remembered Ravel and his shadowy offer.

I can help you.

A child like one of these could have been hers for the asking, probably at no charge. A benevolent gesture arranged by a man who honestly cared for her and thought he was doing the right thing.

She felt nauseous and leaned over to vomit before mounting the stairs. She retched once but managed to keep the bile down.

Danielle retraced her route off the *Lucretia Maru,* no longer nauseous but still in shock. She barely remembered her confrontation with Ben and Mathilde Faustin from Interpol when she reached the dock again. All she could focus on was coming here, to Hershel Giott, to challenge him with the truth. To find the answers that had been denied her at every turn.

WHAT DO YOU expect me to say?" Giott asked when she had finished. He was sitting down on the carpeted steps now, thin patches of uncombed hair a disheveled mess atop the crown of his head usually covered by a yarmulke. He suddenly looked very old and frail.

"I don't expect you to say anything until I ask."

"What?"

"I have some questions for you," Danielle said flatly. The man before her, once mentor and protector, had let her down terribly. She had not thrown away her career; it had been stripped from her, punishment for coming too close to a secret that had been buried too long.

But what was that secret?

"Is this an interrogation?" Giott asked.

"I prefer to call it a discussion. I came here out of courtesy, out of respect. If at all possible, I will keep your name out of the investigation."

"The investigation ended yesterday afternoon, Danielle. You were suspended, remember?"

"By someone potentially affected by the results of that investigation. I think you should take a voluntary leave of absence, Rav Nitzav."

"And if I disagree?"

"Tell me what I need to know and I will keep your name out of this."

"How very gracious of you." Giott slapped the knees of his pajamas and stood up again. "Very well, what you need to know is that you have no idea of the depth of what you have stumbled upon."

"I think I do."

"*No*, you don't. The offer I intended to extend to you in your time of need was genuine, from my heart."

"But you didn't make the offer yourself."

"It was not my place. I knew Levy and had some knowledge of his dealings. I made one phone call, gave him your name and room number. That's all."

"Did Ravel kill him?"

"I don't know."

"Why was Levy killed?"

"Who can say? A hundred reasons!"

"And could there be a hundred reasons for his phone calls to Max Pearlman too, Rav Nitzav? Or his calls to the man he knew as David Wollchensky for a good part of his life? What happened two months ago to spur those calls? What was Levy afraid of?"

Giott shook his head haplessly. "Besides my call in reference to you, I hadn't spoken to Levy in a long time."

"So why suspend me?" Danielle demanded. "Who are you protecting?"

"You, Danielle," Giott told her, the old compassion back in his suddenly sad eyes. "I was protecting you from yourself. You were dredging up the past, and the past for all of us has secrets better left where they were. Have you forgotten the lessons of Solomon's Pillars?"

"Forget the past! Forget the Pillars of Solomon! Palestinian children are being smuggled out of the West Bank, sold into slavery, and Israelis are intimately involved!"

Giott seemed unmoved by her assertion. "And what do you think men like Ravel do when they are cornered? What do you expect would have happened had I let your investigation proceed?"

"The risk was mine."

"But not the responsibility. As your superior, that rests with me."

"As my superior, you should want this case pursued wherever it leads."

Giott looked at her blankly. "It led you to my door this morning, Danielle. How many other doors would you like to knock on? How many more locks do you intend to pick?"

"The involvement is that widespread. That's what you're saying, isn't it?"

"I've said enough. It's over for you, Danielle. Leave it alone. Don't touch it. The doors are all closed and these doors don't have locks you can pick. Stop trying and it might not be too late. You might be able to save yourself."

"I can handle Ravel," she insisted.

"Haven't you heard anything I've said? I don't know why Levy was killed. But I know enough to realize the reasons for his death are not accessible to people like you and me."

"So we give up? Let his killer go unpunished?"

"You can't touch these people, Danielle, nobody can. You think they will not come after you because you're a woman, a hero?" He seemed to brush her aside with a flap of his hand. "Israel has more than enough of both. This is not a time to interfere. This is a time to let things be."

"All this from a man who claims not to know who's involved."

"I'm doing this for you, Danielle. I know you don't want to believe that now, but my main concern all along has been keeping you alive."

"No one bothered to keep Levy alive."

"My point exactly."

"And Pearlman would be dead now too, if not for Ben Kamal. What about David Wollchensky, or Wolfe, if you prefer?"

"He was contacted through the proper channels and advised of the situation."

"Advised," Danielle repeated. "Is that the same thing as warned?"

"Much is left up to individual discretion in such matters."

"In other words, no one ever says what they mean. That's the unwritten law and you're following it to the letter now."

Giott's tired face sharpened. "You want me to speak plainly? Very well, I will. Yes, I tried to provide you with the option of adopting a baby and, yes, I knew the men behind that acquisition are also involved in a trade we have looked away from for years."

"Israel condoned the enslavement of Palestinian children, then, perhaps even supported it."

Giott didn't bother denying her assertion.

"That's monstrous!"

"But not worth losing your life over, Danielle. We are an open society only in what we choose to let the world see. I am assuming you have come to me with this first, that you have not taken this information anywhere else."

"You're right; I haven't."

"Not even shared it with your Palestinian friend?"

"No."

Giott sighed a little easier. "Then I can still keep you out of this. No one has to know about your accusations, about the conclusions you've reached."

"How about what I saw on that freighter? Were those

babies coming in or going out? Import and export?"

Giott's face remained impassive. "We're running out of time, Danielle."

"What if I walk out of here and go to the next door?"

He didn't hesitate. "Sooner or later someone will be waiting for you behind one. Maybe Ravel. Maybe it will be your own door. And at that point there will be nothing I can do to help." He reached out to take her shoulders, but she stiffened and backed off. "It's over, Danielle. Let it go."

"What's the secret everyone's protecting? What in God's name is worth so many lives?"

Giott shook his head, shrugging his bony shoulders. "There are some things the rest of us are better off not knowing."

CHAPTER 58

BEN STARED INTO the distance from the raised bridge of the fishing boat.

"I can't see her," he said, lowering his binoculars.

Mathilde Faustin kept their speed steady. "If you could, that would mean she could see us. She's out there, not more than a few miles ahead. Don't worry. I'm familiar with the shipping lanes."

"And if we lose her?"

"We'll close the gap as she draws closer to the island of Crete. There, she'll either take the southern channel toward Algiers, or the northern one for Athens. Any farther than that will tax her fuel supply."

Ben refocused his binoculars, not satisfied.

The *Lucretia Maru* had headed out to sea without any warning just after dawn. Perhaps the crew had taken the missed "delivery" as a warning. Perhaps all the activity on the docks the previous night had spooked them. Either way, it was too early to hire a boat to follow the freighter, so Faustin had stolen a fishing boat used for small charters and day trips. The boat was small enough to hide on the sea and fast enough to stay close to the freighter. Her fuel tank had recently been topped off and Faustin estimated they could easily cover as much sea with it as the freighter before refueling.

Ben slipped on the deck and hit his head shortly after they set out from the harbor. The throb he already felt from strain and fatigue worsened, wooziness added for good measure.

"Get some rest," Faustin advised, and he stumbled into the cabin below, where he collapsed on a waterproof couch.

He awoke to a smell like meat left too long over charcoal and found Zaid Jabral hovering over him, a life jacket wrapped around his tattered suit coat.

"How was your trip to the kibbutz yesterday?"

"Not very informative."

"Perhaps you didn't ask the right questions, Inspector."

"A man told me the ones you asked him. He didn't have the answers."

"He told you the kibbutz's records had been lost when they moved to their current location in 1967."

"That's right."

"That's it."

"What are you talking about?"

Jabral just stood there, his burnt flesh popping and puckering. "What did you learn last night on the harbor?"

"I don't know what—"

"What did Pakad Barnea see on board that freighter?"

"Babies, infants."

"There's your answer," Jabral's ghost told him.

"What was the question?"

Jabral shook his head, like the teacher he had once been, disappointed by a student. "Do I have to do everything for you? I'm dead, remember? You're making me angry. I don't think I'll be coming back anymore."

The ghost turned and his flesh squished across the deck.

"I should have asked someone at the kibbutz about babies!" Ben yelled after him.

"Too late now," Jabral said without turning.

"What did you learn? What did they tell you?"

"You'll have to put it together for yourself, Ben. You've got all the pieces. Think about it, where everything started for me."

"Ramira Taji," Ben recalled, *"the old woman who told you somebody had stolen her baby fifty years ago. By Al Safah."*

What was left of Jabral's features brightened a little. *"Then you have learned something new."*

"She claimed she saw Al Safah again recently."

"You go have a talk with her?"

"She's dead, Jabral."

"That's right. I forgot."

Then something occurred to Ben. *"Ramira Taji and Kabir, the finance minister you interviewed—they lived in the same refugee camp after the '48 war, didn't they?"*

"Much better, Inspector." The ghost started on again. *"You're almost there."*

"Jabral!"

The ghost stopped and looked back over his blackened shoulder. Ben thought he smiled, although without any lips it was difficult to tell. *"That's the best I can do, my friend. You'll have to figure the rest out by yourself."*

When Ben awoke, the sun was high in the sky and streaming through the cabin window onto his face. The throb in his head was not altogether gone, but it had lessened enough for him to move about without getting light-headed again. He found a pair of binoculars and climbed back on deck to rejoin Faustin.

"Where are we?"

"Halfway between Cyprus and Crete."

"How's our fuel?"

Faustin shrugged a little behind the wheel. "We'll be okay as long as the freighter docks by nightfall."

Faustin increased the fishing boat's speed as they drew closer to the island of Crete. The island appeared as a small speck on the horizon several minutes before the *Lucretia Maru* came back into view. Faustin kept her pace steady as the freighter slipped around the island toward the north.

"She's headed to Athens," she said matter-of-factly.

They held their distance long into the afternoon, skirting the islands that dotted the Mediterranean between Crete and Athens. The jagged Greek peninsula that held the ancient port city appeared just as the light began to bleed from the sky. It was a magnificent sunset, close enough along the horizon for Ben to think they could sail right into it if they hurried.

The *Lucretia Maru* sounded her horn and blew huge plumes of smoke from her chimneys as she approached the harbor.

"Is this her final stop?" Ben asked Faustin.

"No," she replied with typical reservation in her voice, "just another port of call."

"Pickup or delivery?"

"We'll see."

C H A P T E R   5 9

CONCESSION WAS A new feeling for her, and Danielle had done her best to embrace it.

From the time she had left Hershel Giott's home outside Jerusalem, she'd been trying to look at life differently. Trying to picture it all at once in a vast overview created a jumble of images in her mind, though, an incoherent mishmash of events and plans that in retrospect seemed forever unfulfilled.

She wasn't ready to give up this fight, but had to face the fact that she had no way to pursue it for the moment. Giott would close all the doors, all the possible venues of information otherwise open to her. She had to be patient. Bide her time until the opportunity to continue her investigation came.

She thought of Ben following a different trail with Mathilde Faustin from Interpol. Perhaps they would find Al Safah. Perhaps that was the only true way to end this.

But Danielle similarly couldn't stop thinking that Ben was alone, out there somewhere, with a woman she was quite certain was mad. Faustin would sacrifice anything to get what she wanted, Ben Kamal included.

I shouldn't have left Haifa without him. I should have made him come with me.

Another in a long line of misjudgments that would haunt her forever. This one, though, might cost her Ben, the cold fear that she would never see him again rising above everything else.

To distract herself, Danielle determined to throw herself into the everyday affairs she had painstakingly avoided since her release from the hospital. That meant giving her apartment a thorough cleaning, to make it feel like a home again. Pay all her bills, return her mail. Stop at the post office and pick up the parcels that must be gathering dust, a third one added to the first two.

But first she stopped at a local market, packing groceries into her wagon until they threatened to spill over the top. She was going to fill the refrigerator and cupboards that had been empty for too long. That task concluded, she made herself breakfast, even though she wasn't hungry. Lose herself in the routine and hope that the next time the phone rang, Ben would be on the other end.

Later, Danielle opened the windows to air the rooms out. The apartment smelled better almost immediately, the staleness whisked away by the soft scents that blew in from the orange and olive groves located to the east. Dust followed the breeze as it always did in old cities made of stone, but she would wipe it away later.

By afternoon, Danielle had washed the floors and counters, vacuumed the rugs, scrubbed the bathroom until her skin chafed and eyes burned from ammonia, and paid twenty-seven bills, many of which were weeks or even months past due.

And Ben still had not called.

So Danielle sat down to make a list of everything else she'd been putting off, only to remember the parcels that needed to be picked up. She located the notices she would have to hand over to receive them and decided to take advantage of the beautiful spring day by walking to the nearby post office.

For security reasons, no packages are ever left at a house unattended in Israel. This leads to tremendous backlogs at all parcel services, necessitating separate windows just for pickup at most outlets. Even then the lines are often long, and around Hanukkah season, virtually unbearable.

But the line was relatively short today and Danielle had to wait only a few minutes to hand over her slips in exchange for three parcels. One was from a catalog company she had forgotten placing an order with. Another was a return of a package of Israeli oranges to an aunt in the United States on which she had failed to put the proper form. The oranges were surely spoiled by now.

Danielle could not identify the third and smallest parcel at first glance at all. It was a ten-by-fourteen-inch padded mailing envelope. The return address was blurred, perhaps purposefully, and Danielle flirted with the notion of asking that the package be run through the security station a second time.

But the line had gotten longer and on a whim she simply yanked the tab on the padded envelope's reverse side and pulled out its contents: a trio of thick, matching notebooks bound in leather, six by nine inches in size. The leather was dry and cracked, faded from its original brown to a kind of distressed tan. It felt rough to the touch, though it still smelled of hide.

Standing near a wall in the post office, Danielle left her other two boxes on the floor and opened the notebook labeled on the cover with the roman numeral I.

Her knees wobbled. She felt a little faint.

The first page had yellowed with age around the edges, but the title was printed in bold, beautifully etched letters:

My Story

The name of the author was scrawled beneath it, the sloping letters perfectly centered and safe from the yellow:

Hyram Levy

Danielle leaned back against the wall, turned the page with a trembling hand, and began to read.

CHAPTER 60

I T WAS AFTER nightfall before Mathilde
Faustin and Ben saw anything at all.

Faustin had motored their craft into an empty berth
squeezed amid dozens of others their size in the port
of Athens. She paid a harbormaster an exorbitant fee
in cash and spoke briefly before the man walked away
without giving her a second glance.

"He says the *Lucretia Maru* is a regular visitor to this
harbor," she told Ben. "Never stays more than one
night. That means we can expect some activity before
dawn."

By ten o'clock, traffic in the harbor had all but died
out. Ben and Mathilde Faustin had left their boat and
found cover upon a dry-docked cabin cruiser with a
stripped-down cabin. They sat beneath the cover of the
gunwale with their backs resting against the starboard
side in full view of the *Lucretia Maru*. Ben's head had
started to pound again and he wondered if the ghost
of Zaid Jabral was serious about having left him for
good.

"Why don't you close your eyes, get some sleep," Faustin suggested. "I'll wake you if something happens."

But he awakened on his own untold minutes later to find her sitting straight up, the ridges of her spine protruding through her sweater. The night had gone cold and he realized he was shivering.

"Look," was all Faustin said.

Ben's eyes followed hers to the head of the pier, where a trio of men were escorting a number of small, shabbily clothed figures along a dock. He snapped to attention, waited for his eyes to focus.

The figures all looked to be young boys, some no more than nine or ten, others in their early teens. Ragamuffins and urchins all, some with bare feet.

"Street children," Faustin explained in that distant tone Ben had come to know by now. "No reason to use elaborate schemes, ruses, or tricks on these. Traffickers collect them like dogcatchers, luring them with lies of homes or work abroad, maybe just a meal."

"In other words, hope."

Faustin didn't bother to nod, her eyes growing as faraway as her voice. "I first picked up the trail of Al Safah in Nepal, where thousands of impoverished girls and young women are tricked every year into accompanying traffickers into Bombay, where they are sold to brothels, the kind I knew all too well, only worse: I was in Bombay once when there was a fire in one of the brothels. It was the middle of the day and screams wailed from inside, but none of the girls tried to flee." She looked at Ben briefly. "They couldn't, you see: they'd been chained to the beds to keep them from escaping.

"The Indian government has made some progress in fighting the practice, but corruption keeps the authorities always one step behind. Once in a while a girl escapes to tell a terrible tale, yet her life under government assistance is every bit as bad as enslavement. That

more than anything explains why white slavery continues to thrive throughout the world: not only does no
one care about the victims, but the life they are sold
into is often better than the one they left."

"Sex slaves."

"For many years, that's all it was. But in more recent
times Al Safah has branched out to provide slave labor,
usually from the Third World or China. Boatloads of
peasants who dig in gold, silver, or diamond mines until they are buried where they die. Others work for less
than pennies a day making merchandise that ends up
in stores all over the world. I have seen these places. I
have seen these people. Both always the same. You look
into their eyes and see the hopelessness. Where they
left just as bad as where they are. They give up, because
every place must be the same."

Ben gestured toward the boys approaching the *Lucretia Maru.* "What about them?"

"A few will join teams of beggars in European cities,
handing over every penny they pocket to traffickers in
exchange for one meal a day and a mattress, if they're
lucky. Others will sell pencils or shine shoes or steal
wallets. A few will become fodder for pornography,
perfect subjects since there is no one to report them
missing or stand up to those who would so degrade
them.

"Except me," Faustin finished.

Ben nodded grimly. "And the freighter continues to
steam in and out of Athens unbothered. More payoffs?"

"Sometimes just apathy. If the authorities raid the
ship, the responsibility for the charges on board be-
comes theirs. Most would much rather let it leave port
and become another country's problem. Next week,
the week after maybe, another ship will come. Or
maybe a plane, even a truck. Different transport. Always the same cargo."

"Some authorities must have acted. At least tried."

She looked away again. "Oh, they tried all right."

"Al Safah?"

"It isn't always the authorities themselves who are punished. Sometimes it's their families. Never a witness. Always an apparently random act. Al Safah prefers to go after families because word spreads better that way. That's how he gets his point across."

"You think that's the biggest reason of all why no one, not a single government, does anything about this, don't you?"

"I know it is."

"So the spook story works."

"Story or not, it makes officials at every level ask themselves why bother, what is there to gain besides coming home one night to find the eyes of their children or their wife gouged from their heads. It's easier to look the other way."

"What now?" Ben asked, watching the boys herded onto the deck of the *Lucretia Maru* like willing cattle.

"At dawn, she will take on fuel and supplies, then be on her way." Faustin turned toward him. "We will keep watch, in shifts. Go back to our boat. I'll take the first one."

CHAPTER 61

EXHAUSTED, BEN DIDN'T argue. His head hurt so much that just walking back to the fishing boat made it feel like something was banging against his skull on the inside. He doubled over twice on the way, dry heaves both times leaving him woozy.

It took all his effort to pull himself on board their boat and then stagger across the deck for the cabin, stumbling down the stairs. He set the alarm on his watch and lay down, hoping Zaid Jabral would be waiting. But the journalist was nowhere to be found after he drifted off, and he slept dreamlessly until the alarm's beep awoke him for his shift four hours later.

He was still exhausted but pushed himself up off the couch. He splashed water onto his face from the sink and drank it at the same time. The throbbing had retreated a little, moving to the edge of his consciousness, where it reminded him of its presence with a hollow pinging in his skull. He was still a little nauseous and passed it off to going without food for so long.

Before moving to relieve Faustin, he scoured the

cabin's cupboards for something to eat, settling on some stale crackers and cookies he washed down with water. They tasted like salty paper and sugary cardboard but they made him feel better, more alert anyway. Chilled, he searched a closet and a pair of footlockers before finding an old jacket he wrapped himself in thankfully before heading back to the cabin cruiser that overlooked the *Lucretia Maru.*

Faustin was waiting when he got there, seeming not to have moved from her original perch. "I'll see you at dawn," she said, and took her leave, eyes on the freighter as she made her way down the dock.

Ben kept his gaze on her until she passed out of sight, alone as she had spent the years of her quest. Then he leaned back against the gunwale and crossed his hands behind his head, taking a deep breath. He wondered if there had been coffee aboard the fishing boat. He should have looked, but it was too late now.

The night currents lapped softly against the cabin cruiser and he watched the *Lucretia Maru* undulating in rhythmic fashion before him. The jacket warmed him, and he felt almost peaceful in the cool night air. To keep himself alert, he tried to focus on his last dreamed conversation with the ghost of Zaid Jabral, when he had been closest to finally putting everything together.

There was Ramira Taji, a woman who had spent her life searching for a child she claimed had been stolen from her by a man no one believed was real. A man she had seen again after fifty years shortly before her death.

There was Palestinian Authority finance minister Fayed Kabir, who had lived in the same refugee camp as she.

Put all the pieces together, Jabral's ghost had advised him. But where had his visit to a kibbutz in search of birth records fit in?

What was he forgetting?

For a brief moment, in the trancelike state Ben felt himself slipping into, it was all clear to him. He held the missing piece, the one that brought all the others together, in his hand.

I need to speak with Fayed Kabir, the minister of finance, again. . . .

As quickly as he had formed that thought, though, Ben forgot why. He lost his grasp on the missing piece and saw himself chasing it the way a child hunts a butterfly with a net.

He was still chasing when the resounding bellow of a boat horn startled him. He snapped upright, the sun beating down on his face.

Morning . . .

Panicked, he checked his watch: eight A.M.

He had slept through his watch!

And the *Lucretia Maru* looked to be making ready to set out to sea again.

Where was Faustin? She said she would be back by dawn!

Damn!

Ben rose on wobbly legs and bounced out of the dry-docked cruiser, cursing himself and not caring if anyone saw him. He was running before his feet were steady beneath him and weaved erratically along the docks as a result, lunging onto the fishing boat with barely any air left in his lungs.

"Faustin!" he yelled. "They're setting off! Faustin!"

He threw open the cabin door and leaped down the steps. She was still sleeping atop the couch; she must have been as exhausted as he.

"Faustin," he said, and shook her.

She shifted limply beneath him, limbs splayed, head lopping toward him.

Ben dropped to his knees.

He saw the neat slice across her throat before he saw the blood that had soaked through the mattress closest to the wall, still wet and shiny, looking like spilled paint. Faustin's mouth hung open in a gasp she had never finished. Her hands had locked in a clawlike grip that had fastened on nothing.

But her eyes, her eyes were the worst.

They had been gouged out, leaving empty, bloodied sockets behind.

DAY SEVEN

CHAPTER 62

THE *LUCRETIA MARU* had been at sea
for hours when Ben finally emerged from a pump shed
near the aft bulkhead where he had been hiding since
just before she set out. The pump shed smelled of stale
oil and diesel fuel, and the rubber on the hoses around
him was cracked and warped. He had managed to
carve out a space inside the shed big enough to sit
down, so long as he kept his knees against his chest,
or stretched only one leg at a time.

The best thing about the hiding place was that the
condition of the equipment clearly indicated no one
on the freighter ever bothered to hose down the deck.
But inside, deprived of all light other than a sliver that
sneaked under the heavy door, after so many hours he
had begun to feel dizzy and disoriented, even claustro-
phobic, which was a new and terrifying feeling for Ben.

According to his watch, it was three P.M. when he
cracked open the pump shed's door and peered outside, gradually increasing the opening. Satisfied there
was no one on deck within sight of him, Ben crawled

out on his stomach, a stubborn section of hose catching on his foot. He kicked his shoe about to free it and eased the door closed again before moving on.

Stiff from his hours in the confined space, he stretched his muscles as best he could and took cover behind the aft chimney to survey the scene around him. Close up the freighter was older and in even worse disrepair than he had thought. Surfaces blistered and bubbled everywhere with rust. The paint, composed of two or three different shades from poor efforts at patchwork, was faded and peeling. Tack welds covered the deck and surrounding structures like scars from jagged knife wounds. Orange streaks of corrosion pervaded. The air stank of dried oil, and the entire deck was filthy with a film of it that blackened Ben's hand each time he touched something.

From this angle he had a view of a portion of the pilothouse through similarly oil-stained glass. There were at least two men inside piloting the ship. Another two hands were on deck, one making repairs to the anchor and the other patching a hole in the fore chimney. The hatch had been removed from a ventilation baffle that rose over the engine room, probably in need of cleaning or repairs as well. It would certainly be warm inside, but the shape and position of the baffle would make it the ideal hiding place. Ben would be able to stand up in it with no trouble at all, hidden from all angles once he replaced the circular hatch top over him.

Before moving toward the baffle, he tried to get a fix on the ship's position. Judging by the sun, the freighter had headed due west from the southern tip of Greece, passing out of the Aegean Sea and into the Ionian. On the distant horizon he saw large landmasses that he thought must be Sicily and the southernmost reaches of Italy itself. On this approach the *Lucretia Maru* could either slide round the bottom of Sicily or motor north through the Strait of Messina. Since they had taken on ample provisions at Athens, the freighter could remain at sea for a very long time indeed. Yet from the way she was burning oil and guzzling fuel, a stop seemed imminent in the next twelve hours.

Ben had no intention whatsoever of disembarking more than briefly, though. He was determined to follow the *Lucretia Maru* all the way to her final destination, just as Mathilde Faustin had planned to do. He knew it could just as easily have been him who was murdered, *would* have been had their shifts been reversed, leaving Ben on the fishing boat instead of Faustin. His near encounter with death only increased his motivation, a rage building inside like none he had experienced since confronting the Sandman in his home years before.

Not being an experienced enough boatman, Ben's only alternative was to stow away and let the freighter take him wherever she was going. Faustin had felt certain that eventually that would be to Al Safah, perhaps to the mysterious island a number of witnesses vaguely recalled.

Ben hoped she was right.

He had managed to sneak on board in the final minutes before the freighter set out to sea at Athens. With so small a crew on board, the hands were too busy with the final departure procedures to notice him slide over the gunwale and take refuge in the pump shed.

From his position behind the chimney now, Ben figured he was thirty feet from the open ventilation baffle. He would be in the line of vision of one of the hands briefly, only if the man happened to turn around. Ben took a deep breath and darted across the deck. He reached the baffle and lowered himself quickly into it, then reached behind him and retrieved the cover. The rusted, sun-baked metal was scalding to the touch and he nearly dropped it, grimacing as he settled the cover back into place. It had openings for ventilation on all sides which provided him with a 360-

degree view of the freighter should he require it, so long as he stood up straight.

For now Ben remained on his feet with eyes peeled through the generous slats. He thought again of the moment he found Mathilde Faustin's body, and shuddered. But it wasn't for her he was doing this, at least not solely. It was because the end of the journey would bring him to children who had been stolen from their homes, who would die the same death Mathilde Faustin had died long before Ben had met her, if someone did not intervene. He was going to save them, go up against Al Safah himself if that's what it took, but he was determined to save them.

Weeks after the murder of his family, Ben finally agreed to see a police psychiatrist. He had expected no results, had barely even uttered a word when the psychiatrist asked him what he wanted.

Five minutes, Ben had said, surprising himself, *I want the five minutes back that cost me my family. . . .*

Had he returned home those five minutes earlier, his children and wife would be alive today. He would have pumped his hollow points into the Sandman before the killer's knife began its deadly work. The police psychiatrist had responded by cautioning Ben against living his life forever in search of those lost five minutes. Trying to get them back, though, had led him onto the *Lucretia Maru* hours before, and it would keep him on board until he found what Mathilde Faustin had spent much of her bleak life searching for.

Ben continued to scan the deck, wetting his lips. The water he'd drunk straight from the pump-shack faucet had been too warm and rusty to enjoy, yet he missed it now. He wasn't sure how many more hours would pass before he could drink again, never mind eat. He resolved to take his chances leaving the freighter at its next port of call to find food. Of course, he had no passport and carried only Arab currency, which meant he'd have to be creative.

Ben thought if he sat down on the grated floor of the baffle and tried to sleep, maybe Zaid Jabral's ghost would appear and tell him where the freighter was heading, what he should do when she got there. It seemed like a good idea to get some rest anyway, and he nodded in and out of consciousness as the sun sank from the sky. The night breeze first cooled, then chilled him.

Ben had just cradled his arms around himself when he felt the freighter turn and list slightly to port. He stood up and noticed they were going through waters with lights on both sides of the ship. If his earlier bearings had been correct, they had very likely entered the Strait of Messina, passing between the southern tip of Italy and the island of Sicily. Perhaps the *Lucretia Maru* was headed to Rome or Naples or Salerno, all hours from her present position.

But once clear of the strait, she made a wide sweep to the west. The freighter hugged the Sicilian coastline for a time before angling slightly to the north again, where the Lipari Islands dotted the southern stretches of the Tyrrhenian Sea.

The Liparis were a group of volcanic islands located off the north shore of Sicily. Ben had heard of the major islands like Salina, Filicudi, and Panarea. The smaller ones were mostly abandoned, save for geological and archaelogical survey teams that made regular visits. There were boat stops among these and the larger islands, indicating that the coastlines were safe for even a freighter like the *Lucretia Maru* to negotiate.

Ben remembered hearing rumors that a few of the smaller Liparis had been transformed into fortresses by Sicilian Mafia bosses many years before. Places to take refuge in times of gang warfare or flight from the authorities. Abandoned and forgotten now, hidden from view by their larger neighbors. Islands that, for all intents and purposes, no longer existed.

The perfect place for Al Safah to gather his charges, just as Mathilde Faustin had suspected.

Ben could feel his heart beating faster. His mouth had gone bone dry, but he forgot his thirst.

He knew where the *Lucretia Maru* was headed.

And she would be there in a very short while.

CHAPTER 6 3

THE FLIGHT FROM Tel Aviv began its descent into Kennedy Airport after nightfall, two hours late. Danielle would rent a car upon arriving; she had a long drive ahead of her before she reached David Wolfe's home in Greenwich, Connecticut. Before renting a car, though, she would have to get through customs and immigration, a none too easy task if they had been alerted to her pending arrival.

Back in Israel, she had taken every step possible to keep her departure from drawing attention. But she knew if Hershel Giott had deemed her a security risk and alerted the proper authorities, there was nothing she could do. She had waited until the last possible moment to reserve a seat and board the El Al jet, her heart pounding until the flight was airborne nearly eighteen hours earlier.

Only when it had reached its cruising altitude did Danielle turn again to the page she had marked in Hyram Levy's journal, the story picking up almost where Hershel Giott had left off after the three surviving friends had gained revenge for the murder of Jacob Rossovitch. Now, feeling her stomach quiver a bit from the big jet's descent toward New York, she began to read again.

We gathered again at the kibbutz in Sefir, the three of us, six weeks after our vengeful raid, for the birth of our dead friend's child. It was a truly solemn occasion where we came to honor our pledge to Jacob Rossovitch: that we be there for his son and wife always, no matter what it took.

I believe in my heart that had it not been for that pledge our friendship might have ended the night of the raid on the Palestinian refugee camp. I could not resign myself to what we had done, the innocent lives we had taken, no matter how much I tried. And I know that Max Pearlman couldn't either. Wollchensky was different. He had always been different. The War of Independence only expanded his madness, enlarged his capacity for violence. He grew immune to the horror to the extent I thank God I never did. For that reason I believe we would have gone our separate ways, if not for the imminent birth of our dead friend's child.

Jacob Rossovitch's beloved wife Revkah was in the midst of a terribly difficult labor by the time we arrived. Usually midwives were entrusted to handle the entire birthing procedure, but on this night a doctor was summoned early on and had not left Revkah's side for hours. We went together into the kibbutz infirmary to lend her the kind of strength Jacob would have, but she was already fading in and out of consciousness, delusional.

The night passed. We waited. Ultimately the doctor had no choice but to operate. The facilities at the kibbutz, as impressive as they were, were not sufficient for the complicated procedure that needed to be performed. The doctor's primary concern, of course, was for the life of the mother, but outside the walls and closed windows we

*could hear Revkah screaming for him to save her baby
no matter what it took. She begged him to sacrifice her
life for her child's.*

*We spoke not a word to each other while we waited.
We had shared so much, but this night brought back
only the most painful. The horror we had seen, the other
friends we had lost. The glorious victory we had won,
only to be faced with the reality that we would forever be
at war.*

*On this night, for the first and only time, maybe all
three of us, at least Pearlman and I, began to question
even the perilous journey that had brought us to Palestine. What was the use? What had we really accom-
plished? What kind of men were we?*

*Little did I know that last question was going to be
answered once and for all, before the next day was out. . . .*

Danielle looked up from yet another reading of
Levy's journal as the final landing preparations were
announced over the PA. She checked to make sure her
seat belt was fastened and tucked the book against her
side when the stewardess passed by.

She had become party to a secret that until this time
had been kept to the three men who met at the kibbutz for the birth of their friend's child. Again Danielle
considered the impact of that secret Hyram Levy had
revealed to her from his grave. She felt certain it had
been responsible for his death and the attack on Pearlman's life in Tel Aviv. But the journal did not say how
or why, did not explain why a secret buried for almost
fifty years could cause the havoc that had erupted in
the past week. Indeed, there remained one part of the
story left to be told, and only David Wollchensky, now
Wolfe, could tell it.

Danielle had no idea how he would greet her appearance at his door, had no idea if he would own up
to what he had been party to, assuming he spoke with
her at all. She only knew she had to try and make him.

Danielle settled back and returned to Levy's journal as the jet broke the clouds and the lights of New York City flickered in the distance beneath her.

We waited; it was all we could do. We paced, we smoked, we cried but mostly we waited. I remember dawn had just broken when the doctor stepped outside, his clothes covered in blood. We had heard no child crying inside, so we knew even before we saw the tears welling up in his eyes.

"It was a boy," he said.

"Revkah?" David asked, but it didn't sound like his voice at all. It was the most pained sound I had ever heard.

The doctor tried to light a cigarette and failed. "She is holding the baby now in her arms. Humming to it. She keeps looking up and saying, 'What a beautiful boy. What a beautiful boy.' Over and over again. I tried to tell her but—"

Wollchensky grabbed the doctor by the arm before he could finish. His cigarette fluttered to the ground. David's eyes were furious.

"You will tell her nothing!"

"I, I don't understand."

"You don't have to understand! All you have to do is what I say, exactly what I say."

"Please, you're hurting me."

Wollchensky let go, but didn't back off. "We are going inside now, all of us. You will follow my lead, Doctor. Then you will have breakfast and be gone from here. And you will forget last night. You will forget last night ever happened."

Inside we found Jacob Rossovitch's wife Revkah sitting up in bed, cradling her dead child in her arms. Her wet hair was matted to her forehead. Her skin was sickly pale. Blood soaked the sheets atop which she lay before the eyes of the silent and horrified midwives. She looked up at us with eyes that glowed with happiness against this tragic backdrop.

"Isn't he beautiful?" she asked, holding her baby out just enough to see his limp legs. He looked more like a plastic doll somebody had spilled paint on.

"Very," said David Wollchensky, stepping ahead of Pearlman and me.

"Would you like to hold him? It's what Jacob would have wanted."

"Very much," David said, and extended his hands.

Revkah placed the baby in his arms and David cradled its bloody, still form against him, rocking it gently.

"He looks like his father," Revkah beamed. "Don't you think he looks like his father?"

David smiled. "You should rest now."

"I should watch my baby."

"I'll keep him for a time. You've had a long night. You need to get your strength back."

"I'm very tired."

"And very brave. All you went through . . . Jacob would have been proud."

"I wish so much he were here."

Wollchensky gave the baby to a midwife and stroked Revkah's steaming forehead. "We're here, the three of us."

"My son will have three fathers then."

David glanced back at me and then Pearlman. "He will indeed."

"Promise me you'll take care of him. Promise me you'll watch over him always the way Jacob would have."

David didn't hesitate, not even for a second. "I promise."

We waited until Revkah finally faded off to sleep before leaving her room. Outside, I couldn't stop my hands from trembling. Pearlman kept shaking his head.

"What are we supposed to do when she wakes up?" I demanded harshly.

"We keep our promise," David insisted.

"You're as mad as she is!"

He jammed himself close to me. "What did you see in there, Hyram?"

"What did I . . . The same thing you did!"

Wollchensky shook his head. "I don't think so. I saw the same thing Revkah did, and when she wakes up I am going to make sure she sees it again."

"Her baby's dead, David."

"He doesn't have to be."

"She was having delusions. They will pass. And soon probably."

"I don't think you heard what I said."

"You said her baby doesn't have to be dead."

"That's right."

"You can't bring him back to life, David."

Wollchensky was unmoved. "Maybe I can."

The jet's tires hit the runway and bounced, jolting Danielle from her trance. Protectively, she closed the journal and tucked it in the single bag she had taken along.

It was time to focus on the practical considerations of the present, the dangers just ahead. If American officials had been forewarned of her coming, she would know soon enough. They could be waiting for her at the end of the jetway, or lurking just beyond customs. They could even be lying in wait to arrange a more permanent solution, and with good reason.

Danielle had not followed orders. By coming here without assignment or sanction, she had misbehaved in a very serious way. This trip broke almost every rule of intelligence and diplomatic etiquette, as well as procedure, she had ever learned.

She reached the end of the jetway half expecting men in suits to be waiting there for her, their hands tucked into their jackets. But the gate was deserted.

Danielle followed the flow of human traffic toward the customs and immigration area, cautious of everyone who passed her in the opposite direction. She scanned ahead in search of a misplaced stare, or glint of a weapon, intending to be ready if there was any sign of an ambush.

She reached immigration and then customs without incident, though, and handed her passport over. It almost surprised her when the attendant asked her a few routine questions, stamped her passport, and sent her through with a casual smile.

In the terminal she boarded the first car rental agency bus that came along. Ten minutes later she had rented a midsize car and requested explicit instructions to Greenwich, Connecticut. The clerk tore them off the printer at the perforation and handed them across the counter along with Danielle's keys.

She found her car quickly and set out through the night for the home of David Wollchensky.

CHAPTER 64

COMING INTO PORT at night was a godsend for Ben, permitting a freedom of movement he would never have allowed himself during the day. The island's single pier, he could see, had been specially outfitted and reinforced to handle a ship the size of the *Lucretia Maru*. A tugboat was waiting to ease her the final stretch along the coastline.

Once she docked, from his hiding place in the exhaust baffle, Ben was able to watch an additional complement of men join the crew already on board in off-loading the *Lucretia Maru*'s "cargo." The boys who had boarded in Athens climbed off the freighter first, followed by a number of young women and girls he could not identify from this distance by nationality. A dozen babies came last, each man carrying two at a time.

Ben climbed out of the baffle after all had disembarked but two hands on duty on the bridge. He hurried to the gunwale and ducked low beneath the cover it provided, watching a quartet of vans pulling away from the pier down a flattened dirt road barely wide enough to accommodate a single vehicle. The island couldn't be large, so they wouldn't have far to go. And Ben figured following this road on foot would lead him straight to their destination.

Only a short distance from the shore he came upon a well-camouflaged airstrip which seemed to run virtually the entire length of the small island. A pair of small planes lay near one side, not far from a supply transport being worked on by a man wearing grease-splattered overalls. A man in a pilot's one-piece jumpsuit stood nearby, watching intently.

The airstrip indicated that the island was more than just a refuge for the Mafia chieftain who had once resided here. Most likely it had also been used to transport contraband such as guns or drugs on and off the island. With easy access by both water and air, the island could handle virtually anything, although Ben doubted its original owner had ever considered the merchandise it was holding now.

He continued on along the road for another ten minutes before he came to the compound. An eight-foot stone wall enclosed the fortress on all sides. From this angle, Ben could see the sprawling three-story cream-colored structure built within. An old-fashioned bell tower rose another story above it. Ben caught a glimpse of a guard stationed inside, surveying the surroundings with a pair of binoculars.

Ben approached cautiously and noted that two more guards patrolled the exterior of the compound on foot. Their approaching shadows forced him to duck into the cover of a nearby thicket. They passed forty feet in front of him and continued their patrols. Ben doubted they had ever encountered an intruder in this remote place, in which case they would hopefully be less wary and more complacent in their duties. His trip here was worth nothing unless he could gain access to the compound itself.

The fortress, though, was imposing to say the least; impregnable might have been a better way to describe it. Ben crouched in the bushes wondering what Danielle would do. Probably summon reinforcements to stage a commando raid backed up by air power. He smiled faintly to himself. There would be no reinforcements and certainly no air power coming to his aid tonight.

He thought of Danielle and what she might have done with the terrible truth she had uncovered on the *Lucretia Maru*. As personal as this had become for him, it was even more personal for her. But he didn't regret leaving her back in Israel, for he knew Faustin was right: finding Al Safah was the only way to end this once and for all.

It was foolish, even stupid, though, to believe he could do that himself, or even consider trying to enter the compound alone. Perhaps his best strategy was to find a radio and summon help from somewhere, anywhere. There would be a radio back on board the *Lucretia Maru*, and having only two deckhands to overcome on the freighter made much more sense than entering a fortress full of armed men. He would use that radio to summon the Italian authorities, take things from there.

Ben started to rise, intending to retrace his steps, when he felt the cold touch of a gun barrel against his neck.

"Don't move," a voice said.

CHAPTER 65·

DANIELLE HAD READ the final section of Levy's first journal so many times on the flight that she almost had it memorized. To keep her focus, and her wits, during the drive from the airport to David Wolfe's home in Greenwich, Connecticut, she went over it again, seeing the pages turn in her mind as the words came back to her.

"What are you talking about?" I asked Wollchensky, growing tired of this macabre game.

"You heard me."

"I heard you say you could bring a dead child back to life."

"I can."

"When did you become God, David?" Pearlman demanded.

"You're the religious one, Hyram. You're the one who always told me God lives in all of us. I guess I'm finally listening."

"You aren't being fair to that woman," I accused him.

"We should have been the ones to tell her. Now when she wakes up . . ."

"Her son will be sleeping by her side."

I looked at Pearlman. We both shook our heads.

"Are you with me or no?" Wollchensky asked us.

"You are asking a lot, maybe too much," Pearlman told him.

"No. I am asking that you honor your pledge."

"What pledge?"

"To look out for the wife and child of our friend."

"We've done everything we can."

"Have we, Hyram, have we really?" He stared at us both. "I need an answer: Are you with me or not?"

Pearlman and I glanced at each other and shrugged.

"With you in what, David?" I asked Wollchensky.

He checked his watch, looked relieved that we were prepared to join him. "There's little time. We must hurry."

"Make sense, David!"

"Not until we get there. Then you will see for yourself."

Max and I knew we had no choice. We had made a pledge to our friend Rossovitch and had to honor it.

But in later times, when I think of the things I would have done differently given the chance, this is the one that comes most often to mind. None of us realized that the decision we reached that day would change all of our lives forever.

We didn't realize it then, of course. We didn't realize it until . . .

That was where the first journal had ended. The second journal in what was a set of four was missing, and journals three and four contained no reference to whatever Levy had been referring to at the close of number one. He had brought his life into the 1970s in the final journal, but then stopped, as if the rest of his days didn't matter at all or, at least, paled by comparison. His years as the Engineer were not even touched upon, not holding the same weight his earlier experiences had in his own mind.

In Atarim Square Max Pearlman had hinted at the existence of the journals, baiting Danielle to see if she had recovered them. Danielle had no doubt it was only for that he had agreed to see her. And that meant someone else had removed the journals from Levy's shop and then, for some inexplicable reason, made sure she received them.

But what had happened to the missing journal? Why hadn't it been included in the package? The second journal would surely have explained the desperation of the final two months of Levy's life, because Danielle felt certain that desperation was based on what Levy had become party to following the death of Jacob Rossovitch's child.

David Wollchensky would be able to fill in the gaps, since it was he who had hatched the plan Levy and Pearlman had reluctantly gone along with.

Danielle had to stop twice to ask directions to the home of the man who now called himself David Wolfe. The first time at an all-night gas station at a rest stop on the Connecticut Turnpike to find out which Greenwich exit to take. The second time to get more detailed instructions at a convenience store north of the Merritt Parkway where she was the only customer.

David Wolfe's house was situated among other sprawling estates that dotted the most exclusive area in Greenwich. Some of the mansions were set back behind imposing steel fences; others weren't even visible from the road. Wolfe's was accessible by a private road marked KEEP OUT and NO TRESPASSING. Danielle drove down that road through an unchained gate, expecting to meet up with a roving security patrol any moment. David Wolfe could change his name, but he couldn't change the fact that he was party to the same secret as Max Pearlman and Hyram Levy, making him a target as well.

Danielle's intention was to use a direct, as opposed to surreptitious, approach. She had nothing to hide, after all. Once accosted by the expected security guards, she would explain who she was and what had brought her here. Her hope was that the truth was the quickest way to gain access to David Wolfe.

But to her bewilderment, no guard appeared during her drive down the private road. Nor was there a single man in evidence on the lavish well-manicured lawns that fronted Wolfe's mansion, lit by the bright hue of floodlights bouncing off its facade. It felt wrong to her. Either David Wolfe had left his estate to go into hiding like Max Pearlman, or something had happened to him before he had the chance.

Danielle parked her car along a circular driveway and headed up the walk. She longed for the gun international travel regulations prohibited her from taking out of Israel. She noticed fresh dog prints in the soft dirt of nearby gardens. Where were the dogs now? Where were their handlers?

She mounted the marble steps cautiously and approached the front door. Almost there, she saw it had been cracked open.

Intruders rushing away, their job complete . . .

Danielle could see it all happening in her mind's eye. Someone had struck out at David Wolfe as recently as a few hours ago, perhaps after being alerted that she was on her way. Danielle silently dropped the single hastily packed bag from her shoulder to the stone entry before pressing herself against the door and easing it inward. She entered the house behind the thick cover the door provided, half expecting the caustic smells of gunpowder and pooled blood to accost her.

Instead the pungent scent of cigar smoke drifted mellowly out of a room to the entry's right. Danielle followed it through a wooden double door into a vast book-lined study. In the dim, atmospheric lighting she could see the shadow of a person sitting in a chair with his back to her.

Danielle stopped halfway between the double door and the chair, watching as the shape slowly rose from it into a cloud of cigar smoke and turned her way.

"Good evening, Chief Inspector," said the man she recognized as David Wolfe. "I've been expecting you."

CHAPTER 66

"ALL RIGHT," THE voice said, pushing the gun barrel harder against Ben's neck, "stand up slowly with your hands in the air."

Ben did as he was told, feeling the barrel of a rifle pressed against him the whole time. The sharp branches of the bushes scratched at his arms when he raised them over his head.

"Who else is with you?" the voice demanded. "How many of them are there?"

Ben realized immediately the answers to those questions were the only reason he was still alive. The thought that one person could, or would, infiltrate the island was so ridiculous that the guard assumed Ben must have been accompanied by the kind of commando team Danielle would have brought. It was almost funny, thinking of it that way. If he told the truth, the guard would never believe him.

"Where are they holding?" the guard demanded, snapping Ben's head forward with a vicious thrust. The barrel steadied against his neck anew. "What are their positions?"

"They're—"

Ben spun, knocking the barrel aside as he twisted around and lunged in the same motion. Stunned, the guard made the mistake of trying to resteady his rifle on his target, providing Ben the opening he needed. He kept his charge going and smashed his left elbow into the man's face, grabbing the rifle with his right hand.

A crack sounded. The guard grunted and tried to yank the rifle from Ben's grasp. But Ben latched his second hand to the stock and rammed the butt into the guard's stomach. The blow staggered the guard and he sprawled backward into the bushes, back-crawling out of them as he tried to free a pistol from a holster on his hip.

Ben was still holding the rifle butt forward when the guard lurched out of the thicket. He could see the man working his pistol free, no time to swing the rifle all the way around, aim and fire it. So he rammed the butt into the center of the guard's face and heard a crack like china breaking. Blood spurted from the guard's nose, and Ben jerked the butt down again, into his mouth, shattering his teeth.

The guard kept fumbling for his pistol, coughing up globs of blood between gags.

"Don't!" Ben ordered.

But the guard had drawn the pistol in a trembling hand, and Ben brought the rifle butt down against the throat this time. He felt something give before the butt sank deeper, the flesh receding in its path.

The guard's whole body spasmed. He writhed about the ground, twisting back and forth as he gasped desperately for air. Both his hands clawed at his throat. His eyes bulged, continuing to widen until they froze and glazed over.

Ben dropped to his knees, still holding the rifle. He took deep breaths to steady his heart and fought against the urge to flee. There was no reason. If the guard had used the walkie-talkie clipped to his belt to summon help, it would have arrived already.

Like the other guards partrolling the front of the complex, this one wasn't wearing a uniform. Just a jacket and cap to ward off the chilly sea breeze through a long night outdoors.

Ben eyed his attacker. They were about the same size, same build too.

Maybe, just maybe . . .

Ben dragged the guard's body into the center of the bushes and emerged again after donning the man's jacket, cap, and gun belt, the automatic rifle shouldered casually. Anyone who saw him from inside or outside of the compound would now assume he was the guard whose body now lay cooling in the night air.

But Ben did not approach the fortress directly. Instead he quickly retraced his steps over the road for the airstrip. A single hangar, camouflaged by a brush-colored roof and walls, lay at the south end of the field. Gaining access was as simple as raising a rear window out of sight of the workman and pilot who continued to linger near the large supply plane. Inside the hangar he quickly located a vat of airplane fuel and siphoned off enough to fill two large cans. Then, for want of a match or lighter, he wedged a single emergency flare in his pocket.

The weight of the cans forced Ben to stop a few times to ease the burden on his way back to the compound. Once there, he spilled the fuel out in a straight line near the edge of the clearing in which the compound was contained, draining one can and then doubling back while emptying the other to create a more dramatic effect. He backed up behind the cover of a tree a safe distance from the fuel-soaked ground before pulling the emergency flare's top.

He heard a brief sizzle and then the flare was alive in his hand, flaming bright. He tossed it toward the thick patch of fuel and thought at first he must have missed when no flames shot up.

Then, suddenly, there was a loud *poof!* like a sudden gush of air, followed by a rippling blast that sounded like the ground itself had exploded. Instantly flames jerked out of the earth, running along the path he'd laid and burning white hot as they shed ugly black smoke into the night that was at once aglow.

The sounds of guards screaming for help briefly preceded the rumble of activity from inside the compound. Seconds later, the heavy gate swung open and men in various stages of dress poured out. A few had forgotten their shirts, but all had remembered their rifles or shotguns to turn on their expected attackers.

Ben imagined their surprise when there was no enemy to greet them.

He chose the moment some of the men began lugging heavy hoses through the gate to make his approach. He emerged from the woods coughing and stumbling, after blackening his face with dirt and pulling the guard's cap down low over his forehead to further disguise himself. He waved off assistance and headed straight for the front gate, through which more hoses were being dragged, connected to aboveground pipes somewhere inside the compound.

Ben entered the fortress half doubled over and coughing, looking to be on the verge of collapse. He continued through the black smoke that had begun to blow noxiously into the compound and moved for the first door he saw, left open by the frantic surge of men through it. He didn't know how much time he had before sabotage was confirmed to be the source of the fire; certainly not enough to manage the entire evacuation, but plenty, he hoped, to at least find his charges.

Five minutes, Ben thought, *just give me five minutes. . . .*

And with that he unshouldered his rifle and rushed down the corridor.

CHAPTER 67

"YOU WERE EXPECTING me," Danielle said, dumbfounded, as the man with the cigar faced her, standing beside his chair.

She had read and heard so much about the exploits of David Wollchensky this past week that she had trouble reconciling the slight, stoop-shouldered old man with the image conjured up by her mind.

Like Hyram Levy and Max Pearlman, though, Wolfe would be in his seventies now, many of those years grindingly hard. Yet in spite of that there was something resolute and forceful in this old man's eyes that spoke of the David Wollchensky from the tales told her by both Giott and Pearlman, as well as what she had read of him in Levy's journal.

"Are you surprised, Chief Inspector?" he asked her. "I would have expected it would all be clear to you now."

"Nothing is clear," she told him.

"Except what brought you here."

"Hyram Levy's journals . . ."

"One of which, regrettably, was missing."

Danielle's breath caught a little in her throat. "How did you know that?"

Wolfe reached down to the table set along the chair's side. "Because I have it here," he said, holding up a volume perfectly matching the other three, cigar dangling in his other hand.

Danielle took one step forward, didn't speak.

"I see, Chief Inspector Barnea, I have surprised you again."

"May I have one of those cigars?" she asked him after she collected herself.

"I didn't know you smoked."

"Now I've surprised you."

"On the mantel," Wolfe directed. "Behind you and to the right."

Danielle pulled one from the box labeled PARTAGAS LISITANIA and picked up a nearby wooden match. The cigar was longer and wider than the one Sabi had provided. "You were the one who sent me the journals."

"Indeed."

"You tricked me."

"I baited you."

"The missing journal—what's in it?"

"The bait."

"Why?" Danielle asked, and lit her cigar.

David Wolfe frowned. "I expected more of the great Danielle Barnea, someone who has done a remarkable job of putting so much together already."

"If you wanted to talk, why not just pick up the telephone and return the messages I left for you?"

"Good question. You're the detective, so tell me."

"I think I'll just enjoy my cigar and let you supply the answer."

"Deniability," Wolfe started. "So long as you came here on your own, against the express and explicit orders of your superiors, I could deny any involvement. Certain secrets could remain safe, since your credibility would be nonexistent." Wolfe stepped away from his chair toward her. "Do you not think that your superiors and other Israeli authorities are already aware of your trip to the United States?"

"You told them, of course."

"I made sure they found out."

"Why?"

"Insurance."

"What do you need me for?"

"How's your cigar, Chief Inspector?"

"Disappointing," Danielle said, and snuffed it out in the nearest ashtray.

"You've had better?"

"Only one."

"You're quick to judge, aren't you?"

"Leaves time for more important things. Like reading, for instance."

"Then go back to what you read in those three journals and everything else you have been able to learn or put together. Start with a common denominator."

"Children."

"More specifically . . ."

"Babies," Danielle said, thinking of the offer Esteban Ravel had intended to make her in the hospital, the wife of Jacob Rossovitch, who had suffered an ironically similar fate, and also of the twin rows of cribs she had seen on board the *Lucretia Maru*. "Infants."

"Keep going."

"Hyram Levy was involved in trafficking for a white-slavery ring."

"Was he the leader?"

"No, merely an underling for a criminal of legend, a monster the Arabs call Al Safah."

"And?"

"Levy had arranged for me to receive one of the babies he stole or purchased after I . . . miscarried."

"I'm sorry."

"I never had the chance to say no. I'm not sure I could have."

"And what of Revkah Rossovitch?"

"She gave birth to a stillborn. Was almost driven mad as a result."

"Something," Wolfe started softly, the regret in his voice genuine, "you sadly can relate to. But, of course, Hyram Levy was not yet able to make her the same offer he intended to make you."

Danielle's head suddenly cleared. She felt lighter, relieved, the way one does when coming to the end of a long journey. "What happened that morning fifty years ago? What did you and the others do at the kibbutz, Mr. Wollchensky?"

The old man nodded expectantly. "I would say it's time you heard the rest of the story. . . ."

CHAPTER 68

BEN SAW AT once that the entire inside of the sprawling mansion had been gutted and rebuilt to fit the new specifications required of it. He had entered through a long one-story section of the structure that was now lined on both sides by small dormitory-style rooms that must have served as barracks for the complex's guards. Ben shuffled by those doors, past a few men still emerging without paying them a second glance. His coat, cap, and rifle still made him appear as one of them, so long as he didn't give any of the men too long a look.

At the end of the hall, Ben turned right up a single flight of steps, the wood paler in the center from where a runner had been removed. He opened a door at the top of the stairs and found himself standing at the head of what looked like a prison wing. Directly before him a pair of guards armed only with batons and Mace spray rose stiffly.

"What the hell's going on?" one of the guards asked Ben in English, already edgy from all the commotion downstairs.

Beyond them, large, heavy wooden doors lined both sides of what must have once been the mansion's second floor, at least one wing of it. The doors had steel-barred portals at face level and iron bars slung into slots across the front to prevent them from being opened from the inside. Judging by the irregular distances between the doors, the rooms beyond them varied in size; they were easily large enough to accommodate several dozen prisoners.

All children, he hoped.

This, Ben realized, was the chance he had been awaiting since his own children had been murdered. This was his chance to recover the lost five minutes that had changed his life. Begin the process of bringing down the mysterious Al Safah's network here and now, so no more children would be stolen or coerced into a life of misery and degradation.

"The house is on fire! We've got to evacuate this floor!" Ben ordered the guards, making his voice sound desperate. "The whole place might go up!"

"Jesus . . ."

"I think it's an attack. They haven't said, but I think—"

"Let's get them out of here," the other guard interrupted anxiously, pulling his arms through the sleeves of his jacket.

"The front's not safe," Ben said.

"We'll use the back way," the first jailer said.

Ben blessed the thick scent of burning that had begun to drift up from the first floor. No smoke trailed it, but the stench was more than enough to roust the jailers into taking quick action. With Ben bringing up the rear, feigning a protective watch, the jailers moved down the prison hall, throwing back the iron bolts and opening door after door.

Instantly children of all ages began spilling out unsurely, appearing sad and terrified in dirty clothes that were their only possessions. The vast majority of the children were girls, divided into the rooms by age. The youngest were little more than seven or eight; the oldest were probably in their midteens.

"Let's go! Let's go!" the guards continued to yell as they banged their batons repeatedly against the walls.

Ben moved on down the hall, prodding the laggards on with his rifle as he brought up the rear. Speed was of the essence now. Escaping the grounds before the rest of the keepers of this prison realized what was going on. He searched for Leila Fatuk amid the sea of frightened, unhappy faces but couldn't find her and fought the temptation to shout out her name.

He stole glances into the now abandoned rooms as he passed them. Thin springless cots were squeezed in with barely any room between them. Garbage was scattered everywhere. Grime coated the walls and floor. A sickening sewerlike smell sifted out of some of the rooms, evidence of backed-up or broken-down sanitary facilities.

He made a rough count of nearly sixty children on this hall alone. The infants he had seen carried off the *Lucretia Maru* were not among them, and he was almost reluctant to leave without searching for the wing on which they had been imprisoned as well. But he couldn't take all the children and adults imprisoned here back to the world from which they had been stolen, or had left for a lie. Try for more and he would likely lose his chance to free even these relative few.

Free how?

It was a question to which Ben had not yet found an answer. His ruse could only last so long, and pursuit was a certainty once the guard in the bell tower noticed these children fleeing.

He followed the charging tide of bodies down another set of stairs and through a door out into the rear of the compound. The two guards he had tricked upstairs led the way to a single locked gate built into the wall enclosing the fortress at its rear. Ben could see one of them fumbling with the lock and angled himself sideways so he would be the first to see anyone coming. The guard finally got the lock off and yanked open the door, leading the way out, while the other guard herded the children through.

"What about the others?" that guard asked when Ben reached him.

"They're coming!"

The children and other guard had moved for the road that ran beyond the back of the property, leaving the two of them alone.

Something in the jailer's eyes changed. "If this was an evacuation, then—"

Ben didn't wait. He brought his rifle up in an underhand motion that cracked into the jailer's chin and snapped his neck sideways. Dazed, the man reeled backward, unable to steady himself before Ben lashed the stock against his skull like a baseball bat. Ben could feel the bones give, splintering on impact. The guard collapsed, and Ben hurried to catch up with the pack of children.

The second jailer was moving ahead of them, a pistol Ben hadn't noticed before in his hand.

"The airfield!" Ben said, surely, as if that had been his plan all along. "That's where we're supposed to go! They'll be waiting for us!"

The second jailer gazed back down the road in search of his partner.

"He'll catch up!"

The second jailer nodded, reluctantly turning back to the front. "Let's go, then."

And he set out in the lead, while Ben drifted to the rear again.

CHAPTER 69

DAVID **W**OLLCHENSKY OFFERED
her a chair before he began, but Danielle didn't take
it, preferring to stay on her feet. He picked up the
story exactly where Levy's first journal had left off, with
the three surviving friends huddled outside the kibbutz
hospital where Revkah Rossovitch's baby had just been
born dead.

*"If you're with me, get into the jeep and let's go," Wollch-
ensky said adamantly.*

*Levy and Pearlman could only look at each other and
shrug. Their sense of honor overcame their reluctance to
follow the man whose methods had grown increasingly
violent over the years. But loyalty blurred their sense of
right and wrong. In that instant they were younger men
again, with much less to lose, following the man who
had saved their lives and fighting a war in which they
made up the rules as they went along.*

*Wollchensky drove the jeep out of Israel into the West
Bank almost to Jericho. David knew the back roads that*

were never watched and hardly traveled; they had taken a similar one the night they had raided the refugee camp from where Jacob Rossovitch's killers had come. He took a different one today, longer since they did not have the night for cover. But both Pearlman and Levy sensed Wollchensky didn't care if they drove into a full-scale ambush. Nothing was going to stop him today. Nothing.

He drove to the entrance of a refugee camp that seemed almost identical to the one they had raided only a few weeks before. He parked in plain view and turned to his friends.

"Keep your rifles where they can see them, but don't aim or steady them unless you have to."

"They know we're Israelis." Levy could tell that already from the huddled stares being cast their way from within the camp.

"That's what I'm counting on. They're far less likely to attack Israelis than each other." Wollchensky handed Pearlman a long-dead walkie-talkie. "Pretend to talk into this from time to time. Make them think there are plenty more of us patrolling the area."

Pearlman took the dead walkie-talkie and nodded. He and Levy watched Wollchensky shoulder his rifle and unhesitantly enter the squalid refugee camp composed of dilapidated, makeshift structures and tents. He passed quickly out of sight, and the two men fought to keep their faces hard and fierce.

Some minutes later, it seemed much longer than it was, Wollchensky appeared walking side by side with a Palestinian about his age. The Palestinian seemed to be very short, but as they drew closer Pearlman and Levy could see he was stooped over and hunched, something obviously wrong with the spine. The two moved like old friends, no one they passed challenging David's presence in the camp.

This in spite of the fact that David was holding something in his arms, something wrapped in a tattered blanket. At the entrance to the camp, the Palestinian slapped

*David's shoulder as a friend might and David extracted
a hand from the blanket in order to shake. There was
something orderly and businesslike about the transac-
tion, whereas Pearlman and Levy had been expecting
something else entirely.*

*"Here," Wollchensky said routinely when he reached
the jeep, "take it."*

*He passed the blanketed bundle to Hyram Levy and
settled in again behind the jeep's driver's seat. Levy
pulled back the tattered, soiled blanket and winced.*

"My God," Pearlman gasped from the back.

"It was a baby," Danielle said when the man who was
now David Wolfe stopped. "You went and stole a Palestinian baby to replace the one Revkah Rossovitch
had lost."

"I didn't steal the child, Chief Inspector. I purchased
it. And for the going rate."

"Going rate?"

The old man shrugged. "The Palestinians, I'm
afraid, had very little else to sell at that point."

"So they sold their children?"

Wolfe nodded. "To brokers who came from all over
the Middle East in search of boys to enslave to labor
and girls to use for prostitution. The practice began in
this one refugee camp, but quickly spread throughout
the West Bank, fueled by desperation and eventually
overseen by a single individual."

"Al Safah," Danielle realized.

Wolfe suddenly seemed unsteady on his feet. He
reached over and grasped the chair back for support.
"I see you have uncovered more about all this than I
had heard."

"Al Safah's real and you know who he is, don't you?"

For a time it looked as though Wolfe would not respond. Then, suddenly, he nodded.

"That man you bought the baby from?"

The old man shook his head. "No. Not him."

"You brought the baby back to Revkah Rossovitch at the kibbutz."

Wolfe nodded again. "Normally in those days, we had a much more civilized way of dealing with such tragedies. Recent Jewish immigrants from Yemen were kept in camps until they could be resettled. Here we were a young country ourselves, without the social or economic strength to support even ourselves, opening our doors willingly to all comers. But we knew then that our future security lay in building our numbers, so no one was turned away."

The old man smirked, the expression one of irony and regret at the same time.

"But we also were secure in our own racial superiority to these new immigrants who were, in fact, no different from what we had been at the beginning. This was *our* country they were coming to. So when an Israeli woman's child died, it seemed more than fair to replace it with a Yemenite baby stolen from the camp after its mother had been told it was dead. Unfortunately, we didn't have time to take those steps with Revkah."

"Because you wanted her to think the baby you had acquired for her was really hers."

"It was what *she* wanted to think, Chief Inspector. We returned to the kibbutz to find her sleeping with her dead infant against her chest. I replaced it with the infant we had obtained at the refugee camp without her ever knowing."

"What happened when she woke up?"

Wolfe's expression softened, became almost dreamy. "I can't be sure, but to this day my heart tells me Revkah still believes the child we brought back to be hers."

"She's alive?"

"In her eighties. She has more bad days than good. I call her from time to time. Sometimes we can talk."

"Honoring the pledge the three of you made to your dead friend . . ."

Wolfe shrugged humbly. "Do you recall what that pledge was, Chief Inspector?"

"To protect and watch over his wife and child for as long as you lived."

"That pledge is why you are here today," David Wolfe told her.

"I don't understand."

"You will in time. You will understand everything in time."

"Will I also understand how Hyram Levy became involved in smuggling Palestinian children out of Israel?"

Wolfe turned and sank wearily into his chair. Danielle walked up around it in order to face him. He looked to her suddenly like an old, tired man losing a race with the years.

"It goes back to that day we made sure Revkah Rossovitch would have a son," he said, his voice weak and strained with fatigue. "Word spread of the service we could provide. Jews—Israelis—were desperate to have children. It was considered a sin not to."

Danielle swallowed hard and Wolfe's eyes met hers knowingly before he continued.

"We began preventing that sin from occurring, Chief Inspector. We filled a great need. We convinced ourselves we were doing nothing wrong."

"But it didn't stop there, did it?" Danielle challenged. "Levy wasn't just doing great deeds, he was involved in the white-slave trade. He got mixed up with Al Safah, didn't he?"

Wolfe started to take a deep breath, then stopped in the middle. "Yes, I'm afraid he did. We were a young nation and funds were always short. It was sometimes difficult to obtain the goods we needed, especially guns. On these occasions we often relied on less than savory operators."

"The black market," Danielle nodded. "Did the government know what you were doing?"

"No. They never would have tolerated our actions.

We crossed a terrible line, Chief Inspector, but that was nothing new for us. The stakes were everything. We were willing to accept the risks."

"Until it got out of hand."

Wolfe's gaze was faraway. "Did you know that it was predominantly Jewish immigrants who brought the white-slave trade to America? It was strictly women in those days, imported for prostitution in the early 1900s. The original centers were New York, Philadelphia and Chicago, but it spread to other cities over the years."

"And eventually to Israel. That's what you're saying, isn't it?" Danielle charged.

But Wolfe remained calm. "With the settling of Palestine, some of these Jewish traffickers immigrated and brought their trade with them. A new part of the world, after all, meant new opportunities. The original Jewish white slave traders became more like middlemen, brokers, procuring the women—"

"And children," Danielle added harshly.

"—from one country and placing them in another. They began to centralize the practice on an international level, taking over the trade of other traffickers all over the world."

"Monsters replacing monsters. How could you let them get away with it? How could *anyone*?"

"I told you, Chief Inspector: because we needed the money," Wolfe answered emotionlessly. "We used the profits to purchase the weapons Israel so desperately required."

Danielle shook her head slowly. "I don't believe this. . . ."

"No one ever did. No one even knew."

"The government included."

"We had gotten extraordinarily good at covering our tracks." Wolfe took a deep breath. "Are you sure you don't want to try another cigar?"

Danielle realized the first one had made her a little

sick. Her legs suddenly felt weak. "The white-slave trade is how you made your original fortune, isn't it? That's why you were already a wealthy man when you immigrated to America and became David Wolfe?"

"There was plenty to go around, Chief Inspector, I assure you. I'm not proud of what I did but, given the same circumstances, I'm sure I would do it all over again." His expression changed, became that of the storyteller, instead of the confessor, again. "But we needed a way to seize control of the trade everywhere, even from our fellow Jews who had opened the door for us. We needed to make people willingly give up the trade to us. So we created a myth, a monster, to terrify them."

"Al Safah," Danielle realized. "You made him up."

"Not exactly. See, to create the effect we were after the legend had to be given credence, backed up in all the countries so it could spread. Many of the tales, even most, you have heard of Al Safah are actually true."

"So he did exist once. That's what you're saying."

"He still does, Chief Inspector," Wolfe said, his expression utterly flat. "You see, I am Al Safah."

CHAPTER 70

THE GROUP OF children reached the airfield without incident, Ben breathing easier as soon as he emerged from the woods onto the cleared ground at the edge of the strip. But his relief was short-lived.

"Where are the others?" the surviving jailer demanded, storming toward Ben through the children. "You said they'd be here. What's going on?"

He started to bring his pistol up, eyes flaring. Ben fired his rifle first. Three quick shots, all of which found their mark. The jailer stood there for a moment, looking puzzled, then staggered forward a few more steps before he collapsed.

The children screamed. Some backed away. Others began to run.

"No! Don't be afraid!" Ben called to them, angling himself to cut off the fleeing group. He hoped they could understand English. If not, he would have to rely on the power of his tone. "We're all leaving. I'm getting you out of here, to someplace safe. Follow me!"

And with that Ben waved a hand in the air and led

a charge to the transport plane that was parked fifty yards before them in the center of the paved airstrip.

The pilot had been checking off items on a clipboard when the shooting led him to duck for cover on the other side of the plane. Ben rolled under the nose and raised his rifle.

"Don't shoot!" the pilot pleaded, arms up in the air.

"You're flying us out of here!" Ben brought the rifle to his shoulder. "You're going to fly these children off this island!"

"*What?*" The pilot's mouth dropped.

"How many times would you like me to repeat it?" Ben threatened.

The pilot flapped his arms. "All right, all right!"

"Then let's go!" Ben urged, prodding him around the plane's nose back into the spill of the airstrip's floodlights, where the frightened children had clustered into a tight mass.

Shouts from the edge of the clearing made Ben swing around in time to see five armed men from the fortress running out of the woods with automatic rifles and submachine guns leveled.

"Get down!" Ben yelled at the children.

The ones who understood English dove to the asphalt instantly. It took the first barrage to make the rest follow suit.

Ben fired over them into the night, felling a pair of the gunmen with his initial barrage as return fire dug pockmarks in the transport plane's steel skin. Still clacking off rounds, Ben swung his eyes back on the pilot, who had ducked beneath one of the plane's front wheels.

"Get on board or I'll shoot you next! I swear it!"

Risking bullets, the pilot climbed quickly into the cockpit.

Ben's next spray took a third gunman in the leg and dropped him. The final pair held their positions at the edge of the woods and continued to fire, hoping for reinforcements.

His sole clip almost exhausted, Ben switched to single shots as he zigzagged back and forth near the children hugging the asphalt for cover. Behind him the pilot had released a metal ladder that reached down to the runway from the center of the plane's fuselage.

"Go to the plane! Go to the plane!" Ben ordered, rousting his charges from the concrete. "Get on board!"

The children didn't have to know English to understand his command this time. They rose and rushed the plane en masse, the older ones helping the younger. Ben planted himself at the rear of the pack, firing toward the two remaining gunmen until his rifle clicked empty. Then he drew the pistol from his holster and clacked off sixteen shots in rapid succession, still in the open, daring the bullets to take him. He felt invincible, because these five minutes, at long last, belonged to him. This was the payback he had been waiting for.

Backpedaling, he ejected the spent clip and jammed home the single extra stored in a slot on his gun belt. By then all but a few of the children were on board the transport, and he tried to hurry the rest along.

A bullet took a boy high in the leg when he was halfway up the ladder. He screamed and dropped hard to the ground, clutching his thigh near the final two children waiting to climb aboard.

"Go! Go!" Ben yelled to them, and moved to offer cover, firing eight rapid shots toward the gunmen left near the woods as the transport plane's engines fired up.

When the last of the children was through the hatch, Ben grabbed the downed boy with one arm while he continued pulling the trigger until the slide locked open. With enemy fire dappling the plane's fuselage, he climbed half the rungs and then hoisted the wounded boy into arms dangling from the hatch. He lost his footing at the top of the steps, feeling the sting of bullets pulsing past him in the night. His legs dangled and he clutched the rung of the ladder for dear life.

Strangely, in that instant the words of Zaid Jabral's ghost fluttered through his mind. The revelation he had finally grasped, only to lose, on the *Lucretia Maru* returned to him, and this time he held tight to it, as tightly as his hands gripped the ladder.

My God, that's it!

The truth had been there all the time, but it had taken a ghost to show it to him. Ben looked up toward the transport's doorway.

Zaid Jabral extended a hand to him, smiling.

Ben stretched upward and squeezed his eyes closed. When he opened them, Jabral's ghost was gone and a pair of the older boys he had freed leaned out the doorway, hands reaching down. They latched onto Ben's shoulders and yanked him up into the plane.

Intent on getting airborne, Ben shoved away the children around him, shouldered the door closed, and twisted the wheel into the locked position. Then he stormed forward into the cockpit, brandishing his empty pistol.

The pilot gazed back at him fearfully. Through a corner of the cockpit glass, Ben could see the sweep of flashlights coming through the woods seconds before a large number of the compound's guards rushed onto the tarmac. Muzzle flashes flared through the darkness, and gunfire he couldn't hear over the rumbling sounds of the engine clanged off the plane's skin.

"Get going!"

The pilot shoved the throttle forward and the plane began to move, picking up speed quickly. A bullet thumped into one side of the windshield, but the glass didn't shatter, holding together through the spiderweb of cracks. The last thing Ben saw through the glass was the gunmen rushing to keep up as the transport gradually pulled away from them down the runway.

It lifted into the air with surprising agility, a graceful bird rising toward the safety of the sky. Ben slapped the pilot gratefully on the shoulder, started to move to check on the children.

"One thing," the pilot said, and Ben turned back toward him. "Where are we going?"

Ben smiled, realizing he had barely considered that question yet himself. "Israel," he said. "Lay in a course for Tel Aviv."

CHAPTER 71

DANIELLE STOOD LOOKING down at David Wolfe, trying to picture this frail old man as the mythically brutal killer feared to this day in dozens of countries. The shock of his revelation had worn off, cold logic replacing it. Everything in David Wollchensky's life, it seemed, made a twisted kind of sense, this included.

"You still haven't told me what I'm doing here," she said finally.

"You stated it pretty well yourself before."

"I've been discredited, disowned. My career's finished. You want me to do your dirty work because I'm the perfect fall guy."

"Close enough."

"How did you get Hyram Levy's journals?"

"That doesn't matter, believe me."

"Who killed him?"

"That doesn't matter either."

"Then why am I here?"

"To prevent another death before it's too late."

"Max Pearlman?"

Wolfe shook his head. "Not Pearlman."

"Why did Levy call you two months ago?"

"To tell me something he had decided to do. Something I could not let him do."

"But Pearlman must have listened. That's why they spoke so much."

"Pearlman was on his side."

"Meaning you were on the other? But these men were your *friends!*"

Wolfe looked away from her. "And so they will always be. But we came to a parting of the ways."

"Over what?"

"The past . . . and, even more, the future."

"I can't help you if you don't start making sense."

"Try to remember the date of Levy's first phone call to Pearlman. What happened that day, or the day before? Think!"

"I don't remember."

"Neither did Levy. Neither did Pearlman," Wolfe said more softly, somberly. "That was the problem. They had forgotten the greatest pledge we had ever made, the pledge that bonded us together with a secret forever."

"To honor the memory of a dead friend." Danielle nodded. "To be there for his wife and child. You told me all that."

"Not all of it, Chief Inspector. There is still one part of the story left to tell. . . ."

DAY EIGHT

CHAPTER 7 2

WE'RE APPROACHING ISRAELI airspace now." The pilot glanced behind him toward Ben. "They'll never let us land."

"So you keep telling me."

Ben had spent much of the flight back in the hold, making sure his young charges were as comfortable as possible. With the help of a first-aid kit on board he managed to stanch the flow of blood from the leg of the boy who'd been shot. Then he again checked the cluster of still-fearful and uncertain faces one by one until he came to that of a teenage girl cradling her knees with her arms. He felt a great surge of warm excitement go through him before he spoke, forcing the words past the clog in his throat.

"You are Leila Fatuk."

The girl looked up at him, eyes suddenly bright with hope.

"I'm going to take you home," Ben told her. It all seemed worth it now, everything he had done.

Back in the cockpit, though, the pilot was less than

optimistic about their chances. "The Israelis will shoot us down if we keep going," he insisted.

"Maybe."

Seconds later a pair of advanced F-16s appeared on either side of the transport, seeming to have dropped out of nowhere. Then the radio began to squawk.

"Attention unidentified aircraft, you have violated Israeli airspace. Repeat, you have violated Israeli airspace."

The pilot snatched the microphone off the instrument panel. "Israeli control, this is Navistar seven-one-seven Roger Tango."

"Attention Navistar, please divert from your present course or our fighters will be forced to shoot you down. You have thirty seconds to comply."

"Israeli control, we are low on fuel and declaring an emergency. Request immediate clearance for Ben-Gurion Airport."

"Twenty-five seconds, Navistar. State the nature of your emergency."

Ben grabbed the microphone from the pilot's grasp before he could continue. "Israeli control, this is Inspector Bayan Kamal of the Palestinian police."

"This is *who?*"

"Please be advised that we are low on fuel and carrying sixty children on a rescue mission. If you shoot us down, you will kill them all."

"Ten seconds, Navistar."

The F-16s dropped off to firing distance.

"Israeli control," Ben said, "we are on direct approach to Ben-Gurion. If we turn off now, we will crash at sea. So shoot us down if you must. Let the deaths of these children be on your conscience."

There was no response, the ten seconds gone.

"Navistar, this is Israeli control. Change your heading to four-zero-niner and descend to five hundred feet. Be advised that our fighters are holding at your rear."

Ben clamped his free hand on the pilot's shoulder and handed him back the microphone.

"Acknowledged, Israeli control. That's four-zero-niner at five hundred feet. We'll see you on the ground."

AFTER LANDING, THE transport was directed to a separate, isolated part of the airport, where it was surrounded by a brigade of troops and vehicles. The frightened children were ushered off under heavy guard, weapons trained on them the whole time. They were loaded onto the back of trucks and taken away; to what destination, Ben had no idea. The only exception was the boy who'd been shot back on the island, who was carted off in an ambulance. Leila Fatuk stared at Ben from the final truck's rear as it pulled away, and he lifted a hand for a slight, reassuring wave from the doorway of the plane.

He descended the ladder and was immediately ordered to spread-eagle on the ground. He was searched roughly, handcuffed, and brought to a detention center within the airport, where he was locked in a small windowless room, a pair of armed guards standing on opposite sides of the wall.

The interrogation began twenty minutes later when a surprisingly young soldier entered the room and began pounding him with questions. The young man was in his mid-twenties, with bushy eyebrows that seemed almost to grow out of his thick head of dark hair. Already exhausted, Ben totally lost track of time, saved only by the hearty meal his captors served him after he asked for it. He answered all their questions truthfully, although it was obvious from their faces that they were having trouble making sense of his fantastic tale.

"You say you went to this island all by yourself without a plan. Is that correct?"

"That's right."

"And then you rescued these children, also all by yourself."

"Yes."

"Why?"

"I don't know."

"Why bring them to Israel?"

"Because it was the only country within our flying range I could trust to take them."

Ben's young inquisitor wrinkled his brow.

"You've got to let me go," Ben said simply.

"So you keep telling me."

"You don't understand."

"You keep telling me that, too. Why don't you help me to understand."

"I can't."

"Why?"

"Because I'm not sure myself. I need to see someone in Jericho. Then I'll know."

"Know *what*, Inspector?"

"You wouldn't believe me if I told you," Ben said, thinking of the incredible discovery that had finally dawned on him outside the plane on Al Safah's island.

"But that has not stopped you from leveling serious charges here against prominent Israeli citizens, Inspector," his inquisitor snapped.

"Check them out, Captain or Major or Colonel, or whatever you are."

"Lieutenant," the officer said, and he leaned farther over the table, almost nose to nose with Ben, when a knock came on the door.

The lieutenant backed off and opened it, then spoke briefly to a figure in the hall. When he turned back toward Ben, his face was red and his expression fuming. He said nothing, just signaled his men and the guards to leave the room with a stiff wave of his hand. Then he removed Ben's handcuffs and followed them out, disappearing into the hall.

"Not a very pleasant young man," said Colonel Nabril al-Asi, entering in the lieutenant's wake.

Ben could scarcely believe his eyes.

"I would have been here sooner, but I couldn't resist stopping in the duty-free shop."

Ben saw he was holding a shopping bag in his hand. "Ties?"

Al-Asi nodded. "No Armani, unfortunately."

Ben rose. "How did you . . ."

Al-Asi waved him off routinely. "I received a call from one of my Israeli counterparts. I promised him the arrest of two terrorist leaders in exchange for you." He stroked his chin. "Now if only I could decide which two they will be . . ."

"Maybe you won't have to."

"Really?"

"I may have something much bigger for you to trade with, Colonel."

CHAPTER 73

FAYED KABIR WAS again at his construction site in eastern Jericho, this time holding the plans of his house-to-be in his hands as he watched the crew begin work on the framing. He turned on hearing Ben's approach and spotted Nabril al-Asi hovering outside his Mercedes.

"Good afternoon, Minister," Ben greeted affably.

"I'm surprised to see you again so soon, Inspector," Kabir said, but his gaze continued to stray toward the colonel.

"We didn't finish our discussion the last time we spoke."

"We didn't?"

"Apparently not. You left out a few things I have since become aware of."

Kabir's eyes shifted nervously from Ben to the colonel. "Is this an official investigation?"

"That depends. If you cooperate with me, no." Ben glanced over his shoulder in the direction of the Mercedes. "If Colonel al-Asi gets involved, well then I'm afraid you will not be here when your home is finally completed."

Kabir hunched over a little more than usual. "What is it you want to know?"

"You told me last time we spoke that in the refugee camp where you grew up, you did whatever it took to survive."

Kabir eyed him warily. "We all did, Inspector. You would have too."

"Of that I'm sure. That's why I'm not here to accuse you of anything. You are, however, part of another investigation. Only if Colonel al-Asi gets involved might that change."

"I will tell you anything I can."

"Zaid Jabral came here as a result of a story he had recently published. A story about an old woman, a resident of the same refugee camp as you, who claimed her baby was stolen from her fifty years ago. Jabral's research indicated you had something to do with the theft of that baby. Yes or no?"

"I told Jabral no."

"Is that what you would like to tell me?"

The Palestinian Authority's minister of finance looked once again at al-Asi before responding. "That woman's was not the only baby taken, and I was not the only one involved."

"But you dealt with Jews, didn't you? At least once. They would have come from a kibbutz," Ben said, thinking of Jabral's mysterious visit to a kibbutz in search of birth records.

"I don't know where they came from. They paid extremely well, in American dollars."

"It was a boy, wasn't it?"

Kabir nodded.

"And this would have been 1950."

"Yes. In the spring."

"Forty-nine years ago . . ."

"Almost to the day."

"And the woman's name, it was Ramira Taji?"

"After all these years you expect me to remem—"

"Yes, I do."

Kabir tried to look away from Ben's intense stare, couldn't. "I don't know. It could have been. I mean, the name sounds right."

Ben suddenly felt revulsion for the man hunched over before him. "You don't know what you started, do you?"

"I looked into your file, Inspector. I know what you're working on, and I can tell you that I had nothing to do with these missing children you are investigating. I haven't been involved in such things since I escaped that refugee camp."

"Not directly. But the ones who are involved today are your successors. For that, you bear part of the blame."

Kabir cast his eyes fearfully toward Nabril al-Asi. The colonel's white dress shirt billowed in the wind. His tie flapped against his chest.

Kabir swallowed hard. "Why does it matter? After all these years, why bring this up again?"

"Because somebody else already has."

DANIELLE'S FLIGHT BACK to Israel seemed to take much longer than the one to New York. She did not have Hyram Levy's journals to occupy her time, nor endless questions to ponder. She had answers now, enough, perhaps, to make her wish she had never left Israel to find David Wollchensky in the first place.

"There is still one part of the story left to tell . . ."

Danielle knew before it was told that she didn't want to hear the rest of the story that had begun on a beach in Caesarea on a night in 1947.

"Our pledge did not end that day we gave Revkah Rossovitch back her baby," David Wolfe had continued. "The three of us continued to watch over them, remained a part of their lives even after Revkah remarried." He smiled sadly at that memory. "None of us blamed her; she was still a young woman and she deserved a rich, full life. She married a doctor, but he had been a soldier first, much decorated on the battlefield for all the lives he had saved by stitching men back together as bullets hummed over his head. I served with him in the '56 war at Mitla Pass in Egypt."

Wolfe said that as if it was very important to him. Then his face emptied once again of both emotion and color.

"Revkah named her son Ari, and two years later the boy was given the last name of the only father he would ever know." Wolfe's despondent eyes locked with Danielle's. "Bar-Rosen, Chief Inspector. The Palestinian baby we took from that refugee camp is now the prime minister of Israel."

CHAPTER 74

IN THAT INSTANT, Danielle had been struck not by fear or shock, but by the cold logic behind David Wolfe's words. She took strange comfort in the fact that she now understood everything that had taken place in the past week. But that comfort lasted only until Wolfe spoke again.

"Levy called me after the special election two months ago. He asked what I thought we should do. I told him nothing. I told him it wasn't our place. He said we had made it our place when we gave Revkah Rossovitch a Palestinian child. How could we have known this would happen?"

"And if you had known, would it have changed anything?"

Wolfe shook his head. "The boy was raised a Jew by the only mother he ever knew. Today he is as good a Jew as you or I."

"Then the truth . . ."

"The three of us never shared it with another living soul. I say living because we all shared the truth with Jacob Rossovitch."

"So Ari Bar-Rosen doesn't know."

"He couldn't. It's not possible."

"But Levy and Pearlman did. They disagreed with you, decided they could not let a Palestinian become prime minister of Israel."

"They were worried for themselves, not Israel. Responsibility for the stands Bar-Rosen has advocated was something they could not accept. They believed he was going to make Israel weaker and that it was their fault, *our* fault. They decided he could never take office."

"Bar-Rosen takes office officially in two days."

"At Masada. In a public ceremony."

"My God, Pearlman and Levy planned to assassinate him there! That explains it. . . ."

"Explains what?"

"Levy's connection to a black bag Mossad agent named Ravel. A killer. And the plan must still be active!"

Wolfe didn't look surprised, just grim. "You must stop it. You're the only one who can."

"No. You've got to call someone else, someone official."

"I can't. You know that."

"Why?"

"I would have to tell the truth. What do you think the truth would do to the State of Israel, Chief Inspector?"

"I don't know, I don't know."

"I do. You must believe me, my way is best. This secret must be kept, and so must my pledge. I cannot go back on that pledge now, even after all these years."

"You couldn't have known all those years ago."

"Do you think it would have made any difference if I had, Chief Inspector? Would betraying my pledge then be any worse than betraying it now?"

"You made me the fourth person to know the secret, but you haven't asked me if I believe what you did was right."

"Because what happened in the past doesn't matter. What matters is Israel's present and her future. You *will* stop those who would destroy that future, Chief Inspector. No matter how you feel yourself, you will not let this happen. You will stop them and that will ensure the secret remains safe."

"And you never once thought Pearlman and Levy might be right?"

"I told you, it doesn't matter."

"But you haven't told me how you really felt about having a man born a Palestinian serve as prime minister of Israel. Do you really think his moderate stance, his desire to make the concessions necessary to achieve a full and total peace, are merely a *coincidence?*"

"He is a product of his times, Chief Inspector, more even than his upbringing and certainly more than his birth."

"What if he learns the truth someday?"

"He won't."

"But Pearlman—"

"Pearlman is dead now too, Chief Inspector. I can assure you of that." Wolfe's eyes moistened. "I knew him too well, you see. He could not evade me long. There remains only this assassin Ravel and whomever else he and Levy might have retained."

"They don't need anyone else, not with Ravel. You don't understand. You believe the mystery of Al Safah begins and ends with you. But it's not true. The story of Al Safah may have been just a legend, but somebody else has been keeping it alive for the last few years. That means a trail of bodies left of anyone who gets too close or tries to move in. Who do you think Levy used to leave that trail? I've seen this man," Danielle said after a pause, recalling her one brief meeting with Ravel in the hospital. "And believe me, he's someone I don't want to see again."

"You'll find a way to stop him."

"Find someone else!"

"There is no one else," Wolfe said flatly, and for a fleeting instant his eyes were young and sure again, the dedicated soldier fighting to make a country. In that same instant, Danielle saw him the same way the younger Pearlman and Levy must have: a man they would have followed to the grave. "The day after tomorrow, Chief Inspector. At Masada. Go with God."

NABRIL AL-ASI LISTENED to Ben's story impassively, without comment, but growing visibly shaken by the tale's end. "Your friend Jabral figured all this out himself?"

Ben nodded. "Someone killed him because he was on the verge of breaking the story of the incoming Israeli prime minister's true background." Ben watched al-Asi shift uneasily in the backseat of his Mercedes. "It bothers you, doesn't it, Colonel?"

"It bothers me that I didn't figure it out myself. I think I may be slipping. Can you imagine the outcry if this had come out? Or if it ever does?"

"I was thinking that letting it out might be in our best interests."

"Whose interests exactly, Inspector? The Israelis would never allow Bar-Rosen to stay in office, and the Palestinians would cry foul when another election was called for. The end result would almost surely be the reelection of the old hard-line government, and that would serve no one."

"You think Bar-Rosen may favor our cause because he's Palestinian, even though he doesn't know it?"

"An interesting moral dilemma," al-Asi agreed. "I wish I had the answer. Perhaps he is the one we should tell. Let him make his own decision."

"If he ever gets the chance. Jabral could only have been murdered by an Israeli faction determined to make sure the truth is never revealed. That same faction can never allow Ari Bar-Rosen to take office."

"He takes office tomorrow in a ceremony on Masada. Puts us in quite a spot, doesn't it, Inspector?"

"We need to be there, Colonel."

"To stop the Israelis from assassinating their own prime minister," al-Asi said, sounding as though he didn't believe it himself.

"Can you get us on Masada?"

Al-Asi thought briefly. "Bar-Rosen has invited a rather large Palestinian contingent to be present at the ceremony. I think I can secure places for you and myself."

"That's a start."

Al-Asi didn't look pleased with the prospects. "We'll have to go unarmed, Inspector, and if we so much as look at Bar-Rosen the wrong way, Israeli security will bury us with the rest of the skeletons on that rock."

"We'll think of something."

DANIELLE STOOD ON the mountain plateau of Masada, looking down upon the desolation that surrounded it. She had come here many times as a child, always in the company of her father, who very early wanted to ingrain the Jewish fighting tradition in her and her brothers. Except for the day she had raced up the serpentine Snake Path with the rest of her graduating army class, she had never been here without him. For that reason she had walked up that same winding path from the mountain's base this afternoon.

But reaching its buffeted summit out of breath and drenched in sweat did nothing to ease her melancholy or make the task at hand any less daunting. She pulled a mineral water from her backpack, drank it quickly, and then went to work on another as workers swarmed over the site, readying it for the next day's ceremony.

Gazing around her in the afternoon light, Danielle found it easy to understand why Ari Bar-Rosen would have chosen this place to officially become Israel's prime minister. More than any other single symbol, Masada typified the plight of the Jewish people through history. King Herod built it originally as a royal sanctuary and fortress. But its historical significance came over a half century after his death, when Jewish Zealots, who had revolted against Rome, took refuge on its rock-strewn precipice. The Zealots held the mountain stronghold for three years, the final one against the continuous onslaught of the entire Tenth Roman Legion, which outnumbered them by more than ten to one. Entering the fortress to claim their victory at last, the Romans found 973 corpses, victims of a mass suicide, waiting for them inside the walls it had taken them three years to penetrate.

And no wonder. Standing on the border between the Judaean Desert and the Dead Sea valley, Masada rises 1,400 feet above ground level on a summit that covers five acres. The past lives and breathes on the desert wind and amid the reconstructed buildings, swirling with the ever-present dust. Her father used to tell Danielle and her brothers that if they listened hard enough, they would hear the cries of those who had died here on that wind.

And tomorrow she would come to Masada to prevent one more from joining them.

DAY NINE

CHAPTER 75

THE PALESTINIAN DELEGATION had been asked to arrive at the base of Masada three hours before the ceremony. Although Israeli security would not subject the members to the indignity of a search, the officers did escort the Palestinians through an elaborate metal detector and then an explosives sensor. Their identities were carefully checked and matched against a list received from the Palestinian Authority the night before.

After learning of the precautions to be taken, Yasir Arafat had opted out of attending. Five members of the Palestinian Council had come in his place. As with the the rest of the delegates, they were required to leave all bags and briefcases behind in a designated area. When all that was done, they were confined under constant surveillance to an open tent that had been erected at dawn.

A buffet table had been set up inside and Colonel al-Asi was one of those to take full advantage.

"You really should eat something," he advised Ben.

"I'm not hungry."

"These bagels are excellent. I understand they used to be shipped frozen from New York. Now the Israelis bake their own. I have two dozen sent to my office every week," al-Asi said, and took another bite.

Ben rose from his folding chair. "It's no good."

Al-Asi looked up at him between chews. "You haven't even tried one."

"I was talking about our plan. The Israelis will be watching us like hawks. We won't be able to make a move."

"What did you expect?"

"You could still call your Israeli counterparts. There's time."

The colonel held off taking another bite. "They're probably here right now, eating breakfast in one of the other tents. But we discussed this yesterday, and the problems haven't changed: if I tell them an Israeli is going to assassinate Bar-Rosen, they will want proof. And if I tell them a Palestinian is going to assassinate Bar-Rosen, they will cancel the ceremony, and the assassin will choose to strike another time when we are not so close."

"Makes sense," Ben acknowledged.

"It's what you told me yourself yesterday, Inspector. And you also told me we can't even be absolutely sure there's a plan to assassinate Bar-Rosen at all."

"I'm as certain as I can be."

"Can I ask you something else?"

"You never needed permission before, Colonel."

"That's because you never hijacked a plane at gunpoint to whisk sixty children away to freedom. I understand the Israelis are in quite a quandary over what to do with them. It seems you have created an international incident."

"What about the ones I didn't get out?"

"I filed your entire report with Interpol, on behalf of their late Inspector Faustin. I'm sure they will act quickly, but I doubt it will be quickly enough."

"Of course," Ben sighed, as if that didn't surprise him.

Al-Asi returned his half-eaten bagel to his paper plate. "When was the last time you slept more than two hours straight, Inspector?"

"When my wife and children were still alive, Colonel."

WORK CREWS HAD labored through the entire night to ready Masada for the ceremony to install Israel's newest prime minister. Chairs had been set up in neat rows all across the summit's northern front, just beyond the reconstructed remains of Herod's palace. The extensive restorations to the large bathhouse, terraces, and labyrinth of storehouses, completed years before, made them the ideal backdrop. The ceremony would take place on the flat plain between the palace and the remainder of Masada's structures scattered across its dusty vastness.

With constant surveillance by security personnel and regular stops for random explosives checks, the process of setting up took much longer than it ordinarily would have. A stage was erected, angled so Ari Bar-Rosen would not have to look into the sun and canopied so the heat and blowing debris would not conspire to dishevel him. Power for the event would be drawn from the same underground lines that fed Masada's lights, which had burned throughout the night.

But the lights could not show everything. No one was watching when late at night the gaunt figure of a narrow-shouldered workman, whose skin seemed painted onto his skeletal face, buried something just beneath the surface of the dry ground.

*   *   *

IN ALL, ONE thousand guests were expected, including delegations from a dozen countries. Because of the inordinately long period of time it would take to ferry so many up by cable car, all foreign delegations had been asked to arrive early. They would be the first to be seated. By protocol, the Palestinians would be the second to the last to take their chairs and the Americans last, just before the nonpolitical invitees were channeled up.

Since they had been the first group to arrive at the base of Masada, Ben Kamal and Nabril al-Asi were able to watch the entire process unfold from the start. They estimated there were two soldiers present for every guest expected. The security precautions were unprecedented in Israel, those in charge having learned their lesson from the Rabin assassination several years earlier.

Ben watched al-Asi return with a third cup of coffee and retake his seat in the Palestinian tent. "Our Israeli friends seem to be expecting something."

"If they were expecting something, the ceremony would have been canceled. They're just going by the book on this one."

"I noticed a few with those earpieces the American Secret Service uses."

"What's your point, Colonel?"

"I think we will witness history being made today; we will not witness an assassination."

"I hope you're right."

"On the summit I'll bet our delegation will be seated facing the sun, to make sighting for a quick shot all the more difficult."

Ben had a thought. "Have all the members of our delegation been checked out?"

"Three or four separate times. You saw the precautions being exercised yourself."

"But not by you."

"Not personally. Why?"

"Nothing," Ben muttered. Something still nagged at him, even though he couldn't identify exactly what it was.

Al-Asi rose and deposited his coffee cup on the table. "Our escorts are coming for us, Ben. It looks like it's time."

DANIELLE, TOO, HAD arrived early, but the lines to board the cable cars were already backed up. Everyone at ground level was doing the best they could; the cable cars just ran too slowly to comfortably accommodate all those present.

She had hoped to arrive in time to search for Esteban Ravel. Find him at the base and whatever he had in store at the summit could be preempted altogether. Professionals like Ravel never worked in teams, especially in a situation like this one, where a single, crazed gunman would make for the best explanation for an international tragedy.

Danielle thought she caught a glimpse of Hershel Giott riding up to the summit in the cable car just ahead of her. Her heart fluttered briefly, and then she remembered she was here as a citizen who had been privately invited. She doubted he would cause a scene, even if he noticed her.

Danielle reached the summit in one of the last five cars to make the climb, one hour after the ceremony's scheduled start, a start that had already been delayed twice. Upon reaching the northern front, she was horrified to see Ari Bar-Rosen mingling with the crowd, concentrating his efforts on the foreign delegations. Were his security men crazy? Did they think their high-tech earphones would prevent a single man with the skills of a Ravel from extending a pistol instead of a hand?

She tensed when she saw Bar-Rosen had reached the front of the Palestinian delegation, the delegates rising en masse to shower him with greetings. It was almost as though she was the only one here who knew the punch line of a joke. Still she scanned the faces of the Palestinians with whom Bar-Rosen exchanged hand-shakes to see if one of them might have somehow known it as well.

Bar-Rosen stopped before he reached a pair of fig-ures seated near the end of the row she was approach-ing. When his security detail moved to one side, she recognized Colonel Nabril al-Asi and then . . .

Ben Kamal!

What was he doing here? A guest of al-Asi's, perhaps, or could it be that his investigation had led to Masada as well? She would have to get his attention when she passed by his chair. A slight squeeze of his hand, a shift of her eyes—anything to let him know she was here to stop an assassination.

A man seated a dozen rows behind Ben amid the Palestinian delegation looked briefly up, then down again. But his face was visible long enough for Danielle to note the skeletal wedge-shaped head, sunken cheeks, and olive skin that looked shiny with makeup.

She had found Esteban Ravel.

CHAPTER 76

"QUITE A SPECTACLE," noted Nabril al-Asi. "Don't you agree?"

"I hadn't noticed."

"Relax, Inspector. The Israelis have everything under control."

"I'd like to believe you're right."

"I think you may have overreacted."

Ben looked away from al-Asi just in time to see Danielle Barnea heading straight for him up the aisle.

DANIELLE PRETENDED TO lose her footing on the rocky earth. She went down hard, breaking her fall with her hands.

She saw Ben bounce out of his chair to lend assistance, picking up on her ruse. She felt his hands upon her and whispered,

* * *

Ravel . . ."

It was all Danielle had a chance to say before a sea of hands joined his in hoisting her back to her feet. To the crowd that had turned their way, she looked simply embarrassed.

But Ben could see something else dancing in her eyes as they continued to glance sidelong to the rear of the Palestinian delegation. Could she be telling him that Ravel, the master assassin he recalled from an Israeli artist's drawing, was hiding among the Palestinians?

Ben sat back down and turned to al-Asi. "He's here," he whispered, fighting an urge to swing round and search the killer out.

"Who?"

"Ravel. The assassin. He's sitting in our delegation."

Al-Asi's features suddenly went pale. "The Palestinians will be pinned with the blame after he strikes."

"Not if we stop him."

A rumbling like a thunderclap shook Masada.

THE OVATION BEGAN just as Danielle reached her seat. She fought to keep her focus on Ravel, twelve rows back from where Ben Kamal was sitting. But the members of all the delegations had risen to their feet, cheering and applauding as Ari Bar-Rosen strode across the stage.

Bar-Rosen walked hand in hand with his wife, their three teenage children following slightly behind. The prime minister was smiling, beaming to the crowd, a picture for the ages that captured both the family man and the war hero who had served under Danielle's father. Bar-Rosen exuded confidence and charisma, the perfect man to usher in a new millennium as well as a new government.

Bar-Rosen reached the dais with his arms raised triumphantly in the air. His family settled into chairs set immediately behind him. Danielle turned away from the stage and began searching the crowd again for Esteban Ravel. Even if she could find the assassin, though, it seemed impossible to cover the distance between them with security so tight.

But maybe she could make that security work for her.

She knew where the killer was. If she pointed Ravel out to any of the multitude of soldiers and police, they would have to act on her claim. None of them would dare take a chance she was making the story up.

"People of Israel and the world," Ari Bar-Rosen began as Danielle rose again and slid toward the aisle, "a new era . . .

. . . Is upon us."

Ben gripped his knees hard with both hands and tried to concentrate on the words of the new prime minister of Israel, a man who had been born fifty years before to a woman named Ramira Taji in the squalor of a Palestinian refugee camp. Bar-Rosen spoke without benefit of notes, rotating his gaze from group to group, from his own people to the representatives from dozens of countries.

"The time has come to cast aside a past marred by prejudice and antagonism, where each side, in thinking only of itself, betrayed the goals of both. I speak of an Israel that after fifty years of bloodshed rightfully demands that her people live in peace. . . ."

The words faded from Ben's consciousness as he tried to picture the assassin Ravel seated somewhere behind him.

"He couldn't have been part of our delegation," al-Asi whispered. "He never would have gotten through."

"Then he was already up here. Somehow. It doesn't matter."

"What are we going to do, Inspector?"

Ben cocked his head backward, trying futilely to find Ravel in the mass of tightly clustered bodies. "I don't know."

. . . I SPEAK OF THE Palestinians, who have the right to a homeland just as they have a right to be treated as neighbors and not outcasts in the land where they have lived for centuries. If we are to continue to deny them this right, and the hope that goes with it, then we must expect them to turn away from the one hand we extend in friendship while the other clings fast to a gun. . . ."

A second rousing ovation echoed through Masada as Danielle finally reached the aisle. A pair of soldiers intercepted her before she took even a step.

"Listen to me," she began, "there's an—"

Danielle felt something slam into her from behind and suddenly she was being taken down, a sea of arms engulfing her, holding her against the ground.

"What are you doing?" Danielle tried to ask, but almost all her words were swallowed by the dust and rubble she sucked into her lungs with each breath.

Hands brutally frisked her. A pair of handcuffs were slapped on her wrists. The ovation ended as she was rushed up the aisle by her captors. She glimpsed people shuffling around in their seats, casting their eyes upon her.

Hershel Giott turned away too late to avoid her gaze.

"Rav Nitzav!" she managed before a hand clamped over her mouth.

But their eyes met again until Giott's turned away uncertainly.

"You've got to listen to me!" she rasped into the oily palm covering her mouth. *"I know what's—"*

Giott had just looked uncertainly back at her when a third standing ovation drowned out the rest of her words. Danielle tried to pull free of the soldiers, hoping to lose herself in the crowd long enough to find Ravel. She had almost succeeded, when a soldier slammed a baton into the back of her skull and she crumpled to her knees at the feet of her former superior.

THE ONLY WAY to wipe out terror is to wipe out its reason for being!"

Ben caught only the barest glimpse of Danielle as Israeli soldiers hustled her limp form away from the area. He knew now he was the only person standing between Ari Bar-Rosen and an assassin's bullet. And he also knew that the stir caused by Danielle's arrest and struggle would likely spur Ravel to action quicker than expected.

"The only way Israelis can live safely in their homes is to make sure all Palestinians have homes where they can live! . . ."

Ben judged that Ravel could not take the risk that the soldiers would finally listen to Danielle's ravings once they dragged her out of the area. He would enact his plan at the earliest possible time now and take his chances. For a killer of his level, improvisation would be nothing new.

"The only way Israel can heed the wishes and fulfill the dreams of the many is to stop obliging the nightmares of the few!"

Ravel would activate his plot from this section, assuring blame would be cast upon the Palestinians. But how was he planning to escape? Ben wondered as yet another ovation shook Masada.

Ben pictured delegates seated on either side of the assassin. What would *they* do when Ravel made his move? His plan must have taken their presence into account, his precise location among the crowd chosen strategically. The gun would have been planted beneath his chair by a workman, perhaps even Ravel himself in a different guise, explaining how he had joined the Palestinian delegation without ever having been at the base with the rest of its members.

"The only way Israel can remain truly strong is to realize that the Palestinians cannot remain weak. And the only way the Palestinians can establish their nation is to accept the inalienable right of Jews to maintain theirs as well."

The latest ovation jarred Ben and he bounced up to his feet, twisting around. Behind him, about a dozen rows back, a man had stooped over as though to retie his shoes. He cast his gaze up furtively, and Ben caught a glimpse of his face before his view was blocked.

"I think I see Ravel," Ben said to al-Asi, just loud enough for the colonel to hear. "I'm going after him."

"You're *what?*"

The crowd sat down again en masse, but Ben stayed primed on the balls of his feet, ready to bounce up. He would wait until the next ovation to lurch backward through the crowd, hoping the cover of bodies would keep Israeli soldiers from firing at him. Create a moment of confusion and hope that moment was enough for him to reach Ravel.

"The Jews and Palestinians have lived as we have lived for thousands of years. Together, yet apart. Close, yet far. Identical goals that have long canceled each other out in mutual exclusivity. Are we to continue this for another thousand years? Is that what we want for our children? Or has the time finally come to tear the signposts of the past away and venture down a new uncharted road we will pave with hope."

Ben could feel the audience springing for another ovation. He lurched up from his chair and pushed himself into motion, plowing backward.

THE SOLDIERS DROPPED Danielle harshly to the ground a safe distance from the assembled throngs. A pair of hands held her face tight against the earth, and she sucked in mouthfuls of dust and dirt

every time she continued trying to scream her warning.
"*Let her up! Let her up now!*"

Danielle recognized the voice of Hershel Giott even
as the hands holding her suddenly weakened.

"Do it!" Giott ordered, his eyes meeting Danielle's
when she was able to turn her head. "And come with
me, all of you!"

B EN LED WITH his shoulder and caught his fellow Palestinian delegates so off guard that they shrank
aside as chairs tumbled in his path. He never looked
back to see if pursuit was coming, determined to keep
his surge going until it brought him to Ravel.

Hands began to flail away to stop him, and Ben
mounted chairs to avoid their grasp. He hurdled from
one to the next toward a figure hunched in front of a
chair four rows ahead on his left. When the man finally
straightened, Ben recognized him clearly as Esteban
Ravel from his picture.

Then he saw the odd-looking rifle in his hands. It
resembled a simple length of pipe, but Ben was certain
the trigger and hammer assemblies were hidden from
view.

Ravel raised his rifle, using the tightly packed cluster
of bodies for camouflage and angling the weapon so
it almost rested on the shoulder of the man before
him. Ben saw one of Ravel's eyes close as the assassin
aimed through a narrow sight mounted on the shaft
and felt for the trigger.

Ben leaped up onto one last chair and lunged off it,
hurling himself through the air as Ravel fired.

Something that felt like a kick from a steel-toed boot
hammered Ben's ribs and twisted him around in mid-
air, but he crashed into Ravel before the assassin could
make another move. The collision spilled Ravel over
backward to the hard earth, his hot steel weapon now
smoking against Ben's side.

Ravel tried to free himself, but Ben clamped his hands on his shoulders to stop him. He tore the assassin's jacket and part of his shirt away in the process.

Ravel was wearing an Israeli army uniform beneath his dress clothes! In the chaos that ensued after his bullet struck home, that was how he had planned to escape!

Ben felt suddenly weak; something was spilling out of him, like a leak in his chest, and he realized it hurt very much to breathe. Still, he wouldn't let go of the killer, not even when Danielle Barnea tried to pry him off, not until he was sure Ravel wouldn't be going anywhere either.

EPILOGUE

THE SHIVA, THE traditional Jewish memorial service, for Hyram Levy was held in his Jerusalem home three days after Ari Bar-Rosen was officially installed as prime minister of Israel. Since Levy had not actively practiced Judaism for years prior to his death, the more stringent traditions of covering mirrors and sitting only on crates were abandoned. The simple, open gathering drew an eclectic group composed of business associates and customers of both Israeli and Palestinian descent, as well as high-ranking politicians from both sides.

Danielle Barnea arrived at the beginning of the second hour and was greeted at the door by David Wolfe. He took her gently by the arm, transferring a cup and saucer from his right hand to his left.

"Chief Inspector, what a pleasant surprise."

"When I heard you had returned to Israel, I couldn't resist, Mr. Wolfe. Or do you go by 'Wollchensky' again when within our borders?"

Wolfe looked disappointed. "I should think you would have come to pay respect to the deceased."

"We can discuss our levels of hypocrisy another time."

Wolfe smiled and rested his cup and saucer upon a mantel set over a small fireplace. "Actually, I'm glad you came. It gives me a chance to congratulate you on your reinstatement to the National Police."

He extended his hand and Danielle took it. "It hasn't been made public yet."

"I know. I understand your superior, Giott, has regrettably retired."

"I believe he's taking a leave of absence, and that hasn't been made public either."

"Yes, well, he had an excellent career. He deserves a long and healthy retirement."

Danielle realized Wolfe's eyes had not left her for an instant since she entered the room.

"I'm also glad for the opportunity to thank you in person, Chief Inspector."

"You don't owe me any thanks."

"I have been fully informed of your efforts at Masada."

"It was the efforts of a Palestinian detective that saved the day."

Wolfe nodded. "Ben Kamal. I'm well aware of that too."

"Then you probably also know that he and the officer in charge of the Palestinian Protective Security Service are privy to the same information you shared with me about Prime Minister Bar-Rosen."

Wolfe's expression remained utterly impassive, noncommittal.

"In the minds of some," Danielle continued, "that could pose a rather uncomfortable problem. I came here today to let you know you have nothing to worry about on that account."

"Is that all?"

"No," Danielle said, and ever so subtly she removed Wolfe's cup from its saucer and placed it on the mantel. Then she tucked the empty saucer into a small plastic bag and slid it into her pocketbook. "It's funny, but two things still stick in my mind about Hyram Levy's murder. The first is that a number of witnesses reported seeing an old beggar in the street the night he was killed. And the second is the claim of an old Palestinian woman, who was among the first to have a child stolen, that Al Safah had returned to Israel."

"How interesting."

"I thought you'd feel that way. I understand you were quite partial to disguising yourself as a beggar during your undercover days with the Haganah."

"I was indeed. Tell me, what happened to this old woman?"

"She died."

"Pity."

"Don't worry. There are still a number of fingerprints we have not identified from Levy's shop." Danielle felt the shape of the saucer through the fabric of her handbag. "I bet if I had the prints lifted off that saucer, we would find a match. I think I will hang on to it. Just in case anything happens to Inspector Kamal or Colonel al-Asi, you understand."

"I think I do."

Danielle started for the door, followed step for step by Wolfe. She turned back after opening it and grasped his arm, just as he had grasped hers.

"I'm sorry for your loss," Danielle said, and closed the door behind her.

BEN WAS FINALLY able to receive visitors that night, having been taken upstairs from intensive care. Colonel al-Asi had stopped by briefly. During his short stay, he informed Ben that Captain Fawzi Wallid had been promoted to chief of police for the district of Jericho, thanks primarily to his excellent work supervising Ben's most recent investigation.

"You will also be happy to hear that Leila Fatuk has been returned to her parents," the colonel told him. "They are most grateful."

"What about the rest of the children?"

Al-Asi shook his head. "She was the only Palestinian."

"Then the others are still on that island. . . ."

"Italian commandos raided the island this morning, Inspector. They found it deserted."

Ben sighed and worked his morphine pump, a measure of the drug dribbling instantly into a vein in his arm.

Al-Asi glanced at the table by Ben's bedside. "I had your phone turned on. In case there was anyone in the United States you wanted to call."

Ben felt his mouth going dry. "I don't believe there is."

The colonel smiled. "I'm glad to hear that, Inspector. I truly am."

BEN WAS STILL groggy when Danielle arrived that evening. A plainclothes security guard closed the door behind her.

"I'm surprised he let you in," Ben said.

"It's been taken care of. He'll be gone by morning."

"Who'll guard me?"

"That man is the kind you need to be guarded *from*, believe me."

Ben stiffened a little. "What about Ravel?"

"He committed suicide in his cell."

"How convenient."

Danielle sat down on the edge of the bed and took his hand. "I understand Prime Minister Bar-Rosen wants to meet with both of us."

"What do you think we should tell him, Pakad?"

"I think we should congratulate him on a great speech."

Ben squeezed her hand back. "And leave out the results of our latest joint investigation?"

Danielle looked at him unsurely, surprised.

"Our investigation pertaining to the white-slave trade," Ben elaborated.

"He could help us eradicate it," Danielle said, and breathed easier.

"At least end the practice forever in Israel and Palestine. Once and for all."

"A start, anyway. I quite agree."

Ben nodded. "And while we're at it, perhaps we should ask his permission to see each other."

"I'd say he's already given it, if his speech was any indication."

"Gives you hope, doesn't it?"

"For now," Danielle said, and kissed Ben lightly on the lips.

DAVID WOLFE FOLLOWED *his granddaughter's gaze out beyond the shores of Caesarea.*

"This is where it happened," Tali said excitedly, pumping his hand up and down. "This is where the story of the four friends began!"

Wolfe looked out to the sea and for an instant, just an instant, saw a rusted freighter renamed the Gideon *making a dangerous run through the British blockade for the beach-head. Then he nodded.*

"I'm so glad you took me here, Papa. I love this country, I love Israel."

Wolfe brought his granddaughter to him.

"You'll tell me the story again, won't you?"

"Of course. Don't I always?"

His eyes wandered back to the sea, following the lifeboats in their desperate race for the sand. Then he turned to the right and imagined the British patrol jeep converging on the men who would become the greatest friends he had ever known in his life.

"Papa?"

"Yes."

"I'm glad the story had a happy ending."

"So am I," David Wolfe said, hugging his granddaughter tight against him so she wouldn't see his tears. "So am I."

Look for

A Walk in the Darkness

by Jon Land

available in hardcover from Forge Books
April 2000

CHAPTER I

DANIELLE BARNEA FLIPPED the air-conditioning switch up higher as the hot sun of the Judean Desert baked her through the car's glass. The wave of nausea she had felt passed quickly, and she returned all of her attention to the road. She had gotten the call while sitting in the doctor's waiting room and had driven from the clinic straight to the West Bank.

The final stretch of the drive to the crime scene took Danielle east through the Judean Desert toward the Dead Sea along a flattened dirt route. Around her the land was arid and scorched, only thin patches of gray vegetation scattered across the rock-strewn landscape. She could feel the dryness even in the cool air flooding the Jeep's cabin. Besides occasional nomadic bedouin tribes, she knew there were no settlements anywhere for miles.

At length, Danielle approached a makeshift military checkpoint just up ahead. She flashed her ID and an Israeli soldier swiftly waved her through toward a campsite set in the lee of the hillside another mile up the road. Israeli Defense Forces vehicles rimmed the encampment, along with enclosed Jeeps bearing medical markings. White rectangular tents erected over worktables fluttered in the wind. Four miniature Quonset huts with canvas flap fronts rose haphazardly out of the desert like unwelcome brush, now watched over by armed soldiers. Danielle noticed wooden plates nailed to boards driven into the desert ground named three of the huts after American hotel chains in hastily scrawled printing: HOLIDAY INN, MOTEL 6, and HOWARD JOHNSON'S. A trio of old Land Rovers were parked to make use of what little shade there was, while not far away a pair of covered cargo trucks roasted in the sun. Up a steep rise, just beyond the camp, she could see a doorway-sized opening into the jagged stretch of hillside, also guarded.

As she drew her Jeep to a halt near the others, Danielle got her first glimpse of the bodies covered by white plastic that crackled in the heat and wind. She climbed out of the car and walked toward the scene slowly. She noticed an Israeli army captain conferring with an old bedouin man in flowing white robes that billowed outward and headed toward him. The bedouin's hands trembled badly, his eyes red, drawn, and gazing somewhere else. The Israeli captain saw her and slid away from the old man.

"Pakad Danielle Barnea, Captain," Danielle greeted, handing him her ID.

The man took it reluctantly. "Captain Dov Aroche. We weren't told anyone from National Police was coming," he said, returning her identification after a cursory inspection.

Danielle chose to ignore his words. "You were first on the scene?"

"Yes."

"Then someone from your office was simply following procedure."

Captain Aroche did not relax. "I was under the impression this was a military matter, military jurisdiction."

"If there are security issues, yes. But the murder of foreign nationals is a civilian matter, unless terrorism is involved. Do you have any reason to suspect that here?"

"We have fourteen bodies, all shot to death, apparently from very close range as they slept. Beyond that, I don't know what to suspect at this point, Pakad."

"How many were American?"

"Twelve."

"Archaeologists, I was told."

The captain nodded. "I guess no one told them these hills were picked clean years ago."

Even though no stranger to carnage, Aroche sounded plainly unsettled. Danielle could smell tobacco smoke on him and a half-empty cigarette pack protruded from the lapel pocket of his shirt, the plastic hanging down over his nametag.

She looked over his shoulder toward the old bedouin man. "He found the bodies, I take it."

The captain nodded. "There were four bedouins bringing supplies not long after dawn. The old man sent the others to go for help. They came upon one of our patrols three hours ago now."

"What else has he told you?"

"Nothing. We can't make sense of his language, even if he stopped ranting."

"Ranting?"

The captain nodded. "He seems to know one of the dead. We have just finished compiling a list of their names from IDs we were able to recover."

"Show me this list."

Aroche hedged. "I'm not sure if I have—"

"Now, Captain."

Aroche shrugged and reluctantly led Danielle to the hood of a truck that had become his temporary headquarters. Atop the hood lay an assortment of wallets, passports, and identification cards. Aroche snatched a pair of pages from beneath a rock that had kept them from blowing away in the breeze.

"It's preliminary," he explained, handing it to Danielle with some reluctance, "but we still believe it to be complete."

"Very good, Captain," Danielle said, grateful for the time Aroche had saved her.

She scanned the handwritten list cursorily, until the ninth name stunned her. She swallowed hard, took a deep breath and felt the hot, dusty air burn her mouth.